SEASONS OF CHANGE

Book One of The Rosemeade Chronicles

JANIS JOHNSON REESE

Seasons of Change
An Uplifting Small-Town Women's Fiction Novel of Love, Loss, and Starting Over
The Rosemeade Chronicles Book 1

This book is a work of fiction. Names, characters, businesses, organizations, places, events, and incidents either are the product of the author's imagination or are used fictitiously. Any resemblance to actual persons, living or dead, events, or locales is entirely coincidental.

REESE, JOHNSON, JANIS, Author
SEASONS OF CHANGE
JANIS JOHNSON REESE

Published by:
ELITE ONLINE PUBLISHING
63 East 11400 South
Suite #230
Sandy, UT 84070
EliteOnlinePublishing.com

ISBN: 978-1-961801-96-7 (eBook)
ISBN: 978-1-961801-97-4 (Paperback)

Library of Congress Control Number: 2025912554

FIC027660
FIC044000

QUANTITY PURCHASES: Schools, companies, professional groups, clubs, and other organizations may qualify for special terms when ordering quantities of this title. For information, visit JanisJohnsonReese.com

For Resources and updates visit:
JanisJohnsonReese.com

ROSEMEADE COUNTY
MUNICIPAL BLDG.
VILLAGE GREEN
PUBLIC LIBRARY
DINER
BOOKSTORE

DEDICATION

*I*t is with my sincere love and appreciation that I dedicate this book to those who buoyed my spirit during its writing. First off, I owe tremendous gratitude to both my family and my extended family for their unwavering confidence in my ability. To lovely Allison, who read my first rudimentary draft and gave it praise; all this from a woman who candidly warned me that she was not a big fan of fictional writing! Allison's true encouragement spurred me even further forward.

As well, I dedicate this book to my late parents, Wayne and Beverly, and to my two beautiful sisters, Julie and Suzi, who are currently challenged with dementia. May all four of you never forget how much I have loved you.

Though this has been a somewhat lengthy project, I find that others who have gone before me in writing their first book have expended years of their time, as well. So, it is with great joy that I willingly share **Seasons of Change** with those of you who do not know me, but with whom I hope to become a friend. Thank you for investing your valuable time in reading my work.

With every affection,
Janis Johnson Reese
Wife, Mother, Daughter, Sister, and Friend

A SINCERE WELCOME
TO MY WORLD

*H*ello, dearest Reader, I am so happy you've decided to accompany me today on a road trip in my little red car to historic Rosemeade County. It is such a pretty place where I have friends that I can't wait for you to meet. The seasons there meld into one another with stories of love and laughter, people you won't soon forget, and it's also an idyllic place where you'll want to stay for a while. Since summer is almost upon us, I've got my little red car all gassed up, I have a picnic hamper loaded with sandwiches and chips, cubed watermelon with blueberries, savory potato salad, and two slices of pecan pie for dessert.

And, Reader, I want you to know as we begin our journey, that though ***Seasons of Change*** is based on true events, historic Rosemeade County and its denizens have been fabricated within my imagination. My story could be in many places under the brilliant blue skies and wide-open spaces of the western United States. Some of my readers might even find their historic Rosemeade County on the western slope of Colorado or nestled within the beauty of Oregon's Willamette Valley, or even along the tree-laden Wasatch Front in Utah. As well, let's not forget scenic northern California or my forever-treasured home state of Idaho… The choice is yours, my friend, as to where your imagination might take you.

As we embark upon our drive to historic Rosemeade County, enjoy the rolling hills that are strikingly encrusted with pines, scrub oaks, and aspens. During the winter season, these splendors are covered with pristine snow whose spring run-off empties into a myriad of tiny lakes that also dot the landscape. However, it is not just the physical beauty of this beautiful place that sets it apart. Instead, it is that Father Time has seen fit to surround historic Rosemeade County and its burghs with a specialness that comes straight out of an artist's painting. It is

America at its very best…much like the years following World War II when the Greatest Generation had just returned home after defending the world against horrible tyranny.

Yet, in historic Rosemeade County, there ***are*** cell phones, cable television, live streaming, and the internet, but its commerce is not dominated by big-box stores or shopping malls. Instead, local ranchers and farmers provide the regional population with their farm-to-market offerings at the community grocery store. There are restaurants where the daily fare is prepared one dish at a time for patrons, bookstores that have been family-owned for generations, and a town square with a carillon chiming out the hour of the day. Local vendors know their patrons by name, and in the event of an accident or illness, neighbors are always there to help. Small businesses abound, and there isn't a need for just one day a year to applaud their commerce; it is celebrated all year long!

Finally, within historic Rosemeade County, we will visit two memorable smaller towns, Reedsburgh and Rosemeade Township. Both places retain a captivating atmosphere of community pride and patriotism. Reedsburgh is the larger of the two, and Rosemeade Township is considerably smaller. Yet, Rosemeade Township is a hub of inviting industry; most particularly, The Old Vineyard Road Nursery. Within the confines of this memorable small burgh, our story begins.

I hope you will put my writings into your memory bank, and let me captivate you with new friends whom you will never forget. Here's hoping you will want to join me in historic Rosemeade County time and time again. Watch for more of my stories and, of course, my colorful postcards! With affection, JJR

WINTER SEASON

*L*iliana Rawlings** was tired…so very fatigued for a woman of a mere thirty-two years. Recently, Liliana's world had imploded, and since that time, she had been trying to keep up with huge changes that would have tired three women, let alone one. By today's standards, she had it all, and yet…what did she really have to show for it? There was no happy home, no children to nurture, nothing to look forward to, and no hint of what had become of the hopeful, young woman she had once been. Her hand had even been forced to give up her teaching job, and she felt somewhat like a prisoner in her own home. There was nothing left; not one shred of her young life, that had once been so hopeful, was left.

There are those who would say that Liliana had wasted the best years of her life. And, she had to admit that if she were to be truthful with herself, she would have to agree. At last, Liliana acknowledged to herself that she was, in fact, sorry that she had ever married Richard Rawlings. There had been a few good times during the early months of their ten-year marriage, but would she have done it the same way again? No, not really. It seemed that Richard's volatile disposition and job changes had always seemed to keep their lives in perpetual upheaval. She was fatigued even thinking about all the turmoil that she had endured.

By nature, Liliana was a happy person, not at all prone to wallowing in self-pity or regret. She was quite creative, yet she also thought with the other side of her brain. Such thinking and its related discernment had served her well. She felt she could accurately assess people, but she had been dead wrong about her husband. Today, she needed a good cry to purge the anger she had been harboring. Anger rarely showed itself in her demeanor; but on this early winter afternoon, anger was manifesting itself in record amounts toward her husband, toward her husband's business ventures, and toward the countless partially-completed projects around their home that Richard had started and never finished. Lastly, exhausted Liliana Rawlings harbored anger toward a certain life insurance company. She was Richard's beneficiary. Why had Grace Mutual not sent her any papers to sign if Richard had, in fact, cashed out his life insurance policy? Today, any vestiges of emotional support or financial security had flown out the window with the waning afternoon sunlight.

The late-afternoon setting sun cast a slightly pink tint upon the wall of Liliana's upstairs guest room which was painted a soft blue. The combination of the two colors lit the wall a subtle lavender hue which exemplified how Liliana was feeling. She was resident in her guestroom because her husband had died a day and a half ago, and she just couldn't quite bring herself to sleep in the room which spoke most vocally about Richard. His designer jeans were still draped over the back of a tapestry-covered chair in the walk-in closet; numerous keys to who knew what were tossed upon the bureau; and mixed with some loose change in a leather dressing case were various business cards of recent contacts. His receipts were strewn about, too…way too many reminders to do something with right now…so she had just moved down the hall for the time being. Though this home was not on the market, Liliana knew she would be moving again and starting over. "Why does this make me feel so very tired?" she asked of herself aloud.

Though unexpected, Richard's death had not really been surprising to her, as she had somehow felt deep in her gut that this was how their marriage would end…Richard leaving her with a mess to clean up. And now, she did have a disaster to attend to; coupled with the added burden of Richard's creditors. Yet now, she could not even question him as to *why* he hadn't shared with her the vast array of debt that he had encumbered. She knew Richard was a gambler of sorts, but he had never gambled at any gaming table. No, he had only gambled with their lives…high-risk investments, high-end real-estate acquisitions, and speculative deals…each of which was sure to be, "***the one***."

Richard was gone, and Liliana could no longer face sleeping in the bedroom which smacked of dead Richard and his betrayals to her. An investigation into the pockets of her husband's expensive overcoats and designer suits, as well as into the dark recesses of his desk, had provided Liliana with the answers to some questions she had been harboring for some time. A receipt from a pawn broker for a diamond tennis bracelet which could not be found in her jewelry chest explained what had happened to her first anniversary gift from Richard. He had said he would get in touch with their insurance agent to file a claim. Her husband had lied to her.

As well, she had found cancellation notices from Grace Mutual Insurance Company concerning the large insurance policy that Richard had taken out when they were newly married. He had insisted that, "Three million dollars in life insurance was the least he could do for her in the event something happened to him." Now, Liliana discovered that her late husband had recently borrowed from the principal on his universal life insurance policy; then, had let the policy lapse for non-payment. A conference call to the insurance company confirmed the worst of Liliana's fears. There would be no life insurance money to settle Richard's affairs; he had already spent it. But what had he done with that money?

Also, of notable concern, were sketchy promissory notes Richard had hidden deep within his personal files to a handful of friends and to hard-money lenders who apparently were funding short-term loans for his most-recent real estate acquisitions. Richard had assured her that all his dealings were being underwritten by his local banking contacts. To her horror, Liliana also found documents from the federal government informing her late husband that his financial licensure was being suspended due to allegations of insider stock trading and irregular business practices. Liliana knew that such allegations were surely punishable with nothing short of a prison term. She was now beginning to understand why he had always insisted on keeping a post office box near his office. He had wanted to hide his meddling from her and to keep her in the dark on his business transactions. Why would he purposefully do such a thing? Evidence surely confirmed things she had wondered about him but had dismissed as too accusatory on her part. She now knew she had been correct in her assumptions.

Things worsened when the local ***Money 4 U*** check-cashing agency contacted her inquiring why their required payment was overdue. Further investigation into the black abyss of yet another set of Richard's designer pockets did, in fact, produce a contract for $2500 of fast cash in exchange for the title on ***her*** late-model European luxury car; a car she had never even wanted, yet her husband had insisted on purchasing for her. After telling the check-cashing agency clerk that she would come in with cash that afternoon to make the payment, she went to the zippered pocket in her purse where she kept an emergency stash of cash only to find that all the money had been taken. It had been there two days ago; she knew it was, as she had borrowed a twenty-dollar bill from it to buy some sundries for Richard at the hospital gift shop. All these recent "finds" volleyed even more questions Liliana's way. "No…" she murmured. She began to dread what further investigation into their finances and Richard's secrets might provide.

Lastly, there was the phone call to her old friend, David Renton, who was an attorney. Somehow, David did not seem totally surprised at the things which she was sharing with him. Was Richard that transparent? Liliana had needed to seek out David Renton's help when she tried to make arrangements to take Richard's body to Reedsburgh, her hometown, for burial. She related to him how she went to her bank to withdraw cash only to find that all of her accounts had been frozen. The young teller, whose face had turned ashen, had said, "Mrs. Rawlings, there is some type of problem with your accounts. I'm sorry, but I cannot give you any money. Let me take you to see my manager." The bank manager, though gracious, had been very affirmative that there was no way she was going to be able to get her money. He had quietly stated that he was very sorry her husband had died, but he could do nothing when the federal government froze anyone's bank accounts.

David, too, had quietly informed her that this was a sign that Richard had been in serious trouble and was, most likely, being investigated for fraud or misappropriation of his financial clients' money; maybe even unpaid taxes. He said, "Liliana, we need to do some investigative work here. I don't know what may have gone down with Richard, but this situation appears to be very grave indeed. Let me get started on checking into it. I'm suspect that Richard was in far deeper trouble than you even suspect. I'll be in touch with you when you arrive back in Reedsburgh. But listen, do you need some money to get home to your parents?"

"Thank you, David, but my father has taken care of things. I'll be okay," she sighed. "I suspect that Dad will want to confer with you on all of this…he may be retired, but he is still a lawyer at heart. Do you mind?"

"No, I do not mind at all, Liliana. I would welcome his expertise and his case experience in this situation. Rest assured that we'll get to the bottom of this for you. Just know, too, that you have legions of friends that admire you, and no matter what kind of trouble Richard may have gotten himself into, it is no reflection on you or your character. We will all be here for you."

Liliana could hardly believe this was happening… An automobile accident had taken Richard from this world in less than a week. Yet, she somehow felt that he had embraced the situation as the perfect exit. Richard always relished playing the victim, so he accepted his injuries with gusto and, for once in his life had fully completed a task; that of exiting from this life at one hundred percent efficiency.

Even his death had been questionable, but Richard's departure from this life hadn't really left Liliana so very alone, as she had pretty much been on her own the last few years due to Richard's extensive travel and his self-imposed exile from friends and family. Yet, his death had left her facing hardships, and those hardships were not of her own making. She lay down upon the soft duvet covering the guest bed and closed her eyes for some hard-fought rest. "Oh, Richard, what have you done?" she whispered to herself. Exhausted Liliana Rawlings would consider her options when she awoke. It was all she could do on this chilly winter afternoon.

PART I

SUMMER'S FREEDOM

CHRISTOPHE

*C**hristophe Riordan* was happy. It was May, and this was to be a summer to remember. Not only was he to have the company of his special god-daughter to work in the nursery this year, he was soon to enjoy the expertise of his second cousin, Declan Ryan. Declan was due to arrive next Tuesday from Christophe's beloved Scotland, and Declan was sure to ramp things up a wee bit at the nursery. Mary Ryan was Christophe's cousin, and her son, Declan, had not long ago graduated from university with a degree in horticulture. What a find…a young man with the latest technical knowledge and skills to help with Christophe's life's work. Things were looking up, indeed!

As Christophe unloaded freight, he thought about how he had arrived at this juncture in his life. He wasn't particularly old, but he didn't quite have the stamina he had once had when it came to working a twelve-hour day. He wasn't lazy, but he truly desired to spend some time with his wife, Annie. He wanted to travel with her to some of the places that she was so desirous of seeing. He wanted to make sure that she would be able to immerse herself in the local culture and cuisine of their destinations. Having Declan join him at The Old Vineyard Road Nursery would ensure that he and Annie would be able to get away more often without concern for the welfare of their nursery, its patrons, or its expansive stock of trees, plants, and flowers.

Christophe's musings also brought to mind his own arrival from Scotland years ago. It had started as just a trip to the United States, but his travels had brought forth many new experiences and a certain affinity for this giant piece of land they call, "The Red, White, and Blue." Yes, America had beckoned him to stay for a bit longer than three months. It invited him to stay and help at a pretty, little diner in a small township called Rosemeade, which was the county seat for historic Rosemeade County. Perhaps, it was the lay of the land, the friendliness of the people, or the beautiful raven-haired waitress at the said diner. He really couldn't quite put his finger on it, but America called to him.

Because the little township of Rosemeade was not much more than a little village (much like his own back in Scotland), he realized that he could probably secure a position as dishwasher for a few weeks, then he would travel further west. But the weeks turned into months, the months into almost a year, and his relationship with the raven-haired waitress, Annie Jarvis, bloomed; and when it came time to leave, he found he could not. He loved the United States of America and Annie Jarvis; but not necessarily in that order.

After filing the necessary governmental papers to stay longer, Christophe found himself advancing from dishwasher, to short order cook, to applying for US Citizenship. The lovely Annie Jarvis, the brilliant blue skies, and the green, rolling hills of historic Rosemeade County and its village namesake had wended their way into his heart to a point where he knew staying was his only option. Oh, he missed his ancient Scotland and its heritage, but there was nothing left for him there. His mum and dad had both died within months of each other several years before his departure. Their beautiful long house, grazing fields, and sheep were leased out to his Uncle Silas, so he really had no worries about staying away from the old country a bit longer. And, that lovely smile belonging to Annie Jarvis had him mesmerized.

Annie Jarvis came from a hard-working family whose roots went back five generations to a fledgling America. Her great, great grandfather had homesteaded in the Rosemeade County area under the provisions of America's Homestead Act. She was homegrown, true blue, and vehemently faithful to her family. She had tried not to love him, but things couldn't be helped. There was something big going on between them. He, a giant bear of a Scotsman, who really didn't have much to offer her, became the sweetheart she yearned for and, two and a half years later, he was saying, "I do." underneath the rose bower at the little village church in Rosemeade Township.

He had then taken Annie to Scotland to see where he had come from; she had met Uncle Silas and had slept in the slate-roofed stone house where he had grown up amidst fields of grazing sheep alongside his special cousin, Mary. He was so happy that Annie could finally meet those who meant so much to him. For close to four weeks, he and his new bride had honeymooned their way through the Highland moors and the rugged beauty of his beloved homeland. Yes, his Annie had been a gem. She had made him feel complete; something he hadn't felt since the death of his parents. Yes, he had Uncle Silas, who was a confirmed bachelor of seventy-five years, and his beautiful cousin, Mary Ryan, but that was all that was left of his Scottish roots. Yes, Annie, fitted into a hole in his chest that he hadn't realized was slightly gaping until he met her.

A year or two into their marriage, Christophe and Annie had become acquainted with Jenny and Stephan Lylestrom. The Lylestroms lived in Rosemeade Township, where Stephan was a young law clerk for the only attorney in the tiny town. Neither couple had babies yet, so it was natural that they had much in common. By then, Christophe and Annie were hoping to buy the diner and add a few traditional Scottish dishes to the menu, and it was Stephan who had assisted them with their foray into American Capitalism. The business relationship blossomed into fast friendship, and they found themselves attending the cinema together, dining together on Sunday nights, and spending every special occasion in each other's company. It was a solid relationship with all parties knowing this was a life-long bond.

Stephan and Jenny, who were about ten years older than they, had wept with them when Annie had repeatedly miscarried three babies in a row, and Christophe and Annie had comforted the Lylestroms each month when no pregnancy had occurred for them, also. It was that time in their lives, when they all desired to start young families, but for some reason, the Good Lord had not seen fit to bless either couple. It had been discovered that Annie suffered from an extremely small uterus which had come about from her mother taking a drug called, Thalidomide, when her body had threatened to miscarry Annie years before. Scientific research continued to discover the ill effects of Thalidomide, and there were many. Christophe and Annie came to accept the fact that they might never have children but found solace in each other. As for Jenny and Stephan, doctors still could not find anything wrong with either partner, but children somehow eluded them.

Just after he and Annie had celebrated their fifth Wedding Anniversary, Jenny and Stephan announced that they were moving about forty miles away to a larger town in historic Rosemeade County, called Reedsburg. Stephan was planning to open a private law practice. This was something that he had been very desirous of doing for several years. It was very hard for the friends to say good-bye, but they all knew such a move was a good decision for Stephan. Even though the miles separated them, they found themselves still getting together for any and all special occasions. Jenny Lylestrom threw a whale of a good Fourth-of-July celebration, and he and Annie always hosted Thanksgiving. There were high spirits and happy memories made whenever they got together.

Not long after the Lylestroms had moved to Reedsburgh, Christophe started looking into purchasing an abandoned vineyard that was located just north of the highway on a picturesque road, most appropriately named, Old Vineyard Road. The vineyard sat nestled just below the rolling foothills that surrounded historic Rosemeade Township. It had been abandoned during the Great Depression years and had let Mother Nature take her course; which had been to cover the rolling hills with grapevines run amok. Yet, this ramshackle old property boasted a charming vintner's cottage built of stone and an old barn whose wooden structure was leaning off its sturdy stone foundation. Since the vineyard was located at the end of the road, Christophe felt it could easily be fashioned into a tree and flower nursery. He and Annie loved to garden, and he felt this old property could accommodate them and, hopefully, their children.

Christophe and Annie were doing well financially, as they were both thrifty. When Uncle Silas had passed on, Christophe had gone back to Scotland and had sold the family's home, property and grazing land where he had grown up. Old Uncle Silas had done well by him, as the estate had been maintained beautifully. Everything was in fine condition, so it didn't take long to ready the house, sheep, and land for sale. It turned out that a close neighbor and friend was desirous of adding Christophe's acres to his own expanding farming operation, so a fair price was negotiated.

In the end, Christophe was back home to his beloved Annie within about six weeks. The funds from the sale of the family estate and sheep had paid off the bank note on the diner and had purchased the entirety of the dilapidated old vineyard property. All he needed to do then was build a snug family home on that old acreage, and his wonderful Annie knew exactly what she wanted and where.

Fast forward fourteen years...that picturesque family home was surrounded by roses and covered with flowering vines. The nursery boasted an arborist's dream come true, and there were many handsome old farm tables groaning from the weight of the hundreds of colorful flowers. In addition to all that, there were also three very large green houses. The old, stone-foundation barn had been refurbished; it housed supplies, offices, and a loft apartment for the property manager whom he still hadn't managed to hire. As for the vintner's cottage, Christophe had left it pretty much as it was, and Old Jim, who was once down on his luck, lived there quite happily. Nowadays, Old Jim spent his days watering trees, pottering in the green houses, and thanking Christophe for helping him to turn his life around.

It turned out that Christophe had anticipated correctly, as The Old Vineyard Road Nursery flourished under his care and had become a destination shopping experience. Clients came from miles around to "make a day of it." They ate a gigantic breakfast at Annie's Diner which now also featured a full Scottish breakfast of eggs and bacon, sausages, baked beans, grilled tomatoes, and haggis alongside fried toast and tea. Those same returning customers, who had learned to enjoy haggis, had then driven the short distance from the diner over to The Old Vineyard Road Nursery and shopped for healthy, eye-catching nursery stock for their gardens. Christophe knew he loved the Free Enterprise System, here in America. One could arrive without much in his pockets and end up a successful businessman with a little hard work.

The next few years continued to speed by, when Jenny and Stephan happily announced that they were expecting a child the next June. Annie cried; both for herself and for Christophe and their childless home, but with great joy for Jenny and Stephan Lylestrom. True to their best friends' loving nature, when their beautiful daughter, Liliana Rose Lylestrom, was born on a balmy June day, Christophe and Annie were asked to be her godparents. Such an honor was hard to pass up and neither of them could imagine not taking the lovely child into their home should something happen to her wonderful parents.

So, Liliana Rose Lylestrom had grown up enveloped in the true love of her parents and that of her Uncle Christophe and Aunt Annie. And now, that beloved soon-to-be-nineteen-year-old girl and her tag-along dog were coming to Rosemeade Township to spend the summer working at his nursery. What joy she brought wherever she went. He couldn't wait to introduce her to young Declan. That lad would see that America turns out some bonny lasses, too. "Oh, this is to be a memorable summer," Christophe Riordan chuckled aloud to no one in particular as he very happily hulked yet another weeping crabapple tree off the truck.

DECLAN

*D*eclan Ryan was apprehensive. Though he was embarking upon a new chapter in his life, Declan was slightly nervous. Had he made the right decision in moving to America? Would his precious mum have approved of this decision? Though he was already a man and soon to be twenty-three years of age, he would have enjoyed deferring to his mother for her advice on such a huge life-change, but his mother, Mary Ryan, was gone. She had passed from this life, praising her Lord and Savior, but leaving Declan, her only child, heartbroken. She had died three months ago, and since that time, Declan had been dealing with death taxes and auctioning off his family's business in Inverness.

Declan's father, James, had gone home to be with the Lord when Declan was a mere boy of eight years of age. James had left Mary with a small village grocery store which had provided enough income for Mary to make ends meet while she raised their son alone and for Declan to be university educated. Life had been kind to Mary and Declan. They had enjoyed a quiet solitude and comradery as Declan grew old enough to be a help to his mum in the little store, and Mary had taught him the lessons of hard work and honesty. Locals commented that, "James would have 'busted his buttons' with pride if he could see what a fine job Mary had done in raising his son."

There are those who say, "It takes a village to raise a child." And they would, indeed, be correct as residents in Mary Ryan's little hamlet within Inverness had made sure she and her son were never forgotten on holiday celebrations, church events, or summer junkets. James Ryan had been a friend to all in his life-time, and his friends made sure that his sweet wife and young son were rewarded with repayment for all of James' kindnesses to them.

In short, Declan Ryan's young life had been idyllic, even though he was fatherless. He was never wont of male role models, as the parents of his young friends made sure that Declan was always included on fishing trips, football teams (Soccer to us, Yanks!), and cycling. Declan's teachers encouraged their small charge to be curious about his world and to study the plants, rocks, and trees about which he was so fascinated.

In classical fashion, Declan documented, drew, and watercolor painted his botanical specimens in an old, leather-bound journal which had once belonged to his father. Sometimes, his mother would despair of all the nature strewn about Declan's small room, but she couldn't have been any prouder of the young man whose life God had entrusted to her. Several years later, it came as no surprise that Declan desired to study botany and horticulture while at university, and to these facets of personal interest, he also added the mastery of language, literature, and business as his life's goals. So, with a lump in her throat and a fracture in her heart Mary Ryan launched Declan into this new phase of his life at the University of Edinburgh. And, with Declan's mangy old dog, Bob, beside her for company, Mary Ryan knew that no matter what life might bring his way, her son would do well.

Declan's university years flew by quickly. He received high marks in his studies and graduated first in his class. Graduation was marked with time-honored traditions, and scholastic honors were bestowed upon Declan with much pomp and circumstance. But the celebratory mood was slightly marred for him when he saw how frail his mum looked since the last time he had been home. Mary Ryan assured him that she was, "just fine," but Declan instinctively felt as if something was terribly wrong. After many serious pleas from her beloved boy, Mary grudgingly agreed to visit the doctor. The old village physician, Dr. Haynes, was surprised and saddened by the suspicious symptoms Mary presented, and referred her to a young oncologist in Edinburgh for further testing. The news was not good.

Ever the dutiful son, Declan spent the next two years caring for his precious mum while she battled brain and lung cancers. Declan turned a blind eye to the ugliness of cancer and the toll it took on his mother by daily carrying her up and down two flights of stairs to her room, regaling her with stories from his university days, and discussing the pros and cons of hybridization (his choice of subject…

not Mary's). When time permitted, Declan minded the grocery store with the help of Jane Ross, an old friend of his mum's. When she felt that the end was coming, Mary Ryan requested that Declan stay in touch with his only blood relative, Christophe Riordan, in America. Declan reluctantly agreed, if only to make his mother happy.

After the last vestiges of Mary's life were cleaned up and packed away, Declan embarked upon what was to become the next chapter in his solitary life. He was an only child; his parents had had no siblings either, so it appeared that Christophe Riordan really was the only remaining familial tie from his mother's family. Christophe was her cousin, and they had remained close until he traveled to America for an extended visit, and in the end, had decided to stay. Christophe, too, loved nature and owned his own tree nursery on what was once an old vineyard that had been abandoned during America's Great Depression. Slowly, but surely, the old place had come back to life under Christophe's ministrations, and Declan was interested in hearing about his cousin's life's work; thus, the phone call was made.

Christophe Riordan was quite saddened to hear of Mary's passing, but he also recognized the sound of a broken young man over the phone and the miles of distance between them. He knew of Declan's close relationship to his mother, and he also knew the feeling of losing one's only remaining parent at such a young age. Christophe was quick to encourage the young man to come to historic Rosemeade County for an extended visit… "I could really use some help at this old ramshackle property of mine. Your knowledge and expertise would be of great value to me. Please consider it, Declan, as it would be a real gift to me to have your assistance."

When the last of the death taxes had been dispatched to the government, and the little grocery store's inventory and fixtures had been auctioned off, Declan Ryan left his homeland and headed to America to visit his mother's cousin and to begin the second act of his young life. Though he hardly even remembered meeting Christophe Riordan when he was younger, Declan felt fully acquainted with him from his mother's stories of their shared childhoods and from the ribbon-bound packet of Christophe's engaging letters to her. Declan read all those letters hoping to glean some insight into his only remaining relative's story and came away liking what he had learned.

It appeared that after James Ryan's death, Christophe had looked after Mary Ryan from afar with gifts and, occasionally, money which had provided some extras for Declan. And, now, Christophe Riordan was offering Declan an opportunity to really use his education and skills in America. In the end, it was quite an easy decision to make, and Declan Ryan found himself on his way to The Old Vineyard Road Nursery in historic Rosemeade County in that huge land they call, The United States of America.

After a long and somewhat tedious flight from Scotland, Declan finished the last leg of his travels on a commuter train from the Brookings City International Airport to a bus station, where he caught a connection to Reedsburgh which was just over the historic Rosemeade County line. From there, he traveled another forty miles to Rosemeade Township and, finally, in a taxicab to The Old Vineyard Road Nursery. What he found astonished him, as his mother's cousin, Christophe, had managed to prod the old, ramshackle place into a charming destination for his clients. And, clients there were…the parking area was jammed with late-model cars and wealthy-looking patrons were buying up healthy nursery stock and colorful flowers. There was an older gentleman who was trundling flats of flowers and hanging garden baskets into the trunks of all those late-model automobiles, and he seemed to know each patron by name. Those clients, in turn, were saying, "Many thanks, Old Jim!" to the aging fellow who was carrying their purchases.

Declan was slightly mesmerized by the whole scene until his taxi driver cleared his throat and said, "Anything else you need, sir?" Declan shook himself out of his reverie, paid the cab driver and approached the man whom he now knew to be, Old Jim.

"Excuse me, sir. I'm looking for Christophe Riordan. I'm his relative from Scotland."

Old Jim's wizened face broke into a big, toothy smile. He extended his large, boney hand in greeting to Declan, and said, "Oh my, is Christophe ever going to be glad to see you, my man. We've been busier this year than in all my seasons of working here. He's in the office; let me take you over there." Old Jim led the way up a meandering path to a large barn which was perched on a handsome stone foundation. It reminded Declan of his homeland immediately. Once inside the giant barn, the two walked to the east end of the building wherein rustic offices were constructed, and his mum's cousin sat negotiating prices via the telephone.

Christophe Riordan looked up, motioned both Old Jim and Declan into his office, and signed off on his telephone call. He then jumped up from his seat, and embraced Declan in what could only be termed, a bear hug, exclaiming, "Declan, you look exactly like your father; good looking indeed. I'd venture to bet that you left a lot of girls in Scotland weeping when you left!"

Declan laughed at Christophe's humor and quipped, "Well, I don't know about that, but I'm indebted to you, Christophe, for giving me such a fine opportunity. It's very good of you. Rest assured that I will do my best job for you."

The big man squeezed Declan's palm in a hearty handshake and said, "Oh, young man, the pleasure is all mine. You'll be doing me a great favor. Come, Declan, let's all go over to the house, so you can meet my Annie again. She's been cooking up a storm for you, so I hope you're hungry." And so, began Declan Ryan's extended visit to America.

LILIANA

*J*enny and **Stephan Lylestrom** had been ecstatic. After twenty-four years of marriage and just as many years of trying to get pregnant, they were expecting their first child. Yes, some would say that they were crazy to take on raising a child this late in their lives. Yet, Jenny and Stephan repeatedly acknowledged to one another, "Who cared if they were to forever be the oldest parents attending the kindergarten orientation, the most-aged couple participating in parent/teacher conferences, or the grayest-haired couple attending their child's college homecoming?" Jenny and Stephan were to finally be the parents of a precious baby. They were to know the joys of parenthood that they had only watched and envied from afar for so very long.

It did not matter that Jenny's obstetrician was encouraging them to proceed with earnest caution, forcefully encouraging them to schedule an amniocentesis procedure as soon as possible. In addition to advising them that Jenny's eggs were old and probably wouldn't produce a healthy child in response to Jenny's declarations of great physical health, "Dr. Cautiously Optimistic" tried to ramp down their hope just in case things went awry. These things were of no matter to Jenny and Stephan…they had prayed for a child for years. No matter what the outcome, they were committed to this baby. Come what may, this child was to know only that he or she was sorely desired and very-well loved.

Despite raised-eyebrows from long-time friends and tongue-clucking from hip salespeople who assumed they were the grandparents, Jenny and Stephan sailed through three trimesters in good form. The day of the baby's arrival floated in with the scent of honeysuckle in the air, with warm breezes wafting through the lace-curtained nursery, and with the perfect temperature of seventy-five degrees. Their vegetable and cutting garden boasted young cabbages and sweet peas as well as fragrant rosemary, basil, and chives. Jenny was just cutting a bouquet of tender yellow roses when her water broke, and the pains began. Five and a half hours later, Liliana Rose Lylestrom was born…perfect in every way.

Liliana was nurtured and loved by her parents; so much so that she grew to be a happy, content baby, a sweet toddler, and cherished little girl. Liliana was never spoiled, though many were fearful that she would be due to her doting parents. Her parents were firm, always requiring respect, and she grew up knowing that she was secure and thoroughly loved. Factor in a chubby Golden Retriever puppy, named Iris, and there was no denying that young Liliana lived an idyllic life. Both the silken-haired girl and prancing retriever were an inseparable duo.

Fast forward to age seventeen, and you would frequently witness a slightly shabby, pale blue Volkswagen convertible toddling through the streets of a picture-perfect home town with a smiling young Liliana at the wheel and her aging, white-muzzled Iris riding shotgun. On those occasions when Iris had to stay behind, she was replaced with her mistress's fresh-faced young friends. Liliana Rose Lylestrom was never wont of close friendships. She was one of those rare creatures with whom everyone felt at ease. In short, Liliana kindled life-time, heart-felt relationships wherever she went.

The watershed events of Liliana's young life ebbed and flowed with an ease. It seemed to Jenny and Stephan that they merely blinked a time or two before their sweet girl was finished with her first year at university. But, this summer season, Liliana desired an adventure after a long year of heavy studies. In short, their girl wanted to spread her wings and soar just a little bit. Not wanting to stifle his daughter, Stephan Lylestrom contacted someone who subsequently offered up a great opportunity. His life-long friend, Christophe Riordan, also Liliana's godparent, had an opening at his tree farm and nursery in Rosemead Township about forty miles away. Christophe had kindly offered Liliana a job at the said nursery attending to and watering the nursery stock. Liliana could find a studio apartment in town and work for him and his wife, Annie, during the busy summer season. Stephan knew his daughter would be safe, but not smothered, with Christophe. Liliana's face lit up like a candle when the proposed opportunity was presented, and before they knew it, Jenny and Stephan Lylestrom's baby girl was embarking upon the newest adventure of her young life.

The old V-Dub was serviced, received a new set of tires, and was loaded with girl, dog, and three giant suitcases of shorts, shoes, and girly things. Yes, Iris, the aging Golden Retriever was also offered a job that summer…that of greeting clients, chasing squirrels and snoozing under a robust weeping cherry tree at the front entrance to the nursery. Jenny and Stephan earnestly waved good-bye to their beloved duo then proceeded to the back patio for a sandwich and a good cry, as they were learning that it is never easy to see your children grow up and fly away.

The trip to Christophe's home flew by and before she knew it, Liliana was pulling into the drive. The house was a comfortable salt-box style with an attached breezeway and a pergola covered with flowering vines; underneath which was parked Annie's aging Porsche roadster. The old home was picturesque, and now the front door was opening to reveal a smiling "Uncle Christophe" and "Aunt Annie."

Christophe embraced his young charge with a huge hug and kisses to both cheeks and exclaimed, "Oh, my Lily Girl, how you have grown and turned into such a pretty young thing, too. I had thought you might never grow into that big smile of yours, darlin,' but I see that you have… well done! Now, where is your doggie? Has she taken off toward the barn? There are plenty of new scents to explore up there, but I'm sure she'll be right back when she sniffs the aroma of my Annie's roast beef sandwiches!" And with that, Christophe began to unload Liliana's bags from the car.

Liliana sighed contentedly. She was so very happy to be in Rosemeade Township for the summer and to be helping Uncle Christophe at The Old Vineyard Road Nursery. As they proceeded to the house, Christophe exclaimed that he was especially happy to have Liliana meet his young relative, Declan Ryan, who had just arrived a few days earlier from Scotland. "You'll be working closely with Declan this summer, Lily Girl. He graduated several years ago with a degree in Plant Sciences, so I'm hoping to finally get some time off for a nap! He's only been here since Tuesday, but he's already helped me tremendously. You know how much a new pair of eyes and a fresh perspective can do to implement worthwhile changes. I'm sure Declan will find plenty to keep both you and Iris busy, Liliana. Only the Lord knows how much he's kept me on my old toes in just under a week. Now, what do you say to a nice lunch on the back patio?"

Christophe was right about Iris' return because just as Annie proceeded out the back door with a luncheon tray loaded with sandwiches; Iris came trundling up the back walk with a hopeful look on her face. Iris was no fool. She had consumed one of Aunt Annie's roast beef, arugula, and horseradish sandwiches before, and she was hopeful she just might be given another.

As the picnic luncheon was consumed, the conversation naturally turned to the nursery and to Christophe's second cousin, Declan Ryan. Again, Christophe was very complimentary of Declan's strengths and some of the new ideas he had brought with him from his university studies in Scotland.

Christophe's brow furrowed slightly, and he said to Liliana, "You should know this, though, that he lost his mum recently, so he's a little subdued. His father also died when he was just a young lad, so you see, Liliana, our young Declan is an orphan of sorts. It's up to us to heartily welcome him to America and show him some of our hospitality. It's the least I can do for his dear mum. She was a playmate to me when we were children, and we continued to stay in touch even after I moved to America."

The day passed by with unusual speed, and at day's end, Liliana found herself sated with Annie's delicious cooking, and Christophe's continual topping off her iced tea. She was fearful she might be wide awake at three o'clock in the morning due to the copious amounts of caffeine she had consumed throughout the evening. And true to her misgivings, Liliana was wide awake at quarter to four in the early morning. Though she had not drunk any iced tea, Iris was restless, too, and rustled about in her dog basket. When she sensed that her mistress was not sleeping very well either, she whined to go out. Liliana acquiesced to her and opened the French doors which led to a small patio off the guest room.

The evening air was scented with a mix of newly-bloomed roses and freshly-mowed grass, and as Liliana breathed in the fragrance, she said to no one in particular, "Such a scent needs to be made into a perfume. It would sell very well." She perched herself on the edge of a small rock wall that enclosed the little patio and stared up at the brilliant moon. It lit the night sky so well that Liliana could easily identify familiar things scattered throughout Uncle Christophe's nursery and vineyard; even the old stone barn had lights glowing. She ruminated on what an adventure she was embarking upon.

Tomorrow, she was to move into a little attic apartment that was located over the local bookshop. Liliana knew that it wasn't large, but it was still the very first piece of real estate that she, Liliana Rose Lylestrom, would lease in her life! She couldn't wait to get started on making it her own. Just then, her thoughts were interrupted as Iris bounded over the little wall surrounding the patio and shot across the yard toward Uncle Christophe's nursery. "Oh, dear..."

Liliana Lylestrom had run track in high school, so she hopped over the wall and ran after Iris with admirable speed, but the wayward Golden Retriever still managed to elude her. Iris ran as if she was on a specific mission and knew exactly whom she was to meet. So, a chase, of sorts, ensued with the golden dog hightailing it toward a light in the barn and her mistress sprinting behind her. When Iris tore through the open doors to Christophe's old barn, Liliana followed her in without any hesitation. She had played in that barn many times as a young girl, so she, too, flew through the front doors only to stop short at what she was witnessing. A mahogany-haired young man was ruffling Iris' head, and saying in a heavy brogue, "So, you're back again, are ya, now?" Instinctively she knew he had to be Christophe's relative.

That traitor, Iris, was angling her broad head to make sure that she received adequate "pets" and looked at Liliana in a way that bespoke, "Hey, this is my guy; go find your own."

Liliana Lylestrom, who was rarely at a loss for words, could only whisper, "Oh!"

The young man raised his head and looked first, at shapely young legs wearing pink bunny slippers, and second, at a dark-haired stranger whom he immediately guessed to be Christophe's special summer visitor. In a quiet, deep voice that was accented by his Scottish heritage, the stranger spoke, "Hullo, now who might you be? Are you related to this runaway lady?"

Coloring slightly, Liliana answered, "I'm Liliana Lylestrom, and yes, I do know this runaway lady. I guess that explains where she went when I arrived yesterday afternoon. As soon as she jumped out of the car, she was off." She then extended her hand and said, "You must be Christophe's relative from Scotland, and why are you here in the barn in the middle of the night?"

Looking quite serious, the young man replied, "Yes. I am, indeed, Christophe's second cousin from Scotland. I'm Declan Ryan, and you must be the university coed who's to do the watering this summer. *And*, as to why I'm here… I live upstairs in the loft, and I can't sleep…I'm still a bit off my sleeping schedule; the time change, you see. I guess you'd call it jet lag. So, while I was up and awake, I was rearranging some things to make my work easier this summer."

Feeling exceedingly silly in her tiny pajamas and bunny slippers, Liliana extended her right hand to Declan in greeting. After they shook hands, Liliana pointed toward her errant pooch and said, "This is incorrigible Iris." And to herself she noted, "What a traitor!" Iris, the Golden Retriever, hadn't even given her mistress a wag, let alone acknowledged that they had been inseparable for years by coming over to stand next to her. "I guess I know to whom your fidelity is given, Iris!" she quipped. Liliana noticed Declan had to bite his cheek to keep from laughing, but he did a terrible job of it.

Then, surprising Liliana with one of the most engaging smiles she had ever seen, Declan responded, "Off you go then, Iris…it's time for you to be getting back to your bed to chase some rabbits in your dreams!" He then gently nudged the big dog toward her mistress and said, "It's been a pleasure to meet you Liliana. I've heard very complementary things about you from Christophe and Annie. I will surely appreciate your help this summer." Extending his arm toward the barn door, he gallantly said. "Let me get you both back to the big house before someone discovers you're missing."

As they walked down the path toward the house, Liliana could not think of a thing to say to Declan. He seemed likable enough, but he was quite serious. Perhaps, it was the loss of his family and of finding himself in a new country that made him seem so serious, but even young Liliana could tell that he was far different from all the fraternity boys she knew at Brineforth University. He seemed far more courteous. Perhaps, it's because he was raised to be a gentleman…she mused to herself.

Upon arriving at Liliana's little patio, Declan extended his hand and assisted her, her bunny slippers, and her rogue Golden Retriever over the rock wall and back onto her tiny walled patio. He then bade her, "Good night, Liliana. I look forward to working with you this summer." Declan Ryan then disappeared into the night…the perfume of freshly-mowed grass, roses, and shower soap trailing behind him.

Liliana rolled her eyes and looked toward Iris, "Did you really just do that, Miss Iris? I had to meet Uncle Christophe's family member in my pajamas. I'm quite embarrassed. Don't you even think of running away like that again, young lady!" Attempting to look displeased, youthful Liliana Lylestrom walked back through the French doors to her guestroom, and a not-very-penitent Iris followed her.

RICHARD

*R*ichard **Rawlings** was ashamed. He was embarrassed about many things in his life. He was ashamed of his parents, his three younger sisters, his family home, ***and*** his family car. Factor in his shame regarding his height and its accompanying skinniness, and you would understand why Richard had a perpetual scowl on his face. In short, Richard would have traded his life for another if such a thing were possible. In his mind, he wished one could just step up to the return desk, much like the customer-service counter at the local department store and ask to be re-assigned to a new family. Unfortunately, life does not work that way for anyone, and Richard had to face shame and embarrassment on a regular basis.

First, there was the ugly evidence that his family was not well off in the form of the rental home in which they lived. It was situated on a nice lot, had a fair amount of large trees, yet both the front and back yard had been neglected so extensively that the grass had withered, and the flower beds were laden with so many weeds that the flowers his mother had attempted to plant had been choked out. His home was the only eyesore in the entire neighborhood. Richard would have mowed the grass and cleaned up the flower beds, but his mother cautioned him against it. Such actions would make his father feel even more inadequate and bring on a drinking binge. Young Richard knew his family could not afford such an outcome; both literally and figuratively.

Richard could remember such a time when his father did not have a problem with alcohol; they had been a happy family. His mother had been a stay-at-home mom, and she had cared for him and his little sisters. Once, he had had the family and the life that he was now forced to envy from afar. Things had started to change when Richard was about ten. No one ever shared with him why his father had started to feel so badly about things, but a certain cycle began to repeat itself every year and a half. There would be a move, a new job, a new school for Richard and his little sisters, and just when things would start to settle in, his mother's face would take on her look of worry and helplessness. His father would start to be missing from the dinner table several nights per week, and his mother would try to reassure her young ones that their father would be himself again soon. Yet, Richard's father never did start to act like his old self ever again.

By the time Richard was twelve years old, he realized that he was going to have to become an academic achiever if he wanted out of his situation. He began to apply himself to his studies, but still found himself stifled. Too often, he was called upon to be a care-giver to his three younger sisters. Why? Because his mother took on the role of bread winner since her husband could not stay sober long enough to stay employed. Richard's mother went back to teaching school; her vocation prior to becoming a wife and mother. She looked to Richard for help because her husband could not be trusted to care for his own young children. Though Richard would have done anything for his mother, he found himself resentful of the position to which he had been assigned. Any respect he had for his father eroded, as he watched his mother take on not one, but two jobs, to provide for her children. As for Richard's father…he fell further into the stranglehold of alcoholism. There were times when his father, Robert Rawlings, tried to escape his entrapment to alcohol, and he could go for several months without a drink, but when he fell off the wagon, he fell deeper and deeper into his self-propagated despair.

Things hit rock bottom, when Richard was fifteen years old. His father's drinking had become so problematic that Richard elected never to bring his young friends to his home ever again; no matter what the circumstances. It was too nerve wracking. Everyone else's father held down a job, they cheered on their kids at baseball and football practice; they took good care of their children; but not his father. It had once been alright if his friends met his mother, she was great, but Richard could never feel comfortable bringing anyone home to meet his family, now. If he did, he ran the risk of his father being in a drunken stupor and embarrassing him in front of his friends. Everyone knows that being a teenager is hard enough without having to cover for one's inebriated dad. At age fifteen, Richard could only feel shame for his father's behavior.

Because Richard had figured out early on that he would need to achieve high marks academically to eradicate himself from his family situation, it came as a crushing blow when the scholarship he had earned for his college education had not included money for housing and food. In pleading with his parents to help him cover these costs, his poor mother only shook her head with tears in her eyes. She firmly told him how proud she was of his accomplishments, but he was going to have to accept a different scholarship…one from the local community college. "If dad is handling his drinking problem better by the time you graduate from a two-year school, perhaps we can talk about trying for Richland University again, son. As things stand now, I am unable to give you money for much of anything. I am so very sorry Richard."

That night, Lorena Rawlings had to endure the upbraiding Richard gave her regarding the family's meager earnings. His father, Robert, was just cowardly enough to let his wife take the brunt of Richard's ire. Instead, Robert Rawlings went to the local bar to drink away his regrets. Angry eighteen-year-old Richard found himself forced to attend a much lesser-expensive community college with the hope of earning a full-ride scholarship later for his upper-division education. This was when Richard honed his propensity for lying in earnest.

Richard found that he could make up excuses as to why he gave up his scholarship that would make him appear to be a caring son to his parents and a loving brother to his younger sisters. Statements like, "Yeah, I'm just so very close to my mother and sisters that I can't bring myself to leave them; not when my mother works so very, very hard providing for the family. While she works, I am helping to raise my little sisters. I'm also taking care of my dad, too, because he was injured in an accident, and he is unable to work right now. That's one reason why our yard looks so bad…my mother and I are just too busy to care for it, and my father is still too injured to help with the yard. When he's back on his feet, we'll get things in order."

More than once, as they read between the lines, his friends' families gave Richard gift certificates for the local grocery store or money for a night out at a nice restaurant, but these gifts never made it home to be given to his hard-working mother. Richard used them for himself. It never even occurred to him that his benefactors might wonder why his mother never mentioned or thanked them for the gifts that they had sent to her. Poor, silly Richard.

Besides learning to lie proficiently, Richard also learned something of human nature, too. It began with his lovely mother. Richard found that if he nagged his mother long and hard enough for something he wanted or thought he needed; she would eventually acquiesce to his demands. At first, she gave in to his pressure just to get him to be quiet, and later, it was to keep the peace. All hard-working Lorena Rawlings wanted was for her family life to go smoothly. In short, she wanted everyone to get along. It was then that Richard realized that his mother was an appeaser. He handily learned to use his mother's peace-making nature again and again, until he left home to attend State College

By the time Richard was ready to attend State College, his propensity for lying had practically taken on a life of its own. Richard found he could schmooze clerks in the registrar's office with his impeccable manners, his sad stories of his family's misfortune, and his handsome good looks. Before he knew it, he was accepted to "State," as it was called, and the next chapter of his life was ready to begin.

It was at this same time, that Richard made a life-altering decision. Late one summer evening, Richard's parents and his three younger sisters were involved in an auto accident that proved to be a turning point in everyone's life. As it happened, Richard's father, Robert Rawlings, was driving his wife and three young daughters home from the County Fair as it was just getting dark. It had been an enjoyable day together, but Robert had consumed enough alcohol that his reflexes were impaired; a serious accident ensued. Though no one involved was mortally injured, Robert's alcoholic actions destroyed two automobiles and thoroughly inconvenienced two families for months as they endured physical therapy and restorative surgeries. Though this incident was his first infraction with drunken driving, Robert Rawlings was ordered to meet with a court-ordered counselor in lieu of a jail term.

Richard was so fed up and ashamed of his father by this time that the automobile accident was the last straw. Couple that accident with a court-ordered counselor, his father's entry into Alcoholics Anonymous, and driving an old beater car until something better could be arranged and Richard found that he could take no more. Several weeks later, he left for college. He vowed to himself that he would never return to his home or to his embarrassing family ever again, and he kept that vow.

At first, he fabricated excuses to his mother as to why he would not be home for the holiday season, but by the time his second year of college arrived, he made sure that he was always in receipt of an invitation to the home of one of his buddies. You see, Richard told the most egregious lie of his young life: He sorrowfully related to one and all that the entirety of his family had been wiped out in a fiery automobile accident just before his first year of college and that he was totally on his own...he had no one.

This lie endeared him to State's registrar, and she helped Richard to secure a student loan to ensure that he was properly educated. Somehow, wily Richard was able to produce false death certificates and fabricated tax records to secure that student loan. That same lie also made young women fawn over him and invite him home to meet their families. Lastly, Richard's lies also encouraged his young male friends to always pick up his tab for beer and pizza. In short, Richard had a very good thing going. He knew that if there were an award for proficient lying, that he would take home the coveted prize, indeed. He was proud of himself.

Back at his home, his poor mother worried because Richard was unaware that his father had been successful in his counseling. Robert Rawlings had finally overcome his debilitating alcohol habit and was working again. That frightening and very horrible accident had made him see the light. Yes, there was still an old beater car in the garage for a little while longer, but the yard was free of weeds and well-groomed. Their once-shameful family home was no longer neglected, and life was good again. Her husband had asked Lorena for her forgiveness and had vowed to be the man that he had been when they had married. Richard's three younger sisters were now enjoying the kind of father that they had only admired from afar before the accident. In short, Robert Rawlings was making up for lost time with his beloved family… everyone that is, except Richard.

Because of his staunch unwillingness to stay in touch, Richard never knew he had missed out on the salve that would have healed his wounds of inadequacy, seething anger, and festering frustration. Angry young Richard…he had shot himself in the foot, and he didn't even have the good sense to realize it. His sweet mother fretted that she might never see him again to share all the blessed changes that had come to the family. When Lorena Rawlings thought about her son, all she could ever say was, "Oh, Richard, why are you doing this to yourself?"

IRIS

ris, the Golden Retriever, was a good dog. She loved visiting one of her favorite places, The Old Vineyard Road Nursery. She had been there many times over the last fourteen years. Yes, Iris was considered an old dog now, but in her heart, she still felt like a puppy. When her girl (Everyone called her girl, Liliana.) had let her out of the car earlier in the day, Iris had bolted up the foot path to the barn.

Oh, she knew that barn!! It had all the scents a city dog longed to smell. Today, Iris honed in on something new: a human she didn't know. Yet, that new human's scent was mingled with all her favorites from the barn. Following her nose, she raced up to the open barn doors and stopped short. There was a new human there alright... He looked young, like her girl. Iris then remembered her training and refrained from galloping up to meet him. Instead, she just stood there and watched him. That young man was carrying some little trees in big black pots.

"Well, look at you! Where did you come from? Do you live around here?" he had said to her.

That nice young man had then held out his hand to her with his palm up, and Iris had taken that as an invitation to walk over and get to know him. Her radar told her this was a good person. She sniffed his palm, and then she wagged her tail. Iris knew a first-rate person when she met one. But just as they were getting to know each other, Iris had smelled something else that made her even happier…roast beef sandwiches!

Now, if she could have spoken, Iris would have told you these weren't just any roast beef sandwiches, they were that nice Aunt Annie's roast beef sandwiches with Swiss cheese, arugula, and horseradish. She had eaten one of those sandwiches before when one had been knocked off the luncheon tray and had landed on the stone patio floor. Iris had "hoovered up" that yummy treat before anyone could take it away from her. Faced with a dilemma, pets or roast beef, Iris had jumped sideways, dipped her head, wagged, and woofed. Her decision made; she was off.

As she darted back to find those sandwiches, she heard that young man say, "Well, good-bye, then!"

Iris knew she would go back to the barn later. She liked that person!

A SPECIAL FIRST SUMMER

he Old Vineyard Road Nursery looked beautiful this year. It was always picturesque, but the heavy snows from the just-finished winter had left it lush with vegetation and wild flowers that weren't always known to bloom. Though the grapevines were still in disarray, their wildness just seemed to add to the character of the property. Everywhere, there were hanging floral baskets, huge tables filled with flowers and vegetable starts, and platoons of blooming trees and vines. There was the scent of honeysuckle and wisteria floating on the air and heavily mulched flower beds adorned every available space. All in all, the old vineyard was coming back from its abandonment with vigor.

This morning, Declan Ryan, who hailed from Inverness, Scotland, watched petite Liliana Lylestrom walking hurriedly to keep up with her Uncle Christophe's long strides. It was her first day of work at the nursery. Christophe greeted his customers enthusiastically and made sure that they all met his "beautiful god-daughter, Liliana." Everyone was cordial to the lovely young ingénue. She, in turn, showed impeccable manners. Declan couldn't help looking at her; there was something about her that piqued his interest. Oh, he had had plenty of girlfriends while at university in Scotland, but none of them had ever put his heart into overdrive…somehow, when he had escorted her home earlier this morning, at four o'clock, to be exact, he had intuitively known she was very different.

For some reason that only his Creator knew, they had met in the middle of the night. Her crazy, old dog had shown a marked preference for him, and that canine had come bounding into the barn in the middle of the night followed by adorable young Liliana. She had been wearing pink bunny slippers; something Declan had heard about but had never witnessed firsthand. Couple those bunny slippers with green eyes, long brunette hair, and the most elating smile he had ever seen in his almost twenty-three years of life, and Declan Ryan was slightly fearful for his heart. Yet, this young woman had no clue that she was so very pretty. It was her sweet innocent demeanor, coupled with a lovely personality, which made her so unforgettable.

This morning, after their middle-of-the-night meeting, which was unbeknownst to Christophe Riordan, both he and Liliana had had to work hard to stifle their smiles when introductions were made. Declan took the high road, and extended his hand and his greetings to her, but she had to work a wee bit harder to stifle her laughter when they shook hands. Thus, their friendship began. Later that same day, he had been assigned to help Liliana move her things into a tiny, little attic apartment over the local bookshop. Declan had helped her to carry three huge suitcases up to her new attic abode in addition to her dog's bed, a forty-pound bag of senior dog kibble, and a portable sewing machine. Declan had asked himself, "Why on earth does she need a sewing machine when she's to spend the summer working at a nursery?"

After he had helped her finish moving her things into the little apartment, Liliana had offered to buy him a late afternoon snack at Annie and Christophe's diner which was just down the street from her little garret. Declan had heartily accepted. Over iced tea and scones, they had gotten to know each other better.

Liliana had asked, "Declan, I know you just lost your mother a few months ago, but what made you decide to come to America? I'm so insulated here with my family and friends, that I feel it would be hard for me to make such a life-changing decision."

"Well, you see…" he began, "I graduated almost two years ago from university. My area of emphasis for my science degree was in botany and horticulture. My mum cared very much for Christophe, her first cousin, as they had grown up together. Shortly, before she died, she asked me to be sure to stay in touch with him. He is really my only living relative. So, I did call him and, after we visited for a while on the phone, Christophe just up and asked if I would be interested in helping him with his nursery and his vineyard. He said he could use my expertise, but I think he knew I needed a change of scenery. Since I hadn't worked in my field after graduation because I was caring for my mum, it seemed like a good opportunity for me. So far, I like what I see, and I have enjoyed learning from Christophe. He is a very good man."

Liliana had then given him her electric smile and said, "I hope you enjoy it here in Rosemeade Township. I think it is one of the prettiest places in the entire world; though I've only seen the United States and Canada very extensively. How about you? Have you seen much of the world?"

"Yes, I saw a fair amount during my school years. Since the United Kingdom and the Continent are rather close in proximity, it is much easier to travel Europe on a student's budget than an American student can. I've visited Italy, France, Germany and Austria…I went on a skiing holiday in Switzerland…pretty much the top highlights. They were all very interesting and quite scenic," he answered.

"How long was your mother ill, Declan?" she asked softly.

Declan sensed she didn't want to bring up a sad subject, but she was just being a caring person. "Mum had brain and lung cancers. She had a very hard last year and a half. She was diagnosed right after I graduated from university, that's why I chose to care for her in lieu of going right into the workforce. Now, I'm glad that I did. She was a very good mother to me, and I wanted to care for her during the last days of her life. We had some very special times together."

Liliana looked at him earnestly, and said, "You'll never regret your choice, I'm sure. My parents had me when they were in their late forties. They had waited a long, long time to conceive a child, so you might say I was given the very best of their love. I hope that when their time comes, that I might show as much honor to them as you have shown to your mother, Declan. I quite admire you for what you did for her."

With that one little statement, Declan Ryan found that he had fallen just the tiniest bit in love with young Liliana Lylestrom.

Earlier that same day, Liliana had noticed Declan Ryan working very hard. She smiled when she thought about him. When she had met him in the middle of the night, she had felt so silly. She had been in her pajamas and slippers. But Declan had been a gentleman. He hadn't ogled her like some other guys from college might have…no, he had made sure that she and Iris had gotten home safely to Christophe and Annie's house. "What a nice guy," she thought.

Then, after work, Uncle Christophe had asked Declan to help her get her things moved up to her attic apartment. She had secretly admired his muscles as he had carried her hefty luggage up the stairs. He hadn't complained once about any of her stuff. She was sure that he must understand women, having been raised by his widowed mother. Reflecting on him…he was tall, broad shouldered, and he had hair that would make all her dorm friends squeal with admiration… very dark, wavy hair, combed back off his face…it was just a little long, but not too long. That hair, coupled with brilliant blue eyes, flawless skin, and perfect lips made him one of the most-handsome guys Liliana had ever seen. Her room-mate, Suzette, would say that he looked like one of those hunks painted on the cover of a romance novel. Liliana had to admit that she agreed.

All Liliana knew was that when she offered to treat him to refreshments after all his hard work in helping her to move in, he had accepted. It made her very happy. They had a nice conversation. She found that though serious, Declan was easy to talk with... She guessed that his serious demeanor had something to do with losing one's parents. She was so loved; she could easily understand why he chose to care for his mother in the last years of her life. If their roles had been reversed, she knew she would make the same choice that he had. Not very many young men of her acquaintance would be so thoughtful. Knowing this about his character had made her tumble just slightly in love with Declan Ryan.

When their afternoon refreshments were finished, he had covered her hand with his own when she reached for the check. He had simply said, "Where I come from, we look out for the fairer gender. Let me pay for our tea. It is my pleasure." Liliana thought he was the most gallant man she had ever met, besides her father. So began a very memorable summer in the lives of the two young friends…

Liliana Lylestrom's summer employment took off with alacrity. Under Christophe Riordan and Declan Ryan's tutelage, she learned to love the ebb and flow of working in the nursery and caring for its beauty. She had an innate understanding of what spurred young seedlings into growing lush and strong. Christophe was delighted to find that she would not only water his precious plants and trees, but she would rearrange them daily to present them at their best to his customers. She dead-headed everything and nipped off broken fronds or damaged buds. As if that weren't enough, the clients loved her. She had a knack for remembering their names, which pleased them tremendously. In the fast-paced lanes that were hurtling the world toward a new millennium, she gave them old-time courtesy and service. In short, Liliana Lylestrom was a natural.

Old Jim adored the ground that her garden-booted feet trod upon, and he delighted in visiting with her and hulking around anything that was too heavy for her slight young frame to move. He acknowledged to Christophe that, "If I were just sixty years younger, I would ask her to marry me." Christophe knowingly smiled; it was no news to him that everyone adored Liliana.

As for Declan Ryan, he was the biggest beneficiary of Liliana's charm. Because she worked closely with him, he spent a lot of time in her company. This did not bother Declan at all; in fact, he welcomed it. She was bright and articulate and was a stellar assistant when there was time for research. In short, Liliana helped him to feel like his young life had begun again…he felt alive; something he hadn't felt in quite a while.

Within weeks of her arrival at Old Vineyard Road, Liliana was an old pro at her job. Because she was efficient, and because her efficiency helped Declan, Christophe began to find that things were, indeed, getting caught up. On those occasions, he encouraged Liliana to show Declan around the area; it was always the same scenario: Liliana, driving; Declan Ryan, passenger; and Iris, the Golden Retriever, in the back seat of her little, robin-egg blue Volkswagen convertible. Somehow, Annie Riordan always knew when to pack a picnic hamper for their excursions, so showing Declan around the area always proved to be great fun.

No matter where they went, they always ended up at one of the larger lakes in the district. Liliana kept a big colorful old quilt in the trunk of her little car, so she was always ready for a picnic, star gazing, or warming up after a swim. She loved to swing out over the lake on the ancient rope swings that others had installed years ago. Her brunette ponytail always flew behind her as she swung out over the blue water. Declan always made sure that he was out in the lake first, just in case something happened. He couldn't stand the thought of her ever being hurt.

Sometimes, Declan invited her out to the cinema. He would call for her at her tiny apartment, and then, they would walk to the theater together. On those occasions, she always said, "Oh, Declan, I just adore the movies." And she did…it didn't matter whether it was an action movie, a comedy, or a romance…She truly enjoyed becoming immersed in someone else's story on the giant screen. Declan loved to sneak a peek at her sweet profile while she was completely engaged with the story. Afterward, they would walk to Christophe and Annie's old diner for something to eat. There was always delightful conversation on those evenings. The special days of Declan's first summer in America were to become treasured memories, but the memory which meant the most to him was when Liliana invited him to her family home for the Fourth of July…

Though they had only just met a very few weeks ago, Liliana had insisted that Declan join Christophe, Annie, and her family for his first American holiday. He wasn't completely sure he should accept, but both Christophe and Annie had insisted, as well. "You're family now, Declan!" Christophe had boomed with vigor. "Of course, you'll join us. It wouldn't be the same without you."

On the morning of the Fourth of July, Declan had driven Liliana and Iris to Reedsburgh in one of the company trucks, while Christophe and Annie followed behind in Annie's old Porsche. It had been a brilliant morning. The temperature was perfect, and the sunlight shimmered off everything. Liliana had sat near to him on the truck's bench seat because Iris required a wide berth. It had felt good to have her so near.

She smelled of something nice, but he couldn't quite put a name to the fragrance. "Oh, she is a sweet thing," he had thought to himself.

When they had arrived at her family home, Declan couldn't believe his eyes. Her home was beautiful. It was situated on a sizable lot with handsome trees planted in perfect proportion around the perimeter. A huge vegetable garden embellished the south side of the property, and there were roses in bloom everywhere. A rose arbor, adorned with pink climbers, marked the entrance to the side yard where a perfect patio beckoned. It, too, was planted with colorful beds and containers showcasing cascading petunias, sweet potato vines, and geraniums. There were blue delphiniums in full bloom as well as hollyhocks and foxglove. Mr. and Mrs. Lylestrom knew a thing or two about English cottage gardening, it was obvious. No wonder Liliana had taken to her new job like a duck to water.

Her parents, Stephan and Jenny Lylestrom, had welcomed him as if he were the most-important guest they had ever entertained. Declan was humbled by their hospitality and by their interest in him; never had anyone shown such interest in his family or in his vocation. These were truly nice people. He could now see why Liliana was so good natured; it had been modeled to her by loving parents. Stephan Lylestrom had taken him aside shortly after their arrival and had thanked him for helping Liliana to get moved into her little apartment and for tolerating Iris's antics. Jenny Lylestrom had hugged him and thanked him for being such a good friend to "her girl." Declan liked them both immensely.

As the day had progressed, Jenny Lylestrom had served them a delicious meal of southern BBQ. She had toasted soft sesame-seed-topped buns, filled them with a layer of pulled BBQ pork, topped that layer with her coleslaw salad, and lastly, had laid sliced dill pickles on top of the coleslaw. Finally, a buttered-and-grilled top bun was added atop all those tasty layers. Declan thought the sandwich was one of the most-interesting things he had ever seen assembled in the kitchen, and after his first bite…one of the most-delicious things he had ever tasted…that is, until Jenny served her home-made blueberry pie, topped not with ice cream, but with whipped cream. He found himself quickly deciding that Americans really knew how to enjoy their bountiful food.

After their delicious meal, Liliana had taken him on a tour of her home, and he was fascinated with the chronology of her life in photographs…such a cute little baby, then a pretty little girl, and finally, a fresh and very attractive young college coed. Yes, it seemed to Declan Ryan that Liliana Lylestrom had led a charmed life, but it hadn't spoiled her disposition. Quite the opposite, she fostered happiness wherever she went. "No wonder, Old Jim is so crazy about her," he laughed to himself.

As evening drew near, all six of them had walked the short distance to a handsome city park not far from Liliana's home. There was a band shell, and an eclectic group of musicians were playing songs from every era of America's colorful history. Declan could see why Americans were always so proud of their country. The Fourth of July was definitely a fine holiday.

Finally, after a spectacular and very colorful fireworks intermission, the musicians started to play music for dancing under the stars. He and Liliana had danced together quite a few times that night. He had thoroughly enjoyed himself. As they all walked back to her family home, he had tucked her hand into the crook of his arm, and had held that small, but very capable, hand. It had been a day to remember. On the ride back to Rosemeade late that evening, she had snuggled just a wee bit closer to him than she had on the ride earlier in the morning, her head occasionally lying on his shoulder when she dozed. Declan's day went from, "a day to remember," to one of his best days ever. "Happy Birthday, America!" Declan Ryan had whispered.

Liliana had awakened when Declan pulled the company truck up in front of her bookstore garret. She was slightly groggy and kept shaking her head to wake up. Declan knew that she could tell that he had enjoyed himself with her family, and for some reason, he also knew it had meant something to her. So, when Declan escorted her and Iris to their door, she hugged him. He had then kissed her good-bye very softly on the cheek. Unbeknownst to him, Liliana went into her tiny garret apartment and relived her day several times before she went to sleep. As for Declan, he drove the battered company truck home to Old Vineyard Road with a secret smile on his face.

Summertime was waning; the slant of the sun was starting to look more like September than August. Both Liliana Lylestrom and Declan Ryan were sorry to see it come to an end. This summer had been a renaissance of sorts for Declan; he had felt youthful again. For Liliana, she had experienced many firsts: a real job, a tiny apartment of her own, and a friendship with someone who possessed the admirable qualities always modeled by her father…someone fun loving, yet respectful and responsible. The summer had been a heady time for both young people. Though neither of them spoke of it, they both knew the Thanksgiving break seemed a very long time off.

LATE SUMMER'S POSTCARDS

*L*iliana *Lylestrom* sat in her dorm room. She looked out the open window and noticed that a few of the trees were just beginning to change colors. Enjoying the panorama, she began to think of the wonderful summer she had just spent at Uncle Christophe's tree-and-flower nursery, and then she began to think of Declan Ryan. When he came to mind, she unknowingly sighed, and if she could have seen her face in the mirror atop her chest of drawers, she would have seen the flush of first love on her face.

Thinking of Declan, then brought a smile to her countenance, and she found herself missing him immensely. She had already started counting down the days until the Thanksgiving break, but she didn't think she could go that long without his wonderful company. She sighed, took a deep breath, and began to do mathematical calculations that were due tomorrow morning. It was hard to stop thinking of him.

Unbeknownst to young Liliana Lylestrom, just a little over one hundred miles away, Declan Ryan was quietly mulching seedling trees at The Old Vineyard Road Nursery for the chillier temperatures which would be upon them before long. As Declan labored at his work, he was secretly thinking of one thing only that afternoon: Liliana Lylestrom. The more he thought about her, the more he wanted to see her. She buoyed one's spirits whenever she was around, and everyone at the nursery had missed her very much after she had left to return to her university studies. Funny thing, though, Declan felt as though he was off kilter without her company.

Knowing that he likely wouldn't see her until America's Thanksgiving holiday, Declan decided that he would write to her… not a letter, not even a short note… he would send her a postcard from his late mother's colorful collection with just a couple of sentences.

He knew Liliana would truly enjoy such a small reminder of their friendship, but little did he know that he was starting a tradition that would mean so very much to the two of them.

That night, when returned to his loft at the end of a very busy day, he went straight to the small chest of belongings from his old life in Inverness, Scotland. Opening the said chest, he inhaled the scent of the cedar wood that lined his mum's old chest, breathed in her scent on several beloved items of hers that he had saved for no particular reason, and found the rectangular box that held his mother's collection of postcards.

Declan thoughtfully went through the colorful stack of cards in his mum's collection and chose one that he felt sure Liliana would enjoy. It was a very old depiction of Edinburgh Castle underneath a truly azure sky with fluffy cumulus clouds scudding across that colorful sky. Needless to say, its artist had captured the castle perfectly. Here is what Declan wrote to his special new friend…

Hello, sweet Liliana,   *September 17th*

I've been missing you these last two weeks. It's just not the same without you here at the nursery. Thank you for sharing "Your America" with me. It was my finest summer ever, and I am indebted to you for making it so special. Best regards to your parents and to your wagging Iris. Warmly, Declan

Three days later, Liliana went to pick up her mail, and was so delighted with Declan's postcard that she went straight to the bookstore in the Student Union Building to look for a postcard to return to him.

For some reason, she had remembered seeing postcards with reproduction prints of floral botanicals adjacent to the art history books last year, and true to her memory, there they were… she chose a very beautiful reproduction print of an old-world red rose. She could almost inhale its exquisite perfume.

Here is what she wrote back to her memorable Scottish friend…

Hello, Declan!   September 20th

I agree with you. It was a wonderful summer, and I was happy to drive the backroads of Rosemeade County with you. I am sorry you had to navigate to get us back to the nursery some days, though! Perhaps, you might like to come up to Brineforth for homecoming in October… My whole family will come, and now you are a part of it, too. Please consider it.

With affection, Liliana

And so began what would serve as a continuing connection between Declan Ryan and Liliana Lylestrom. The thread of their respective postcards would bind them together until they could see one another again that first autumn.

One might query why they chose this method of connection in this age of technology, but both felt there was such a sweetness in handwritten words. For Declan, it was his desire to make sure his lovely young friend never felt any pressure from him.

And for Liliana, she loved how gallant Declan had been in corresponding in this fashion with her. It truly gave her something special to look forward to each week amidst the sea of homework, quizzes, and examinations that she was swimming through. Somehow, his written words truly buoyed her spirit.

A MEMORABLE SECOND SUMMER

Though **Liliana Lylestrom** had visited her parents and had seen Christophe and Annie, and occasionally, Declan over the course of the school year, she found herself eagerly looking forward to the summer break. She could have enrolled for a summer session of school to help expedite her studies, but she suspected that her heart would ache if she could not get back to her work at the nursery. Of course, in her heart of hearts, she knew working with Declan Ryan was one of the real reasons why she was so anxious to get back to The Old Vineyard Road Nursery.

At last, finals week was over, she had received good marks, and her dorm room was packed up and ready to be transported home. Stephan and Jenny arrived at ten o'clock in the morning the day after grades had been posted, and all three of them enjoyed their leisurely trip back to Reedsburgh. Both Stephan and Jenny had exchanged knowing looks when their sweet girl kept reiterating how much she was looking forward to her summer job.

Miles away in Rosemeade Township, young Declan Ryan was busy sprucing up The Old Vineyard Road Nursery for Liliana's arrival. He was tanned already, had been smiling unceasingly for the better part of a week and frequently commented to Christophe Riordan that, "He would be glad to have Liliana's help once again, as things were getting busy." Christophe Riordan and Old Jim had exchanged knowing winks.

At last, the day of Liliana's arrival came. It was a warm, sunny day with billowing white clouds floating in the brilliant blue sky. Around noontime, that slightly shabby blue VW Beetle came toddling up the drive with an even prettier Liliana at the wheel and a whiter-muzzled

Iris riding shotgun. True to form, as soon as the car stopped and Liliana opened her door, Iris shot out of the car and over to the nursery to seek out Declan. Liliana thought for sure that her dog must have radar for that guy, but she did not blame Iris one bit.

Minutes later, a smiling Declan escorted Iris from the barn. He was followed by an eager Christophe, and a very happy Old Jim. Annie, who had heard some commotion, came down the path from the house. She articulated it best, "Now, we can finally usher in the summer season. Our Liliana has returned to Rosemeade Township, at last!"

It goes without saying that hugs abounded for the next little while. Annie announced that dinner would be served promptly at half past six that evening and that all of them were invited. She then dispatched Declan to go with Liliana to her little apartment and carry her things up the stairs once again. Minutes later, an Old Vineyard Road Nursery truck, loaded with French Blue chairs and orange geraniums that had spent the last nine months in the greenhouse, was seen making its way into town. It was followed by a convertible-top robin-egg blue V-Dub up to the junction, and both vehicles turned into town.

As Christophe Riordan and Old Jim walked back to their offices, Old Jim elbowed Christophe in the ribs and queried, "Do you think Declan is happy that she's back?" He and Christophe then proceeded to double up in laughter.

Declan Ryan was happy to do the "carrying and fetching" of anything that belonged to adorable Liliana Lylestrom. He bounded up and down the stairs with her giant suitcases, Iris's dog basket, and that blue-and-white portable sewing machine once again. He still wondered why she carried it with her. The last thing he carried up was a little cooler.

While Declan carried her things up from the car, Liliana had arranged her tiny patio with its resident French blue chairs and orange geraniums. She was quite impressed with what a few months in the greenhouse could do for already pretty geraniums; but now, they were huge and so very vibrant. Their new size and repotting (thanks to Declan) really added even more charm to her roof-top getaway.

When Declan joined her, she opened her little cooler and presented him with a bottle of cooled water, and a small tin of Scottish shortbread. "I made these for you, Declan; I hope you like them. They are likely not as good as your mother's, but they are a gift from my heart. I tried several recipes, but I thought this one was the best."

Declan was touched that she had even remembered what his favorite cookie was, let alone that she had baked it for him. He opened the tin and recognized the perfect crumb and the perfect pale color of her work, and he immediately knew these were to be the most-delicious shortbread triangles he had ever tasted. Declan felt slightly guilty that her shortbread was even better than his dear mother's. "Forgive me, Mum," he thought to himself.

"I have one other thing for you, Declan," she said shyly. "I hope you don't think me forward, but last summer, when I picked you up at the loft for one of our lovely trips to the lake, I noticed that your bed looked slightly plain. I took the liberty of making you a quilt, because Mrs. Addington, my landlady, was teaching me how to do old-fashioned quilt making after hours last summer. I finally finished the hand stitching just a few weeks ago." She then handed him a parcel wrapped in plain brown paper and tied with hemp garden twine.

"Liliana, how very thoughtful of you," he said softly. His large nurturing hands carefully opened the parcel which revealed a classic quilt done in deeply-colored, jewel-tone stars on a background of very pale blue. It was obvious from her intricate work, that Liliana was very talented; even *be* could see that, and all the while, he had wondered why she toted around her sewing machine.

"This is very handsome, Liliana. I had no idea you were so very artistic, and what a thoughtful gift, too." He then gave her his teasing smile and quipped, "I guess it goes without saying that I shall probably dream of you every night from now on, as I slumber beneath your special gift to me." He reached for her and kissed her soft lips. "Thank you, Liliana."

Declan reluctantly broke their embrace, and said, "I guess today is the time for gift giving." He then proceeded to pull something from within his shirt pocket. "While I was in Reedsburgh on business a week or two ago, I chanced upon a jewelry store that had something made just for you in the window. I could not pass by without purchasing it for you. Here…"

Liliana took the small square box he offered. It was wrapped in bright blue paper and bound with white ribbon. She blushed and said, "Declan, this is very sweet of you to buy me a gift; thank-you." With slightly trembling hands, she opened her box. Inside, nestled within sky-blue tissue paper, was a sterling silver linked bracelet, upon which hung charms that would delight any ardent dog lover. Yet, this bracelet contained a miniature Golden Retriever, a perfect little dog house, a tiny dog dish engraved with Iris's name, a minute chew bone, and a red-glass fetching ball. The bracelet opened and closed with a dog-bone shaped fastener that fit through a tiny, circular dog collar. Liliana was delighted, "Oh, Declan, what a perfect gift!"

Declan replied, "I know your wrist is small, so I had several links removed to ensure that it fits you properly."

"Oh, Dec," she chirped. "You are so very thoughtful." She then leaned over and kissed his cheek.

Declan Ryan gave her his beautiful smile and thought that he had never been happier to see anyone in his life.

About six weeks later, something happened that left Liliana Lylestrom broken-hearted and Declan Ryan thankful that he had made the effort to purchase that special gift for her.

It had been evident to everyone for several days that aging Iris had not been feeling well. Liliana had tried to ply her with special dog treats, but Iris was not interested; she only wanted to lie beneath the shade of the vine-covered pergola that housed Annie's car. Christophe who had grown up on the farm recognized the signs of an animal whose life was coming to an end. He knew the expense of a veterinarian visit would be useless. Iris had simply grown too old to last much longer, but he made sure that Iris was comfortable in a little nest that he fashioned for her from blankets that had long been out of service but were clean and comfortable.

Large Christophe Riordan had gently picked Iris up like a baby lamb and had cuddled her in his embrace. He moved her to a nearby grassy spot below a vine-covered section of the beautiful yard that surrounded his property. He tucked her gently into the soft bed of blankets. Here, Iris would be protected from the afternoon sun. Iris had locked eyes with him, and her soulful gold-brown ones had communicated her thanks.

Throughout the day, Liliana had continued to check on her dog every few minutes. Each time, Iris would look toward her, but she could no longer thump her tail in greeting. Declan, too, had visited her and had smoothed her soft ears with gentle hands and had crooned an old Scottish lullaby to her.

Around five o'clock that afternoon, Christophe knew the end was not too far away. He dispatched Liliana to stay with her beloved companion. Liliana lay down on her side in the soft grass next to Iris. She held one of Iris's big golden paws in her hand and she stroked the dog's face and ears with her other.

"Iris, you are such a good girl, and you have been a good friend to me for most of my life. I love you, and I thank you for being my sweet companion. I can't tell you how much I will miss you, and who will ever be able to greet Christophe's customers with such enthusiasm when you are gone? Iris, please know how much you are loved and how much joy you have brought into all our lives. You will be sorely missed," Liliana had sobbed.

Iris turned her soft big head slightly, lifted it, and then laid it down upon her girl's left arm. Her eyes continued to look steadily into Liliana's eyes. Liliana embraced her sweet dog as best she could and looked back into Iris's soulful eyes saying, "Yes, you're a good girl, you're a very good dog, and you're *my* dog." until she saw the light of life leave those pretty gold-brown eyes. Liliana had then hugged her old dog tightly and sobbed uncontrollably.

Annie, Christophe, Old Jim, and Declan had watched the poignant scene from several feet away. Each of them had wiped tears from their eyes as well. Christophe, who knew Liliana like she was his own, put his huge hand on Declan's shoulder and said, "It's you she's going to want right now, son. Go to her. Jim and I will dig a grave for Iris on the crest of the foothill over there. I'll let you know when it's ready."

Declan Ryan, who had faced too much loss in his young life already, knew just the right things to say to Liliana. In just a minute or two, he had her up and on her feet, his arm around her slender shoulders. He mopped up her tear-stained eyes with his clean handkerchief and guided her over to Annie's loving arms.

Annie had then held Liliana close and brushed her long hair off her face. Liliana tried to smile but started to break down again. Annie kissed her on the cheek and said, "I'm going in to make Iris's favorite roast beef and arugula sandwiches in her honor for dinner. You sit for a while with Declan. He'll take good care of you, sweetheart." Annie then put a tartan throw that she had been clutching for the last half hour over Iris' still body, but she left the dog's broad head uncovered. Iris looked as though she was enjoying a long, winter's nap

Declan and Liliana sat on the grass near to where Iris lay in repose. Declan's heart was heavy, because he knew that Liliana and her dog always came as a matched set. Neither he nor Christophe had ever worried about her staying alone in town, simply because she had that great big old dog to protect her. While Liliana looked unseeing out over the wild, old vineyard rows, deep in her own thoughts, Declan Ryan was making a punch list of the things he would need to buy at the hardware store to ensure her safety in town.

When Christophe and Old Jim had finished digging the grave for Iris, they carried her up the hill hammock-style in an old blanket, Liliana and Declan had followed them up to the grave site, and Liliana said a last good-bye to her old dog. Declan had held her hand. Christophe had again picked Iris up like a little lamb. Old Jim had removed her lavender-colored bandana and had snipped off a lock of her silky golden fur. He soberly handed them to Liliana. Jim, wound the blanket completely around Iris; then, both men folded the tartan throw over her blanketed body. When they were done, Iris's remains were lowered down into the deep grave. Christophe gave Declan the signal, and he walked Liliana back down the hill to Christophe's home.

After a quiet meal with Christophe, Annie, and Old Jim, they each raised a toast to Iris's life, and Declan drove Liliana back to her little apartment. He immediately noticed that entry up the stairs to her place was not nearly so noisy without Iris's nails tattooing their tune upon the wooden treads. When Liliana opened her door, the first thing they both spotted was Iris's half-eaten bowl of kibble and one of her chew toys. Liliana, who was pretty much cried out, had sighed heavily. "Do you want me to drop off her things at the Humane Society, Liliana?" Declan had asked.

"No, Declan, not just yet, I'd like to keep them for just a little while longer. Thanks, though," she smiled. "Would you like to go out on the roof for a while?"

"That sounds great, it's a clear night. Why don't we do some star gazing?" Declan replied.

At the end of their star gazing, Liliana had admitted that all the constellations looked like Iris to her this evening, and they had had a good laugh. When it was time for him to go home, Liliana said good night with a tear trickling down her cheek.

Declan Ryan, who knew how she felt, hugged her and said, "Why don't I stay for a bit longer…I could tell you about my mangy old dog, Bob, from when I was a boy."

In the end, she had fallen asleep on her tiny sofa still dressed in her work clothes, and Declan had slept on her floor.

When he had awakened early the next morning, his head ached and his back felt about a hundred years old, but it was all worth it when she had said, "Declan, thank-you for comforting me yesterday. I just love you for it." Declan Ryan had driven home slightly crippled, but with a smile in his heart.

A week later, when Liliana arrived at work, Christophe had met her with a tender smile on his face. "There is something I want you to see, Liliana." They had walked together up to where Iris was buried. There, on top of her grave, was a small, ornately carved, white cross. The cross was inscribed, and it simply said, "Iris, a good dog."

Christophe had quietly said, "That is Old Jim's way of showing his love for you. Why don't we pick out some blue flax or some forget-me-nots, and I'll plant them on her grave."

Liliana had been very touched by everyone's affection for her, because she realized that losing Iris had been the first real bump in the road of her young and happy life. She knew there would be more bumps along the way, but so appreciated everyone's sincere kindness to her.

The remainder of the summer had sped by in much the same fashion as last year. There had, again, been many hours of hard work, frolics at the lake, drives through the back roads of Rosemeade County, and nights at the cinema. This year, Liliana and Declan had also added antiquing to their repertoire of fun, so his loft no longer had only a bed for its inventory. On a regular basis, Christophe would shake his head when Declan and Liliana arrived toting yet another piece of someone else's life into Declan's abode. But Christophe had to admit that both Declan and Liliana had an eye for design. That old loft had never looked so good!

When the first week of September arrived, Declan and Liliana picnicked together one last time. She wore the bracelet that Declan had given her. On this junket, Declan drove one of the nursery's small trucks, and Liliana sat right next to him, though she had not been deprived of space by Iris. She had tucked her hand around his arm and smiled up at him. It felt good to be with her. Declan truly wanted her for his own; but for some reason, he felt he needed to hold back. She was still such a young thing.

Declan always seemed to wrestle with the reasons he held back his sincere feelings for her. "Why?" he wondered. He knew that he cared deeply for her. He knew that what he felt for her was, most-likely, love. Was it because he didn't want to change the dynamics of their relationship by declaring his feelings for her? He did not want to drive her away if she did not feel the same…but she always seemed very happy to be in his company. Was it because they worked together? No, that had never been a problem, because it was a family-run business, and it was obvious that Christophe and Annie would like nothing better…

All he knew was that he had never spent time with anyone as special as Liliana Lylestrom. She was still in school, and he didn't want to deprive her of any special experiences there. But Declan Ryan finally had to be honest with himself…it was because he had nothing to offer her. "Liliana deserves someone who can give her the best of everything. Will I ever be that man?" He had asked of himself. The logical part of him felt that such thinking was unwise. "I am an educated man, and I have amassed some money over the last year. Yet, she is so very special. Does she deserve someone better?" He had wrestled with these questions many times. He decided he could not tear himself up with such thinking as he drove along the lake road. "Today must be special, as it will be the last time that we'll be able to share time with each other for a while," he had wisely decided.

In the end, Declan Ryan kissed Liliana Lylestrom several times that day. He held her hand, he laughed with her, and he shared a meal with her. When they returned to her apartment, they, again, stargazed on the roof-top patio. When it was finally time for their summer to be over, Declan loaded most of her things into her little V-dub, and then he loaded her French blue chairs and her gigantic orange geraniums in the company truck. He bounded up her steps one last time. He embraced her and looked into her eyes, and he said, "Liliana Rose Lylestrom, you are the sweetest young woman in this world, and I shall miss you tremendously. But I will think of you each night as I fall to sleep, because I'll be wrapped in that handsome quilt you made just for me." He kissed her one last time. "I'll see you soon sweet Lily…"

Liliana had smiled at him radiantly, "I'll be counting the days, Declan."

A month later, Liliana Lylestrom answered the door of her new, off-campus apartment. She gasped in delight. Declan Ryan stood there holding a brown cardboard box. "I've brought you a pie," he said with a pleased smile. "I just happened to be in the neighborhood, and I know your feelings about pie… Also, your mum told me where to find you!" he laughed. It goes without saying that her roommates swooned when Liliana delightedly ushered him into the room.

AUTUMNAL POSTCARDS

*D*eclan Ryan had brought a peach pie to present to Liliana at her tiny apartment on the outskirts of Brineforth University, and that day, it seemed as though their affection for one another had increased ten-fold. He felt so much fondness for her that it was hard for him not to hold her close that afternoon. She, too, was so elated to be with him that she could hardly tear herself away from him when the time came for them to say, "Good-bye."

That Autumn, postcards were sent again and again, but this year's cards became increasingly more poignant. It was also becoming apparent to both of her parents as well as to Christophe and Annie that the two sweethearts were on the precipice of falling in love. Stephan and Jenny Lylestrom adored Declan and were very pleased that their daughter had chosen such a kind and thoughtful man for her beau. Knowing that Liliana was so very fond of "Their Declan" pleased Christophe and Annie immensely, too.

About a week after Declan's memorable pie delivery, Liliana received a beautiful old-world postcard depicting perfectly ripe pears; just recently plucked from the tree. Here is what Declan wrote to her…

Dearest Liliana,   3rd October

I know that I just saw you a little over a week ago, but I'll be candid. I miss you so much. Today, Annie baked a fresh pear tart because she is missing you, too. It was delicious, but it just wasn't the same without your lovely company at the tea table in Christophe's library.

With every affection,

Declan

Young Liliana Lylestrom was so struck by the beauty on the front of his postcard, as well as by his written candor on the back, that all she could do was hold the card to her heart and dance around the room. Her roommates smiled at one another knowingly as they witnessed her antics. They were very happy for her because they innately knew Declan Ryan was a prize.

A day or two later, Liliana found just the right postcard for Declan at a tiny little bookstore about three blocks from her apartment. Its artwork depicted a small square print of a little yellow bird with blue wings. The little bird print had been affixed upon a background of water-colored botanical leaves and a small wood cut of printed plant fronds. It was a unique postcard, and here is what she wrote to Declan in return…

Oh, Declan,   *October 10th*

What a perfectly beautiful postcard you sent to me. You know how much I love Annie's fresh pear tart, but I have to say that it would never be right for me to have it without you, either. Again, precious Declan, thank you for coming to see me and know that I am truly looking forward to your homecoming visit very soon.

Affectionately,
Liliana

And so, the autumn progressed onward toward Brineforth's homecoming celebration and then on to Thanksgiving when the two special friends would be able to again give thanks and enjoy a meal together at Christophe and Annie's home. The two young sweethearts were anxiously looking forward to both reunions.

A SPECIAL THIRD SUMMER

*I*t was late May, and everyone at Old Vineyard Road had been anticipating the arrival of Liliana Rose Lylestrom. Liliana was the sparkler that always turned summertime into an event. Though he would never admit it to anyone, Declan Ryan had been counting the days until she arrived. They had seen each other periodically throughout the last nine months, but their time was always limited. Now, they had all summer long to spend catching up; Declan Ryan couldn't wait to see her.

As always, her pale blue Volkswagen convertible had pulled in the drive shortly after noontime. Again, Declan had been blown away when he saw her…she was even prettier than she had been at Easter time. She was maturing into a beautiful young woman. But that wasn't what had caught Declan's eye, yet again. No, it was her spirit; she just reached out and touched his very soul, and he was never the same afterward. Liliana had soothed his heart when it was aching from the death of his mother. She had brought him back from the dark recesses of cancer care-giver and into the light of being a young man who wanted to participate in life again. He loved her for that…

Today, she had jumped from her little car, and she had hugged him tightly while she laid her head upon his chest. It had been a completely unabashed demonstration of her affection for him. Christophe had laughed when he saw her hug Declan so fervently, and Old Jim had pouted saying, "That crazy young Scotsman is moving in on my girl. I don't know if I like that or not." Seconds later, Old Jim was beaming when she hugged and kissed him on his withered cheek.

As always, Annie had come down from the house and held her "special girl." Again, she had proclaimed that summer season was finally upon them, "Our Lily Girl is here, at last!" Annie had then announced that dinner would begin that evening at half past six, and everyone was invited. Then, she had charged Declan with getting Liliana moved back into her little attic apartment. As always, Declan Ryan had no complaint about his assignment.

Earlier that day, Declan had repotted Liliana's orange geraniums into even bigger containers and had dusted off her French blue roof-top chairs. They had had some fine times getting to know each other on those chairs, and he was glad he had repaired and strengthened their joints when she had pulled them from the trash bin two summers ago. Then, he had carefully loaded her precious cargo into a company truck. Now, all he needed to do was load Liliana and her luggage into the truck too.

As they had driven toward the junction and then turned into town, Declan had looked over at Liliana. Her eyes were closed, yet she was slightly smiling and breathing deeply of the fresh air. When she opened them and had seen Declan watching her, she had said, "I guess I'm no different than my sweet old Iris, I just love a draft of fresh air coming in the window of the truck. Only now, I don't have to fight Iris for your attention when I'm in the truck with you!"

Declan Ryan had heartily laughed.

When all of Liliana's things had been unloaded, she had invited him out to her patio. The clouds had overtaken the sun the last hour, so it was cool on the roof-top, even though it was mid-day. Declan Ryan had reached for her hand and pulled her into an embrace. He had kissed her several times. She looked seriously into his eyes. He found himself mesmerized and softly said, "Liliana, you have my full and complete attention. You need never fight anyone for it." He wanted to kiss her again many more times and to hold her tightly, but he did not. Something inside made him keep his affection for her in check.

Liliana smiled up at him, "I'm very happy to hear that, Declan Ryan, because I have been waiting for three-quarters of a year to spend some time with you. I'm so delighted to see you."

Declan's strong arm came a little bit further around her waist and pulled her closer to himself. "I'm glad to know you've missed me, Liliana Rose."

Still serious and looking deeply into his eyes, she whispered, "I *have* missed you, Dec…tremendously."

Minutes later, when Declan and Liliana emerged from the door of her little attic apartment, she was slightly flushed from being thoroughly kissed, and he held her closely to his side as they came down the stairs. Both were delighted. It was a good beginning to the beautiful summer.

Liliana knew that Declan Ryan was only three years her senior. She had always teased him about being "old," but something had changed within her. She was soon to be twenty-one years old, and she no longer felt like a young girl in his presence, she felt different somehow… Perhaps, it was more on equal footing. Liliana viewed Declan as someone whose company she not only wanted, but as a man who seemed to summon emotions from her like none she had ever experienced before. She knew she had always been slightly in love with Declan, but now, she suspected that what she felt for him might be much more. She thought that Declan Ryan might just be her soul-mate.

Christophe and Annie had noticed that things were different that first night of her return. Both Liliana and Declan were obviously very pleased with each other. Though they had not even held hands or touched one another, it was obvious to everyone at the dinner table that there was something going on. Christophe had winked at Annie after dinner, when Liliana had said that she had a big day tomorrow, so she had better get home to get some rest. Declan had stood up immediately and had said that he would get her bundled into her car. Both had excused themselves, and Old Jim had shaken his head and laughed.

"May I come by to see you a little later when I get things buttoned up here?" Declan had asked as she got into her car.

She smiled, "Yes, Declan, I would love to have you come by. What time?"

Declan's serious face then broke into a smile, "How about in an hour?"

"That would be perfect. I'll see you then."

An hour later, Liliana Lylestrom answered her garret door. She wore a short blue and white floral sundress. Her eyes were sparkling. Declan Ryan stood on her stoop, and he held a bouquet of wildflowers in a mason jar. His hair was slightly damp and combed back off his face. He just smiled. He was prepared to give her his full and complete attention.

That night, they walked around the town square and then through the quiet streets of tiny Rosemeade Township. They walked closely together; nothing much was said. They were just so delighted to be back in each other's company again. At evening's end, when Declan Ryan had delivered her to her little apartment. He had held her close and had kissed her quite tenderly.

Liliana went sleepily to her tiny bed. She dreamt about Declan Ryan. She awoke refreshed, yet still feeling Declan's kisses on her lips. She couldn't wait to start working at the nursery that morning. She thought to herself how he always looked so ruggedly handsome in his work clothes, yet, he had no idea that women, young and old alike, always took a second glance at him while he worked so diligently. That was one of the things she liked best about Declan, there was not even a hint of arrogance in his demeanor.

So, the happy days of a third summer flew by in Rosemeade County once again. Declan and Liliana worked hard and enjoyed countless hours with one another. As always, they swam at one of the lakes, built bonfires after dark, and delighted in the cinema; but now that she was twenty-one years of age, some things did change. Several times, Declan took her across the county line into metropolitan Brookings City where they went to the discotheque and danced the night away. One night, Declan drove her north of Rosemeade Township to the next county for a rodeo and a western dance…

When he arrived at her little garret over the bookstore, she opened the door and surprised him. She looked reminiscent of a Spanish senorita that one would see on a very old travel poster from the 1940s. She had her hair curled in waves which flowed down her back, halfway to her waist, and she wore a crocheted-lace blouse slightly off her tanned shoulders. The blouse was coupled with a very colorful skirt that floated when she walked. Golden earrings dangled from her ears and twinkled against her dark hair, and golden bracelets wound around both her wrists. She looked quite striking, and as Declan unabashedly admired her blossoming good looks, a wayward dimple deepened in his left cheek.

That night, Declan realized that Liliana was budding into quite an exquisite rose. Though she wasn't trying to garner attention at all, Declan noticed that many men looked at her appreciatively while she danced with him. As much as he did not want to admit it, he found it slightly disconcerting that other men were now noticing her in that way. She had always been his lovely young companion, and he had never had to share her attention with anyone. It niggled at him that other men were now starting to notice her distinctive beauty, yet he could not blame them. Declan Ryan now had to admit to himself that Liliana Lylestrom was no longer a young ingénue; she was quickly hurtling toward womanhood.

On the last dance of that evening, she had surprised him by pulling her flowing skirt to mid-way up her calves and swishing it back and forth as she danced around him. Her golden sandals caught the light. When the music stopped, she looked into his eyes and exclaimed, "I adore you, Declan Ryan. Thank you for a perfect evening. I'll never forget it."

At this juncture, a rugged young rodeo cowboy walked up to Declan and said, "You, sir, are a very lucky man! Don't ever let that beautiful woman get away. She's perfect." Liliana had blushed, and Declan had again found himself feeling slightly ill-at-ease because other men were openly admiring her.

He winked at the young cowboy, then responded in a very heavy brogue, "Aye, she is a keeper, isn't she?"

That night, Declan admitted to himself that it wasn't that he was jealous of their regard for her, but it tugged at him that other men could, perhaps, try to pursue her…she had always been his…his sweet, sweet secret love.

When the slant of the late summer sun again signaled that it was time for Liliana to return home and prepare for her last year at Brineforth, they had both felt melancholy. Each September, it seemed as though it was harder to part than the year before. This year, on the night before she left to go back to school and resume her studies, Declan took her to their favorite lake for a midnight swim.

They rode to the lake on his old Harley Davidson motorcycle that he had bought and refurbished during the long winter months. Funny thing about that old motorcycle, both Declan and Liliana loved it. He had high regard for it because it gave him freedom; but moreover, it gave him the thrill of Liliana's arms hugging him tightly around his middle while looping her fingers through the belt loops of his worn-out jeans. Liliana loved Declan's cycle because she could hug him very tightly and lay her head upon his muscular back while they cruised through the back roads of Rosemeade County without anyone thinking she was brazen!

That night, they had picnicked under the late-night stars, and Declan had given her a pair of handsome silver earrings. He had said, "When I saw these in the jewelry store window, I envisioned you wearing them whilst the wind blew through your dark hair. It is hard to say good-bye, and I am sorely going to miss you, dearest Liliana."

He had kissed her much as a man kisses a woman he loves deeply. She had responded in kind. Yet, he had refrained from those three little words which would enlighten her as to how much she truly meant to him. He loved her profoundly, but he still did not want to pressure or scare her off. He did not feel right taking anything away from her happy youth. Declan Ryan told himself that she would be graduating soon. He could wait for her a little while longer; then, he would propose spending the rest of their lives together.

On her doorstep that night, tender Liliana Lylestrom told Declan that she had never felt so close to anyone in her life. "I feel as if I'm losing a part of myself in leaving you tomorrow, Declan," she had seriously admitted.

Very touched, Declan responded, "Believe me, Liliana; I feel the same way, too. Each fall, when you leave to go back to school, I always feel off kilter somehow…as though I've lost a limb or something. Every year, it becomes more difficult to say good-bye to you. I've never known anyone else like you before, and I have very deep feelings for you." Declan had then enfolded her in his arms and had kissed her quite ardently, yet again. It had been an especially sweet parting.

A TREASURED
HARVEST SEASON

That Autumn, the weather was perfect. It had been an extremely wet winter season, so the fall colors were especially brilliant and very beautiful. Once again, the chain of postcards connected Declan and Liliana every week, and it was always exciting for each of them to see what type of artwork the other would choose for their tiny missives. Both looked forward to the daily mail delivery; just in case it might hold something special.

As Declan continued to send Liliana caring messages via postcard, he was secretly hoping that she would extend another invitation for Brineforth University's homecoming weekend. And soon, true to her caring fashion, she extended an especially warm invitation to him to come for the highly anticipated event. And, on a day when he least expected it, Declan Ryan received something which made his heart turn a full somersault in his chest.

A vellum envelope of a soft pink hue arrived in the mail at The Old Vineyard Road Nursery, and Old Jim was selected to be the bearer of its happy greetings to Declan Ryan. That afternoon, Old Jim made his way to the eastern corner of the nursery where he found the lucky recipient of Liliana's letter. He said, "Young man, I suspect I have something which will touch your heart. Seeing the softness of its color and the feel of its heavy paper with just the slightest hint of fragrance, I suspect it is from your Liliana. Take some time to savor it, son, as you have been working very hard since she returned to school."

Declan Ryan wore a big smile as he took the pink missive from Jim and sat down underneath the shade of a large burlap wrapped conifer to read the sweet words from the woman he adored above all others of her gender. He held the letter up to Jim as if he were toasting to its content's happiness and simply said, "I thank you for this special delivery, Jim. It means a lot to me."

Old Jim replied, "Declan when I encouraged you to savor her letter, I meant it. As you read Liliana's letter, imagine where she might have sat in the library while she wrote it; envision her walking across campus to post it to you; but most of all, recall her sweet face and beautiful smile. Tuck all of these images away in your memory bank because I suspect you're falling deeper in love with her, and you'll want to relive them again and again until you see her once more." Enjoy your well-deserved break, son."

As Declan unfolded Liliana's letter, he did think about her as Old Jim had suggested. And in his mind's eye, he saw sweet Liliana, he inhaled her essence, and he read the words that she had carefully printed in calligraphy letters; especially for him.

It was a heady experience just to receive a postcard from Liliana, but to receive a letter that she had taken the time to compose and write to him meant everything to Declan Ryan. But the little remembrance of her that she had tucked into her letter wrenched Declan's heart and made him feel an even stronger fondness for her. Perhaps, we should read on to find out what that tiny surprise was...

September 20th

My dearest Declan,

Oh, how I have been missing our summer fun together! Even the hard work at the Nursery is memorable when it is with you. So, now that you know how much I miss you, I'm wondering if you would like to join me for Brineforth's Homecoming weekend which begins the 16th of October?

On Thursday evening, there will be a special dinner and the announcement of the Brineforth University Homecoming Queen and her attendants. Since I am a finalist, I wonder if you might be my escort for Thursday evening; then again, for the homecoming dance on Friday night? I know you have been finished with university activities for several years, but it would bring me great joy to have you as my guest and my partner for Friday evening's activities, too. It would also be a lot of fun if you could come a bit early, as well…say Wednesday night? There will be a huge bonfire and some parties on that evening, so I do hope you can join me a bit earlier.

Then, on Saturday afternoon, my Brineforth Bulldogs will play football against "State" for first place in our division and a berth in the Bulldog Bowl which you know my school always hosts. It's bound to be a wonderful afternoon, and my parents have invited Christophe, Annie, and Old Jim to attend the game with them, too. Since I am a student, you will sit with my roommates, their dates, and me for the game. Later, after we hopefully "win" the game, my Dad wants to treat all of us to dinner at the Cottontail Grill, here in Campus Place. They serve wonderful international food as their specialty. Please tell me that you will come; it definitely would mean a lot to me.

The attire for the Friday night dance is formal, but you can wear your father's tartans if you would like, Declan… I will be looking forward to your answer.

With every affection,

Your Liliana Rose

P.S. The ribbon-tied lock of hair is mine, Declan. I'm sending it to you, as it is an old-fashioned gesture of affection. You know that I hold you in the highest esteem, so I wanted you to have it as we look forward to Homecoming. I suggest that you put it in your botanical painting folio or in your beautifully-worn Bible. That way, you'll always know that I am thinking of you!

As Declan Ryan read Liliana's thoughtful invitation to him, he twirled the lock of her hair wound round with pale pink ribbon between his fingers. That simple act released the beautiful scent of her hair and once he finished reading her letter, he smiled and touched the snippet of her hair to his lips. Declan chuckled to himself, "This is not going to be a hard decision at all. I can't wait to accept Liliana's Homecoming invitation."

Later that evening at about nine o'clock, Liliana's cell phone rang, and when she answered, it was Declan's voice woven with the heavy Scottish burr that she adored. He said, "I received a very special letter from you today, Liliana. It brought me great joy. And, yes, it would be my sincere pleasure to escort you to your homecoming festivities. I know that I will be the luckiest man alive to have you on my arm everywhere we might go that weekend. Thank you for inviting me, dear one."

Liliana was very pleased that Declan had accepted her invitation and little did Declan Ryan know that she was dancing around her apartment with great happiness written across her sweet face while she politely said, "Oh, Declan, I will be so happy to see you, and if perchance, you can stay over for part of Sunday, we could spend extra time together; just the two of us. Perhaps, we could picnic on the University Village Green, or I could show you some of my very favorite places in my little university world."

A thoroughly pleased Declan answered, "Liliana, that sounds wonderful, and I can't wait to spend time with you again. I'll plan on taking the commuter plane on Wednesday in the late afternoon, and I'll rent a car, so we can spend a little bit of extra time together then, too."

"Liliana happily sighed and said, "Declan, you could probably sleep on the sofa at our little girly apartment, or I could try to secure visitor housing for you in the dorms."

An amused Declan Ryan answered, "Sweet Lily, I don't want ever to offend your father by staying at your apartment, so I will find out where Christophe, Annie, Old Jim and your parents will be staying, and I will secure lodging there, as well. But, if I were of a different ilk, I would have gladly taken you up on your offer to stay at your 'girly apartment.' Alas, I'm going to be a gentleman, so your innocence can never be questioned! I am, however, quite honored that you volunteered your sofa."

Feeling silly, Liliana responded, "I only offered the sofa; not my tiny little twin bed, but thank you for being so gallant, Declan!" The two of them then had a good laugh.

They chatted a while longer, then Declan signed off, "I'll be honest with you, Lily, I'll be counting the days until I am able to see you. Again, thank you for your very kind invitation as well as a lock of your beautiful brunette hair. I've already got it tucked safely into my tatty old Bible, but know this: Even King Solomon would have wanted you for his own, if he had but known you. I consider myself a very fortunate man to flourish in your friendship and affection. Good night, sweet girl."

"Good night, dear Declan… Thanks for calling me and sleep well tonight.

"Good night, precious Liliana… I will be seeing you soon. Take care. Goodbye.

That night, Declan Ryan slept deeply and dreamt of Liliana Lylestrom. He awoke once again feeling Liliana's sweet kisses from their recent summer junkets on his lips.

WARMEST MEMORIES

Declan Ryan's commuter flight arrived at the tiny Campus Place Airport at half past six on Wednesday evening just as the Brineforth Homecoming festivities were getting underway. When he arrived at Liliana's apartment, his heart was quickening with every beat. At last, he would be able to hold her again. Liliana Lylestrom was the only woman who had ever fascinated him, and he couldn't wait to see her.

Upon seeing his arrival through the front window of her apartment, she burst out the front door and ran to him. Declan held her to himself savoring her embrace, then he set her back slightly, cupped her face with his large hands, and kissed her quite tenderly. Liliana returned his kiss in equal measure as Declan felt his heart melt at her returned kisses. Yes, the homecoming weekend was beginning in fine fashion…

After sharing a pizza together at a local Italian restaurant, Declan drove them back to Liliana's apartment to join her roommates and their boyfriends for the huge bonfire on campus. The festivities were lively, and Declan met many of her friends and even some of her professors. Liliana was vivacious and very happy to introduce Declan to everyone, but he instinctively knew that what they both truly wanted was to just be alone with one another.

Later, when Liliana suggested that they might drive to Mercury Point to do some star gazing, Declan found himself all in for her suggestion, but there was one thing he wanted to take with them. It was pie. So, they drove to the only bakery that Declan knew of in Campus Place and were lucky enough to find it open. Its owner was just closing for the evening, but he smiled when they walked in.

He looked directly at Declan and said, "I'll bet it's a pie you'll be wanting, young man. Am I right?"

Declan smiled his unforgettable smile and replied, "You, sir, have noted my habits of late, haven't you? And now you know the discerning young woman who has definite feelings about pie!"

The bakery owner then looked at Liliana and teased, "If it's a peach pie you might be wanting this evening, miss, I'm sold out, but you look like you just might be a fan of blueberry, too. I have one in the back which I baked just this morning! Let me pack it in a box for you."

Liliana beamed at him and chimed, "My Scottish friend must have described my love of pie to you very well!"

When the shop owner returned with the boxed pie, he had also included a sample size spray can containing whipped cream, some plastic cutlery, napkins, as well as two colorful paper dessert plates in a separate bag. He laughed softly and said, "You two go and enjoy your pie and some time under that big, beautiful harvest moon that is easing it way further up and into this evening's starlit sky.

Via Liliana's directions, Declan drove them to Mercury Point to watch the stars. For the next hour, there was delicious pie, plenty of holding each other, lots of talking, and a fair amount of kissing interspersed with their stargazing. There was also the palpable joy of being together once again; just the two of them. Under the striking harvest moon that night, honorable Declan Ryan and tender Liliana Lylestrom tumbled even further into love, though neither of them had ever mentioned it to the other.

During their last few minutes at Mercury Point, as they held one another, knowing they would soon have to part, Liliana put her small hand on the base of Declan Ryan's face and stroked his three-day stubble. She said, "I love this on you."

At Declan's intake of breath and his whispered declaration of, "Oh, Lily!" as he held her a bit tighter, she found herself moving her hand down the warm length of his neck and slightly inside the collar of his shirt. She gently moved her soft hand over his collarbone as he murmured, "Sweet girl, you're killin' me. I'd best get you home."

Though they could hardly bring themselves to break up their reunion, Liliana did confess that she still had a tiny bit of homework to complete for her classes on Friday morning. Finally, being firm with himself and still feeling her touch on his skin, Declan drove her home to her apartment and walked her to the front door.

As she twisted the doorknob to let herself in, she turned and said, "Declan, I am so happy that you came early. Thank you for always making me feel so special."

"You *are* special Liliana," Declan quietly murmured. Then, very moved, he gave her a knowing look, then pulled her into his embrace once again. His large hand stroked an errant brunette curl back into place, and he confessed, "Lily, please don't think I was spurning your touch tonight. If anything, the precious stroke of your hand ignited my affection for you even more, but I must always look to your safety, even if it's protecting you from me. If given the chance, I would stay out until the wee hours of the morning just talking with you, holding and kissing you, but I don't ever want to lose Stephan and Jenny's trust when you are in my care."

Declan then smiled somewhat wryly and shared, "I am making every effort to be an honorable man for you and your parents, Lily." I don't ever want to disappoint you, Stephan or Jenny, in any way. Sometimes, I feel as though I might have saddened my lovely mother's heart those first couple of years that I was away at university with my less-than-stellar behavior…drinking too much and chasing women. It really wasn't who I was or who I am now. I truly hope that I didn't grieve her. And nowadays, I find such great pleasure in my relationship with you, Liliana, that I don't ever want things between us spoiled because I was not respectful of you."

Very touched, Liliana answered, "Oh, Declan, you've never shown anything but the utmost care and tenderness toward me, and I adore you for it. You always show your honor to Annie and Christophe, to my parents, and to me. You needn't ever worry about your mother feeling saddened about you. Though I never met her, she surely knew clear up to her last day on this earth what a wonderful man and son you were to her. If she could see you today, helping Christophe achieve his dreams for The Old Vineyard Road Nursery, her heart would be very full and oh so proud. Don't ever doubt yourself, dearest Declan." Liliana then hugged Declan Ryan tightly to herself then turned toward her partially opened front door. She looked him earnestly in the eye and whispered, "Why don't you join me for breakfast in the dining hall tomorrow morning.

There is a special little table that I have reserved just for the two of us… before I have to go to class."

Declan gave her his rare smile, but Liliana could tell that he was also moved by what she had just said to him about his late mother being full of pride for him. He then answered, "Sweet Lily, I will be counting the hours until I can break bread with you. What time shall I call for you in the morning?"

She flashed him her electric smile and replied, "How about eight? My first class isn't until nine-thirty, so that will give us plenty of time to linger over our coffee. Sound good?"

"It sounds perfect!"

That being said, Declan Ryan bussed Liliana on the cheek and tucked her inside the entry of her apartment. "Sleep well, dear one, " he whispered as he turned to walk back to his rental car. He noted how Liliana watched him walk to the car before she closed her window blinds. The festivities thus far had only whetted Declan's desire to savor his beautiful friend's company even more…

The remainder of their weekend together was laced with much joy, as Liliana was named first attendant to Brineforth's new Homecoming Queen, and Declan was very glad he had opted to bring his black-tie formal wear from his university days. He was proud of his Scottish heritage, yet he hadn't wanted his evening apparel to be too markedly different from that of her peers. And when he escorted Liliana upon his arm to the stage where they presented her as the first runner-up, he found himself very touched when the master of ceremonies acknowledged, "And our first runner-up this evening, Miss Liliana Lylestrom, is being escorted by Mr. Declan Ryan, a former graduate in Plant Science and Business from the University of Edinburgh, Scotland. Let's all give him a warm Brineforth welcome, too!"

And so, Declan and Liliana's special weekend together continued with a colorful homecoming parade throughout the picturesque tree-lined streets of Campus Place, an exciting buzzer-beater Brineforth win on the football field, and plenty of comradery with Liliana's parents,

Christophe, Annie, and Old Jim. In all, it had been a very poignant weekend for them all.

For Stephan and Jenny Lylestrom, they recognized that love was truly blooming between Declan Ryan and Liliana as they witnessed how sweetly he attended to their daughter's every need that weekend and how he would quickly kiss her palm when he thought no one else was looking. It especially pleased Stephan to witness these things, as he knew his daughter was an extraordinary young woman, and he wanted only the most honorable of men to, one day, marry her. In his father's heart, Stephan Lylestrom knew Declan Ryan modeled these qualities in every way.

WINTER'S POSTCARDS

***A**s the autumn progressed* toward Thanksgiving, Declan and Liliana were finally able to spend precious time together again at Liliana's family home along with Christophe and Annie. It was a heartfelt holiday that day, and even Old Jim was there to celebrate at Stephen and Jenny Lylestrom's Thanksgiving feast.

After putting the leftovers away and cleaning up the kitchen together, Declan and Liliana found time to enjoy one another. It was evident to everyone just how much they cared for each other that day. All had watched as Declan had lovingly attended to Liliana throughout the meal and later, tried not to watch when he took a small parcel from his jacket pocket and presented it to her as they sat together across the room.

Her gift was a very pretty postcard upon which was a print of sweet pea flowers in full bloom. The tender flowers were painted in clear pink, soft apricot, deep burgundy and pristine white. Declan had had the lovely postcard framed in a very attractive silver and gold molding, and his eyes shone as he presented it to her.

He whispered simply, "Sweet peas are so delicate and at home in a cottage garden; they always bring great joy to the gardener who is caring for them, too. The frame shop built the framing so you can open it and read the back of your postcard whenever you like…"

Unlocking the tiny hinges on the back of the frame and lifting it open, Liliana was rewarded with words she would never forget.

My dearest Liliana,　　　　　　　　　　　　　　　　*Thanksgiving Day*

Since we've known one another, I have been trying to decide which flower or botanical plant would best illustrate who you truly are. Recently, I stumbled upon this postcard, and I knew the exquisite, fragrant sweet pea blooms illustrated both your inner and outer beauty. You are my treasure, sweet one.

Always yours,

Declan

Just about a month later, Declan received a very similar Christmas gift from Liliana. He was equally as touched as she had been at Thanksgiving.

Her postcard gift portrayed a very handsome shepherd-type dog whose portrait had been water colored upon printed newspaper. The purity of the watercolor paints had let the typed newsprint show through on parts of the dog's beautiful coat.

In addition to the intricacy of the dog's handsome countenance, the artist had also captured the dog's essence…a kind spirit, a willingness to protect…but there was also a whimsical addition sitting atop the dog's snout; a yellow water-colored rubber ducky. Liliana's postcard gift was also framed; Liliana had chosen a simple black molding with a special hinged back that opened to read the message. This is what Liliana had written to Declan…

Dearest Declan,   *December 25th*

The striking dog depicted on this postcard illustrates your honor, strength, and kindness; as well as your willingness to care for others. You are very generous in your caring, too, Declan. The little rubber duck represents me and how you have been my loveliest friend, honorable teacher, and protector as we have navigated our way through a beautiful friendship these last three years. I hope you know that I carry you in my heart always.

With every affection,

Liliana

That Christmas morning Christophe gave a slight nod and a quick wink to his best friend, Stephan Lylestrom, and both surreptitiously watched as Declan Ryan reached for Liliana and held her to himself after he had opened his gift from her.

Stephan noted how Declan cradled his daughter's head with his large and very capable hand while he held and whispered his thanks to her. This very gesture told Stephan volumes about how much Declan

Ryan cared for his daughter. It pleased him, but it also tugged at his heart. His baby girl had grown up into the loveliest of women. He knew that he would soon face giving her protection and care to another man. Yet, he also knew that if that man turned out to be Declan Ryan, both he and Jenny would be heartily pleased.

As January melded into February, weekly postcards were still sent, but as March arrived, the time between Declan and Lilianna's correspondence waned just slightly. Declan queried why, yet he knew that Liliana was very busy with her senior capstone project along with her studies. He still continued to send her a postcard every Tuesday morning, though, because he wanted her to feel supported and adored while she labored with her studies.

A SERIOUS FOURTH SUMMER

Summer season arrived differently at The Old Vineyard Road Nursery that year, with overcast skies and chilly temperatures. Yet, everything was still very green and lush. The nursery looked beautiful with colorful hanging baskets positioned everywhere. Brightly-painted wooden tables again groaned under the weight of hundreds of colorful flowers and vegetables just waiting to be scooped up by avid gardeners. The flowering trees were in bloom, and there was the perfumed scent of late spring in the air. Yet, something was slightly off. Christophe Riordan attributed it to the weather, but Declan Ryan knew in his heart that things that they had enjoyed in years past might not ever be the same again. He knew why, too.

At Easter, two months ago, Liliana had come home to spend time with her family. As always, he had been invited to share the holiday with them. It was always such a sacred and beloved holiday. They all attended church together, then enjoyed Jenny Lylestrom's delicious Easter dinner. Afterwards, it was always the same. He and Liliana spent precious time visiting together for the remainder of the day. They usually caught up on all her news from school and began to look forward to the hard work and summer fun that they both knew they would soon be enjoying. It was usually such a happy time.

Declan had driven the forty-mile stretch to Liliana's family home, along with Christophe and Annie, but the three of them had been quite surprised to find that Liliana had brought home an additional guest. His name was Richard Rawlings. Apparently, he was a friend of hers from school. Though Liliana had greeted them all with her usual sparkle, and had given Declan her customary effusive hug, he had felt immediately ill at ease because Richard had looked at him with disdain. Richard had also been aloof and somewhat rude to friendly Christophe. No one was ever rude to Christophe Riordan; he was a beloved man throughout Rosemeade County. Declan could not abide anyone treating his dear cousin and friend in such a fashion.

The day had progressed with Stephan Lylestrom apologizing for their houseguest's manners and admitting that he felt Liliana had been pressured by Richard to include him in her Easter vacation. Jenny, too, had apologized for their daughter's slightly-rude guest. Both had said that he had no parents; they had been killed in a horrible automobile accident when he was still a teenager. Each of them had gone on to speculate that was likely why he was so sullen.

While Richard had been engaged in conversation with Stephan, Liliana had sought out Declan. "Dearest Declan, I am so very happy to see you!" she had chirped as she reached out to hold both of his hands. "It has been such a busy semester at school that I've barely even had time to write my weekly post card to you. Can you forgive me?"

She then continued on, "Oh, Dec, I'm getting close to finishing, though. I do my student teaching this fall. I would probably have benefitted from taking several classes in the summer session these last three years, but I couldn't bring myself to do it. I could have even graduated by now, but I guess one more semester won't hurt me! You have no idea how I'm looking forward to working with you and Uncle Christophe again this summer, and how I am sorely in need of some deadheading in the greenhouse and a swim at our favorite lake with you!" She had given him her electric smile, and her green eyes had looked at him like they always did…with marked affection. Declan's doubts had then eased up, but he hoped that his misgivings about Richard escorting her home for Easter break were nothing to worry about. Somehow, he wondered.

When late May finally chugged in, Christophe, Annie, and Old Jim were in high spirits when the day of her summertime arrival came. Yet, Declan felt somewhat uneasy. It had been an overcast day, and an occasional raindrop pelted the graveled walk. So very happy that her "special girl" was arriving that day, Annie had prepared some of Liliana's favorite dishes for dinner, and they were all looking forward to kicking off the summer fun that her arrival always heralded.

Before any of them saw the car, Old Jim heard it. "Why that's someone who's looking to soothe their poor self-esteem with a powerful and probably expensive car. Let's brace ourselves for a cantankerous customer!" They had all laughed at his insight.

Just seconds later, that powerful automobile came into view with Liliana sitting in the passenger seat. A somewhat-surprised Christophe opened her door to help her out. When she alighted, she was slightly subdued, but still very happy to see them all. Richard then came around the car, and aloofly shook hands with Christophe. He simply nodded his head to Declan.

Liliana looked between Old Jim, Christophe, and Declan and said, "Richard recently finished his internship with Bruxton Reed. He did a great job, and they offered him a permanent position. This is his new *baby*… a gift to himself for a lot of hard work," she said as she inclined her head toward Richard's vehicle. Both Declan and Christophe caught her cue, and heartily congratulated Richard on his accomplishments. Richard seemed smugly satisfied with their compliments. Poor Old Jim just stood there looking dumbfounded; he couldn't believe Liliana would be in the company of such a man.

Declan was the next to speak, "Liliana, are you not bringing your little V-Dub to Rosemeade Township this summer? Where are your things?"

Liliana looked flustered, "They are in the trunk, Declan. Would you mind?"

As Richard unlocked the trunk, he ignored Declan's presence. Declan swallowed his irritation, looked at Liliana, and said, "Why don't I put your things in the company truck along with your roof-top furniture and plants…we'll drive everything over later." With that Declan Ryan left carrying her things. He was not seen the remainder of the day. Even when Annie's special dinner was served that evening, Declan Ryan was not in attendance. Christophe and Annie, along with Old Jim, were left with the odious chore of entertaining an aloof and condescending Richard Rawlings. Everyone was heartsick. Summer season was not starting well.

Later that evening, after Richard had roared back down Old Vineyard Road in his powerful automobile, Liliana had walked over to the stalwart stone barn. She was glad to be back at The Old Vineyard Road Nursery again. Everything looked so very beautiful; vivid with brilliant color and verdant with lush foliage. Yet, she felt somewhat uneasy. She had quietly knocked on the door to Declan's loft. Seconds later, he opened it and greeted her. He was friendly enough, but Liliana could sense something was off.

"Declan, will you be able to take me over to my place tonight?" she asked. Her heart was beating a little too fast. She had never before felt any trepidation with her beloved Declan.

"Certainly, Liliana, are you ready to go now?" Declan quietly replied.

"Yes, I am ready," she answered. "Anytime you are, Dec."

"I was just changing my clothes. Come in, I'll only be a few minutes."

Liliana came into his loft and sat down in his slightly worn leather chair. His personal things were strewn about on a handsome old table that he used for his desk. She saw his keys and his change tossed into a colorful glass dish, several photos of the two of them were tucked into a corner of his leather desk blotter, and his weathered and well-read Bible lay open. His new lap-top computer and a somewhat battered leather journal that he frequently carried with him had been relegated to a corner of the desk.

His journal was open as well, and his flowing script annotated a water-colored replica of some type of plant. It looked right out of the Eighteenth Century. That was one of the things she loved about Declan, it was as if he had been plucked out of some other era; as if he had been given the classical education that she had only read about in books. Declan spoke several languages, he could draw and paint well, and he played the piano; though he had never played for her, yet. Once, he had also sheepishly admitted that his mother had insisted he learn to dance, and she knew from experience how special it was to be held in his arms while he led her around the dance floor.

Though Declan was artistic and had the best of manners, he was very masculine, too. Liliana laughed to herself about all the times she had secretly watched him lift adult trees as if they were saplings; his muscles rippling under his shirt. His strong, yet gentle, hands could work miracles with damaged trees and plants; always restoring health. Then, there was his ability to build or fix anything… he had worked wonders with some of the broken-down old pieces of furniture they had hauled back to his loft several years ago. In short, Declan Ryan fascinated her like no other. Besides her father and a few professors at Brineforth, Declan Ryan was the only "real man" of her acquaintance. He made her heart soar whenever she was in his company, and tonight, she felt badly that she might have made him cross.

She heard the water in his shower turn off, so she called into the other room, "Declan, I missed you at dinner. Why didn't you join us?"

Declan appeared in the doorway clad only in a large dark-colored bath towel that was slung around his hips. His hair was wet, and his smooth, muscular chest still had water droplets upon it. His attractive face was hard to read, "I was busy today, Liliana. Besides, Richard was your guest."

She stared at his physique as she said, "But, Declan, I haven't seen you since Easter break. I was so hoping to catch up with you. We hardly got to visit then, either." she quietly retorted.

"I know, Liliana. Richard was your guest then, too," Declan replied as he walked back into his room.

Liliana was stunned. She waited quietly for Declan to finish dressing. When he returned, she spoke; her voice barely above a whisper, "Declan, please don't be out of sorts with me. I can't bear it…"

"I'm not out of sorts with you, Liliana. It's just that we've been very close since Bineforth's Homecoming, Thanksgiving, and Christmas, I'm just a little surprised that you arrived with Richard, that's all. Come on, let's get you over to your little garret," he smiled.

As they drove the short distance to her apartment, it was quiet between them, yet Liliana sat close to him on the truck's bench seat. She so desired to be near him. Somehow, Richard Rawlings bringing her to Rosemeade Township and to the nursery had put a strain on their long-awaited reunion. Declan bounded up and down the wooden steps to her tiny apartment carrying her bags and sewing machine, just as he always did. They enjoyed sparkling drinks and watched the constellations from her rooftop, just as they always did, yet he remained slightly guarded. It was the first time Liliana had ever felt unsure around her beloved Declan Ryan.

When their quiet starry evening came to an end, Declan asked her how she planned to get to the nursery without her car this summer. She shook her head and said, "I think Richard was so anxious to get his new automobile out on the open road that he never even considered that I would need transportation to and from my work. Would you mind picking me up for a few days, Declan? Then, I'll take the bus to Reedsburgh on Sunday morning and drive my car back."

Declan smiled, "Why don't we make a day of it? I'll go with you. I hate to have you riding on the bus all alone."

Liliana's face lit up, "Oh, Declan, I would love that…"

"Well then, let's plan on it," a smiling Declan answered. "In the meantime, I'll pick you up first thing tomorrow morning at quarter after seven. Sleep well, Liliana." With that, Declan Ryan descended her stairs and drove off into the night. He did embrace her, but there were no sweet good-bye kisses. Tonight's reunion was off-kilter, somehow. Both were quite saddened at how her first day back at the nursery had turned out.

When Sunday morning came, Liliana and Declan had to be at the bus station by six o'clock. Both were tired from a very busy work week. Liliana was the first to nod off, and she vaguely remembered holding onto Declan's muscular upper arm with both of her hands and laying her head on his shoulder. She awoke as the bus rolled into Reedsburgh. Declan, too, had been sound asleep, and he stretched and gave her a sleepy grin when the bus came to a stop. When Stephan and Jenny

Lylestrom saw the two of them framed in the bus's window, they were relieved.

Jenny whispered to her husband, "Perhaps arriving with Richard didn't do too much damage after all."

"I hope you're right," a sober Stephan replied.

As the summer progressed, both Declan and Liliana realized their idyllic relationship was changing. She was soon to graduate and begin teaching. Neither of them knew where teaching might take her. Liliana fretted because she had had such a rocky start to her summer with Declan, and he regretted how their relationship seemed to be fraying around the edges. Like always, they still spent a fair amount of time together, but the dynamics of their relationship had somehow changed. Things were no longer easy between them. Somehow, Richard Rawlings always seemed to intrude on their outings, even though he was miles away.

Richard called Liliana quite frequently, and he came to Rosemeade every other weekend to see her. And it seemed that his visits always came just when Declan and Liliana seemed to be getting back on solid footing again. Then his visits made everyone uncomfortable. Christophe and Annie felt remiss if they didn't invite Richard for dinner, and Declan found it impossible to be in Richard's company, so he never joined them. Liliana always felt heartsick and on the verge of tears on these occasions.

Poor Declan endured Richard touching Liliana affectionately and acting quite possessive of her. And, those actions tore at him, too. Declan had truly planned to tell Liliana of his devotion to her just as soon as she returned to the nursery that summer and to, hopefully, make plans for a future with her, but she had arrived with Richard; opening a fracture between them that continued to grow larger and larger.

Declan fought hard to keep his grievous regret at bay, but he feared that he may have, indeed, waited too long to tell Liliana how much he cared. He had assumed she knew something of his love and desire for her; yet he still hadn't truly verbalized it to her. Now, it appeared that wealthy and successful Richard Rawlings just might usurp him. Declan hated to admit that Richard might be a better candidate for her affection, but he was. All Declan knew was that he wanted only the best in this life for precious Liliana, and he knew in his aching heart that he hadn't been able to offer much of anything to her until just recently, but odious Richard could. Declan Ryan sadly suspected that he was too late.

Though Liliana liked Richard Rawlings well enough and had enjoyed some excursions with him while she was away at school, their friendship was not even on the same plane as her bond with Declan. In her heart, she knew that her desire was to spend precious time alone with her dearest Declan only. Her memories of their beautiful homecoming weekend last October assured her of just how much she adored Declan, but there was still a tiny niggling doubt in her heart because he hadn't yet told her that he loved her, though his caring attention always indicated otherwise. And this summer season, every time that she and Declan found themselves getting comfortable with one another again, Richard would arrive in tiny Rosemeade Township for a visit, spoiling their small strides toward renewing their exquisite relationship. These days, it seemed to Liliana as though Declan was purposefully stepping away from her. Why?

Sweet young Liliana Lylestrom began to question whether she had misread Declan's Ryan's affection for her after all. Manipulative Richard Rawlings, on the other hand, made every effort to let her know that he wanted her even though she had turned down his crazy offer of marriage earlier in the year. Unbeknownst to Liliana, Richard's mission of late had been to erode her relationship with Declan at every turn, and he was succeeding. Poor Liliana was quite torn up about how things were turning out this summer at The Old Vineyard Road Nursery, and she was finally concluding that Declan did not have feelings for her after all, nor did he want to have a relationship with her. These revelations saddened her tremendously and fractured her very tender young heart…

Two weeks before Liliana returned to school, Declan tried to smooth things over with her, but things went terribly wrong…

Liliana had found herself out of sorts; something that was rare for her, but she knew the cause. Soon, she was to return for her last semester at Brineforth University. Ordinarily, she enjoyed school, even though it meant that she would be counting the days until she could see Declan again. But, today, she grieved. Nothing was the same; all was changing, and she didn't like it one bit. Achingly, she questioned herself, yet again, about what had gone awry with Declan.

As she organized containers of brightly-colored chrysanthemums on a freshly-painted display table, she ruminated on what she might have done wrong. "No one has ever made me feel the way Declan does," she thought, "but he doesn't care for me anymore. Richard Rawlings is educated, well-off, and poised to be very successful, and we have had some good times together; yet the only man I truly desire is Declan Ryan. Declan hasn't even kissed me, all summer long, though he's always been very engaged with me in every other respect." Liliana sighed heavily as she arranged the last of the pretty chrysanthemums. She sighed so heartily, that Declan Ryan heard her and watched as wisps of her dark, wavy hair rearranged themselves around her face.

Minutes later, her reverie was interrupted by the one person who was causing her to be so out of sorts. Declan Ryan stood on the other side of the display table, backlit by the slant of the mid-day sun. Frustrated Liliana thought to herself, "He always looks so blasted handsome, even in his muddy work clothes." She grudgingly greeted him with none of her usual sparkle.

"Hello, Dec…" she grumped.

Looking slightly wary, Declan inquired, "Everything okay, Lily?"

"Oh, I'm just a little cranky and out-of-sorts today," she replied.

Declan Ryan then laughed. "Liliana, in all these years, I've never once seen you cranky." Sobering, he said soothingly, "Is there anything that I can do?"

She shook her head in the negative, as she silently declared to herself, *"Yes, Declan, you can love me back!"* But to him, she simply responded, "I'm sure, I'll snap out of it soon." Once again, her heavy sigh rearranged her dark hair.

"I'll tell you what, why don't you meet me at my loft in about twenty minutes. I'll take you over to Annie's Diner for a cup of "cranky tea" and you'll be yourself in no time," he suggested.

Feeling a bit ashamed, Liliana's face then brightened as she said, "Thanks, Declan, I would enjoy that very much."

"I'll see you in a bit then," he said, as he walked away.

Twenty minutes later, Liliana was tucked into the cab of Declan's shiny new Chevy truck. He looked over at her; and with just the slightest bit of hesitation in his manner, said, "So ya don't wish to sit next to me, eh?"

Liliana bristled and retorted somewhat petulantly, "Do you want me to, Declan?"

"I always want you beside me, dearest Liliana," he said quietly. He then reached over, undid her seatbelt, and hooked his arm around her waist. He pulled her across the bench seat until she was seated next to him. He then proceeded to buckle her in. "That's more like it," he said, as he put the keys into the ignition. Not much was said as they drove over to the old diner.

When they arrived, Declan helped Liliana from his truck. He put his hands around her waist and lifted her down. She looked into his vivid blue eyes and thought she saw reproach. And for some reason, that incensed her, too.

There wasn't much conversation over their cups of tea, either. Liliana was quiet and Declan tried to broach several subjects of interest to her, but she would not be soothed. At last, Declan decided to be abrupt.

"Liliana what's gotten into you? I've never seen you like this," he said firmly.

She shook her head, "Declan, I'm sorry. I don't know what's gotten into me, either. I apologize. Here you are being sweet to me, and I'm an old grouch."

From there, they quietly made small talk until Declan decided to inquire about Richard. He asked questions about things he thought he had a right to know…Who Richard was? What did he mean to her? Where was Richard from? And what were Richard's intentions?

Lastly, a stone-faced Declan Ryan inquired, "Why does Richard act as though I am the interloper in his friendship with you, Liliana? Have I been mistaken about any feelings you may have for me?" Then, the sparks truly began to fly.

"Declan, my relationship with Richard is none of your concern," she petulantly retorted as she remembered doubts that Richard had planted in her unblemished mind about Declan and if he even cared for her.

Feeling as though he had been slapped, Declan bit out, "I think you're exceedingly wrong on that, Liliana! Richard definitely seems to have come between us this summer." Declan looked at her with an unreadable countenance. "Our very special relationship is suffering right now, and it is of great concern to me. I suspect that Richard Rawlings may be far more serious about things than you even realize, Lily."

"Declan, please don't find fault with Richard," she snapped.

"I am not finding fault, Liliana, I just want you to be on your guard." he answered wearily. You are so precious. I don't blame him for heartily pursuing you; just don't let him rush you into something that you don't want or may not even be ready for!"

With her frustration reaching the breaking point, hot tears filled her eyes as she fought for control. "I don't want to talk about this with you, Declan. Can you take me back to the nursery now?" she spat out.

"I don't want us to be at odds either, Liliana! This conversation is rapidly breaking down. Let's go." Declan then got up to pay for their unfinished afternoon tea.

Back inside the truck, Liliana sat as far away from him as she could. She was heartsick that they had quarreled. Declan started the engine; then, immediately put the transmission into neutral. He again reached across the bench seat and unfastened her seatbelt. For a second time that afternoon, he curved his arm around her waist, and pulled her closer to himself. This time, he held her tightly and looked deeply into her eyes. Liliana desperately wanted him to kiss her. Her heart was racing in her chest. Instead, he cupped the back of her silken head with his large hand and lovingly kissed her cheek, murmuring, "I didn't mean to be harsh with you, Lily. Believe me, I'm truly sorry."

"I'm sorry too, Declan," a sad and very disappointed Liliana softly answered back.

The ride back to Old Vineyard Road Nursery seemed long, and the feelings of each occupant in that shiny new truck seemed brittle, at best. It was unsaid, but both Declan and Liliana knew their summer was ending badly.

The remainder of that afternoon, Declan Ryan felt tormented about his quarrel with Liliana Lylestrom. He had truly wanted to hold and comfort her when she was feeling out of sorts. Never did he suspect that their afternoon junket to the diner would end up with bruised feelings. In his mind's eye, Declan kept seeing her lovely countenance with brimming tears floating before him, and he felt wretched about making her feel so very upset.

It was close to midnight, and Declan could still not forget what had happened between them during the afternoon. He tried to close his eyes for sleep, but all he could see was her sweet face, with anger toward him written all over it. Then, he heard his own voice snapping out clipped questions and retorts to her.

"How had everything between them gone so wrong?" Declan asked of himself for what seemed like the one hundredth time since he had gone to bed. "I cannot be at odds with Liliana over anything," he whispered to himself. "I care for her too much to be alienated like this. We must smooth things over."

Declan rose from his bed, dressed, and drove to Liliana's attic apartment. Sure enough, her tiny bedroom window was lit up. He knocked softly on her door, "Liliana, it's me, Declan. We need to talk." Soon, she opened her door; she was wearing a tiny pink satin nightgown and her tanned feet were bare. He saw that her eyes were swollen from crying.

"Hello, Dec, come in," she invited resignedly.

"You've been crying, Liliana. Why?" he asked softly.

"Oh, Declan, everything is wrong right now," she said. "I'm upset about everything. You and I are not getting along like we usually do. It seems that we've hit a rocky patch in our lovely friendship, and it tears me up. I'm not excited to go back to school in the least, and all I have left is my student teaching. Everything is changing for me, Declan, and I'm not sure that I like it!"

She then broke down and wept, but what she had neglected to say was that Richard had been harassing her about her feelings for Declan and suggesting that Declan had little or no affection for her; let alone any love. At Declan's knock, Liliana had cut their conversation short in order to admit him to her little apartment.

Declan had only seen her cry once before when Iris had died two years ago, but there was something different about her tears tonight; they were bitter. He sat down on the sofa and pulled her onto his lap. He held her in his arms, and she leaned into his comfort. She hiccupped and sobbed; all the while laying her head on his shoulder. Finally, her tears were spent, and she quietly continued to let Declan hold and soothe her. She tightly held a tuft of his cotton-knit tee shirt in her hand, as if she was afraid that he might vanish. Both were silent. Liliana could feel the solid beat of his heart.

Finally, Declan took hold of her upper arms and set her slightly back from himself. He stroked her wet cheek, then kissed her quite tenderly on the lips, and quietly said, "Liliana, I'm so sorry about arguing with you this afternoon. We both have been on edge and we were snapping retorts at one another. Lily, we've never treated one another thus…"

At this point, Declan's Scottish brogue grew heavier with emotion, and he knew he could wait no longer to declare himself to her. Sweet girl, these last several years have been the best of my life…" At this point, Liliana let go of the tuft of his shirt that she had been holding and smoothed the stubble on his cheek with her hand. From there, just like she had done at Homecoming, she continued smoothing her hand over his cheek and down into the neck of his tee shirt and caressed his collarbone taking his breath away. Fighting for his composure, Declan began again, "I want you to know how much I…"

Just then, with extremely poor timing, her cell phone rang. Declan's heart sank; he knew it was Richard Rawlings. He suspected his knock on the door had likely interrupted a call. Resignedly, he said, "It's late, Lily. Do you know who it is?" Liliana said nothing.

Declan tried again, "It's Richard, isn't it?" She still said nothing. She just looked down at the floor. A very-saddened Declan interpreted her actions as affinity for Richard. She had obviously made her choice.

Quietly, Declan murmured, "Go ahead…answer your phone, dearest Liliana. I will let myself out."

As a miserably resigned Declan Ryan drove home, he hopelessly wondered what might have happened if he had gotten a few more words out in his declaration of love for her before Richard had called back. Declan then looked out at the brilliant night sky. He whispered aloud, "Those stars are very bright tonight, but sadly, my world has dimmed."

Miserably, Declan Ryan admitted to himself that he would let Richard Rawlings have Liliana. Richard would be good to her. Successful and wealthy Richard had won. Though Declan disliked him, he knew Liliana would be provided for, and he hoped that her beautiful spirit would bring out the best in sullen Richard's disposition.

Liliana was not the only one who wept that night. Unbidden tears rolled down Declan's cheeks as he turned onto Old Vineyard Road. He felt physically ill because he knew his achingly sweet relationship with Liliana Lylestrom had somehow come to an end.

Though Liliana tried to seek him out, Declan made it a point to be away from the nursery for the next week and a half. He made sure their paths did not cross. When it came time to move Liliana out of her attic apartment, he sent Old Jim to help her and to bring her French blue chairs and vibrant orange geraniums from her roof-top patio back to the nursery. Jim was also assigned to drive Liliana's little V-Dub back to Reedsburgh the next weekend because Richard had again insisted on picking her up at the nursery and driving her home to Reedsburgh. It seemed that Richard never gave thought to what might be the most convenient for Liliana. He considered himself only and proving to everyone at The Old Vineyard Road Nursery that Liliana was **his**, now.

When Old Jim returned from Liliana's attic apartment with her plants and her French blue chairs, he seriously said, "Declan, why do you tarry? I can tell that that wonderful young woman loves you, and I know with certainty that you love her, too. Don't let arrogant Richard have her. I don't care how much money and status he might have. Young man, you are worth a thousand of him. Please, Declan, don't do this to yourself or to tender Liliana. I speak from experience here… **don't** let her go," he urged.

Declan sadly responded with, "Jim, I waited too long to let Liliana know how much I truly cared. Richard Rawlings swooped in and had things set in motion long before she even arrived here in his expensive automobile this summer. Richard is highly educated, he touches her possessively, he lavishes her with his attention, and he can give her things that I cannot. He has even won her allegiance now. I find it very hard to compete with him."

Old Jim looked over at the foothills; they were covered in grapevines run amok. He was quiet for a moment or two and when he looked back at Declan, he had tears shimmering in his aging eyes. "I was like you once, Declan. I foolishly let the love of my life go, and I have been regretful of that choice for a lifetime. I don't want to see you follow in my footsteps. If not for Christophe pulling me out of the muck and the mire, then sharing his faith with me, I don't know what would have happened to me. I shudder to think of it."

Kind Declan put his hand on the old man's shoulder. "Jim, I thank you for sharing with me, and for caring. You are a good man." Then, a defeated and heart-broken Declan Ryan turned around and walked resignedly to his loft.

The next day, at mid-morning, Declan heard, rather than saw, Richard's powerful new automobile. Outside his open office window, he could hear Christophe, Annie, and Old Jim saying their good-byes. He had a splitting headache, so he was holding his head in his hands, with his elbows propped on his desk when he heard her voice. He looked up and saw that she had been watching him.

She looked fragile and slightly pale; she simply said, "Declan, I hope to see you again soon. I'll miss you so very much."

Declan Ryan quickly rose from his chair, crossed the length of his office in several strides. He put his hands upon both sides of her face and lightly rubbed his thumbs across her tender cheeks. He looked into her memorable green eyes and kissed her softly on her full lips. He then pulled her tightly to himself, and kissed her again; this time, very fervently. She held on to him tightly, too, and returned his kiss in earnest. When he broke their kiss, he heard her sharp intake of breath that bordered upon a sob. He smiled and said, "I'll miss you more than you'll ever know, my lovely Liliana. There is no other woman quite like you. I want you to know how much I truly…"

"Are you ready to go, Liliana?" a stone-faced Richard Rawlings interrupted from a few feet away. He did not look pleased.

Declan wondered if he had seen their affection for one another, but continued to encircle her within his arms. He didn't care what Richard might have witnessed.

"Yes, Richard, I am ready," she resignedly answered.

"Good-bye, Declan," she said, on the verge of tears.

"Good-bye, dearest Liliana. I will miss you." Declan then gently kissed her one last time and whispered something private to her all the while still holding her in his embrace; not concerned about Richard's presence in the least.

Richard Rawlings then walked further into Declan's office and pulled Liliana from Declan's arms with some abruptness. He then wrapped his arm possessively around Liliana's shoulders; all the while openly showing his disdain for Declan. He ushered her out of Declan's turf and walked her down the pebbled path to his car.

Declan followed them out to the path. "Richard!" Declan called.

"***What do you want?***" Richard sneered.

"Please, take good care of her, mate."

"I have been," a clearly-displeased Richard Rawlings spat out.

In anguish, Declan Ryan watched as the most-important person in his life walked away with another man. He couldn't believe that such a thing had happened. How had he and Liliana arrived at this point? What an egregious mistake he had made in not telling her how ardently he loved her. He had erred critically and now, she cared for someone else. Both his aching head and his aching heart felt as though they might burst. It was stunning to realize that the only remnants of his relationship with Liliana were her tender letters and the prized postcards she had sent to him.

PART II

AUTUMN'S CHANGES

TEN YEARS
OF LIFE'S SEASONS

QUESTIONS

Everyone at The Old Vineyard Road Nursery was disappointed when the invitation arrived in the mail. Liliana was to marry Richard Rawlings on the twentieth of November. Annie Riordan cried, and her husband retreated to his library to weep in privacy. As for Declan, his already-wounded heart became so painful that he sometimes wondered if he would ever mend. Not only had he lost Liliana, but it was obvious that Richard had, most-likely, forced the issue of marriage upon her.

When the autumn leaves were in full color, Stephan and Jenny Lylestrom came to Rosemeade Township for a long weekend. Declan joined them all for dinner their first night there. When the after-dinner conversation came around to the preparations for the upcoming wedding, Declan Ryan thanked Christophe and Annie for their hospitality, kissed Jenny's cheek, and shook Stephan's hand. "Pardon me, friends, but I've got to meet a vendor in town," was his excuse. After Declan exited the room, Stephan Lylestrom, shook his head.

Stephan began, "For the last several years, I was pretty sure that young man would be the one eventually taking Liliana for his wife. I'm sorry to say this, but we are very surprised by Liliana's choice," Stephan admitted rather sadly. "Oh, Richard is a nice enough young man, but Liliana doesn't seem as taken with him and she has always been with Declan."

Jenny Lylestrom sighed, "I'm not sure what might have happened, but Liliana was really down when we took her back to school. Ordinarily, she is excited to get back to her classes, and she knows exactly how many days there are until she can see Declan again. Last year, Declan drove up to Brineforth quite a few times to see her, and she was so elated. This year, it's Richard who escorts her to exciting places…the theater, the symphony, and to art galleries in the city, but she seems listless and tired."

"Well, that's two of them feeling that way," Annie Riordan commented. "When Declan arrived here from Scotland, he was grieving the loss of his mother. He was sweet, but very serious; yet, when Liliana arrived, we watched him bloom, if you'll pardon the pun. He and Liliana just clicked right from the start.

This year, when Richard brought her to the nursery, we could tell that Declan was very hurt. There were times when she and Declan seemed like themselves, but whenever Richard drove down for a weekend, it was hard on both of them. I don't know what exactly happened, but just about two weeks before she left, they had a falling out. Declan practically vanished from the property, and your girl looked miserable."

Christophe looked at Stephan and said, "I know Richard is soon to be your son-in-law, but I have to be candid. I feel that he hounds Liliana, and she is so sweet-natured that he gets away with it. I'm suspect that getting engaged was the result of real pressure on her. I wasn't going to say anything, but when Richard helped Liliana into his fancy car the morning he picked her up here at Old Vineyard Road, I heard him raise his voice at her. He was quite angry. Liliana had gone up to Declan's office to tell him good-bye, and when she didn't return instantaneously, he got upset and went looking for her. Apparently, he saw Declan embrace and kiss her good-bye, and he was furious."

Christophe looked uncomfortable, but he soldiered on, "Pardon me, Stephan and Jenny, but I feel like our Declan is the one who was wronged here. Richard has barged his way into Liliana's life and pushed away people who mean a lot to her. It is okay if Liliana does not want to have a serious relationship with Declan. Really, it's all right…but I feel she was somewhat badgered by Richard Rawlings this summer, and that's why both she and Declan are unhappy right now. Their heartfelt relationship did not take its natural course. I hurt for them both."

"Oh, my poor girl…" Jenny sighed.

"I'm glad that you two have been frank with us," Stephan acknowledged. "We both want to support our daughter in her choice, but something *is* definitely off here. Why is Richard rushing this wedding? It's been hard on Liliana to plan for a wedding and to focus on her student teaching, too. I know that *I* would like her relationship with Richard to take its natural course, because I don't think it would lead to ***the altar***. If Richard is the man Liliana truly wants, then we'll support her, but I don't want her hand forced on this issue at all."

"Let's talk about something else," Jenny suggested, "Otherwise, we're going to have six unhappy people instead of just two…anybody for a movie in town?"

A FRACTURED HEART

Declan Ryan had hardly noticed that it had been a colorful fall. The arrival of the invitation to Liliana and Richard's wedding had been a brutal blow to him. Though he had practically given Liliana to Richard Rawlings, in his heart, he had somehow hoped that she might still want him. He had been dead wrong. There had been absolutely no communication from Liliana. This was hard on him, too, because he had spent the last four years actively involved in so many facets of her life, and he had come to enjoy the way the seasons wrapped themselves around her. He felt disconsolate without her, and now, concrete proof had arrived in a cream-colored vellum envelope that she was no longer "his," so to speak. It was an ugly and very bitter feeling.

Declan also wrestled with whether he should attend her wedding. He knew if he saw Liliana, it would send him reeling again. He was just barely coming to terms with the fact he had been too slow in letting her know his sincere love for her. In the end, he decided that he had to see her one last time; even though he knew it would be a setback for him.

November twentieth arrived…the day of Liliana's wedding. It was a cloudy, gray, rainy day. A cold wind blew throughout Reedsburgh and, somehow, it befitted the way he was feeling. Liliana was an exceedingly beautiful bride, but Declan knew her too well. She wasn't as happy as her smile might lead one to believe. As she came down the aisle on her father's arm, she locked eyes with him. His stomach had clenched, and he had wanted to howl out in pain. In her eyes, he had seen reproach. Something was very off, but Declan couldn't be sure what it was. Richard had looked rather severe as he waited for his bride at the altar. But Declan knew that no matter what was going on between Liliana and her fiancée, it was none of his concern. She belonged to Richard now. She had made her choice.

Wedding toasts had been very hard on him, because he could not bring himself to toast Liliana and her new husband. The dancing had been difficult for him, too, because he had wanted to hold her in his arms just one more time. In short, the whole affair had been exceptionally hard on him. At last, he could take no more; he sought out Stephan and Jenny Lylestrom and told them he had to be going. Both were disappointed, but he suspected they knew how he was feeling. As he was departing, Liliana crossed the room and surprised him.

"Declan, why are you leaving so soon?" she had asked. "You haven't even danced with me, yet. Please don't go."

Declan had answered, "Liliana, you are such a lovely bride; you don't need me to escort you around the dance floor. You've quite a few anxious young men who desire to dance with you. You needn't wait for me to be your partner."

"On the contrary, Declan. I do need to dance with you one last time. Please come back," she answered with tears glistening in her green eyes. Those tears got to him. Because it was Liliana, and because he wanted desperately to hold her in his arms, he acquiesced.

Minutes later, they were dancing together looking intently at one another. The fact that it was her wedding didn't seem to matter to either of them. Many in the crowd were watching them with unspoken questions as to what might have happened between them. Halfway through their dance, Liliana said, "Declan, please know that I miss you so very much, and I'll never forget all the wonderful times that we have shared these last four summers." She looked earnestly up into his eyes and said, "Do you know that you mean everything to me, Declan Ryan?" Again, those tears shimmered in her bottle-green eyes.

Declan tried to keep his sanity in check as she said these things to him and answered, "I will miss you too, Liliana, and you are right; we did share some very beautiful times together. I will treasure them always." Just as he took a breath to tell her all that she had meant to him as well, Richard had walked over to them and ruined the moment. He cut in and somewhat viciously pulled Liliana from Declan's arms.

"Pardon me, Mr. Ryan, but she is *my* wife; not yours," he had venomously spat out.

Declan stepped away and said to Richard, "I do understand that she is yours now, Richard, but you needn't be rough with her. She is your precious bride."

"That's right, Declan, she is my bride; not yours. I don't know where you get off acting like you've some kind of claim upon her just because you've known her longer, but she's made her choice, don't you get it?"

Declan Ryan looked grimly at Richard for several seconds, and then he stepped back and away from them. He nodded to Liliana and quietly said, "Good-bye, Liliana." He then turned and strode away. He did not look back. It was hard for the wedding guests not to notice that Liliana looked wary as Richard angrily strode to the other side of the reception hall pulling her behind him.

Hours later when Christophe and Annie returned home from the wedding, they saw Declan Ryan, still in his wedding clothes, his sleeves were rolled up, and he was pruning the abandoned rows of wild, unruly grape vines with a vengeance and tossing the cuttings into a roaring fire.

They watched this same scene play out for several days. Knowing that it would not stop until the entirety of the vineyard had been pruned and put to rights; Old Jim joined Declan in the vineyard and worked tirelessly beside him for the remainder of the autumn. They both continued until the winter snow prevented them from the cathartic madness of Declan's project.

As soon as the snow melted again, Declan was back out in the vineyard pruning as if mad dogs were chasing him. Again, Old Jim stayed by his side. This behavior lasted for months until the entirety of the huge vineyard had been pruned extensively and put back into working order for summer harvesting of its fruits. At the end of his project, Declan Ryan felt indebted to and very close to Old Jim. And, he had finally purged the constant, wrenching ache from his heart. Though he was not particularly happy, Declan Ryan was finally able to get on with his life.

THE WEDDING NIGHT

*R**ichard Rawlings*** sat and stared at his sleeping wife. It was two o'clock in the morning, and he had just returned to his honeymoon suite after sleeping with a woman he had just met in the hotel lounge. That woman had soothed his ruffled feelings but could not take away the guilt he felt. Now, here he was watching his new bride in slumber. In the low lamp light, he could see the sheen of dried tears upon her porcelain cheeks. Liliana was clad in an attractive satin nightgown. Her long, wavy hair tumbled across the sateen pillowcase, and her honeymoon ensemble fit her exquisitely. She looked reminiscent of a 1940s movie starlet, yet, Richard could only find fault with her.

Richard preferred the fuller curves of his recent lover and not the small bust of his new wife. As well, his wife was slender and not nearly as voluptuous as the woman he had just sullied himself with… he preferred more flesh. And, as he sat with his elbows propped on the bedside desk, he steepled his fingers, rested them lightly on his upper lip, and thought about what he had just done. No, not the tryst with the woman two floors down, but the guilt he harbored for purposefully pressuring Liliana into marrying him. Richard Rawlings knew that by marrying Liliana, he had irreconcilably severed her bond with someone who was truly devoted to her, and for some reason that made him feel a bit of remorse right now.

Shamefully, Richard Rawlings admitted to himself that he was so selfishly bent on besting everyone to win scholarships, stipends, internships, and now women, that he had tenaciously pursued Liliana because she would be the definitive wife. She would always look beautiful on his arm, and she was very intelligent. Yes, the picture-perfect wife for his master plan. Richard was never going to be the drunken loser his father had been. He was going to be the most highly-visible and the most-successful man in his industry…no matter what he had to do to get there.

Scanning the rumpled sheets on his side of the bed, Richard saw the bloody evidence of his wife's virginity, and it angered him. Liliana had come to their marriage a chaste woman, but Richard knew that her virginity should have gone to someone else who revered her; namely Declan Ryan. Richard laughed somewhat bitterly to himself…it had all been a game. It had almost been too easy to knock honorable Declan Ryan off the playing field. As he had suspected the first time they met, there was something inside that made Declan vulnerable.

Seeing the events in his mind's eye, Richard thought about how he had hotly pursued Liliana on the Brineforth campus. First, securing a coffee date, then outings for fancy dinners, trips to the museum and the theater, and finally bald-face lies to Liliana and her parents about his academic accomplishments. It had been easy to dazzle Liliana because she was used to college venues with beer and pizza. Going to high-end restaurants and the theater with him had made her feel like a woman. She had been somewhat easier to throw off the playing field than Declan Ryan had been. He had easily planted doubts in her unblemished mind…sizable doubts about Declan's affection for her, doubts about the lifestyle she would have with an immigrant who, until recently, didn't even own a car…and finally, doubts about why Declan had never declared his love for her. Seeing the hollowness in her green eyes when she, at last, considered that Declan Ryan might not care for her had been the turning point. All he had had to do thereafter was erode their relationship at every turn with his presence.

Now that Liliana was his, he could only find fault with her. Their marriage had been consummated with him hastily taking her with no consideration for her feelings. Afterward, he had rolled off her, dressed again, and had gone down to the hotel lounge for a drink. He knew she would never cross him for this behavior because she had lain there pale, silent, and humiliated. Richard smiled to himself…she had tried to be an earnest lover her first time, but he purposefully had laughed at her efforts. Richard wasn't interested in honing her skills… love-making could give a woman power over you.

Richard continued to sit next to the bed until half past five that early morning, watching Liliana in her sleep. At last, he finally began to feel true remorse over his actions last night and made a decision. Yes, he would still pursue his dreams no matter the cost, but he would also try to be a kind husband to Liliana. She deserved, at least, that much.

Liliana awoke with a start. She had been reliving her dance with Declan from yesterday in a wildly-vivid dream. In her nightmare, things had turned out quite differently…Richard had hit Declan with his large fist and had killed him. Then, he had carried her up to their honeymoon suite to consummate their marriage…she was wildly kicking and trying to call for help; but for some reason, she couldn't make a sound no matter how hard she tried. Now that she had her bearings, she realized she had been dreaming.

The clock on the night stand said half past five. The room was still illuminated by a lowly-lit lamp, and Liliana thought she could hear water running. She looked over to Richard's side of the bed and saw the bed sheets in disarray and the proof of her virginity in a small pool of dried blood. With last night's memories flooding back, tears stung at her eyes.

Just then, Richard emerged from the bathroom. He came to her side of the bed and looked down at her with remorse. "Liliana, I was not kind to you last night. Please let me make it up to you. The last few days have been hard on both of us emotionally. Can we start anew?"

Liliana found it hard to look into Richard's eyes, and tears pooled ready to overflow. He took a hold of one of the wavy locks of her hair and tugged on it. She found the wherewithal to look up at him and saw that he was smiling down at her. His hair sparkled with droplets from the shower, and he was freshly shaved.

"Come on, baby, let's try it again," he said softly as he held out his hand to her.

Richard then led her to the sizable marble tub in the bath and switched on the water. He removed her satin gown. He then helped her into the warm water that swirled around her from the water's pressure. Joining her in the tub, he gently cleansed her with soap that smelled of fresh rain and washed away all remnants of their first coupling from her body. He then wrapped her in a warmed towel and carried her to the bed. Throwing back the sheets, Richard unwound the fluffy towel from around Liliana's slim frame and laid her in the bed. Joining her, he covered them both with the sheet and held her in his arms, telling her again that he was sorry for his actions.

As Richard held her, Liliana thought about what had happened last night. She was learning that Richard could be quite unfeeling. He had treated her callously on their wedding night; but she was willing to forgive him. Surely, he knew that if such treatment were repeated, it could erode one's affection. Liliana was already slightly wary of her new husband, but she was willing to give him the benefit of the doubt.

That morning, Richard made love to her with considerably more affection, and held her until they awoke at noon, but Liliana still queried why things had gone so awry on their wedding night.

Two floors down, unknowing Sierra Monroe wondered when she would get to spend time with tall, handsome, and well-to-do Richard Rawlings again. The poor girl had no idea he was a new bridegroom and hadn't even been married twenty-four hours.

THE OTHER WOMAN

*S*ierra Monroe** found herself watching and waiting for Richard Rawlings to get in touch with her. In the three weeks since they had met, he had sent her roses with a personal note telling her he was out of the country but would contact her as soon as he returned; little did she know Richard was on his honeymoon with his wife.

Though she knew she would never be a rocket scientist, Sierra Monroe knew one thing. Richard Rawlings had eagerly made love to her as no one ever had…she knew her largesse of intimate experience had captivated him, and he had been a very vigorous partner. As well, there had been a slightly dangerous aura about him that night that made him very exciting. In short, Sierra wanted Richard for her own.

Never again, could she settle for a man like Henry Carlson, her current boyfriend. Henry was an accountant. He made very good money and treated her well, but there was just something about Richard Rawlings that made her want to sigh. She was fearful that she had fallen in love with him during their one night together. She was thankful that Henry had been delayed that evening and had called off their night out. That night, when she had entered the luxurious lounge at the hotel for a drink, she would never have guessed that she would meet a man who would sweep her off her feet.

Years from now, Sierra knew that the date of November twentieth would always be a precious memory of her first meeting with Richard Rawlings, and she hoped that he would be back in her arms again very soon.

Poor, poor Sierra…Richard had played her like a harp, and she had unknowingly entered his web of deceit. It hadn't even crossed her mind that he might be married.

ANNIE'S TRIBULATIONS

Annie Riordan became ill three years after Liliana was married. During a long and snowy winter, it was discovered that she had Stage III Breast Cancer. She took the news well enough, but Christophe Riordan was out of his head with grief. Anything remotely resembling suffering tore at Christophe's heart, but when that suffering belonged to his wife, he almost couldn't stand it. Now, it was Christophe's turn to be a wild man with his grief. Since the vineyard was groomed impeccably these days, thanks to Declan's sorrow, Christophe was left with nothing to do except build stone walls along the perimeter of the vineyard and the nursery. Declan, who knew the heartache and the rigors of battling cancer, became the "strong one" that the Riordans both needed for Annie to fight her cancer battle.

Shortly after she was diagnosed, Annie asked for Declan to come see her. Declan, who had been down this road before, knew what she was going to ask for even before she began to articulate her thoughts. Declan knew that she wanted him to keep Christophe occupied enough that it would take his mind off her illness. She had said, "Declan, you took care of your mother, so you know what I am about to embark upon; it's not pretty, and it is not easy. I may even die, but I don't want Christophe worrying about me. Please keep him occupied, so he doesn't fret."

She had smiled wanly, "Chris does need to build those rock walls around the vineyard section; especially now. He wants them to look like those handsome walls throughout the old country. You know what I mean…old-world stone walls, surrounded by rolling green fields… and in our case, vineyards, barns, and a pretty nursery. You have an eye for the style, Declan, and the cost is of no matter, please just keep him occupied and focused while I do my best to get well." Serious Declan had held her hand, kissed it, and had given her his vow that he would keep Christophe occupied and that the finished product would look straight out of Scotland.

Within hours, Annie was in surgery for a radical mastectomy. She came through with flying colors, but next, she faced both chemotherapy and radiation treatments. Declan drove both Christophe and Annie to Reedsburgh Medical Center for her treatments every other week, and Stephan and Jenny Lylestrom traveled regularly to Rosemeade Township to help care for her. These were challenging times but filled with loving help from friends and neighbors. Christophe and Annie had been friends to all during their lifetime in Rosemeade County, so once word got around that they needed help, the community came to their aid.

Old Jim, who was starting to be a wee bit fragile himself, sat at Annie's bedside and sang the old church hymns to her. Rosemeade neighbors mowed, raked, mulched, and helped Declan prepare everything the next spring at The Old Vineyard Road Nursery. All the while, Christophe toiled… building the beautiful stone walls that he cherished from his youth. With all the added help from the Rosemeade community, Declan was also able to help Christophe on his project, too. Together, they prayed for Annie's healing, talked about the fragility of life, and found comfort in one another while they labored on a project that brought them the salve that they both needed for their wounds.

At about the 18-month mark in her battle with cancer, Annie began to feel like herself once more. Her hair had grown back again, but it was no longer dark, it was a very pretty silver. Those who didn't know her or what she had just gone through tended to ask her, "Who colors your hair? It's simply beautiful."

Annie just laughed on those occasions and said, "Oh, Mother Nature is my stylist!"

Everyone was optimistic about a full recovery now, as all her tests indicated she was cancer free. Annie had survived, but she would not feel completely comfortable until she passed her five-year anniversary.

It had been a hard fight for Annie Riordan, but she was alive. Her husband had been occupied so he did not make himself ill from worry, and Declan Ryan had, again, proven himself to be the son they had never had. He had cared for them both, he had single-handedly run the nursery and the vineyard for months, and he had shown great strength and compassion under duress. Both Christophe and Annie Riordan were very proud of him. They knew that they already loved him, but Declan's kindness to them during such a difficult time increased the depth of their love for him by tenfold. During all these trials, no one brought up the subject of Liliana, but they did wonder why Stephan and Jenny never heard very much from her. Something seemed quite off kilter; such behavior from Liliana was truly out of character.

THE OLD VINEYARD
ROAD NURSERY

Christophe and Declan were featured in a regional gardening magazine story five years after Liliana's marriage to Richard. When the spring and summer seasons arrived at Old Vineyard Road, the vineyard and nursery were also showcased on two local television stations as garden destinations not to be missed.

The true beauty of the old abandoned vineyard was now harnessed into acre upon acre of tidy rows of exceptionally-beautiful grapevines surrounded by old-world stone fencing. Christophe and Annie's lovely old family home was also shown looking its best, with the new stone wall also surrounding it.

And, the nursery itself shone like a handful of brilliant, multi-colored gemstones in the midst of it all. Not only did Declan have an eye for design, his eye for landscape architecture had taken the nursery from a "pretty little spot" in historic Rosemeade County into one of the most-photographed garden spots in the region. Even with all this notoriety, no word was ever heard from Liliana.

Now that both the nursery and the vineyard areas were healthy and well-cultivated, Declan suggested to Christophe that they might just want to turn some unused land directly across from the nursery entrance into an organic fruit and gardening venture. Declan also proposed that they might even want to sell produce seasonally from some type of kiosk or old-time fruit stand that would be compatible with the feel of everything else. Part of the impetus for this suggestion was that Declan wanted to make sure that Annie ate the healthiest of foods to help her stay cancer-free. It goes without saying that Christophe Riordan caught his young cousin's vision.

That year, a small fledgling orchard was planted alongside rows of melons, squash, pumpkins, tomatoes, hybrid corn, potatoes, onions, lettuces and peas. The fallow land blossomed with the organic ingredients used to amend its soil, and soon a very handsome fruit and vegetable plot was showing its beauty to clients. On weekends, Christophe, Old Jim, and Declan worked on a striking stone kiosk which would showcase their soon-to-be harvested first fruits of summer.

By summer's end, word had spread throughout the county about the new and very picturesque organic farm stand at The Old Vineyard Road Nursery. People came from miles around to purchase unsullied farm fresh vegetables and berries, and Old Jim was the perfect farm stand attendant. Everyone loved him. Christophe and Declan were pleased with all their recent improvements, but most of all, they continued to celebrate Annie's recovery from cancer.

OLD JIM

Old Jim shared his life story with Declan late that fall, after all the fruits of their labor had been harvested and sold to their rapidly-growing customer base. They were working side by side readying the stone farm stand for the inclement weather that would soon be upon them. It was cold, but the day was very bright and sunny. Old Jim looked up, took a drink from his water bottle and said, "You know, Declan, it was a day just like today, the first time I ever saw this property. It was dilapidated, filled with many years' worth of trash and refuse, and wild grape vines covered everything. That day, Christophe shared his vision for the place with me, and he asked me to help him get things started. Declan, I was recovering from a horrible bout of pneumonia, I had almost died, yet Christophe saw something worthwhile in my sorry soul."

"Jim, you are one of the finest men I know, please don't say such things about yourself," Declan had answered.

Then and there, Old Jim decided that the time had come to fully share his story with his young friend. "On the contrary, Declan. I had lived a very privileged life as a young man in the eastern United States. My family was quite wealthy, and I received a quality education. I went to college and trained to be an engineer, and it was there that I met the woman that I had hoped to marry. As I once told you, I foolishly let her go, and my life was never the same."

"I looked for solace in alcohol, and when it still couldn't numb my sorrow, I started to smoke reefers; I guess they call them joints now. At that time, I was working for an engineering firm, and most of the time, I was able to hide my love for alcohol and weed from them. But after several years, I began to embrace hard drugs. By the world's standard, I had it all, but you can probably guess that I eventually brought much shame to my wealthy, upper-class family. After losing a series of jobs and finding my name in the newspaper more than once for drunken driving and possession of narcotics, my father threw me out…out of his home and out of the family. I was so far gone, I didn't even care. My mother, who still saw some worth in me, cried her eyes out."

"So, from there I started living the life of a hobo, that's what they called us, back then. I travelled far from my home where no one knew me. I could work for a few hours at a time without the booze and drugs, so I earned just enough from odd jobs to support my habit. One day, I found myself in Reedsburgh. I was hungry, so I went to a small café to eat a meal. I was still bleary-eyed from the night before, so I wasn't paying much attention to anything in the place. Suddenly on the television behind the counter in that little café, I heard my mother's name. It seemed she had died. But the thing that stunned me the most was that the television reporter who was telling the story about my mother's life, said that she had never gotten over the disappearance of her youngest son. The reporter said that she had searched for him in vain for many years." Jim swallowed almost convulsively, "Declan, that son, was me."

"While I had wallowed in my sorrow at losing the love of my life, my little mother had tried to comfort me. As I dissipated myself with alcohol, then hard drugs, my mother had tried to help me; she exhorted me to stop my behavior and to get a hold of myself, but I was too far gone. The day my father threw me out of the family, her pretty little face was red and swollen from her crying. She ran after me and held me tight. She told me that she loved me and begged me not to do anything to harm myself. Declan, as much as I loved my precious mother, I could not stop myself for her. I would write her an occasional letter, but I don't think she ever received them, as I never heard anything from her again. I suspect that my father made sure she never saw the letters that I wrote to her."

"To hear that television reporter say those things finally crushed what was left of my broken spirit. That morning, I left that café, and I sought out the nearest liquor store and drank myself into oblivion. I don't even remember how many weeks or even months that I binged, but I finally hit rock bottom one night outside of some seedy bar a few doors down from the Rescue Mission; still in Reedsburgh."

"Declan, I don't even remember it, but Christophe told me, it was about nine o'clock on a summer evening…it was still light. I was lying in the alleyway between the bar and a vacant building. Christophe was walking to his car; he had just helped to serve the evening meal at the Rescue Mission. He saw me in the alley, soaked in urine and covered in filth. He heard me choking to death on my own vomit. Though I didn't deserve his compassion, Christophe called for an ambulance and while he waited for the ambulance, he tried to resuscitate me… me, an undeserving, selfish man who had wasted every opportunity that had ever been given to him." Old Jim sadly shook his head, and continued…

"When I finally came around several days later, I was in the hospital in an intensive care unit. I had been washed and cleaned up, but I was suffering horribly from pneumonia. The young physician, who was treating me, said that I had come very close to death that night. That young doctor then went and found Christophe and brought him to me. Christophe was good to me. He paid for my hospitalization, he gave me a little room over his diner to live in, and he gave me a job busing tables and washing dishes at the diner. He drove me to rehab, but more than anything else, he shared his faith in God with me. He told me I could be forgiven and restored to a family again; the Family of God. The day he told me that, I fervently admitted I was a sinner, and I prayed to receive unmerited forgiveness from my Creator. Declan, all desire for alcohol and drugs went away that day, but I still finished my rehab program. I praise the Lord daily for my salvation and for the special friend he gave to me in Christophe Riordan."

"You know, I only have one thing left from my old life, and I put it into my suitcase the day my father threw me out of the family. It is a quilt that I watched my mother make for me when I was a little child in the late 1930s. It was in my pack the night Christophe found me. After I was released from the hospital, that pack was returned to me, and Annie helped me go through my things. When she saw that filthy quilt, she recognized that it had once been something beautiful. She asked if she could take it to Betty Addington, here in Rosemeade. I gave it to her. Betty repaired and restored it. When it was finished,

Betty brought it to me wrapped in tissue paper and bound with a ribbon. Exactly like my mother would have done."

Quiet Declan Ryan was stunned by what Jim had just shared with him. Now, he understood why Jim had been so adamant that he not walk away from Liliana. Old Jim knew exactly what he had felt during those sad times.

That night, Declan awakened from a sound sleep. He had a revelation of sorts. Five years ago, when Liliana had married Richard, he had come home after her wedding and had started a bonfire with cuttings from the wildly-rampant grapes in the vineyard. He had almost been out of his head with the heartache he was feeling, and cleaning up the vineyard had seemed the only way to quell his pain. A day or two later, Jim had quietly come over to the vineyard rows and had started to help him with his huge pruning project. He hadn't ever realized that Jim had been looking out for him; making sure that he stayed grounded…ensuring that he didn't lose himself in his regret. Old Jim had been a solid friend and had worked hard to make sure that the remorse of losing Liliana hadn't chewed him up and spit him out. A humbled Declan then proceeded to thank God for Jim and his constant, caring friendship.

LILIANA'S INTROSPECTION

L iliana had to be honest about things. She had just passed her sixth wedding anniversary, and she had started to feel more than uncomfortable with her husband. The previous five years of her marriage hadn't been easy, but she had been able to maneuver things enough that she could keep Richard's emotive actions to a minimum. But now, the tide was changing. Richard had become openly hostile to her. He had always been condescending, slightly rude, and somewhat emotionally abusive, but the pendulum seemed to be swinging into uncharted territory. She had never really feared Richard, yet she was beginning to feel somewhat ill at ease with him; simply because she never knew what to expect when he arrived home from his work. Richard had recently lost his second job in eighteen months. With the job changes, came relocations.

The first move had been to the Chicago area, and it had been exciting to live in The Windy City. It was with this relocation that Richard had insisted that Liliana give up her teaching position and become a stay-at-home wife. He intimated that he wanted her to give up her job so they could start a family, yet no plans for children were ever made as he had found himself at odds with his regional manager. If Richard felt under duress, which he quite often did, he made sure that Liliana was somewhat to blame for his problems. "If she were more understanding of him, he wouldn't be so upset all the time. And, if she were more supportive of him, he could outsell all of his colleagues…" and the list went on. Liliana tried to appease him, but it wasn't easy.

Just as they were starting to feel settled in Chicago, Richard had an incident with his manager and was placed on probation; he retained his job, but his sales were under scrutiny. Richard immediately began looking for a new position. He soon was offered a new job in Denver, Colorado, so their household was, once again, boxed up and loaded into a moving van.

With this move, Richard vowed to be a better husband to her, so she did her best to make him happy. She also learned that opening their home to his clients and co-workers pleased him immensely, so she made every effort to entertain both his clients and his work colleagues often. Liliana found that she had a knack for making a simple dinner with clients an event, so Richard often found himself gleaning the referrals of their dinner guest's families and friends for a week or two after a dinner party at their home. Consequently, Liliana enjoyed relative calm for close to two years during their tenure in Colorado.

Just prior to her eighth wedding anniversary, the owner of the investment group for whom Richard worked, announced that he was retiring. His son was to take over as head of the family-owned business. Richard bristled over someone younger being in authority over him. Even though his accounts were his own, it was still hard for Richard to bow to someone with less experience. The old anger set in again, and before she knew it, Liliana found herself moving to Seattle, Washington, with a sullen Richard for yet another new job. It seemed that this move was a turning point in their relationship. The subject of starting a family never came up. This was fine with Liliana, because she did not want to subject her child to an emotionally-abusive father.

Richard was in such pursuit of quick wealth that he was rarely home, and when he was, it was hard to be in his company. Venomous comments, mixed with dissatisfaction with his circumstances, were quickly hurtling to the point where Liliana found herself wary of being in his company. The more Richard traveled, the more comfortable she became without him. She still tried to appease his combative temperament when he was in town, but it became more and more difficult to temper his moods. It was also during this time-frame that Richard lost all interest in intimacy with her. Liliana even wondered if, perhaps, he might be cheating on her, yet she could find no concrete proof to support her suspicions.

All in all, their marriage was a subterfuge covering something far more volatile in Richard's disposition. She just didn't know what. Liliana knew she would stay the course with Richard, but her life was becoming more and more walled in. In short, she felt like a prisoner.

It had been a very long time since she had seen her parents, and she missed them very much. She didn't like to even think such things about her husband, but she wondered if he was, in fact, purposefully trying to keep her from them. Any inquiry as to when she might be able to get away to Reedsburgh for a visit always ended with him loudly shouting, so she ceased to bring up the subject.

Liliana suspected that Richard might be battling some type of emotional disorder and felt that if she could just get him diagnosed and, perhaps, medicated appropriately, his volatile disposition might improve. It was really a question as to how she could broach such a subject to him without him becoming vicious. Shortly after her ninth wedding anniversary, Liliana met with a physician to discuss her suspicions and how she might appropriately handle getting her husband diagnosed and treated. She left the consultation with great hope that Richard could be helped.

Little did Liliana know that while she was seeking out professional help for Richard, he was in the arms of another woman, and all the while, he was painting her in a very negative light to his mistress.

A HAPPY TURN OF EVENTS

*O*ld *Jim* awoke one morning feeling quite weary. As he did most days, he wondered about Liliana. They still had not heard anything from her, and she had been gone for ten years. Old Jim still worried about her welfare, and now, it seemed that both Liliana and his lost love, Bette, had been in his thoughts for weeks.

Last night, he had dreamt about Bette, the love of his life, whom he had foolishly let slip through his fingers so many years before. In his dream, he was a young man again, and he hadn't made any decisions that would alter the course of his life. Bette was beautiful and looked into his eyes with unconditional love. They sailed together in a boat on the small lake that was in the heavily-wooded back end of his parent's palatial estate. The sun was warm on their faces and between them was a picnic hamper with sandwiches lovingly prepared by Sissy, his family's live-in cook.

His dream continued with gentle breezes ruffling Bette's long blond hair. Then, the breeze turned to wind and became stronger. Soon, waves were stirred up on the lake. He was having a hard time keeping the little sailboat under control, and the next thing he knew, a large wave hit the boat and capsized it. Bette was flailing in the water calling his name, and Jim could not get to her no matter how hard he tried…

Jim awakened in a sweat and was thankful that it had been only a dream. But the emotion of that dream was so realistic that Jim felt drained and melancholy the whole day. Late in the afternoon, Christophe, who knew him well, inquired if everything was all right. Old Jim hung his head and sadly confided, "Chris, I dreamt about Bette last night. It was so realistic that I woke up quite agitated and unhappy this morning. I've been mulling over that dream all day long, and it's gotten me to thinking. Perhaps, I should try to find out whatever happened to Bette. If she is still alive, I would like to contact her. Do you think David Renton might be able to help me? If she's passed away, it is okay; but if she's still living, I would at least like to make things right with her before I leave this world."

Kind, compassionate Christophe Riordan then put his giant hand on his old friend's shoulder and said, "Jim, I think that's probably a good idea. Why don't we drive to Reedsburgh in the morning and see what can be done? I'll put in a call to David right now.

A week and a half later, David Renton called with news of Jim's long-lost love. She was still living and was in good health. She lived in Phoenix, Arizona. David had, in fact, contacted her and she had been happy to learn that Jim was desirous of getting in touch with her. Old Jim could hardly believe his ears. At last, he was going to be able to ask her forgiveness for his arrogant and thoughtless behavior.

That evening, Jim dialed Bette's number and waited nervously through three trills of the ringtone. The next thing he knew, his beautiful Bette was on the line, and they were chatting as if there had never been a chasm between them. Jim was candid with her about the life of dissipation he had led before Christophe had pulled him out of the muck.

She told Jim that she had prayed that God would protect him for many years. She said, "God has been faithful to us both, Jim. I was reckless myself after we broke up, but I married a man who loved me and helped me to work through what happened between us. He even took on the child that I was carrying as his own. That child was yours, Jim. We have a son, and his name is John. My husband, Charlie, loved him as his own, and John grew up to be a fine man. He is a physician in Chicago. You would be so proud of him. John knows about what happened between us, but I know that he considers Charlie his true father. I think you understand."

Old Jim was stunned. "Was that what it was, Bette? Was that what you were trying to tell me the last time we saw each other? Bette, I am so sorry. I was just a selfish, very privileged young man. I knew that we had gone way too far, and I panicked. I should have offered marriage to you as soon as we went down that road, but I wasn't man enough. Instead, I distanced myself from you. Please know this, I **was** regretful. Believe it or not, I did love you very much, but before I knew it, you were married to someone else. I just couldn't believe that I had been so foolish. I had let you slip through my fingers. Oh, Bette, had I known you were carrying our child, I would have married you. Please, believe me when I say that I would have loved you for a lifetime. Can you ever forgive me? I'm sorry, Bette; so very sorry how things turned out."

"Jim, I had a wonderful life with Charlie. He was a man of God, and he was the pastor of a small church in the south. Just like you see in the movies…a little white church with beautiful stained-glass windows and a cross atop the steeple…we had an idyllic life. We had a small farm, too, and John lived a carefree childhood there. Please don't be regretful, Jim. There is no longer any need for blame."

"Bette, may I come to see you sometime?" Old Jim inquired.

"Yes, Jim. You may come to see me. I would like that very much."

Over the next few weeks, Old Jim and Bette spoke several times via the telephone. They, at last, selected the first week of December for their reunion. Declan Ryan flew with Jim to Phoenix, Arizona. He rented a car and drove his aging friend to Bette's home. It was a little stucco bungalow in a gated retirement community where pink, white, and red Oleander bushes, bloomed and colorfully potted garden plants abounded.

When Bette opened the door, tears shone in her eyes. She held out her arms to Jim and embraced him. Bette was a beautiful older woman. She had a crown of curling white hair, a healthy glowing complexion, and a zest for life. Though Jim had lived his life considerably harder than Bette; his weathered face shone as he was reunited with his true love.

As Declan watched this poignant scene, he found himself feeling wistful. He, too, had erred grievously with his one-and-only true love, but Old Jim had saved him from drowning in the black abyss of his all-consuming regret. Shaking away those old memories, Declan smiled at the special couple, and left them alone to mend things that had gone before.

When the December sun dipped low in the western sky later that evening and all was aglow in a pink and lavender mist on the horizon, Declan returned and took the elderly sweethearts out for a special dinner at Bennochio's. There was much joy for Old Jim and Bette that night as they savored Mediterranean cuisine under the stars adjacent to the restaurant's patio fireplace. A very-pleased Declan raised his glass in tribute to his aging friends who had, at last, been reunited in love.

Much later, while all was quiet in their hotel suite, Old Jim awoke to hear Declan faintly call out in his sleep. Instinctively, Old Jim knew that Declan was likely beckoning Liliana. He prayed that night for his young friend's heart to be healed, too.

One morning, three weeks later, Annie went to Old Jim's cottage with some freshly baked bread. She found Jim lying in his bed clutching a photograph that Declan had taken of him and Bette. He smiled weakly and with labored breath said, "I'm going home today, Annie".

Annie smoothed his slightly fevered brow and kissed his cheek. "Oh, Jim," she said as she sighed sadly. She then dispatched Christophe and Declan to come quickly.

When they arrived, Old Jim, again, smiled weakly. He looked at Christophe with tears in his eyes and wheezed, "I love you, brother. You shared with me just how I could restore my broken soul."

Then, Jim's eyelashes fluttered momentarily, and he barely breathed out, "Declan, I thank you for taking me to see my beautiful Bette. You are a very fine young man."

With very-labored breathing overcoming him, he asked, "Dearest Annie, could you please sing some of the old hymns to me now?" He then closed his eyes.

Old Jim passed from this life two hours later with Christophe Riordan holding his left hand and Annie Riordan holding his right. Declan Ryan sat next to Jim on the edge of his bed. Ever thoughtful, Declan had held his large comforting hand over Jim's heart until the very end.

That evening, Declan was assigned the task of calling Bette to tell her that Old Jim had passed away. Bette quietly said to him, "Declan, I didn't think he was long for this world, but I am so happy that he was restored to me. I have been loved by two very special men in my life, and even though things were painful for Jim and me, I can rejoice that he went home to God with no regrets. When is his funeral?"

"We have planned it for Friday morning, here in Rosemeade Township."

"I will be there for him, Declan"

"Thank you, Bette. I'll text you all the details."

Declan Ryan then signed off and wiped unbidden tears from his eyes. He suddenly remembered how fond Old Jim had once been of Liliana Lylestrom. He wondered how she would feel if she knew that he had passed from this life. Somehow, Declan knew that it would grieve her tender heart.

THE POLICE

Jack Spence drove into the circular driveway on Ferncrest Drive NW, the suburban address where he had been dispatched to check things out. Funny thing, though, the well-groomed property and its quiet location truly belied the fact that he was seeking an individual with multiple drunken-driving complaints filed against him from the night before, as well as a possible arrest for assaulting the owner of a little pub in the "burbs" called, Johnny O's.

Officer Jack Spence was truly surprised, however, when a young woman who looked to be just slightly older than himself opened the front door. She was fully-dressed but looked quite fragile; as if she were just recovering from an illness. She also wore a swollen black eye and bruises on her attractive face and delicate neck.

"Ma'am, I'm Officer Spence from the Edmonds PD. Are you Mrs. Rawlings? Mrs. Richard Rawlings?" he asked as niggling concern crept up his spine. He noticed that the young woman looked wary as she quietly sighed.

"Yes, I'm Liliana Rawlings, officer. How may I help you?"

"Ma'am, is your husband in today? I need to speak with him regarding several complaints that were received regarding erratic driving in a vehicle which is registered to him."

"No, officer, I'm afraid I haven't seen him since very early this morning. Would you like to come in? I'll be happy to help you in any way that I can." She opened the door wider and motioned for him to come into her beautiful brick home.

As Mrs. Rawlings led the way to a family-area just off her shiny chrome and marble kitchen, Officer Spence noted that a formal dining area off the main hallway looked as though a bomb had gone off inside, yet the remainder of the house was impeccably clean. He was already beginning to suspect the erratic driving allegations were just the tip of the iceberg for Richard Rawlings's wrongdoings.

"Have a seat officer, may I offer you something to drink?" she asked.

"No, thank you, Mrs. Rawlings. Is there a chance that you know where your husband might be right now?"

"No, sir. I have no idea where he might be. As I said, he left quite early this morning around five o'clock. I've not heard from him since. Tell me, what has he done?"

"He is accused of physically assaulting the owner of a pub near Olympic View Drive last night. Then, he was reported driving erratically by several claimants who barely escaped with their lives. Apparently, he was driving well over the speed limit. The Edmonds PD does need to speak with him regarding these complaints, ma'am, if it was, in fact, your husband in the pub, and later, for driving so erratically."

"Was he intoxicated the last time you saw him, Mrs. Rawlings?" Officer Spence quietly inquired.

"Yes, Officer Spence. He was quite drunk and smelled heavily of alcohol," she quietly answered. "But, characteristically, he has never been a drinker. His father was an alcoholic, and my husband seemingly eschewed alcohol until last night. Quite honestly, I had never seen him like that ever before. I feel he was likely still under the influence when he left this morning. He seemed to be in quite a hurry when he pulled out of the drive."

"Do you know why he was in a hurry, Mrs. Rawlings?" Officer Spence softly asked.

At this point, Office Spence knew all he needed to know…Richard Rawlings was likely a wife-beating brute, but he hoped his inquiry might lead his wife to confide how she got her injuries. Instead of answering, her eyes filled with tears, and she looked down at her folded hands.

"Mrs. Rawlings?" he asked again.

When she met eyes with him again, she squared her shoulders and replied, "My husband is a harsh man, but I had never seen him out of control like he was last evening. The marks that I bear are from him, but last night was the first and only time."

"It may likely occur again, Mrs. Rawlings, would you like to file a complaint?"

"I would like to, Officer Spence, but I won't at this time."

"Mrs. Rawlings, to ensure your safety and good health, I suggest that you go to an emergency room to get your injuries evaluated and to have your eye sutured, so you don't end up with any scarring. Let the hospital's medical personnel document the incident. You do have injuries that should be reported. Also, ma'am, if you have family in the area, go to them. And, if there is anything else you need, please feel free to contact me at the department. Here is my badge number, too, should you need any help."

With that, Officer Jack Spence got up to leave. At the front door, he turned back to the young woman; she had a petite frame, and she looked so small and vulnerable beneath the twelve-foot ceilings in her entry hall. He kindly said," Mrs. Rawlings, thank you for your time this morning. You've been very helpful, but I will check in with you again in a few more days to see if you've heard anything from your husband. Please, Mrs. Rawlings, stay safe."

Several days later, Officer Jack Spence again checked in on Liliana Rawlings late in the afternoon. When she opened the door, he was relieved to see that she looked considerably better than the last time he had interviewed her, and that she was now wearing stitches just below her eyebrow. He began, "Mrs. Rawlings, I just wanted to make sure you were feeling better and to inquire if you have heard anything from your husband, yet..."

Shaking her head slightly, she answered, "No, Officer Spence, I have heard nothing from him at all. Would you care to come in?"

Opening her front door wider, she again admitted him to her home, and led him to the same family area just off her kitchen. Glancing into the formal dining room on the way through the hall, Jack noticed that there had been some attempt to clean up the broken furniture and refuse, but it was obvious that it was turning out to be a big job for one person.

He queried, "Mrs. Rawlings, I'm not trying to pry, but is your husband responsible for the damage in this room?" He watched as she hesitated just outside of the room. She shook her head affirmatively to answer his question.

"I'll be candid, Officer Spence, he did all of this damage shortly after he was rough with me four nights ago. After I was able to get myself up off the floor, I locked myself in our bedroom, but I could hear the cacophony of his rampage in the dining room. I couldn't call for help because my cell phone was on the kitchen counter, and we don't have a landline."

Looking earnestly up into his eyes, she continued, "From there, I'm pretty sure he drank heavily from the wine and liquor that we did keep in our pantry for guests. I found several bottles shattered along with everything else in the dining area."

"I'm sorry, Mrs. Rawlings, why don't we sit down. I would like to annotate a few details for my dispatch report."

"Of course, Officer Spence."

Liliana Rawlings watched as the officer sat and marked several notations in a small notebook, then he looked up. His face looked slightly tense, "Mrs. Rawlings, do you know what time your husband came home that evening?"

"Yes, it was about 11:30 or maybe even midnight."

"Did he tell you where he had been?"

"No. He just kept begging me to open the locked bedroom door." She sighed and then added, "He wouldn't take "no" for an answer, but I wouldn't let him in. Finally, I heard a muffled thump...I think he sat down outside our bedroom door and either passed out or fell asleep. It was quiet for several hours. Later, he awoke; and he, again, continued to beg for me to open the door for what seemed like another hour or so. At last, I acquiesced just to get him to be quiet. I think he was surprised when he saw my injuries, but from there, it just got uglier because I wouldn't let him touch me... He wanted to 'comfort me,' she said as she made air quotes with her slim fingers."

Reading between the lines, he grimly asked, "Did your husband strike you again before he left that morning, Mrs. Rawlings?"

Officer Spence watched as she looked away and down at the floor. After a second or two, she softly answered, "Yes, Officer Spence, he did." But what she hadn't told compassionate and kind Officer Spence was that her husband had not only beaten her again, but that he had forced himself upon her, as well. Liliana was much too ashamed to share that part of the story with Officer Jack Spence.

"I'm truly sorry, Mrs. Rawlings. Truly," the officer murmured.

Minutes later, as Officer Spence was leaving, he asked, "Do you have **any** family or friends that you can go to in this area for your own personal safety?"

"No, Officer Spence, I don't, and I wouldn't want my parents to see me like this anyway. My parents are older, and I am their only child. It would break their hearts."

She continued, "I don't think you need to worry that my husband will come back anytime soon, as I have learned that he had been fired for serious indiscretions the day he came at me. It would be very hard for him to admit that to me now. Besides, I have suspected that he has been involved with someone else for a while now. He is likely there. And for right now, I am just fine with that… I did have a locksmith come to change the locks, so I am secure for now. There are far worse things for me than being alone, but I will be careful, nonetheless, Officer Spence."

"Mrs. Rawlings, please let the department know if you learn anything regarding your husband. And, again, please stay safe."

With that, Officer Spence drove off feeling slightly apprehensive for Mrs. Rawlings whom he suspected had put up with a lot more bad behavior from her husband than she had even let on.

DISTRESS

*L*iliana *Lylestrom Rawlings* was suffering in silence. Her husband had harshly beaten her almost three weeks ago; then, he had vanished. A police officer had even come to their home to interview him regarding an incident in a tavern on the coastal road as well as for multiple complaints they had received of his reckless driving. Once again, she was left to face questions meant for Richard. He had left her to clean up the detritus of his bad decisions while she healed from the physical wounds that he had inflicted upon her.

This morning over her toast and tea, she had decided she would take no more; she was done with Richard. In the quiet of the early morning, she decided that, never again, would she try to soothe his volatile temper...she was finished. Hurting and slightly fragile, Liliana had determined that she would file for a legal separation from Richard. At last, she was willing to live apart from him for the rest of her life. She was exhausted from the unending task of humoring him. Living alone for the remainder of her life was not what she had once hoped for, but she would carry on. Perhaps, she could even move closer to her dear parents. Innately, she knew solitude was of considerably more benefit to her now than the constant dread of his explosive emotions and their concomitant actions.

All around her, the Christmas season was in full swing, yet she numbly wondered how she had found herself at this juncture in her life. She desperately wanted to see her parents, but she was much too ashamed to let them see her broken like this…she must heal for a while before she could be in their company. And, she really didn't know if she could truly burden them with such shame.

Something had gone terribly wrong when she had married Richard. She had once been a hopeful young bride with dreams of a promising future, yet that future had dawned with the harsh reality that Richard had never really loved her. He had only sought the conquest of her affection. Basically, his marked pursuit of her was only because he desired a trophy. Perhaps, it had even been a competition of sorts…with whom, she could guess. Yes, something had gone terribly wrong.

COMING TO TERMS

Declan Ryan realized something over his morning coffee one December morning just before Christmas. Liliana had been gone for almost ten years. Rarely, if ever, did anyone hear anything of her. Even her parents, Stephan and Jenny Lylestrom, rarely heard from her. They were puzzled, because such silence was so out of character for their daughter. Declan knew that Stephan and Jenny did receive an occasional phone call from her, but those calls were obviously monitored by her sullen husband. Stephan and Jenny had even tried to go visit their daughter, but she had subtly steered them away from coming to see her. Her parents knew she wasn't happy, and Declan instinctively knew Richard Rawlings was behind her out-of-character behavior.

Over the years that Liliana had been gone from her family, Declan had finally spent the last of his energy mourning the loss of her to someone else. Gradually, he had started to see other women, but there was always something missing. Being with other ladies felt hollow to him somehow. Yes, there had been several young women whom Declan had even spent time with and dated for several months and had taken them to meet Christophe and Annie, but he had eventually lost interest in all of them. Finally, he just gave up and focused on his work until he could meet someone that he wouldn't lose interest in... such had been the case with Kristen Bellyer.

She was just a few years younger than he, and she had never been married. She didn't seem self-centered or demanding in any way, and he found he was taking pleasure in her company. If Declan had been honest with himself, he would have admitted that he finally wasn't comparing her with anyone; namely, Liliana.

Red-headed Kristen was the third-grade teacher at Rosemeade Township Primary School. She had moved far away from her home in upstate New York to Rosemeade County. She was adventurous, so she hadn't minded living so far away from her family. They had met one morning outside of Annie's Diner. She had been carrying a small stack of her teaching files, and they had slipped from her grip. Declan had pulled his truck up in front of Annie's Diner and had seen her chasing several pieces of errant paper as they danced in the breeze. Once he had parked his vehicle, he hopped out to help her corral those wayward papers. She had given him an engaging smile and thanked him profusely. It was early on a Saturday morning.

As Declan held the door to the diner for her, she had asked, "May I treat you to a cup of coffee for helping me to save my grade-book pages?"

Declan had answered, "No, but you can let me buy *your* coffee." He had then introduced himself, and that's how it had begun with blue-eyed Kristen.

That morning, they had visited easily on a wide range of subjects, and Declan found that he had enjoyed his time with her. Kristen was bright, and she had entertained him with stories of her third-grade charges. She had also asked him questions about where he was from when she realized that he spoke English with a slightly different accent. It had been an enjoyable hour before he had checked his phone and realized that he needed to be going.

A week and a half later, Declan stopped by her school late in the afternoon when he was pretty sure her students had gone home for the day. He sought out the location of her classroom from the secretary in the school office and minutes later, after receiving clearance, knocked at her classroom door. She was straightening the rows of tiny desks and seemed pleased when she looked up and saw who was at her door.

"Mr. Ryan, please come in," she chimed in her pretty voice.

"Only if you call me Declan, Miss Bellyer!" he chuckled.

"Then, Declan it is, and you may call me, Kristen," she answered with a smile.

Declan had then inquired if she would consider a dinner date with him. She had happily accepted his invitation. Three days later, they had enjoyed their first date. It had been early October.

As the autumn had progressed, Declan had found himself seeking out her company more and more. He had helped her to transform the entrance of her classroom into a fish pond for the Fall Carnival at her school. The children had been delighted when he and Kristen had sat hidden on the other side of the "pond" and had pulled on the ends of their fishing lines before fastening their prizes onto the pipe-cleaner "fish hooks" on their poles.

At the end of October, he had dressed as a western cowboy and she as a cowgirl when the primary school's Halloween parade had been held. That same evening, he and Kristen had handed out candy alongside Christophe and Annie to all the little trick-or-treaters whose parents had brought them to the end of Old Vineyard Road. It was known far and wide that Christophe and Annie Riordan always rewarded those who made the long trek to the end of their street on Halloween. Loads of young children had come for treats. It had been an enjoyable night.

When November had arrived, Declan had invited Kristen to join him for Thanksgiving dinner with Christophe and Annie. Then, before he knew it, the Christmas season had been upon them. Kristen had flown home to see her family over the holidays, so in her absence, Declan had time to think about the last few months with her.

He had enjoyed his time with Kristen very much. She was loving and very warm in her acceptance of him and his quiet manner. Declan finally decided that he might now be able to move forward and, perhaps, build upon a relationship with her. He was even willing to see where it might lead.

Now, it was the Christmas season, and for the first time in many years, he hadn't thought of past holidays spent with Liliana and her family; not once…but he also hadn't thought about his new girlfriend, either. All during the fall, he had been pleased with the time that he spent with Kristen Bellyer. But he did notice one thing that gave him hesitation. He did not yearn for her or picture her beautiful red hair while she was away for the holidays. He knew from long ago that his heart had always yearned for Liliana whenever they had been separated. This gave him pause, and he decided he must proceed with caution with Kristen; he had no desire to hurt her in any way.

PART III

WINTER'S
BURDENS

RICHARD'S SHAME

*R*ichard **Rawlings** loathed himself. It was New Year's Day, and he had been out of town for almost four weeks, purposefully avoiding his wife. He had been holed up like some escaped criminal, hiding from the federal government, hiding from his creditors, and hiding from his wife whom he had beaten.

He had been married to Liliana for ten years, and he had not been forthright with her in all that time. As Richard drove over the mountain pass home to Seattle, he dreaded the thought of finally "coming clean" with his wife, but he knew that his house of cards was crashing down around him faster than he could have ever guessed it would. Amazingly, he felt great guilt consuming him as well, and he had never really felt guilty about any of his inappropriate decisions over the last decade; he questioned why he felt remorse now.

Richard guessed it was because, in his heart, he knew that Liliana was finished with him. She wasn't a stupid woman. In fact, she was very bright, and that was what had attracted him to her in the first place. She had been a popular coed from Brineforth University, and he had seen her at the campus library. Richard had watched her arrive with two other young women, who were both very pretty, but their beauty paled when he witnessed her vivacious greetings to various friends as she and her cohorts sought out a place to study. Liliana had been quite an attractive young lady, but it was her sparkling disposition and her kindness that made those two young friends of hers fade into the recesses of his mind. As that afternoon progressed, Richard had watched as she researched, wrote, and organized what he guessed must be a mid-term paper. Her book bag seemed to supply any and all implements needed to satisfactorily research and write; both for herself and for her study group.

Trying not to appear obvious, he observed her attention to detail, her willingness to lead the study group, and her study skills. In the way she interacted with her group, he was sure that she was exactly the person he was looking for; someone who was a natural leader. Richard had recently hatched an idea that he felt would fly with the help of someone like her.

Richard was hoping to set up a small business that would cater to college students who needed short-term loans. He figured that if his own college experience was the norm, many of the kids on this campus would willingly pay a little extra in interest for a few days; rather than call home to tell "Daddy" that they had used up their monthly living allotment on pizza and beer. He had a feeling such a scheme might just work.

Liliana had seen right through him when he approached her several days later inquiring if she needed a part-time job and had turned him down flat, but she had been very gracious and not the least bit rude. After their encounter, he no longer wanted her as an administrative assistant, he wanted her…she was the wife he needed for his bucket list. She was pretty; she had bottle-green eyes that were so forthright he couldn't bring himself to look away. In addition, that smile tore at his heart. Richard Rawlings was twenty-three years old, and this was the first woman who had ever taken his breath away. He quickly forgot about his scheme, laughed, and said, "Oh, I guess you saw right through my pick-up line!" She rolled her eyes and chuckled while Richard said, "How about this one…I'm supposed to meet the most-beautiful girl in the world here in front of the Student Union Building at ten o'clock this morning," he said, crooking his arm to scan his watch, "I thought you were she."

Liliana had again rolled her eyes, and said "How about losing those stupid pick-up lines, and try introducing yourself?" Elated, Richard introduced himself, "I'm Richard Rawlings, and I was studying for my LSAT in the library a few days ago, when I saw you come in. I'm fairly new here, so I don't know a lot of people yet."

"Liliana," she said, and extended her hand.

Richard thought to himself that whoever her parents were, they had picked out the perfect name for this girl. For now, all his short-term loan scheming evaporated, and he found himself wanting to get to know her. They chatted for a few minutes longer about nothing much and had parted ways. As he turned toward the campus library, Richard asked, "May I buy you coffee some time?"

"Maybe," she smiled. And she had walked away.

From that day on, Richard had made sure he was where he needed to be in order to see Liliana. He inquired of the few people he did know on campus, and all had said she was a very nice girl and not the least bit stuck up. One guy had even gone so far as to say, "You'd better treat that girl right or you're going to have to answer to me."

"What a welcome change," thought Richard every time he received the same response.

Finally, after about three weeks of making sure he encountered her every few days, Richard had invited Liliana for coffee at the Student Union Building, and as they sat opposite one another in a huge, upholstered booth, they got to know one another other better, and Richard was rewarded with Liliana tentatively agreeing to go on a casual date with him. That hard-fought date turned into several, and before he knew it, Richard Rawlings found himself falling in love with the ***idea*** of having Liliana for his own. She would always be the perfect girl to have on his arm ...the perfect corporate wife. There was only one thing that marred his plans for having her for his own, and that was: He had nothing to offer her.

Liliana obviously came from a well-off family, as she had told him her father owned his own law practice in a smallish-place called, Reedsburgh. Richard's own family was not well off, as his father had always struggled to stay employed, and this made him feel somewhat inferior to those who hadn't known such embarrassment. It was hard to see both his mother and his father burdened with having to, yet again, pick up and move the family to a larger city where Dad's reputation and propensity for consuming alcohol excessively weren't known. That was why he had stepped away from his family years ago and had never looked back. As far as he was concerned, they were dead to him.

As their friendship progressed, Richard knew he had to have Liliana for his own. He wanted to add the conquest of her to his bucket list of fame, fortune, and perfect spouse. It was a concern to him that she not ever meet his family. They were an embarrassment to him. It humiliated him even further that even though he was intelligent, his family had not had the resources to pay for his college education. Oh, yes, he had earned a scholarship to Richland University, but his parents had nothing to help him pay for room and board. So, Richland University had flown out the window, and Richard had found himself attending a community college and eventually a state university with the hope that he could win another stipend of some sort to offset his expenses. Eventually, he had earned another scholarship, but still found himself burdened with debt from all those living expenses that hadn't been included in his scholarship package. Most people's first house did not cost as much as his student loans had amounted to, but Richard found it was easier not to think about such a burden when he was with his trophy, Liliana Lylestrom.

Richard's first momentous lies surfaced when Liliana asked him about his family, where he grew up, and where he had graduated from. Before he knew it, his parents had "died" in an auto accident, and he had no other family at all…then, the word, "Harvard," had leaked out. Seeing how impressed Liliana had been at such a declaration, the lie was further embellished to include a major of Political Science, completion of the prestigious Harvard MBA program, and aspirations of Law School. This was the beginning of a relationship built not upon trust, but upon Richard's burgeoning imagination. It seemed that after this initial deceitfulness, the lies came easier and easier to him.

When Liliana's parents drove up to Brineforth University for a long weekend, Richard had pressured Liliana to meet them. From there, Richard's lies seemed to take on a life of their own, and it became apparent to him that he should have, in fact, majored in theater, as he seemed to have an uncanny knack for dazzling others with his fabricated accomplishments. Liliana's parents were no exception. He felt that Stephan and Jenny Lylestrom embraced his lies and his impeccably good manners with elation. It seemed to him that they felt their little girl had found herself a good man, and he could tell that they were so happy for her. Ruminating on those lies now, Richard started to wonder if Liliana's family had seen through him after all. Who was he fooling? Yes, they had seen through him, but had been too gracious to doubt him. Stephan Lylestrom was a lawyer for goodness sake. Yet, in the end, they had given their permission for him to marry their daughter. Why? He wondered. *I* wouldn't even give Liliana permission to marry me. "What ***were*** they thinking?" he asked himself.

Back then, the only fly in the ointment of Richard's fabricated life was in the personage Liliana called, "Uncle Christophe." Christophe Riordan and his wife were Liliana's god-parents, and it seemed that Christophe had an uncanny knack for asking Richard questions; too many questions. In addition, Christophe was entwined in Liliana's life so thoroughly, that Richard sometimes feared that he saw through all of his fabrications. For the last three summers, she had worked for her Uncle Christophe at some dump he called, The Old Vineyard Road Nursery. It was obvious that she thoroughly enjoyed her job and was looking forward to working for him again this coming summer. Richard feared that if she went back to that giant Scotsman yet again this year, she might be grilled with questions on Richard's background and family, and she might become suspect of him.

It seemed that fate was to be Richard's friend that spring, though, and Richard had finally secured an internship that could catapult him into the big leagues and, finally, into some money. All he needed to do was finish strong in his internship at Bruxton Reed Wealth Planners, pass his licensure examinations, and he would be launched. It had really helped to say that he had completed his MBA and had graduated "Ivy League" on his internship application. His old buddy, Jim Ray, had done a bang-up job of impersonating a college "prof" when the call for a recommendation had inevitably come. "Well done Jimmy!" Maybe now, he could stop the charade of saying he was considering Law School and get on with making enough money that he would be able to buy all the trappings that go along with being a high-roller.

Richard did well on his internship, managed to make people believe that his parents were deceased and that he was on his own in this world. Richard passed all his examinations and was now a licensed financial planner. In the fall, much to his delight, he was offered a permanent position with Bruxton Reed. At last, he was launched. Liliana still had to finish what was left of her senior year and then complete her student teaching, so this would give him a chance to bank some money for an engagement ring in the spring; never mind that he knew she had affection for someone she had worked with for the last three years. He could break her down…she *would* be his…he would make sure.

That spring, he went to the jeweler and chose the largest diamond ring he could afford; it was a three-carat solitaire like none he had ever seen. The price was prohibitive, but he knew that he was making good money, so the purchase of the ring was solidified. He just needed to close a couple more prospective clients and that ring would be as good as paid for…

Unsuspecting Liliana was quite stunned when Richard presented the ring to her and asked for her hand in marriage. Not quite as overwhelmed and happy as he thought she should be when she received a proposal of marriage from him, he was encouraged that she smiled when she said, "Richard, did you even ask my father if you could marry me? Somehow, I can't imagine Dad giving anyone his permission to marry me right now. Though we've had some fun these last few months, I'm not ready for marriage at all…I'm not even finished with my schooling. I still have two senior projects to complete, and I've yet to do my student teaching. You know I won't even be twenty-two until this coming June. As well, you also know, too, that I have someone very special who lives in Rosemeade Township. I'm very fond of him."

Richard was crushed, but he was not about to let Liliana off the hook. He skillfully presented the facts as he saw them. He was older than her by three years. He was making good money, so he was surely able to take care of her in the style to which she was accustomed. He was a Harvard "grad" with an MBA, and he would be able to give her anything that she ever desired…what more could she want in a husband? "Am I not a better candidate for your affection than some guy who plants flowers for a living? Oh, isn't he just the most-successful guy on the planet! Aren't I good enough for you and your respectable family, Liliana? Is that it?" he had asked sullenly. Liliana had been taken aback and had tried to soothe him. It was at that moment that he knew he would eventually be able to manipulate her into saying, "Yes." He knew that Liliana Lylestrom was a peacemaker.

As Richard thought back on his behavior from ten years ago, he was ashamed of himself. Liliana had been right. She did have a fair amount of her schooling to still finish, but he had pouted, and acted as if she had been rejecting him. He had manipulated her. Yet, she had forgiven him and had reluctantly agreed to let him come to Reedsburgh for Easter with her parents after he had cajoled her for an invitation. Now, looking back, he could admit it to himself…Liliana had not been keen on the idea of him accompanying her home for Easter Break at all… Richard admitted to himself that he had always known that her allegiance had been to Declan Ryan.

He had observed them both on more than one occasion when Declan had come to visit her at Brineforth…just weeks before he decided that he wanted her for his own trophy. Today, Richard did have remorse that he had purposefully made sure Liliana was prevented from spending time with Declan Ryan. Richard had observed her devotion to the guy, and he had instantly had disdain for him. Anyone could see that Declan had loved her. Now, a decade later, Richard despised himself for his behavior. He had purposefully broken their relationship and wrenched Liliana away from someone to whom she was quite devoted.

That Easter Sunday, her Uncle Christophe and his wife had driven up from Rosemeade to attend church and have Easter dinner with her family; apparently, it was a tradition. But they had the audacity to bring Declan Ryan with them. Richard couldn't stand any of these people, especially Declan Ryan.

When they had arrived, Liliana had been so happy to see them all… kissing Christophe, kissing his wife, and then fiercely hugging Declan Ryan, her face aglow with affection. "Who was Declan Ryan, anyway?" A decade after meeting him, Richard still could not understand how Declan was related to Christophe Riordan, and why he was included as part of Liliana's extended family. Richard found himself getting angry just thinking about Christophe Riordan and Declan Ryan as he drove the treacherous mountain pass. *He* knew he was a liar and a cheat, but it had always seemed as though those two guys had seen right through his ruse. Maybe he hadn't been such a savvy liar after all.

Putting his dislike for Christophe Riordan and Declan Ryan aside, Richard's thoughts began to wander back to the issues at hand. He asked himself, "If he came clean with Liliana, admitted to lying to her for over a decade, admitted to never having attended Harvard, admitted to all the infractions that had cost him his jobs during the course of their marriage, and admitted that he had been unfaithful to her, and then, finally disclosed that he was being investigated for insider stock trading and fraud, would Liliana ever forgive him?" He had embezzled almost all the $2 million in her trust fund which her father had given her on her twenty-seventh birthday. He had spent most of her trust on an illicit affair with Sierra Monroe, the woman he had met, and then slept with, on the very first night of his marriage to Liliana.

The expenses he incurred while keeping a household for his mistress and furnishing her with cars and expensive gifts took a lot of cash. He had kept Sierra with him for the entirety of his marriage. Sierra had moved right along with him each time he had relocated. Through each of his moves, Sierra's comfort and expenses had been covered by him. Eventually, he had turned to Liliana's trust fund to keep Sierra. He had also financed real estate acquisitions with those same monies. Oh, how he had bullied Liliana into letting him handle her trust in lieu of those whom Stephan Lylestrom had carefully chosen. Liliana hadn't wanted to go against those advisors whom her father had selected, and yet, after hours of him hounding and accusing her of having no loyalty to him, she had acquiesced just to get him to be quiet. It had always worked that way…him faulting her for having no allegiance to him, him browbeating her to get his own way, and him ensuring she was taken further and further away from those she loved, so no one would see through his ruse. Today, Richard Rawlings despised himself for what he had done.

There was so much more he would need to confess to Liliana. He had lived a life that would make his mother heartbroken and would shame even his no-good, alcoholic father. But he had been determined not to end up like his parents, and yet, here he was doing the same thing to his wife that he had sworn he would never do to his family. Even after all his lying, cheating, and stealing, the thing that made Richard Rawlings want to weep, was that he had raised his own fist and had hit his beautiful wife and knocked her to the floor just four weeks ago; punishing her for the hatred he had for himself.

After she had collected herself, Liliana had stood up slightly shaking with a deepening bruise on her cheek and blood trickling down her temple. She had calmly said, "Richard, if you come one step closer to me, I will call the police. I've not done anything to warrant such treatment from you. Your actions are barbaric. I have only tried to get along with you as best I can, but you are a hard man. You bully your way through this life and force your guilt upon others when you should be looking to yourself. Do you not even realize that such behavior has eroded my feelings for you? Do not *ever* strike me in that fashion again. I think it is time that you seek the help of a professional. Stay away from me." With that, she had walked into their bedroom and had quietly shut the door; graceful even under extreme duress.

Richard had then angrily proceeded to upend the dining-room table, the chairs, a huge wall-mounted mirror, and finally, Liliana's china cupboard. Yet, during this angry episode, their bedroom door had remained firmly closed. "Why hadn't Liliana responded to such a horrible outburst?" he had wondered. Demolished dining room furniture and shards of broken glass were everywhere, but still Liliana stayed shielded behind their bedroom door.

Richard's ire toward himself could not be soothed that evening. He went into the kitchen pantry and drank most of the partially-full bottles of alcohol that were stored there. Stupidly, he left the house, roaring along the coastal road in his powerful and expensive car until he came to a bar. Because his father had struggled with alcoholism, Richard never drank. But, that night, he had drunk himself crazy. After a half dozen verbal altercations with other patrons, the owner had asked him to leave. Richard was insulted that such a worm would ask *him*, of all people, to leave the place. "I have money, I have a huge home, I have expensive automobiles, and I have prominence in this community," he had said to himself. He turned around and walked back into the establishment and knocked the bar owner to the floor. Only then, did his anger seem to be assuaged. He drove blindly home along the Olympic View Road narrowly missing several cars. Oh, how he hated himself...

The house had been quiet when he returned. Everything was still in disarray, and this puzzled him because he thought for sure Liliana would react and clean up after him. She always did; it was what she was supposed to do...but she had not. "Was she still here?" he had asked himself. All was quiet when he knocked on the bedroom door and inquired if she was alright. He turned the knob, but their heavy bedroom door was locked.

"Liliana, please open the door," he had begged. Still, there was no response. Drunken Richard sat down beside the locked bedroom door and proceeded to fall asleep.

When he awoke, it was still quite early in the morning. He looked at the ruins of what had once been their dining room and felt shame being replaced by panic. "Liliana has changed. She has left me to my own devices," he thought. It unnerved him to realize that Liliana was no longer going to be manipulated with his bullying. He knew that she had long ago reached her threshold but had instead tried to humor him in order to get along. "Oh, no, what have I done?" he asked himself. Pounding on their bedroom door, he cried, "Liliana, Liliana...Please let me come in and apologize. Baby, I'm so sorry that I lost my temper. Please let me in." he begged.

After what seemed like hours of pleading with her to open the door, Richard had finally started crying. Panic was engulfing him... "Oh, what have I done?" he thought in anguish. "Liliana, **please**," he had begged. At last, she had opened the door, and he was stunned at what he saw. Her pretty green eyes were not swollen from crying; only from his fist. He saw that his sizable hands had managed to leave angry red welts on her upper body and to break the skin just below her left eyebrow. There was still seeping fluid and dried blood there. Just below her eye, an angry-looking, purplish-red fist print marked her face, and he had done all of this to her. Richard Rawlings wanted to die. He couldn't believe that he had sunk to this kind of behavior. His tears began to flow even more.

In his frenzy to make it up to her, he held and kissed her and begged for her forgiveness. She said nothing; she did not respond to him in any way. He picked her up and laid her on their bed, leaning over to cradle her. He lathered kisses on her face and found himself wanting to make love to her to ease her pain. "Baby, let me love you," he had begged. "Please, Liliana, let me show you how much I care." In the end, after endless nagging and his acute anger erupting again, he had forced himself physically upon his lovely wife. She had tried to fight him off, but his large fists had battered her once again. Richard was nauseated just thinking about it.

This afternoon, it was slow going on the Snoqualmie Pass. There was an eighteen-wheel truck jack-knifed at the top of the pass, so Richard Rawlings had plenty of time to be introspective while he sat waiting for the truck to be cleared away. He knew Liliana would likely never leave him, but she might ask for a legal separation and just live apart from him for the rest of their lives. She was devout in her beliefs. She had saved herself for marriage, and she had always taken her marital vows seriously. Richard realized that he had pushed her too far this time. Richard helplessly felt that he could do nothing to redeem himself; even with forgiving Liliana.

Richard knew that he would be going to federal prison, and that wasn't nearly as daunting to him as facing his wife to admit that he had embezzled most of the $2 million trust fund her parents had given to her on her twenty-seventh birthday. She had put up with a lot from him over the years, and he knew that she had reached her threshold. He was doomed.

As traffic started to move again, Richard thought about the consequences he was now facing. His life was never going to be the same again. The horrendous choices he had made ensured it. Liliana didn't deserve the trials he had forced upon her. He had been a liar and a fraud. He had brazenly hit and slapped her…then, he had callously raped her. "Yes, he had raped sweet, giving Liliana…Why not just add coward to it," he thought. Killing himself was his only option out of his troubles. He knew Liliana would be fine; everyone would come to her aid. As for his lover, Sierra, he had no allegiance to her; theirs was a relationship based on lust; not trust. Minutes later, he made a very spineless decision and purposefully swerved in front of a large SUV that was lumbering up the opposite side of the snowy mountain road. "It will all be over soon," Richard had reasoned.

The sound of the impact was resounding, yet, all else seemed to happen in slow motion: Ricocheting glass, flying pieces of metal, and suitcases sliding across the mountain pass. Richard awoke later as he was being loaded into an ambulance. He was in pain, but the young medic who was caring for him said, "You've been in a serious accident, man, but we're doing everything we can for you."

Richard groaned and said, "I cannot catch a break." He then lost consciousness again.

He woke up a day and a half later to find Liliana sitting soberly beside him. She could barely look at him. She did not touch him. She only asked, "How are you feeling, Richard? The attending physician says you should make a full recovery."

Yellow-bellied Richard Rawlings lied yet again, "The pain is excruciating. Can you get me something for it, Liliana?" She pressed the call-button for a nurse. While they waited, Richard decided that if he couldn't kill himself with a car crash, he would kill himself with an overdose. "No one will ever know," he thought to himself.

SUSPICIONS

r. Douglas Falcone was stymied. How could a healthy man of thirty-five years who had relatively minor injuries from an auto accident be dead? As much as he hated to admit it, he was suspicious of the deceased. The patient's wife had obviously been wary of him while she sat at his bedside. Dr. Falcone had also noted that she had a recently-sutured scar beneath her left eyebrow, and she had only sighed heavily when her husband had been pronounced dead. There had been no tears. Something was off here.

"Mrs. Rawlings, I'm sorry about your husband, would you like to sit here with him for a while or would you prefer that he be taken to the morgue?"

Looking solemnly into his eyes, the fragile-looking young woman had responded, "I'm sorry if this appears cold-hearted on my part, Dr. Falcone, but is there any way to find out if my husband died of an overdose?"

"Why would you think he died of an overdose, Mrs. Rawlings?" the doctor inquired.

"Because I know my husband, Dr. Falcone; his injuries were not life threatening. Yet, he insisted that he was in excruciating pain. I feel that his prescribed medications were, most likely, managing his pain just fine. He shouldn't have been that uncomfortable."

"He had been experiencing some upheaval in his professional life the last several years and was fearful because the federal government was planning to investigate his business affairs. He seems to have died almost too conveniently. I know I sound quite hardened here," the young woman had gravely admitted, "but would it be possible for you to authorize an autopsy to determine the cause of his death? If he died from his injuries, I'll accept the findings. But if there are too many medications in his body, my suspicions will be confirmed."

Dr. Falcone was surprised by the woman's astute observation of her late husband, and while he questioned her a bit more fully about her suspicions, he looked surreptitiously at her healing eye and the very faint marks of recent bruising on her face. The evidence was enough.

"I'll arrange for an autopsy today, if possible, Mrs. Rawlings. Let me call for an orderly to take your husband down to the Pathology Lab."

Dr. Falcone was still in the room with Mrs. Rawlings when a young orderly came to transfer her deceased husband to the Pathology Department. The young man seemed surprised and shaken when he realized whom he was transporting to the morgue. The good doctor then knew he would not be shocked when the autopsy findings came back. He suspected that his patient had probably coerced that malleable young orderly to get the medications for him.

Dr. Falcone then walked down three flights of stairs to the Medical Records Department. He had a hunch that Mrs. Rawlings just might be right. He also wondered if she might have been in the ER recently herself. Sure enough, the report indicated that she had been evaluated for an injury to her left eye just under a month ago. The resident physician, who had examined her, reported that she had arrived with an acutely swollen left eye and marks upon her face and upper torso which were consistent with physical abuse. Of note, the flesh just below her left brow had been sutured.

Late the following day, Dr. Falcone received a call from the pathologist. Richard Rawlings had, indeed, died from an overdose of medication. His stomach contained a lethal "cocktail" of painkillers above and beyond the medications that had already been prescribed for him. It appeared to Dr. Falcon that his patient was not only a wife-beater, but that he had had no backbone. If that wasn't bad enough, Richard Rawlings had probably taken that young orderly down with him, too. "I'm going to get to the bottom of this," Dr. Falcone said to no one in particular.

When he placed the call to Mrs. Rawlings to inform her that her suspicions had been correct, she had additional information for him. It seemed that since the last time she had used her purse at the hospital gift shop yesterday morning, her emergency stash of cash had been taken from deep within the zippered confines of her handbag. Dr. Falcon suspected Richard Rawlings had bribed that shaken-up young orderly to do some shopping for him. Dr. Falcone then placed a call to the hospital's Risk Management Administrator. "This case just keeps getting better and better," he said to himself sarcastically. He could not believe a grown man, who seemingly had it all, would be so yellow-bellied as to fake his own death; then, take an innocent young man down with him. This guy was one for the books.

RICHARD'S VICTIM

acob Rhines was heartsick and scared when his cell phone rang. He had been sitting at his tiny kitchen table cradling his head in anguish. When he realized the identity of the caller, he started to sweat. His heart was pounding out of his chest. It was Jim Richardson, an assistant administrator at Pinehurst Medical Center. It hadn't taken very long for that smart Dr. Falcone to put two-plus-two together and to get in touch with the proper authorities. Jacob knew he was doomed.

As he sat in his little attic apartment, the twenty-year old orderly realized that he had fallen for one of the oldest tricks in the book… that of being duped into thinking he was helping someone, when, in fact, he had been unwittingly used as an accomplice to something so untoward that it made him want to vomit. Mr. Richardson had said that the patient, whom Jacob had stupidly thought he was helping, had died under questionable circumstances and that an investigation into his death was unfolding. He had then requested that Jacob meet with him the following morning. Mr. Richardson, who reported directly to the hospital's CEO, oversaw Risk Management issues at Pinehurst. Things were not looking good. "My life is over," the frightened young man whispered to himself after he finished the phone call.

By 10:30 a.m. the next morning, an exhausted and frightened Jacob Rhines checked in with Jim Richardson's executive assistant and waited to be called into the hospital's inner sanctum. Minutes later, he was invited to step into Mr. Richardson's office.

Fortunately for Jacob, Jim Richardson was a very kind man. He didn't try to break Jacob's spirit or threaten him, but merely said, "Jacob, I suspect you know why I've asked to meet with you. I'll be upfront with you, son, you are going to lose your job, but if you cooperate, I don't think the Board of Trustees will file charges against you. Just tell the truth, and things will go much easier for you. Rest assured that you have advocates in Dr. Falcone and in Mrs. Rawlings, the deceased's wife. The two of them concluded quite readily that you were used quite abominably by Mr. Rawlings."

As the January sunlight filtered through his office window, Jim Richardson sadly listened as young Jacob Rhines spilled his guts about what had gone down with Richard Rawlings. The morning sunlight backlit the young man's curly blond hair, making him look somewhat like a fallen angel as he sat there sobbing and confessing how he had unknowingly helped Richard Rawlings kill himself for a mere three hundred dollars. Jim Richardson felt compassion for the young man.

In the end, it appeared that the deceased had conned young Jacob Rhines into purchasing several bottles of extra-strength pain killers for him. Richard Rawlings had "confided" to the unsuspecting orderly that his wife suffered terribly from migraine headaches, but she hadn't been able to get to the pharmacy before it had closed that day to purchase any pain relievers for herself because she was so very devoted to him and would not leave his side while he was recuperating from his injuries. Because he couldn't remember which brand of pain reliever his wife preferred, the patient had asked him to purchase two separate brands. Wiley Richard Rawlings had then taken several large bills from his wife's handbag while she had stepped across the corridor to the restroom and had requested that Jacob purchase the pain medications while he was on his dinner break that evening. Apparently, when Jacob had questioned Richard Rawlings as to why he gave him so much money for a relatively inexpensive purchase, the patient had smilingly answered that he was very well off, but he knew what it was like to be a struggling student working one's way through college as a hospital orderly. For some reason, he had guessed that Jacob was saving for a car, so he told the young man to consider the change as a "tip" for his trouble and a contribution to his savings account for a new automobile. Gullible, fresh-faced Jacob Rhines had fallen for his ruse, and had blindly gone down the garden path with lying Richard Rawlings.

His emotions spent; Jacob wanly looked out the window of Jim Richardson's office at the frosty winter morning. Kind Jim Richardson offered him some comfort. "Jacob, I know things look bleak to you right now, but son, your confession is a help to me, too. The circumstances of Mr. Rawlings death are not the only questions being investigated right now. I've been visited by both a regional manager and an adjuster from his insurance company, and the circumstances surrounding his recent auto accident are being investigated, as well. You have done all of us a service."

"If you need a reference for a new job, refer any prospective employers to me, I'll look after things for you. You've had an exemplary record here at Pinehurst, Jacob, but you were used quite abominably. This is a life lesson that has opened your eyes to how cruel this world can be sometimes, but try to forgive yourself."

Young Jacob Rhines looked at Jim Richardson and said, "Mr. Richardson, I cannot keep the money that was given to me to purchase those meds. I feel like I stole from that man's wife. Can you give the money back to her?"

Smiling, Jim Richardson answered, "I'll tell you what Jacob, I'll arrange for a private meeting between you and Mrs. Rawlings here at the hospital. She's meeting with me tomorrow, and you can give her the money yourself then. She knows her husband used you, and she feels terribly regretful about his spineless behavior."

For the first time in hours, young Jacob Rhines felt hope.

REDEMPTION

*L*iliana Rawlings felt badly about young Jacob Rhines. It was obvious that up until a day or so ago, he had been a bright-eyed, bushy-tailed innocent; much like she had once been. He, too, had been a victim of Richard's less-than-stellar behavior. Richard had misused poor Jacob dreadfully. For this, she was exceedingly sorry. How could Richard do such a thing to an innocent young person?

When Liliana had arrived at the Pinehurst Medical Center administrative suite that morning for her meeting with Jim Richardson, he informed her that Jacob Rhines had asked to meet with her to offer his apologies and to return her money. She had been touched.

Jacob waited outside Jim Richardson's handsomely-decorated office. While Jim went to retrieve Jacob, she noted that Jim's office was filled with photographs of his family, and it appeared that he had several sons who were close in age to Jacob Rhines. She fervently hoped that Jim Richardson had shown understanding to Jacob, since he had sons of his own.

When Jim finally shepherded Jacob into his office, Liliana felt much better, as he treated Jacob with real compassion; something she was sure this young man needed right now. She extended her hand to Jacob and said, "Oh, Jacob, I am sorry that we have to meet one another under such circumstances. Can you ever forgive my husband for what he did to you?"

"Oh, Mrs. Rawlings, it is I who should be asking for your forgiveness. I accidentally killed your husband." With that, poor Jacob Rhines proceeded to sit down in a proffered seat and weep once again.

Jim Richardson stood next to him, put a hand on his shoulder and said, "Son, you did not kill Richard Rawlings. He made sure that he died all by himself. Believe me, Jacob, when I say you were used…very ill-used."

"Jacob, you are not the only one whom Richard violated," Liliana interjected. "There is a family upstairs in this hospital who is recovering from injuries they received when my husband most-likely ran his automobile into theirs, purposefully. Believe me when I say that I am just now finding out how determinedly Richard must have desired his death. You see Jacob, he was in trouble, and the extent of the hole he had dug for himself was looming very large. Please don't take Richard's death upon your young shoulders. The fault is not yours."

Liliana Rawlings then extended her slender hand and gripped his slightly shaking one. "Jacob, I absolve you from any culpability in this affair, and I pray that you can forgive yourself. Please know that you have my full and complete forgiveness."

She continued on, "As to the money…it was, in fact, my money that Richard gave to you to buy the medications. I kept it in the event of an emergency, and Richard never told me that he had taken it from me. If you feel you cannot keep it, then give it to the Rescue Mission or a charity of your choice, Jacob. Believe me when I say that something good **can** come from it."

Tall, skinny Jacob Rhines then rose from his chair. His blond curls were backlit by the sun streaming through the glass window, and he gave Liliana a wobbly smile. "Thank you, Mrs. Rawlings, for being so kind to me. I won't ever forget it."

Several minutes later, Jacob heartily shook Jim Richardson's hand, and exited through the door. He looked back at Liliana, and she could see that he looked as though a very heavy burden had been lifted from his narrow shoulders.

Jim Richardson then captured and shook Liliana's hand within his two larger ones and said, "Mrs. Rawlings, you have just given that young man his life back, and I would venture to guess that Jacob will pay your kindness forward many times over. It was very good of you to be so gracious to him."

Slightly fragile, Liliana Rawlings then gave Jim Richardson, her beautiful smile. She shook her head just a bit and said, "It was the least I could do for such an earnest young man." Changing the subject, she inquired, "Mr. Richardson, do you think you could accompany me upstairs to meet Richard's other victims? Oh, how I hope their injuries will not plague them for a lifetime…"

Kind Jim Richardson then answered, "I would be happy to accompany you, Mrs. Rawlings. Let me just call upstairs to the unit clerk and find out if we can come now."

SHOCK AND AWE

*D**eclan Ryan* was stunned at the news. Christophe had come to their offices this morning and reported that Liliana's husband of ten years had died from injuries he had received in an auto accident late last week. Liliana was bringing Richard's body back to Reedsburgh, as he had no family. The memorial service was to be this coming Friday.

Christophe and Annie were headed to Reedsburgh to comfort Liliana's family and help in any way that they could. Declan instantly knew things did not bode well for Liliana. Christophe went on to tell him that her father had always questioned the legality of some of Richard's business practices. Christophe noted that his recent conversation with her parents had been hushed about Liliana not even having enough money to send her husband's body home to Reedsburgh. She had had to ask her father for money to bury Richard. Christophe Riordan had taken his assignment of god-parent to Liliana very seriously over the years, so he was visibly upset at this horrible news that he was sharing with Declan.

"These are troubling circumstances, Declan. I never fully trusted that man to take care of our Liliana, and now, my misgivings seem to be coming true. That poor young woman," Christophe sighed.

"Also, son, I hope you don't mind, but I've taken the liberty of telling Stephan and Jenny that you'll go into Brookings City to pick up Liliana at the airport. Could you do that for me, Declan? The snow has been so heavy this week that I feel your truck will be the only vehicle able to make it across the county line in this storm. She'll be arriving at 5:45 this evening. Check with Annie as to her flight number." With that, Christophe shook Declan's hand, gripped his shoulder with the other, and was off.

Declan's stomach clenched at what was happening. He had once loved Liliana very much and would do anything to help her in her time of need. As the morning progressed, Declan's ire was also raised at the dead man who obviously had not taken care of his wife in the way that he should. Declan ruminated on Richard's boasting of his accomplishments, Richard's purposeful methods to keep Liliana from seeing her family, and Richard's obvious disdain for him because of the bond he had once shared with Liliana.

Declan thought back to when he had just arrived in Rosemeade County from Scotland. Christophe had introduced him to her the morning after she had arrived at the nursery, not knowing that they had already met in the middle of the night because of Liliana's wayward old dog, Iris. Declan had liked her immediately, as she had not shown any propensity to be a spoiled American girl who thought that the world revolved around her. He had seen plenty of them on his travels to the Continent when he was a student.

Instead, she had proven herself to be a hard worker; someone who was not afraid to get her hands dirty. Old Jim, the aging nursery hand, had instantly fallen head over heels in love with her, even though he was at least sixty years her senior. Clients had enjoyed her enthusiasm and started asking for her by name. As for him, he had enjoyed her company immensely. She had shown an interest in everything that revolved around keeping the trees, plants, and flowers healthy and looking their best. She was an excellent plant propagator, and a most-handy assistant when Declan had time to do his research and grafting studies. Often, they would sit in companionable silence, she taking notes while he grafted experimental cuttings into the ancient grape vines from Christophe's old vineyard. Three special summers had passed; each with her arrival in late May heralding the beginning of fun and fine memories.

Then, Richard Rawlings had entered her life sometime during her senior year at Brineforth University. In late May that year, Richard had brought her to Rosemeade County in his expensive BMW roadster. He was aloof and slightly rude to Christophe and Annie who had tried to welcome him to their home, but Liliana had apologized for his behavior and chalked it up to his not having any family of his own.

That last summer, his own tender relationship with Liliana had faltered and had begun to fray around the edges. By summer's end,

Declan could not even find the wherewithal to be in her company; it had hurt too much. Even Christophe had worried that Liliana was too quick to cover for Richard's rudeness, and Christophe's worst fears for her were realized when word came from her parents that Richard had asked for her hand in marriage. Stephan and Jenny Lylestrom had seemed resigned to her choice; not nearly as happy as they should have been. Christophe wept openly for her future. Declan had been devastated.

Declan had found it hard to attend her wedding, as did Christophe. Of course, everyone had tried to rejoice and raise a toast. Others had danced and celebrated for their beloved Liliana, as each one of them truly wanted only the best for her... but, not Declan. She had been a beautiful bride, but those, who knew her well, thought that she wasn't as happy as her pretty smile would lead a stranger to believe, and Declan had agreed. Later, Christophe had related to Declan that when he had danced with her and inquired if all was well, she had leaned into his shoulder and sighed, "Oh, Christophe, I have offended Richard with my love and affection for you all. Last evening after the rehearsal dinner, he complained that my priorities weren't right and that I should have been focusing on us and not upon our guests. I don't agree with him. Today *is* about us, and all of you are here because of your love and affection for *us*."

Poor Christophe, who wasn't fond of Richard to begin with, had looked into her troubled green eyes and said, "I know things haven't always been easy for Richard, but he has you for his wife, now. He'll ease into being happy when it's just the two of you rowing the boat." Somehow, when Christophe had shared these things with him, Declan had known that it was going to be a rough road for Liliana. Now, he suspected that he hadn't even come close to guessing just how hard her life had been with Richard Rawlings.

The marriage appeared to be rough even at the beginning. Though Liliana still had to finish her student teaching that fall semester, Richard had insisted that they move across the county line into Brookings City where he worked in the financial district. Poor Liliana had driven the long commute daily to do her student teaching at an elementary school adjacent to the Brineforth campus, but the commute had taken precious hours from her daily lesson preparation, but she had never complained. Declan had learned much of Richard's selfishness through various comments she unknowingly made to Annie over the next few months. These things had cast Richard into a very self-centered light.

Fast forward several years…Liliana was absent on holidays; always giving the excuse that Richard's work kept them in the city. Her letters, emails, and telephone calls to her parents and godparents were fewer and fewer. Then, it seemed that Richard had had a falling out with his boss and lost his job; and then the relocations began. Each progressive move had taken Liliana further from her family and further into the secretive shell Richard Rawlings called his life.

Her parents, Stephan and Jenny, kept a solid front and tried to make excuses for Richard's problems and why they rarely saw their daughter, but it was easy for Declan to see that their hearts were broken. It had been an idyllic time when Stephan and Jenny Lylestrom had included him in their family events because he was Christophe's relative. And during those first few years of his time in the United States, they had made him feel so very welcome in their home, and Liliana had made sure he was always part of every occasion that included her. Her family had morphed into people who meant very much to him, and she into the person whom he most admired. Declan had to admit that when she had married Richard, an integral part of himself had been wrenched away. In short, his heart had been thoroughly broken.

Old Jim who had watched them work together for several years, had queried, "Are you daft, man? Grab that wonderful girl, tell her you're smitten, and court her. Don't let that arrogant man win her heart. Why do you tarry?"

Declan had had no response for Old Jim on those occasions. He had already finished his university days. He didn't want to deprive her of her youth or her college experience by forcing her into a relationship with someone slightly older. Liliana liked to tease him about how old he was, though he was only three years her senior. But, in her young life, filled with school and friends, Declan knew he probably did seem old to her. Right after graduation from university, he had to travel the long, arduous cancer road that had taken his beloved mother. He probably did seem ancient to Liliana, but life had required him to become a man early. As well, he was an emigrant, without wealth. What could he possibly offer such a rare find like Liliana? He only had himself to offer; nothing else. There would be no "courting," to quote Old Jim.

Shaking old memories from his mind, Declan had to focus on the business at hand…Because he loved Christophe and Annie, because he so admired Stephan and Jenny Lylestrom, and because he had once loved Liliana very much, Declan Ryan loaded emergency provisions into his truck and made the snowy trek across Rosemeade County and into Brookings City to bring his old friend home to her family and to a new chapter in her life. He would rather have never seen her again, but life had dictated things otherwise.

As Declan scanned the teeming crowds descending the airport concourse, his eyes were instantly drawn to her. She was beautiful, even in her grief. Liliana no longer looked like the college girl he saw in his mind's eye. She had been a pretty young thing back then; but now, in her early thirties, she was quite breathtaking. Standing alone at the confluence of the concourses, clothed simply in black and holding a colorful tapestry carry-on bag, she looked subdued. Yet, when she saw him, her face lit up and tears threatened those lovely green eyes as soon as she was close enough to greet him.

"Oh, Declan, thank you for coming to fetch me. It seems I am always a burden to you, but I do so appreciate you making the trip for me," she had whispered, as she leaned into his embrace.

Declan felt tears prick at his own eyes at just seeing her again and almost lost his composure when she thanked him for coming to retrieve her. Granted, he had never wanted to see her again, but would he ever have done anything less for her? Declan hugged her solidly to himself and softly said, "You know that I would do anything for you, Liliana."

After helping Liliana to ensure that Richard's body had been delivered to the waiting hearse at the air freight office, Declan helped her into the cab of his truck and stowed her belongings safely into the rear seat. The trip to Reedsburgh was to be a slow and slightly treacherous one. The storm had worsened, and it was obvious that the snow plows were having trouble keeping up. Since it was going to be a long drive, Declan asked Liliana if she was, perchance, hungry.

"I've not eaten much today, Declan. I guess I am just a little bit hungry."

Knowing Liliana as he did, Declan knew that she would push herself until she was too exhausted to go on, so he suspected that she had not eaten much for several days. "Well, then, Pettigrew's Place it is," he quietly retorted.

The owner of Pettigrew's was an old friend of Declan's, and he recognized something serious was happening when Declan held Liliana's elbow and ushered her into the pub. Declan introduced the two of them and nodded to a corner booth where they could have privacy. Comprehension dawned that this was the woman whom Declan had lost years ago, and Jeremy Pettigrew quickly led them to their seats and proceeded to get them something to eat and drink.

While they waited for the arrival of their meal, Liliana was uncomfortable. She breathed shallowly and her slender fingers trembled. When he could no longer tolerate how distraught she was, he reached over to her fidgeting hands and laid his own large one over them. Her trembling immediately ceased, and he felt a frisson of something akin to fear bolt through himself.

"Do you want to talk about it?" Declan inquired, looking soberly at fragile Liliana.

She looked at him steadily with her soulful green eyes for several seconds and began, "Declan, there was a car crash. Richard was hurt, but not critically. He did, in fact, have an undiagnosed heart condition that they discovered at the hospital, but it wasn't anything that couldn't be addressed medically. He complained bitterly about the extreme pain he was in; constantly asking for pain medication. Three days after he had awakened, he was still complaining about the extreme pain; then, he just died quite suddenly and quite efficiently. He had purposefully killed himself, Declan, and almost destroyed the life of a young hospital employee that he used unconscionably. I'm suspicious of many things regarding Richard. I know that I am sounding callous here, but I'm dealing with some substantial anger toward him."

"He had been a monster for months and was exceedingly hard to get along with…acting secretive, detached, and angry toward me. After he died, I found documents hidden away in his belongings that indicated he owed copious amounts of money and that he was in serious trouble with the federal government. He was being investigated for fraud, Declan, and he had not shared any of this with me."

"Liliana, I am so very sorry. But, why wouldn't he share these things with you? You were his wife."

"I find Richard had been a very proficient liar to me, Declan. But when we married, it seemed natural that he would manage the money. He was the one who had graduated with an MBA from Harvard. If he was entrusted with overseeing other people's finances, he could certainly take care of ours. He was always flamboyant with his spending, and he had a very high risk tolerance when it came to investing, but he had done well at his job. This whole time, he made very good money."

"For some reason, he had recently borrowed the principal from his life insurance policy; then proceeded to let it lapse. So…there is no life insurance money to settle his debts. In going through his things, I found notes that he owes money to several hard money lenders, and he had IOUs to friends for considerable sums of money. There were even payment agreements with several title loan companies for paltry sums. I'm very worried. I put a call in to David Renton. You know him, I'm sure. He was a friend of mine from school, and he is an attorney now. So, he's doing some investigating into Richard's affairs. I'm fearful of what he might find."

"I guess the final blow came two days ago, when I found that all of our bank accounts had been frozen. I literally had no money to get here. Richard had even stolen my emergency money that I keep hidden in my purse. I had to ask my parents to purchase a ticket for me in order to get Richard's body back to Reedsburgh. Declan, I'm mortified."

Declan, again, reached across the table and covered Liliana's trembling hands. "Don't worry. David will help you get things straightened out. You have family and friends who care for you; things can only get better. All will be well, Liliana. All will be well."

Liliana then moved her hands out from beneath his larger comforting one and held on to the ends of his fingers for just a fraction of a second. She gave him a shaky smile. "Let's change the subject, shall we? Tell me, Declan, how is Old Jim?" she asked with just a shadow of her former smile. Declan's heart wrenched, yet again. He quietly stated, "I'm sorry Liliana, but Jim died several weeks ago; just before Christmas. He went happily, though. We buried him in the cemetery in Rosemeade.

Liliana's tears, once again, threatened to overflow, but she kept herself in control. "Oh, Declan, he was such a sweet man. I wish that I could have seen him before he died. That makes me very sad." She then closed her eyes, and rubbed her fingertips across her forehead. When she again looked up, she said, "My return is starting to overwhelm me, Declan. I am so weary. Can you take me home now?" she asked with a trembling lower lip.

Again, Declan's heart ached for her, "Of course, Lily. Let me pay the check."

Thanking Jeremy for his hospitality, Declan then ushered her back out into the storm with his hand at the small of her back; as he helped her into his vehicle, he noted that she felt far slenderer than he had remembered. He suspected that things must have been even harder this last little while than she had shared with him.

The remainder of the trip was quiet with Liliana falling asleep yet resting fitfully. Every time she flinched in her sleep, Declan reached across the seat, and laid his hand upon her shoulder for a second or two. Each time, she would calm down. Declan's ire toward Richard Rawlings reared its ugly head as he considered all that Liliana had shared with him. The honorable part of him wanted Richard to have a reason for all these betrayals to Liliana, yet the protective male part of him wanted to pummel that poor excuse for a man, but he was already dead. He seethed in silence as he carefully drove the treacherous county roads back to Reedsburgh.

It was close to eleven o'clock at night when they finally pulled into the drive of Liliana's family home. The walkway had been cleared of snow, and all the lights in the house were ablaze. Stephan Lylestrom was the first out the door to embrace his baby girl who had been gone so very long, and very fittingly, she fell to pieces when she saw her father; the one man that she knew she could depend upon. Jenny Lylestrom then held her daughter tightly and said, "Welcome home, my sweet girl."

Declan was backing off the porch now that he had Liliana delivered safely to her family, intending to drive the rest of the way back to Rosemeade Township, when Stephan said, "Declan, you are one of our own. Please come and stay the night. We've prepared the guest room for you, and I've not had a chance to thank you properly for bringing Liliana home." I am indebted to you. Please say you'll stay. The roads will be much safer tomorrow, and Christophe tells me you've hired a very efficient fellow to help you oversee things at Old Vineyard Road. Please, do come in."

Seeing as how he had no other choice, Declan shook Stephan's hand, and said, "Thank you, Stephan. I'm happy to help in your time of need."

After tossing and turning for hours and still feeling Liliana's touch from when she had fleetingly grasped his fingers, Declan had a sleepless night fraught with dreams of days gone by with Liliana. He awoke to the sounds of breakfast downstairs. He quickly showered, shaved and descended the stairs, feeling somewhat foolish that he was wearing yesterday's clothing. Stephan, Jenny, Christophe and Annie greeted him warmly; and Liliana, who was looking considerably more rested, brought him a cup of coffee. For some reason, she had not forgotten how he preferred his coffee.

After breakfast and some small talk with the family, Declan indicated that he thought he should get on the road home to the nursery before another storm came through. He thought that he saw disappointment momentarily flicker across Liliana's face, but he dismissed it. As he warmed up his truck and scraped the icy snow covering its windows, she came out of the house bundled in Christophe's giant ski parka to give him a small paper bag of snacks for the road.

"Thank you, again, Declan…for picking me up from the airport, for the meal at Pettigrew's, and for just being you. You were very good to me yesterday. I hope to meet your friend, Jeremy, again when I am not feeling so awful." She stepped toward him, and he embraced her slender frame engulfed within Christophe's stalwart coat. She then looked up into his eyes and smiled slightly.

Declan stepped back breaking the embrace, and looked at his old friend, "I was happy to do it, Liliana. You were good to me when I first arrived in Rosemeade County. I wasn't feeling particularly happy myself back then, and you were very kind." Declan then climbed into his truck, "I'll be here again on Friday for Richard's service. Rest up."

With that, he drove off through the lightly falling snow. As he watched Liliana's diminishing reflection in the rearview mirror, Declan admitted to himself that he felt quite shaken at seeing her again. "I must harden myself against feeling anything for her," he sternly told himself. But if he had been honest, Declan would have admitted that something had reignited last evening when he saw her standing alone and vulnerable in a sea of humanity at the International Airport in Brookings City. He had wanted to hold her again and to ease her pain…he had longed to protect her. Then, when she had unknowingly touched his hand and held his fingers familiarly for just a mere instant, something had sparked within his soul. It had always been that way with her… "I must be impervious to these things," he again reminded himself.

LILIANA'S ADMISSION

*L*iliana Rawlings felt wistful as she watched Declan Ryan drive away. She had once known him so well. They had shared many special times from working together at The Old Vineyard Road Nursery to family events with Christophe and Annie. Declan was exceedingly smart, so talented, and very kind. She had once been hopelessly in love with him, but he had not shared the same affection for her. In those days, Richard had pursued her with a fervor and had flattered her inexperienced heart, so she had finally accepted Richard's proposal of marriage after realizing that Declan Ryan did not love her. It was shortly after her honeymoon that she came to understand that Richard Rawlings had only heaped his attention upon her because that was what he did…he feverishly pursued things that he wanted; compromising himself in order to secure them. After he had won her, she had simply been one more bauble on his bucket list of things he wanted to possess. It was a heart-breaking realization for a twenty-two-year-old girl.

Seeing Declan again made her realize how truly transparent and shallow her husband had been. Even though Declan had never returned her love so long ago, he still had treated her well, and yesterday, when he had brought her home to be reunited with her family, he had been caring toward her. Liliana thought about these things as she watched his truck disappear into a pin-dot. She wondered if, perhaps, they would be friends again. Liliana did have to admit to herself that though it had been under awful circumstances, she had been comforted by his quiet presence and care last evening; even if it was simply driving home in a snowstorm. Declan Ryan had always soothed her, but she must make sure that Declan never feel uncomfortable around her. She must take care not to be overly familiar with him.

The next several days were busy ones for Liliana…planning Richard's memorial service, conferring with her father on reconciling the egregious mistakes Richard had made, and dreading what else might come to light from David Renton's investigation into Richard's business affairs… Even after several nights of catch-up sleep, she still felt so very exhausted; even more so than she had before she left Seattle. Dealing with cleaning up the detritus of Richard's life was proving to be harder on her than she had ever thought it would be. And, looking back at her relationship and marriage with Richard, she was beginning to wonder how earnest he had been with her, even from the beginning. "Why is it that I am seeing things so differently now?" she asked her father one evening.

Stephan Lylestrom summoned up the courage to be candid with his daughter. "Liliana, I feel that Richard may have been less than honest with **all** of us over the last ten years. I don't want to speak ill of the dead, but I always thought there was something odd or off about how he never seemed to want to forge a relationship with your family; especially since he did not have one of his own. We tried to welcome him into ours, but he always wanted to keep us at arm's length. I know newlyweds want to be alone with one another, but I feel he purposely tried to keep you from your mother and me. And, don't get me started on how he treated Christophe, and for that matter, how he treated Declan, too. These are people that you love… people who shared in your youth and helped you grow up into the young woman that Richard wanted so desperately. Why would he treat Christophe with disdain? You, of all people, should know that Christophe Riordan is loved wherever he goes. And as for Declan, he and Richard were close in age. They could have been contemporaries, but why did Richard always behave so abominably toward him, as well? Declan was your very special friend, and I suspect he was your first love. He had no family left except for Christophe. One would think Richard would have jumped at the chance to get to know him better; especially since neither of them had parents left. Do you see what I'm getting at here?"

"Yes, Dad, I do know exactly what you are saying. I must admit that I have wondered the same things. And, yet, whenever I ventured to ask Richard about them, an argument would always ensue. 'You love your parents and those two stupid Highlanders better than you do me.' I finally got tired of going the rounds with him. Dad, he had a volatile disposition and was quite demanding. I just tried to get along with him. If it meant keeping the peace, I figured I would have to accept the distance that he kept putting between me and those I care about so much. I hate to say this, but I sometimes felt it was purposeful, too." Unbidden tears rolled down her cheeks.

"Sweetheart, I want you to be very candid with me because I have not been able to see you, these last few years. Did Richard emotionally abuse or ever strike you?"

Quiet for several seconds, she answered, "No, not really, Dad." She then sighed heavily, "He just kept me on a very short leash. I felt kind of like Iris used to when she had to stay in the laundry room for her own safety when she was just a pup. It was like *I* was a naughty puppy who would get into trouble if he didn't keep watch over me. Only, I was never given a reprieve, you know? When he made me give up my teaching job, he said it was because he wanted to begin a family. Instead, he insisted that I cater to his every whim because 'He worked so hard for us and he gave me everything.' But, Dad, I didn't want big houses, fancy cars, diamonds, furs and the lot; none of it meant anything to me. I only wanted to get along with him and to give him the stability he never had."

"Also, he would never let me plant a garden or flowers because that smacked of Christophe and the nursery. And, Dad, I don't even want to get started on all the faults he found in Declan. I never will understand why he disliked him so much. Again, just to keep the peace, I acquiesced to his demands. You know how I hate confrontation. He didn't want me to have my teaching job or to do any of my hobbies, so Italian cooking and baking became my outlet, because he did like to eat and to entertain his clients."

Liliana brushed tears from her cheeks, yet again, and sighed heavily. "I only wanted to get along with Richard, but you've no idea how I longed to see you and Mom. Sometimes, I just wanted to come home and tattle on him like a school girl. I've spent so much of the last ten years in upheaval due to Richard's problems. I took my marriage vows seriously. Oh, Dad, if I had it to do over again, I would not have married Richard, and I hate myself for saying it. Richard is dead now, but he was not even close to being the man that I thought I was marrying. Quite frankly, I feel that he misrepresented who he was and what he would bring to our marriage."

Stephan looked at his daughter, shook his head sadly, and said, "Baby, if you had had any doubts beforehand, you should have spoken the word. I would have stopped things in their tracks; even if it had been just minutes before you were to marry him."

"I did have doubts about Richard," she sniffed. "I was just barely twenty-two years old, but he just kept insisting that things were going to turn out great. You know how Richard can talk his way into, or out of, any situation he desires. That's why he was so good at selling financial products. I now know Richard never loved me. Or if he did, it was in his own... I guess I can say it now... his own twisted way."

Again, tears filled Liliana's eyes, "I feel like my life is over and that I have nothing to show for it. I'm ashamed of Richard's character. And I'm ashamed of my stupidity, and I'm very ashamed if I have brought disgrace to you and Mom. I hope you both know that I stayed the course in my marriage because of my beliefs. I tried to honor Richard in good times **and** bad. Now, I find that my husband has trampled upon everything that I hold sacred. How could I have been so naive?"

"You know what, Dad? Declan once tried to caution me about Richard, only because he knew me so well, but I didn't listen to him. We had an ugly argument. It was the only disagreement that we ever had."

Stephan Lylestrom looked at his lovely daughter, and his heart ached for her.

DAVID'S NEWS

avid Renton was heartsick. The news he had to deliver to Liliana was worse than he ever could have imagined. He had never cared much for Richard Rawlings, but he thought the guy must have had, at least, some shred of integrity or Liliana would never have agreed to marry him. Even David, who thought he had heard just about everything in his law practice, was flabbergasted about what had been unearthed regarding Richard Rawlings.

David knew that Richard's funeral was today, and it was probably not the time to drop such a bomb on Liliana. Yet, she had insisted that he contact her day or night should anything turn up regarding her husband. The morning had arrived with weak sunshine and clouds scudding across the sky due to a stern wind. It was bitterly cold; and, somehow, David thought the weather befitted the bleak news he was about to deliver to Liliana. As he prepared to dial the phone shortly before nine o'clock that morning, David reflected on things that had gone before…

David Renton had been Liliana's beau during her first year of college, and he had always been sorry that he had let her get away. Being young and stupid, David had made a mess of things when Liliana had flat out told him she would not sleep with him. It was the dawn of a new millennium, and he considered himself a stud of sorts, so he thought she owed him her maidenhood for all the dinners he had bought for her and for all those movies, too. When she still wouldn't pony up, he had dumped her flat. Thinking she would soon come to her senses, he had waited for her call, but that call had never come. A year and a half later, when they ran into one another at a party, Liliana had greeted him cordially, and he had apologized for his horrible behavior. She had accepted his apology graciously, but he knew that she would never give him another chance with her. Now, years later, he was happy with his lovely wife, Claire, and she had given him three beautiful daughters, but there were times when he had wondered what would have happened if he had not demanded such intimacy from Liliana. Now that he had daughters of his own, he wanted them to have the guts that Liliana had shown to him. He quite admired her for it now.

This morning, David thought to himself, if Liliana had saved herself for marriage, she surely had been cheated, as Richard Rawlings was not worthy of such a woman. David had attended their wedding and had wondered why she chose such a guy. Richard was nice enough, but something about him just didn't ring true, and Liliana's face had not been radiant that day. Oh, she was a lovely bride, but she had not been her regular vivacious self. It seemed that day that the only person who could keep her spirits up was that big guy, Christophe Riordan. He had pulled her out on the dance floor and had proceeded to dance some type of a Scottish jig with her. By the end of the dance, she was laughing, but when her new husband came to claim her, his face was grim, and Liliana had looked wary of him. David suspected it had been a rocky start for her.

Now, David had the odious job of breaking the news to her that Richard had passed himself off as someone he was not. The firm's investigation had revealed that not only was Richard Rawlings a pathological liar, but he was a cheat. David's investigative team had uncovered information that Richard had not graduated from Harvard, and he did not have an MBA from their prestigious program, as he had acknowledged. He had graduated from State College, but that school had held his diploma because he hadn't paid his last semester's tuition. Even now, that debt was still red-flagged on his college records. And, if those lies weren't bad enough, Richard Rawlings was not an orphan, but he had two living parents and three sisters a mere three hundred fifty miles east of Reedsburgh.

There had also been accusations of unauthorized trading of the assets of his unsuspecting clients, chronic mismanagement of their portfolios, and unpaid personal bills across a wide swath of the United States. The latest on his growing list of infractions seemed to be an investigation by the federal government for fraudulent stock trading. David Renton considered how such infractions into that arena would have gone down, but Richard had taken his own life in lieu of facing his consequences. It seemed obvious that Richard Rawlings had been on a collision course straight to federal prison. Trouble had followed Richard everywhere he went, and that trouble was of his own making. "Poor, Liliana," he sighed. As David rang Liliana on his cell phone, he felt as though he had been selected to put a hangman's noose around her slender neck.

The phone rang once, and Liliana quickly answered, "David, have you uncovered anything about Richard?"

"Yes, I have. I hope you are sitting down, Liliana, because the things I must tell you are not good. In fact, they are some of the foulest revelations I have ever had to deliver."

"Go ahead, David. At this point, nothing you could tell me would be any worse than what I have already uncovered about Richard. I'm only sorry that you've had to be dragged into any of this horrific nonsense at all. Let's just get it over with…go ahead, tell me everything."

From there, David enlightened Liliana regarding Richard's secret life, the revelation that he had not attended Harvard and did not have an MBA. There was the existence of parents and three sisters; then, there was the issue of money he had stolen from clients, the governmental investigation, and the sizable amount of hard-money lenders Richard was indebted to, as well. It was apparent that Richard Rawlings took big risks and that he had brazenly trampled upon those who entrusted their hard-earned wealth to him.

Liliana quietly listened to Richard's growing rap sheet and felt tired. "How could she and her parents have been so duped?" she asked of herself.

Questions continued to fly through Liliana's mind as she tried to take in what David had just revealed. She questioned, "Did he really have parents just three hundred fifty miles from Reedsburgh, David?

How could he just walk away from them and then have the audacity to tell everyone that he had no family; that he had been orphaned?"

She thought back to Declan's serious young face years ago when he had told her about both of his parent's deaths. Declan had seemed very close to losing control of his emotions that afternoon when he had shared these things with her. Richard, on the other hand, had been angry about losing his parents, saying that his father was an alcoholic who could not hold down a job. He had said they had perished in a fiery auto accident caused by his father driving under the influence of alcohol; always adding that he was angry at his father for being so irresponsible. Consequently, Richard rarely consumed alcohol. "How could he deceive her so?" she asked of herself, yet again.

"Liliana, there is more," David soberly continued, "but I suspect that you already know these things…it seems that the insurance adjusters and the police investigators working on the accident case are suspect that Richard may have caused the accident himself. The skid patterns on the snowpack that evening, and the eye-witness accounts don't add up. I know he was desperate, but do you really think he would have resorted to such an irresponsible act? Witnesses have stated that his car didn't appear to slide into that SUV. They all have reported that Richard turned purposefully into the oncoming car. I'm so sorry to tell you these things, Liliana. The Phillips family, who drove the SUV, is still recovering from their injuries. None of them have given the police a statement, yet. But I must say that things do appear suspect."

A quiet Liliana retorted, "David, these findings go along with Richard purposefully killing himself after the accident. He didn't get the job done the first time, so he was quite determined to die of a drug overdose. He continually demanded medications to quell his pain, but I don't think he was in pain…he wanted those meds to avoid prison. The things you've found enlighten me a lot, but I can't help feeling there are other things that I don't know about."

"David, as Richard's wife, I am responsible for his debts, aren't I?" she quietly stated more than asked.

"Yes, Liliana, there are some things that you are, in fact, going to have to re-pay because your name is also listed jointly with Richard's. The debts are cumbersome, Liliana, and I'm so sorry that there is no life insurance money to help you settle things. You will probably need to liquidate all the property you owned with Richard…your home, your automobiles and more to get started on paying things off."

"I do have the trust fund that my parents gave to me when I turned twenty-seven, and I've not touched any of it. Not too long ago, Richard insisted that he begin managing it, David. I reluctantly agreed, as Dad's people had been doing a great job taking care of it for me, and it was the one thing that was mine; something given to me by my parents. You know that I had an idyllic upbringing. My parents worked hard to give me such a gift. I'm fearful now, that Richard may have done something untoward with those funds…especially since he was managing them. Oh, this does not bode well. You know all the bank accounts were frozen last week and that Dad had to pay my way here for Richard's funeral. I literally had no money, as he had even taken the emergency money hidden in my purse. Oh, David, this *really* does not bode well."

Not only was David Renton heartsick for Liliana, now he was fearful, too. His gut told him Richard Rawlings had stolen from Liliana's trust fund. "Listen, Liliana, I'm going to call in some favors…I'll do my best to see if I can find out what has gone down with your frozen accounts; especially your trust fund. I'll be in touch later this morning."

An hour and half later, just as Liliana and her parents were readying to leave for the funeral home, David Renton had the odious duty of breaking the news to them that Richard Rawlings had, in fact, embezzled almost the entirety of the trust that Stephan and Jenny Lylestrom had given to their daughter. What was left of the funds would continue to remain frozen.

Liliana, Stephan, and Jenny accepted this revelation with great sorrow, but no real surprise. Richard Rawlings had raped them all financially. Liliana's only request had been that David prepare the necessary papers to legally reinstate her maiden name of, "Lylestrom."

"I will no longer be aligned with him, David. Even in death, he has violated me. I must be given back my father's name. Can you please see to it quickly?"

David Renton vowed to begin the process immediately. It was the least he could do for his old friend. After ending the call, he sadly shook his head. He knew Richard Rawlings was a vile man, but David couldn't quite bring himself to unload several other potential bombshells that had been uncovered by his investigative contacts…his suspicions would have to wait for just a little while longer.

David sat at his desk and wondered who Sierra Monroe was and why she was aligned with Richard on the records that were quickly unraveling to expose further deceit to Liliana and her parents. If he could, he would try to catch Liliana's father alone after the funeral, as these suspicions gnawed at him. David knew in his gut that Richard had most likely been living a double life with another woman, but today, of all days, David did not want to heap the heaviness of his suspicions upon Liliana's shoulders. She already looked so very pale and exhausted.

DAVID'S SECRET

*D***avid Renton** was reluctant to break more scandalous news to Liliana and her parents on the day of Richard's funeral; yet, he knew it had to be done. As the guests were departing the Lylestrom's family home later that afternoon, David asked Liliana's father, Stephan, if he could speak privately with him. Stephan ushered him into his library, closed the door, and lit the lamps. The afternoon was waning, and French doors looked out onto what was usually Stephan and Jenny's robust vegetable garden, but it was heaped with heavy snow that somehow belied the fact that in just a few months it would produce brilliant flowers and vegetables. Finally settling into their seats, Stephan Lylestrom opened their conversation by simply inquiring what else Richard Rawlings had done to further violate his daughter. David had to be very candid with him.

"Stephan, when my investigative people researched Richard Rawlings, their report contained several red flags that I wasn't ready to discuss with Liliana this morning. I know she's had a hard go of it, and I didn't want to burden her until I received concrete answers to my questions. You understand. Quite frankly, Stephan, I'm pretty sure that Richard was keeping a mistress."

"David, this is a serious accusation against Richard, but somehow I'm not surprised. Do you have concrete proof?"

"Well, on several of the files I received, his name appeared alongside a woman named, Sierra Monroe, as joint-tenants on three different homes that were bought and sold in Chicago, Denver, and Seattle. It appears that Ms. Monroe followed every time that Richard and Liliana were relocated. If that isn't enough, she owns a money fund account that lists Richard as beneficiary. At present, I suspect that Richard likely used her name to cover himself, but I question whether the monies in that fund account might, in fact, be from Liliana's trust fund."

A very saddened Stephan replied, "Well, David, Richard had a much darker side that I had even speculated."

"Yes, Stephan, I suspect this is just the tip of the iceberg. Earlier this morning, I spoke with the forensic investigator we've retained to investigate Richard's trail of transactions. He has been probing into the allegations that Richard stole money from his financial clients. Richard was in deep trouble. It appears that he may have, in fact, traded and sold his client's assets without their knowledge or consent in addition to accusations of insider trading. As well, I query whether Sierra Monroe even knows that Richard is dead or that he used her name as a front for ill-gotten money. This situation just seems to get uglier by the minute."

"I'm very sorry to hear of it, David, but like I said earlier, I'm not totally surprised. Let's hold tight and see what comes of your investigator's findings before we further burden Liliana… I am quite concerned about her. She is so thin and pale, and she bears scars of recent sutures underneath one of her eyebrows. My gut tells me that something has befallen her besides what's been uncovered by Richard's death. Both Jenny and I suspect he may have harmed her, but she denies any ill treatment. **Yet**, she can't explain what might have happened regarding that scaring. She blames it on her own clumsiness. We'll be patient with her because we know her, and eventually she'll spill things. But as I said, we're very suspicious."

"This grieves me, Stephan. I noticed that telltale scar, too, but I didn't want to push her for an answer. I find myself wondering what might have happened to her, as well. For now, I'll keep you apprised of Richard's forensic trail. I suspect that a visit from the authorities might just lead to Sierra Monroe filling us in on some of the details of Richard's secret life."

"I have to admire Liliana and the great strength of character she has shown during all of this upheaval, but it does sadden me to think she feels a need to cover for Richard. That man's immoral behavior seems to know no bounds. I do hope she will eventually confide what might have happened to her with you and Jenny."

"As do I, David…as do I," retorted Stephan sadly. "Let's keep this Sierra Monroe business under wraps until there is something more concrete. I can't bear to see Liliana's heart and soul violated any more than they already have been."

STEPHAN AND JENNY'S CONCERN

Stephan and Jenny Lylestrom were grieved for their daughter but were thankful that she had come out of such an abominable situation with her life intact. Both knew intuitively that her spirit was in tatters and that she was far more exhausted than she let on, but they knew their daughter well; soon she would eventually broach the length and breadth of her life with Richard.

Even this morning, the day of Richard's funeral, after digesting David's stunning revelations to her, she had simply asked for their forgiveness for the shame Richard had heaped upon their family and had proceeded to call the funeral director. Just hours before the funeral was slated to begin, she had requested that her husband be cremated in lieu of being interred in the plot which had been selected for him. "I will reimburse you for any inconvenience we have caused you, Mr. Bromley," she had said, "but I find that I must take possession of my husband's ashes instead."

Both parents were surprised by her actions but knew that she had her reasons. The memorial service slated for Richard went on as scheduled. Liliana was gracious to all in attendance, thanked everyone for their support at such a difficult time, and encouraged all the attendees to join them at the family home for a meal afterward. Their girl was strong right now because she had to be. She was also angry, but they would be there for her when she was finally able to let down. Come what may, Stephan and Jenny Lylestrom would be there for their daughter.

Except for Christophe, Annie, and Declan, all their guests had departed into falling snow and the darkening afternoon that day. Stephan Lylestrom sat down by the front window and shook his head... unconscionable Richard Rawlings had used them all abominably. Jenny and Annie were in the kitchen area washing dirty dishes, Christophe sat across the room perusing something on his new tablet, and Liliana was in the dining room seated across from Declan. As she spoke to him, Declan started shaking his head. Stephan suspected Declan was just now learning of Richard's reprehensible behavior.

As he watched them, Stephan wondered why Liliana hadn't chosen Declan. She was seemingly crazy about him back when…counting the days until she would be home for a special event that would include him. Declan, too, had shown a very marked preference for her. Liliana's face always shone whenever she related stories about their summer fun. Stephan had always thought they might marry, and he wondered for the millionth time what had happened. Why had she chosen to marry Richard Rawlings? In his heart, Stephan Lylestrom now knew that Declan, too, had been an early victim of Richard's deceit, and his heart grieved for him, too. Things could have turned out so very differently if not for Richard's appalling behavior from the get-go.

Stephan Lylestrom ruminated on this sad scenario for several minutes more; then he stood up and walked toward the kitchen. As he passed by Liliana and Declan, Stephan heard Declan say, "So you've nothing left of your trust? Pardon me, Liliana, but that man was a bastard. How could he treat you and your parents that way?" Stephan Lylestrom found himself in complete agreement with Declan.

STEPHAN'S DISCOVERY

*S***tephan Lylestrom** flew to Seattle with his daughter multiple times during late January and early February. They met routinely with a team of attorneys that David Renton had referred. The Seattle team was working in conjunction with David Renton to set up arrangements for paying off Richard Rawlings huge debts. On one of these trips to Seattle, Stephan discovered something that shocked even him. He couldn't believe his late son-in- law had done such a thing to his family.

Stephan found himself at Liliana's home in Seattle helping her to dismantle the household and portion her belongings into categories that would bring in money to erase Richard's debts through a private estate sale. It was hoped that they could soon get her house ready for sale on the now-rebounding real estate market, too.

While going through Richard's client records, Stephan discovered a secret drawer within Richard's home-office desk. Something told Stephan, this secret chamber was sure to reveal answers for many of his daughter's questions, and he was right…

"Liliana! Can you come here, please?" he called with a sinking heart.

"What is it, Dad?" Liliana asked as she came into the room." He noted that her young face now had a wariness to it, as so many toxic things had been volleyed her way during the last several weeks.

"Sweetheart look at what I just found in a hidden drawer," Stephan sadly replied as he held out several bundles of letters and greeting cards to her. "There are even some parcels, too," he added as he blew out a small sigh.

Liliana took a rubber-banded bundle from him silently and began to flip through the contents. As unshed tears misted in her green eyes, she responded. "Dad, I can't believe he would do this to me…to us… these are all of my cards, letters, and personal gifts to you and mom for quite a few years! Why would he have not posted them to you? It even appears that he opened some and read their contents…"

Stephan gently laid his hand on his daughter's shoulder and added, "Liliana, there's even a bundle of our missives to you, as well. They, too, appear to have been opened and read. Lily, you probably wondered why we rarely communicated with you, too. Oh, baby girl, I am so sorry. Apart from just a few phone calls from you over the last couple of years, your mother and I have always wondered why we never heard much of anything from you. It was so out of character. Liliana, I must admit that we were suspect about your lack of communication, but we did attribute it to Richard, not to you. Yet, we wanted to give him the benefit of the doubt because he was your husband."

Stephan continued, "And now, I find that you were probably feeling the same way your mother and I were, too! You **do** know how much your mother and I love you, don't you, Liliana? We would **never** choose to be estranged from you…you are our special girl, and we love you so very much. You know how long we waited and how hard we tried to have a child, Liliana. We were elated when you were born. We would never choose to be alienated from you; no matter the circumstances. But I am pretty sure that Richard engineered things so they would appear that way…making us look as if we were uncaring of your feelings."

"Oh, Dad, there has never been any doubt of your love for me," Liliana sadly said as she embraced her father. "You and Mom are the most-wonderful parents. I know that I was blessed to be born to the both of you. No, no…I never questioned your love and affection for me not once…even when we couldn't ever see each other, and my calls home were monitored by Richard. I always hoped that you two were reading between the lines, too."

Looking very tired, Liliana then sat down upon a leather footstool. Her slender young shoulders were hunched, and she put her hands over her face. As Stephan watched her, it dawned on him that she really was much thinner than he had ever seen her. His heart ached for his daughter. When she looked up again, she sadly shook her head and said, "Dad, all of these letters certainly explain why Richard always insisted that our mail come to a post office box near to his work. He took my outgoing mail with him every morning when he left for the office, promising to drop it in the out-bound mailbox. I can't believe he would stoop to such a thing! Why would he do that to us, Dad?"

Stephan breathed out a tired sigh and said, "Why would he do any of the things that have been revealed about him since his death? Liliana, we have all been duped by him, and I can't believe that I ever allowed my precious girl to marry him. Oh, Lily, I'm heartsick to find out these things. Richard was far more deceptive and malicious than I ever thought he was capable of being."

"You know, Dad, I was insulted and demeaned by Richard on a fairly regular basis the last few years. I'm sure it is not surprising to you that my feelings for him had eroded, and that I became somewhat impervious to his bullying, but finding these letters that he stole from us hurts me anew." Looking heartsick, Liliana continued, "Dad, I'm ashamed to admit this, but I was considering a legal separation from Richard just before he died. Because of my beliefs, I would have stayed his wife, but I wanted to live separately from him. His moods were getting way too volatile, and now his cowardice has saved me from such a life."

At this revelation, Stephan Lylestrom began to suspect that his peace-making daughter had been bullied and pushed to her limits far more than she had ever let on. He advised himself to wait for Liliana to broach the subject when she was ready. Instead, he once again hugged his lovely daughter and said, "Let's just get that man's business affairs in order, put this house on the market, and go home to Reedsburgh and lick our wounds. How does that sound, Liliana?"

"Good! Let's just get this horrible job done, Dad…"

Two days later, Stephan Lylestrom was again surprised when Liliana took almost the entirety of her handsome wardrobe to a consignment store. She turned a blind eye to the very expensive clothing and shoes that Richard had bought for her and asked the store's manager to try to get top dollar for her things. Then, she packed up a paltry few pieces of clothing to take back to Reedsburgh.

That same day, she also gladly sold her very expensive wedding ring and various pieces of diamond jewelry to a local jeweler who gave her fair market value for her things. It became obvious to Stephan that his daughter had never desired any of the gifts that she was now so readily selling. Lastly, Liliana sold two very expensive fur coats. She kept the money for herself because she needed to pay for Richard's college tuition from years ago. Stephan guessed that the next order of business for his daughter would be to pay a visit to Richard's family. A week or two later, he found out he was right…

LORENA AND ROBERT

L iliana asked Stephan and Jenny if they would accompany her to meet Richard's parents. It was mid-February, and it was a blustery winter's day, but being together in the family car on a road trip meant they could enjoy some freedom from the trials of this world. The five-hour drive to Edison sped by quickly. They checked into a hotel for the night and girded themselves for tomorrow's visit with Richard's family. Always considerate, Liliana had already notified Richard's parents of his death, and today, she had brought along several thoughtful gifts for them; each one a remembrance of their son. Stephan hoped their visit would not be too hard on his daughter or on the Rawlings family.

Lorena and Robert Rawlings waited anxiously to meet the daughter-in-law that they didn't even know they had. It had been two weeks since she had contacted them and told them of Richard's passing. They were grieved that their only son was gone, but somehow, they weren't completely surprised. Richard had angrily left the family at age nineteen when they had been involved in that life-changing car wreck. Admittedly, Robert Rawlings was at fault because he had been drinking, but the accident had been a wake-up call to him. Shortly thereafter, he had gone into a rehabilitation program and had been sober for over fourteen years.

After that pivotal accident, Richard had been so angry with his father that he had moved in with friends and had proceeded to distance himself from his three sisters and his parents. What Richard had never known was that his father was free from the torment of alcoholism, that he had been gainfully employed with a good job for many years, and that he had repaired his relationship with his wife and his three daughters. Only his relationship with his son was nonexistent, but that was because Richard had stubbornly refused to have any contact with his father. Lorena and Robert Rawlings had endlessly tried to get in touch with their son, but after he left for college at State, it was as if he had vanished. That was when they had done their grieving over the loss of Richard.

This morning, Richard's wife, Liliana, and her parents were coming to meet them. Neither Lorena nor Robert knew what to expect, but she had sounded like such a nice person over the telephone, that they had great hope that Richard had led a happy life. When their daughter-in-law arrived, she was lovely. She was dressed very simply, she had beautiful green eyes, and she wore her long, dark hair loosely waved around her face. Her parents were much older than expected, but they, too, were very gracious people.

After a few minutes of small talk, the Rawlings family, at last, asked how she had come to be married to their son. Liliana graciously launched into a story to put Richard in his best light.

"Well, in my senior year at college, I saw Richard in the school library several times. He finally introduced himself and asked me out for coffee. After several coffee outings, he then invited me on a date," she smiled. "I guess the rest is history!"

"Oh, so you met him at State?" Lorena asked.

Liliana looked slightly flustered, so Stephan interjected, "Sweetie, why don't you give Lorena and Robert the things that you brought for them; they will be so pleased to see all of Richard's accomplishments."

"That's a good idea, Dad," Liliana quickly answered.

So, forgiving Liliana Lylestrom opened the large box her father had carried in and presented Richard's parents with his college diploma, mortarboard and tassel. She had had to pay his long-overdue tuition and fees in order to give these gifts to his parents. Next, she handed them the satin wedding album and guest book from the day they were married. Since she no longer wanted to ever see a photograph of her unpleasant husband again, she was happy to present a retrospective of their wedding day to his parents.

As the gifts progressed, Liliana handed Robert a stack of wood and cut-glass plaques that commemorated Richard's many accomplishments. They had once hung proudly on the wall of his office. Poor Lorena and Robert need never know how shamefully

Richard had compromised himself in order to achieve the accolades on those wall plaques. And, finally, Liliana handed Richard's mother the urn containing his ashes. Again, his family need never know that Richard had so shamelessly cheated her family that she could not, in good conscience, bury his body in her family's plot.

To Robert, who grieved for his only son, she gave a stack of photograph albums containing the entirety of the photographs from the ten years of their marriage. She had no desire to keep them, and they were something that would bring Richard to the forefront of their memories.

Tears streamed down the cheeks of both his parents, and Lorena said, "Liliana, I cannot keep Richard's ashes; you must keep them. He was your husband."

Liliana smiled at her mother-in-law and simply said, "I know Lorena, but I had ten years with Richard, and you missed out on that part of his life. I have the memories, so I would like you to have your son's ashes. Please feel free to distribute them somewhere special."

"You are a fine person, Liliana, I can see why our son chose you," Robert Rawlings commented. Richard may have been estranged from us, but it sounds like he was successful in all his endeavors. Thank you for restoring him to us. Even though he is gone, we can celebrate his life and his achievements. I couldn't be any prouder of him. Thank you."

"It's my pleasure, Robert." Liliana politely answered.

For the remainder of the visit and during a lovely meal that Lorena had prepared for them, Liliana and her parents regaled Lorena and Robert with stories from the few happy memories that they had of Richard. Both of his parents were pleased. When it was time to go, Liliana hugged her in-laws and told them she would stay in touch.

It goes without saying that if Liliana Lylestrom had been of a vindictive nature, she could have sullied Richard Rawlings' memory to his parents. But, because she had found it in her heart to forgive him his numerous transgressions, she left Robert and Lorena Rawlings feeling very proud of their son and happy that he had led such an accomplished life. She, in turn, was quite exhausted from all the emotional turmoil. Trying hard to keep Richard's secret life from his parents had been an arduous task for her that day. All she wanted to do was lie down and rest. Since Richard had died, it seemed that time to rest was never enough to rejuvenate her weariness. She felt so incredibly exhausted that she thought she should, perhaps, seek out a physician for a check-up; she really shouldn't be feeling quite this fatigued.

A SINGULAR SURPRISE

*L**iliana Lylestrom* finally had time to meet with a physician in Reedsburgh the first week of March. He said he could find nothing that would indicate she was ill, but he would run a series of tests to drill down just a bit further. She was relieved that she was not exhibiting symptoms of any disease, so she again attributed her extreme fatigue to her circumstances. Three days later, she again met with old Dr. Forsythe at his office. He told her that the tests indicated she was pregnant.

"You should probably see an obstetrician, Ms. Lylestrom, to confirm these findings. Do you have one or should I refer you to one of my colleagues?" Dr. Forsythe had inquired.

A shaken Liliana had retorted, "Doctor, I don't think I could be pregnant, because my late husband had not had relations with me in over two years. Besides, my menstrual cycle has always been quite irregular…sometimes up to ninety days between my periods. Could the test findings be incorrect?"

"These days, testing is pretty reliable, so it would be best if you saw your obstetrician as soon as you can." The good Dr. Forsythe had then exited the exam room, leaving a flabbergasted Liliana in his wake.

A second consultation with an obstetrician the next week confirmed Liliana's worst fears. "That one night…that horrible night when Richard had hit and knocked her to the floor… that night of such ugliness had produced a child. A child born of Richard's angry rage that was seemingly always directed toward her. "How could such a thing have happened?" Liliana posed this question to herself again and again. It seemed that Richard just continued to jab at her, even in death. She sat in her mother's car in the parking lot and wept exceedingly bitter tears.

When she finally could cry no more, she said to herself, "I am too ashamed to tell my parents about being pregnant with Richard's baby.

If I do tell them, I may have to divulge my secret of his abuse. I can't do this to them right now. I simply must wait for a little while longer, but I do need to take care of myself for this child's sake."

As she drove to her family home, Liliana also decided that she would wait until she could no longer hide the child growing inside her before she would tell anyone she was expecting. She mentally added the burden of shame to the growing list of things she was trying to overcome, thanks to Richard Rawlings. "Sometimes, it is extremely hard to be forgiving," she whispered to no one in particular.

DECLAN'S MUSINGS

eclan Ryan was purposefully staying away from any location where he might accidentally find himself in Liliana's Lylestrom's company. He had been introspective these last three months and, at last, had been honest with himself. Declan had to admit that his world had been rocked in seeing Liliana again. From the day he had been dispatched to bring her from the airport forward, he had thought about her, he had even dreamt about old times spent with her, and he had endured hearing reports about her troubles brought about by Richard Rawlings. Yet, he had made no attempt to contact her or to be in her company. *I must be impervious to feeling anything for her,* he thought.

In all honesty, Declan had to admit that the few times he had been in her company since her return, he had felt his resolve to forget about her crumbling. He viewed this as weakness in himself and had vowed to purposefully stay away from her. Yet, even though he hadn't seen her since the day of Richard's memorial service, he had been kept up to date on her by Christophe and Annie. Both mourned for her and the heavy burden that Richard had heaped upon her shoulders. It seemed that Liliana was to forever be a topic at Old Vineyard Road. All these things were starting to bring back a very familiar ache.

Liliana's return to Reedsburgh had also put a pall on his relationship with Kristen. After admitting to himself that he did not yearn for Kristen while she was away over the Christmas holidays, he began to question whether he wanted to continue in his fledgling relationship with her. Kristen was a lovely woman, and he had enjoyed his time with her very much, but why did she now seem to pale in comparison to Liliana? These feelings shamed him, too. "Why could he not just forget about Liliana Lylestrom?" he asked himself almost daily.

Declan also knew that Liliana had not tried to manipulate his feelings in any way. She had been very busy commuting between

Reedsburgh and Seattle with her father the last two months to liquidate her assets and to negotiate financial arrangements to pay off Richard's debts. Somehow, all the ugly revelations of Richard's character had only endeared her to everyone even more, as she had been gracious under fire and had not wilted from her burden. She had demonstrated great strength of character in the face of grueling adversity. Liliana was an amazing woman, but this was something that Declan Ryan already knew.

One morning, on a very dreary day in late March, Declan received a call from David Renton. In the years since Liliana had married and had lived away from historic Rosemeade County, David and Declan had become good friends. Somehow, David understood Declan's trials at seeing her again and had finally broached the subject with him saying, "I suspect you might be feeling slightly unhinged at Liliana's return to Reedsburgh, Declan. I know that you two once shared something very special. I, for one, have always queried why neither of you fought for something that almost seemed ordained."

On the other end of the telephone David heard his friend intake a deep breath and retort, "David that is a question that seems to have found itself at the forefront of my mind again, but I am trying to steel my resolve against ever trying to answer it. That was a long, long time ago, and we were both very young. I'm not going there again."

"Declan, you were never young, you've been a wise old soul in a younger man's physique since I've known you. You immigrated to America a lot more grown up and serious than my peers and I were, and it's taken us all a while to catch up with you!"

Declan Ryan then chuckled, "You're right, I probably have been far too serious for most of my life. I guess I was just born that way…"

"Listen, how are things going with Kristen? She certainly seems like a great lady. I'm still in awe that she got you into a cowboy costume last Halloween, Declan! She just might be a keeper, you know. Sweet girls like that don't come along very often."

"Believe me, I know," Declan replied.

"But?" David questioned.

"But I can't fully commit to her, David."

"Why, Declan?"

"I think we both know why," Declan sighed.

David Renton blew out his breath and said, "I'm sorry, man." He then offered up an idea, "You know all of my beautiful women will be out of town at Grandma's this coming weekend. Our weather is bleak, but I'm up for a game of golf. How about you?"

"Sounds great, David. Even if it is still drizzling rain, that is okay with me. I would enjoy a round of golf."

"I'll get us a tee-time for ten o'clock, Saturday morning, then. I'll grill the steaks for us when we're done. We'll catch up on everything."

"Thanks, mate! It will be good to get out. I'll be looking forward to it."

Before David signed off with his friend, he said, "Declan, maybe, just maybe, you should consider that you're being given a second chance with Liliana. Think about it..."

"I can't go there again, David. It turned out badly the first time. I've got to run now, so I'll see you on Saturday."

GREAT SADNESS

*S*tephan Lylestrom looked tired as he alighted from the car. It was the first week of April, yet the weather stubbornly continued to present freezing temperatures and snow. Stephan had driven to Rosemeade Township and back that day. Liliana and Jenny had accompanied him, and while he and Liliana had had a meeting with an old attorney friend, Jack Petty, Jenny had spent the afternoon with Christophe and Annie.

During their meeting with Jack Petty, Stephan had excused himself to take a call. That call had been from David Renton, and the news he had to share was not good. The intelligence David had relayed confirmed their suspicions regarding Sierra Monroe. She had been visited by two IRS agents, a plain-clothed police detective, and an insurance adjuster; all of whom wanted to know about her relationship with Richard Rawlings. It seemed that Ms. Monroe had been both cooperative and a wealth of information, but the revelations that David shared with Stephan had shaken him to his core.

David had related how Sierra Monroe and Richard had been lovers for ten years. She had shared to the authorities how Richard was trapped in a loveless marriage with a wife who did everything in her power to keep him submissive to her. Apparently, the wife was a trust-fund baby who had been spoiled rotten her whole life, so Richard had sought solace in Sierra Monroe's arms during stolen times from his said wife.

Ms. Monroe had even shared that she had met Richard on his wedding night after the shrew had treated him unconscionably because he was a virgin groom. Sierra Monroe had then proudly related how she had given herself to him later on his wedding night and had shown him how real women treat their men. These revelations about Richard's character had so saddened Stephan that he could barely muster the strength to return to his meeting with

Jack Petty and Liliana. All he could think about was how badly his bright-eyed Liliana Rose had been violated by such an unscrupulous man. Stephan knew in his heart that his beautiful daughter had endured more than any of them could even guess at the hands of Richard Rawlings, but he did not want to divulge any of these revelations to his wife or to embarrass Liliana with his knowledge. He bottled up his aching feelings and returned to his meeting with Jack Petty and Liliana.

When the family arrived back home to Reedsburgh that evening, Stephan excused himself and said, "I'm feeling slightly chilled. I think I might be coming down with something. Would you ladies mind if I turned in early this evening?"

Jenny Lylestrom went to her husband and put her hand upon his forehead. He did, in fact, have a slight temperature, so she urged him to take a hot shower and get a good night's rest. Stephan Lylestrom smiled at his best girls, "I'll see you two in the morning then." He turned and walked tiredly into the bedroom hoping his burdened heart was not noticeable.

"Mom, do you think he's alright?" a concerned Liliana questioned. "He's been pushing himself pretty hard trying to help me get Richard's affairs in order. When he stepped out to take a private call during our meeting today, he looked shaken when he came back into the conference room. When I inquired if anything was wrong, he just waved it off. I hope all of this business with Richard's affairs hasn't been too much for him."

"No, honey," Jenny answered. "He's enjoyed having his best girl as his number-one client!" laughed Jenny. She continued, "He's been invigorated lately. It's been good for him to work again."

"Well, I just don't want to wear him out, Mom."

Jenny Lylestrom kissed her daughter and said, "Your Dad would do anything for you, Liliana. He'll be good as new tomorrow."

The next morning, Stephan did not feel any better. He looked haggard and quite pale. Liliana was concerned and wanted to take him to the doctor, but he insisted he was fine. "Just give me a couple of days to shake this thing," he had said. Three days later, he was still stubbornly insisting that he was okay.

In the interim, Jenny started exhibiting similar symptoms, because she shared a bed with Stephan. Liliana was quite concerned for them both, so she called the local "Ask-a-Nurse" hotline. They assured her that both of her parents were exhibiting normal symptoms of this season's influenza. This reassured Liliana, so she prepared chicken soup and plenty of honey-and-lemon tea. But, by day five, she was starting to be quite concerned, so she called Christophe and Annie for some help.

Christophe and Annie were there within the hour, and both were surprised at how ill their two special friends really were. Christophe took Liliana aside and questioned her regarding the onset of their symptoms. She could not pinpoint anything out of the ordinary except that neither of her parents seemed to be getting any better. "Lily Girl, I don't want to scare you, but I think we need to get Stephan to the hospital. Let's call for an ambulance."

A horrified Liliana called the non-emergency number and requested an ambulance to be dispatched. She mentioned that both her father and her mother were exhibiting the exact same symptoms, but with just three days difference in the onset. The dispatcher was very kind and reassured her that the team would evaluate both of her parents.

While Liliana was on the line with the non-emergency dispatcher, Christophe went outside and placed a call to Declan. When Declan answered, a very grave Christophe said, "Declan, I need you to come to the hospital as soon as you can. Both Stephan and Jenny are quite ill with influenza, and I'm worried. Poor Liliana has been caring for them both, and I can tell she's quite exhausted. I need you to come to Reedsburgh to help us, son. Things are not looking good."

With absolutely no hesitation, Declan replied, "I'll be there as quickly as I can get there, Chris. I'll go directly to the Medical Center." Within thirty minutes, Declan had left his new manager, Tim Hill, in charge at the nursery, and he was headed toward Reedsburg. He was very concerned for both Stephan and Jenny Lylestrom, and his heart feared for Liliana. When Declan arrived at the hospital an hour later, he found Christophe and Annie looking shaken, and Liliana quietly looking out the window, but he could tell she was unseeing.

"How are things, Christophe?" Declan inquired.

"Declan, the doctor seems to feel that both Jenny and Stephan have contracted a strain of influenza that may have mutated into something more deadly. And, due to Stephan and Jenny's age, the doctor is quite worried they may not survive. The hospital staff is doing everything they can to make them both comfortable, but it's not looking good." Just then, the nurse came out into the waiting area and told Christophe that Stephan Lylestrom was asking for him. Christophe's usually rosy face immediately drained of all color as he headed toward Stephan's room.

After he had washed his hands thoroughly and put on a mask and gown, Christophe was led to his good friend's bedside. Stephan Lylestrom was awake now, but he could barely speak. He croaked out, "Chris, you've got to take care of Liliana, as she still does not have Richard's loose ends all tied up. She's going to need more help. I don't think I'm going to be here for her, Christophe! I know she's a grown woman, but you're still her god-parent. Please look after my daughter for me." Stephan Lylestrom then choked up, "I think I'm going home to meet my Maker, Chris, and I'm pretty sure Jenny is going with me, too."

Weeping, Christophe Riordan hugged his beloved friend, and said, "Stephan, I'll do everything you've asked of me and then some. I will see to everything for Liliana and take her on as my own daughter. You need not fear for Liliana; Annie and I will care for her. You are my best friend and my brother in Christ. I love you, Stephan, and you've lived an honorable life. Now, let me bring your sweet daughter in to see you."

"Thanks, man," Stephan wept.

As Christophe Riordan turned to leave, he stopped and took his best friend's hand. With tears in his eyes, and an overwhelming ache in his heart, he said, "Well done, my friend."

Minutes later, Liliana also arrived at her father's bedside wearing a mask and gown. "Oh, Dad," she had wept as she sat down on the side of his bed.

A teary-eyed Stephan Lylestrom reached for his daughter and hugged her as best he could. "My precious girl, I think we both know that I'm not going to get well. Liliana, I'm going home to the Lord…but, sweetheart, I want you to know that you have been such a joy in my life, and I want you to be happy. Better days are ahead for you, and Christophe will be there to help you with everything that is on your plate right now."

"Oh, Dad, please don't leave me, Liliana cried out. "I just barely got you back again, and I'll miss you so much," she sobbed. "You have been the best father in the world. I love you so much, and I thank you for everything that you have done for me in this life. Oh, Dad, you are so precious to me."

Stephan Lylestrom fought to speak, "Sweetheart, one more thing…it's Declan…If you ever loved him, baby girl, then patch things up with him. There is still time for the both of you to be close again… maybe even share a life together. We both know that he was a victim of Richard's deceit, too."

Stephan Lylestrom was then seized with a horrible spasm of coughing. When he finally stopped coughing, he held on to Liliana's hand tightly, and said, "Tell Mommy, I love her." He then wheezed, "I love my beautiful girl." Shortly, thereafter, he went to sleep and lapsed into unconsciousness. Two hours later, he was gone; taking Richard Rawlings' secret life with Sierra Monroe with him to his grave.

Forty-eight hours later, the same scenario played out with Jenny. She asked to see Christophe and Annie first, just as her husband had. She then asked that they look after Liliana and help her to get back on her feet again. Finally, she thanked them for being her life-long friends, and said, "I'm glad that I didn't have to live without my Stephan for very long. Now, please bring Liliana to me. I want my baby girl."

A sobbing Christophe and Annie gave her their pledge to help Liliana, they told her how much she and Stephan had meant to them over the years, and they prayed with her. They then dispatched Liliana to go to her mother.

A shaken Liliana then entered her mother's hospital room. Jenny Lylestrom held her daughter's hand and said, "Liliana, I love you so much, and you have always brought such joy to Daddy and me. I want you to have a happy life, baby. Everything is going to be okay; you'll see. Christophe and David Renton will help you see to things."

"And, Lily, I know that you and Declan once loved each other very much. If you two still care for one another, please fix things. You can still have a happy life together, maybe even a family. Sweetheart, I know Declan was your first choice, but I don't know what went wrong. In my heart, I know Richard had something to do with it. Liliana, mend your relationship with Declan! You won't be sorry. Declan has been so very good to all of us. Baby, I **know** he's the one for you." Jenny then sighed heavily, and a spasm of coughing took hold of her.

When her mother's coughing subsided, she said, "We both know that I'm going home. I'll soon be with Jesus. Don't weep for me, Liliana. I've had a wonderful life, and I want you to have the same."

Swallowing the utter sadness that was welling up within her, Liliana vowed to her mother, "I will have a happy life, Mom, and you have my word that Declan and I will be friends again someday, I promise. Oh, I'll miss you so much. Thank you for being such a loving mother to me."

And just like her husband, Jenny Lylestrom slipped into unconsciousness; only she had the luxury of not knowing anything more of Richard's unprincipled life. Three hours later, she departed from this world. A devastated Liliana just continued to hold her mother's hand until the orderly took her mother's body away.

As he had promised to her parents, Christophe Riordan took on his role as god-parent to Liliana. He comforted her in her sorrow, he helped her to make arrangements for her parent's burial, and he was there for her when the impact of her loss hit her about two days later, but though Christophe knew Liliana very well, when her overwrought nerves got the best of her, he felt paralyzed when she fell apart.

Both he and Annie looked to Declan, as he had once known her better than anyone. Quiet Declan, who had watched everything unfold from a distance the last few days, simply said, "She's gone nonstop for months now; she pushes herself until there is nothing left in the tank. She needs to rest." Declan went to her, as she sat weeping in her mother's bright kitchen, clutching a silver-framed photograph of her parents. He said nothing, but he sat down, pulled his chair closely beside her and put his arm around her shoulders. Overwrought, exhausted Liliana leaned into him and cried even harder. After a while, her tears subsided.

"Dearest Liliana," he said. You have not had an easy go of it lately. I suspect that you are worn down. You need to rest. Why don't you lie down for a while?"

With that, Declan Ryan did what he did best…he was strong, and he was steady. He simply helped her up and escorted her to her bedroom and helped her into bed. He then sat next to Liliana's bed for hours on end quietly reading a book while she slept. He knew she needed rest and a respite from her sorrows. When she briefly awoke or was fitful in her sleep, he would reach out and touch her shoulder or hold onto her hand and speak quietly to her. Somehow, steady Declan Ryan managed to soothe her.

DECLAN'S FAÇADE

eclan Ryan needed to be introspective, but too many changes were being volleyed his way in quick succession. While normally an avid reader, Declan found it hard to concentrate on his book while the woman who seemed to occupy his dreams of late was close by. He finally had to be honest with himself. When he had picked her up at the airport almost three months ago, he had thought he could be impervious to her effect upon him. Yet, when he had immediately picked her out of the teeming crowd, and her eyes had lit up when she saw him, the loving had begun again. He could not stop it; she simply was the only woman who had ever spoken to his soul. Why did she have this effect upon him? He had wanted to avoid her at all cost. What was it about her that was causing his mask of indifference to crumble?

While Declan pondered these questions, he looked about the room in which she had grown up. Much of the paraphernalia of youth had long since been packed away, but there were still a few vestiges of her happy young life scattered there. Tucked in the corner of a wall shelf was a framed photograph of the two of them with her college roommates, Suzette and Tracy. They were all standing just outside of the stadium at Brineforth University. It had been Declan's first tailgate party and his first American-style football game, and all of them had enjoyed themselves immensely that day. He and Liliana were happy in that photo, too. Neither of them had made any mistakes yet, and they did look completely delighted with one another.

Next, he looked at the small vanity table where she sat to ready herself each day…an atomizer of scent and a tube of lipstick lay in residence alongside a sparkling cut-glass dish that contained a few pieces of her jewelry. But the thing that surprised him the most about her personal items was a familiar pair of silver earrings and a silver bracelet adorned with charms that smacked of her old dog, Iris; both of which he had given to her. They were lying atop a small blue velvet bag. She had obviously had them out recently. He had kissed her quite passionately the night that he had given her the gift of those silver earrings. Even now, he could feel her tender lips and inhale her familiar fragrance from that evening, but something gut wrenching came to mind. When he had given her that summer-parting gift, he had failed to tell her that he loved her. Declan shook his head sadly.

There was much in that room that spoke quite vocally about Liliana and why he had once felt such tender affection for her. She had a half-read book open with a photograph of an aging Iris marking the page. Old Iris was sitting in front of the garden gate which was overflowing with June roses. There was a basket with crisply-ironed quilt blocks stacked inside awaiting assembly, and there was a pair of red high heels tucked beneath her nightstand. Liliana had never been an average woman. She had somehow managed to wrap herself in the femininity and the allure of a bygone era. She had always fascinated him. No other woman had…

While Declan sat, he looked at her face in slumber. He again noticed that she had a thin red scar immediately below her left eyebrow. He knew she had never had a scar there before, and he wondered how she had come by it. As much as he did not want to admit it, Liliana Lylestrom was back in his life. Somehow, just sitting next to her while she slept felt right. "How in the world had he found himself here with her again?" he wondered. Maybe David Renton was right…could this be a second chance?

When Liliana, at last, emerged from the cocoon of non-stop slumber the day before her parent's memorial service, she awoke murmuring his name. And, as he had done for the last day and a half, he reached over to touch her. Her eyes fluttered open, and she smiled at him. "You've been here with me while I've been sleeping, haven't you Declan?"

"Yes, Liliana, I have been here, " he quietly answered. "You have slept for almost two days. How are you feeling?" he asked.

"Comforted," she answered quietly. "I was dreaming about swimming at the lake like we used to, but for some reason, I found myself separated from you. I was calling your name when I woke up, and there you were sitting beside me. Thank you, Declan, for staying with me," she said softly.

Declan then smiled and squeezed her hand.

She softly whispered, "Declan, I had forgotten how handsome you are when you smile. You should do it more often, you know."

Liliana continued to look at him and returned his smile with one of her own while he sat there beside her. They continued to peruse each other. Declan knew she probably had not seen him smile once since she had returned to Reedsburgh. He understood, too, that she guessed he had purposefully been avoiding her these last few months. Instinctively, he also realized that some part of his self-imposed barrier between them had come down this morning.

"You're very kind, Declan," she murmured. "Thank you."

Declan Ryan said nothing. He just grinned and squeezed her hand again…the hand he had been holding since she had awakened.

ELUCIDATIONS

*D*eclan Ryan was puzzled. As he had watched Liliana from across the room, he could tell something was not right with her. Her parent's memorial service had been over for several hours, and only special friends had gathered together at her family home for afternoon tea, yet she had not once sat down. Her face seemed pinched, as if something was hurting her. He walked through the archway from the dining room to where she stood. Her breathing was a bit erratic, and she had light perspiration across her forehead.

"Liliana, are you alright?"

"Declan, can you get me out of here?" she whispered.

He took her by the elbow and moved down the hallway to ensure privacy. "What's the matter?" he asked, his heart beating faster.

"I think I'm having a miscarriage," she choked out as she turned toward the wall biting her pale bottom lip.

"How can this be Liliana? Richard has been dead these three months."

Liliana took a shallow breath and answered, "I know. I'm four months pregnant, Declan. Please, just tell Christophe to finish up with our people here at the house. Can you take me to the hospital? I think we need to hurry."

Stunned, Declan walked back into the dining room to where Christophe and Annie Riordan were seated chatting with old friends. Declan put his hand on Christophe's shoulder and whispered into his ear.

Christophe's quick look back at Liliana showed his deep concern, yet he knew her need for privacy. He handed Declan his keys and said, "Take my car, she'll be more comfortable. Annie and I will take your truck and meet you at the hospital later. Oh, and Declan, take good care of her; Annie and I know what she's feeling." Christophe then murmured a prayer, "Please, God, protect her."

Declan hurried back to where he had left Liliana, only to find that she was gone. The downstairs powder room was empty, and so was her room. He finally found her sitting in Stephan's little library, cradling her abdomen. Knowing he couldn't take her out to the car in front of guests, he opted for the French doors that led from Stephan's library through the frozen remains of the garden. Once outside, he lifted her slight frame into his arms and carried her to Christophe's auto.

As he hurriedly drove her to the hospital, feelings of fear flooded his heart. Nothing could happen to Liliana; they had just gotten her back. She had suffered so much loss these last few months. What if she died?

All these thoughts swirled through his mind. Liliana said nothing. She simply just sat there with her eyes closed clutching her abdomen. Her breathing was quite rapid and very shallow, now.

Finally, Reedsburgh Medical Center came into view, and he drove straight to the emergency entrance. The glass doors slid open, and an orderly hurried out with a wheelchair. Declan helped her from the car only to find that heavy blood had soaked her silk dress and lay coagulated on the lining of her coat which she hadn't worn; had only sat upon. He easily lifted her into his arms once again, and Liliana's head slumped into his shoulder as she began to lose consciousness. "Oh, Lord, please don't take her from us," Declan prayed. He ran through the doors carrying her while the young orderly abandoned the wheel chair and ran behind him, telling him which way to turn. Two female nurses appeared and directed him into an exam room.

"Do you know what's wrong?" one of the two women asked.

"About twenty minutes ago, she said that she thought she was having a miscarriage." Declan retorted. "She is four months pregnant."

"Okay, let's get her settled. I suspect she may have hyperventilated," said the nurse, whose name tag said, "Julia."

Declan sat down in a nearby chair feeling helpless. Why had Liliana not told them she was pregnant?" he wondered. It seemed to him that she would have been overjoyed about it. Something was not right here.

"Here she is…your wife is coming around, sir.

"Oh, she's not my wife. I'm just an old friend."

"Then, I'm afraid you're going to have to step out. It's 'family only' here," directed the younger of the two attending nurses.

Liliana, who had been lucid enough to understand what was going on, cried out, "Please, please don't send Declan away. He *is* my family." She then started to weep.

Julia Edmonds, the older of the two caregivers, saw the anguish on the young man's serious face, heard the panic in the young woman's voice, and knew instinctively that something more was going on between these two than met the eye. She didn't know what exactly was happening, but it screamed of devotion. Julia Edmonds had compassion, and she had tenure, so she took charge of the situation. "No, Kara, I don't think this gentleman needs to leave. Obviously, our patient needs his support. We'll overlook things today. Go tell the admitting nurse to come in."

Declan solemnly nodded his head, "Thank you, ma'am."

"Thank you, Nurse," Liliana hiccupped, as another spasm seized her. Declan Ryan was out of his chair and holding her hand before Nurse Edmonds could even retort.

He stroked Liliana's cheek with the back of his fingers and whispered, "All will be well Liliana. All will be well."

Julia Edmonds left the room with tears stinging her blue eyes. "Those two definitely care for each other," she thought to herself.

Minutes later, the physician came into the exam room. He shook Declan's hand, "I'm Dr. Caprizo. I understand your lady here is trying to miscarry."

Dr. Caprizo then looked into Liliana's eyes and said, "Let's just take a look at you and see what's happening." The doctor then proceeded to examine her. "I'll need you to scoot down just a wee bit further and put your legs into the stirrups." Declan was horrified, but Liliana held on to his hand tightly. There was no escaping this, so he stepped back toward her shoulder and looked away to his side.

"You are right, young lady; you are in the throes of a miscarriage. It shouldn't be too much longer. I'll be candid with you. In these situations, the chromosomes usually have not stacked up correctly. When that happens, Nature just takes its course. It's not easy, I know," he said gently. "Would you like something for the cramping?"

"No, thank you, doctor," Liliana replied solemnly.

Kind Dr. Caprizo patted her arm, "Don't worry, dear. You, and this young man of yours, are healthy people. There will be other babies for you. I'll be back to check on you in a while." With that, gray-haired Dr. Caprizo left them alone, turning the lights low as he departed.

"Is there anything I can get for you, Liliana?" Declan inquired.

"No, Declan. I'm okay," she said softly. "I'm sorry if I have embarrassed you in any way. I guess we really do know each other well, don't we? And, look…I got blood all over your lovely new shirt."

Declan shot her his rare and beautiful smile and said, "Oh, Liliana, my mum used to make me do the laundry when I was a boy. There isn't a stain that I can't get out. She taught me well." He then proceeded to roll up his sleeves and loosen his silk tie. Liliana loved him for it.

In less than an hour, Liliana passed the tiny fetus. Afterward, she felt emotionally and physically drained. She was wheeled to the fourth floor to a private hospital room, where a kind older nurse helped her to bathe and put on a fresh gown. Declan stepped out into the hall to place a call to Christophe and Annie.

"Oh, Declan, we have been worried sick, but have just now gotten everything buttoned up here. I'm sorry that we weren't there for the both of you," Christophe sighed. "Is Liliana alright?"

"Yes, Chris, she was a trooper. She cried when they tried to toss me out of the emergency area, and a kind nurse took pity on her and let me stay. I must say, I was ready to bloody someone's nose if they had not. I know those people had no idea of what has happened to her lately; they were just doing their job. But her tears got to me when she begged for me to stay with her."

"Oh, Declan. This has been a very hard day for all of us. I'm so sorry for Liliana. Since it is so very late, Annie and I will stay here at Stephan and Jenny's. Would it be a problem for you to stay with her tonight at the hospital, son? She needs someone to be there for her."

"No, no…it is no problem for me. The hospital staff assumes that I am her husband now, so they would think me an ogre were I not to stay, Christophe. Her doctor feels she can be released in the morning, if everything stays static, so I'll bring her home to Stephan and Jenny's house tomorrow."

"Thank you, Declan. I know this hasn't been easy for you either. We'll talk tomorrow, then," and Christophe signed off.

Declan entered Liliana's room to find her sleeping, so he went to the hospital dining room and had something to eat. From there, he found himself in the hospital gift shop where he purchased some flannel pajamas and slippers for her to wear home. He was sure that her dress was ruined. All the while, he was pondering why Liliana had told no one she was carrying a child. Not sharing such a thing was so unlike her. It was almost as if she was ashamed. His gut told him that Richard Rawlings had something to do with her shame.

When he returned to her room, the lights had been turned out, so Declan sat down in the recliner next to her bed. He heard her stir.

"Declan, is that you?" she inquired softly.

"Yes, Lily, it is I," he quietly answered.

"I feel you need an explanation about some things," she whispered.

"Only if you want to..."

"Please, Declan, lower the rail on the bed and come sit here with me. What I have to say is not easy for me, but I feel I must share it, for you to understand my silence about that poor, tiny baby."

Declan, lowered the rail, turned up the lighting just a bit, and perched on the side of the bed facing her. He noted that her coloring had improved, but her respirations were still shallow and slightly irregular. He attributed it to her duress.

"I know that the things that have happened to me these last three months are more than you ever cared to know about me, Declan, and I wouldn't blame you for feeling that way. But, because you had to help me today, I feel you need to know why I had told no one about being pregnant."

"I'll admit it has been puzzling to me, Liliana, but your private life is none of my concern. You are a grown woman."

"Well, lest you think I've been dallying with a lover, Declan... No, I have not," she gulped out.

Liliana soldiered on, "The last few years of my marriage with Richard were pretty much a nightmare. Even from the beginning, things were never easy between us, but I tried my best to make him happy. The deeper Richard found himself in trouble, the more disdain he had for me. After ten years of cruel comments, harsh criticism, and his constant anger toward me, my feelings for him had completely eroded. But I continued to stay the course."

"Four weeks before he died, Richard sunk to a new low. He was physically abusive to me, Declan...over nothing. I had not crossed him. I had not found fault with him, yet he came home from his office and was immediately quite violent with me. He handled me very roughly; then, he slapped me several times. He took hold of my upper arms and shook me until I thought my teeth might fall out; all the while screaming obscenities at me. I tried to get away, but he slugged me with his fist so hard that it knocked me to the floor. I was dazed and could not immediately get up. He towered over me with a look of disgust on his face."

"When I was able to get to my feet, I told him that if he came near me again. I would call the police; he knew I was serious, so he backed off. I locked myself in our bedroom, and he began to demolish our home. He broke our dining-room table and all its chairs into kindling. He demolished a very large wall-mounted mirror into pea-sized bits of glass, and he overturned a china cabinet destroying the entirety of its contents. The cacophony from his rampage was deafening."

"From there, he went on a drinking binge. And, know this, Declan...Richard never drank. Several witnesses reported to the police that he had verbally abused patrons in a little bar along the coastal road. The police officer, who came looking for him at our home the next day, indicated that Richard had hit the owner of the bar and knocked him to the floor. After he left that bar, several motorists contacted the police about his erratic driving. That same policeman saw my bruised upper body and my blackened eye. He read between the lines, Declan. That kind young officer encouraged me to see a physician to stitch up my eye. I was pretty shaken up. He could have hurt someone that night with his anger and his drunken driving."

"He did hurt someone, Liliana, he hurt *you*," a horrified Declan bit out.

Liliana continued, reliving the events of that horrible night. "When he came home very early in the morning, it was obvious that he was drunk. He kept trying to get into our room. He cried and banged on the door apologizing for his behavior. I did not let him in. Then, he was silent. I was pretty sure that he had fallen asleep or had passed out. Several hours later, when he did wake up, he again knocked on the door, begging to apologize. After what seemed like hours of his begging, I finally opened the door just to get him to be quiet. He couldn't believe his eyes. His knuckles had torn the skin just below my left eyebrow. It was still seeping bloody fluid. The entirety of my eye was pretty much swollen shut and was very badly bruised, and I had purple knuckle marks on my face from my cheek up to my brow. His large fist had done its work well."

"As if his violence wasn't enough, he then wanted to make love to me to apologize for hitting and hurting me. He kept trying to hold me and kiss my wounds. He wouldn't stop kissing me," she sobbed. "It was awful, Declan. I think his ardor for me was flamed only because he had entered new territory, and it was exciting to be violent. He begged and begged to let him demonstrate how much he cared for me. He just wanted to assuage his own guilt, and I didn't want him to touch me. He kept nagging to let him make love to me. After hounding me and hounding me, he became violent once again, and he then forced himself upon me. It sickened me. I could not tolerate his touch. Prior to that night, he hadn't wanted me or even touched me for well over two years. I am pretty sure he was involved with someone."

"He left town as soon as he had selfishly "shown his love" for me. I didn't even know where he went, and I didn't care. It was a relief just to be left alone. He was gone for four weeks, Declan. I learned that he had lost his job once again; otherwise, he wouldn't have stayed away that long. I was left to clean up the damage from his rampage and to make up excuses to the physician who sutured my wounds. Richard was gone for the entirety of the Christmas season. The accident happened when he was returning home on New Year's Day. He died four days later, and I turned up pregnant…too ashamed to even tell my parents that I was carrying their grandchild."

"But Declan, know this: I had no idea I was even pregnant until two weeks ago. This is a bit embarrassing to tell you, but my cycle has never been regular. I can go thirty to ninety days without a period. They have always been that way…I never even suspected I might be pregnant. I only went to the doctor because I was **so** tired; I thought for sure I had something wrong with me. Oh, Declan, I could not believe it when the panel of blood work revealed that I was pregnant. My feelings for Richard were dead long before I ever conceived his child in such an ugly way. I wept bitterly at the news, and that sounds so very hardened on my part, I know. That baby had **not** been conceived in love, but I would have done my best for it."

With that, Liliana started to cry.

Declan Ryan was speechless. His heart ached for her, and he could not believe how horribly Richard had treated such a wonderful woman. Intuitively, Declan knew Old Jim would have wept his eyes out had he known what had happened to her. It was merciful that he had passed.

"Oh, Liliana, I am so sorry that Richard hurt you. How could he have treated you thus? Richard was an odious man. You should have called someone to help you. Didn't you know any one of us would have come for you if we had only known you were suffering?"

With tears glistening in his eyes, a heartsick Declan Ryan could no longer keep a mask over his emotions. He passionately entreated her, "Liliana, I have queried myself dozens of times over the last ten years as to why you chose Richard Rawlings. Why did you marry someone who treated you so abominably?"

She looked down, was quiet for a few seconds, and softly stated, "You really don't know why I married Richard do you, Declan?" She was shaking her head slightly. Her pallid expression was somewhat strained, and her brows were slightly knit together, and she said quite simply, "I married Richard because you never asked me. You didn't want me. Did you not ever feel anything for me?"

Declan felt as though he had been struck. He looked at her steadily. His countenance was sorrowful, and he inhaled deeply. He began to shake his head in disbelief. Then, he closed his eyes as he tried to rein in the anger that he was feeling. When he finally opened his eyes, he looked squarely into her tear-filled green eyes. He raised his quiet voice slightly, "Do you *not* know that I have loved you…almost from the very first time I saw you?"

"Do you *not* know that I had nothing to offer you, so I let you marry Richard? You saved yourself for him, but I wanted it to be for me," he bitterly choked out. "My heart was thoroughly broken the day you married him. I have suffered, Liliana. My soul could not forget you… Do you *not* know these things?"

"I have lived my life trying to be content with others, but I *cannot*. You are the only woman I have ever wanted. I cared for you enough to give you up once because I thought you deserved someone better. I thought you wanted Richard, and he seemingly appeared to be able to give you everything that I could not."

Declan continued, his Scottish burr thickening as he spoke. "Richard was a detestable man, Liliana. He trampled upon you. He hit you. *He* hurt you! These are things that I cannot stand to even think about," he said passionately. "How I wish I had been selfish and declared my feelings for you, even if I had nothing but myself to offer you. At least, I would have been honest; something Richard *never* was!"

Liliana looked steadily at him, her breath now coming in gulps. She was fighting for control and her face was already slightly swollen from crying. Looking at him with an unreadable countenance, she said, "Declan, did you *not* know how much I wanted you to care for me?" Liliana continued with fervor. "I would have been over the moon to know that you loved me. Yet, you never let me know your feelings for me. Oh, you were very sweet to me Declan Ryan. I knew you missed me every year when I went back to school, but you still never told me that you loved me! Why, Dec? I still ache to know. You are not the only one who has suffered!"

Declan wiped an unbidden tear from his cheek and responded, "I cherished the time we spent together, and I wanted only the best for you, Liliana. I was already a man; you were still a precious young woman. I felt so much older, and I did not want to force a relationship upon you that you might not have been ready to embark upon. Believe me when I say that I loved you very much, Liliana, but I knew you deserved and needed to have life experience before you married, so I was waiting for you. That, coupled with the fact that I didn't have much to offer you those first few years that I was here in America, held me back."

"I know that I had my chance for four beautiful summers in a row, and I never told you how much I truly cared. I will be regretful of that choice for the rest of my life. Lily, I felt that you held a lot of affection for me, and I had planned to declare my sincere love for you that last summer when you arrived back at Rosemeade Township. I wanted to make plans with you because I had so much more to offer you by then, but I was too late. Richard delivered you to Old Vineyard Road in his expensive automobile. I ***thought*** he was more educated than I, and that he possessed a job that was proving to be quite lucrative. How could I compete with that, Liliana? I watched you let him touch you possessively. I thought you wanted him, too, and I was devastated."

"Late, that last summer you were with us at the nursery, just before you left to go back to school at Brineforth, I tried to say something to you. Do you remember, Liliana, that you became defensive? We had a falling out. That night, I couldn't sleep because we had never quarreled before, and I ached for you."

"Because I wanted so desperately to right things between us, I drove over to your little apartment at midnight, and when you answered your door, I could tell you had been crying. That night, I held you until your tears were spent, all the while deciding to declare my love for you at last. I was even going to ask you to make plans with me for a future together, but Richard's call interrupted us just as I began my declaration… Do you remember that you wouldn't answer me when I asked if it was Richard? Sweet Lily, I interpreted your silence as your choosing Richard instead of me. I left with a very heavy heart."

"A week and a half later, I watched you drive away with that man…that horrible, ***lucky*** man. Though I did not care for Richard,

I tried to respect your choice. Before I knew it, you were wearing his expensive engagement ring. You had made your decision, Lily. But now, I wonder if you were, perhaps, coerced, manipulated, or maybe even bullied into marrying before you even had time to finish your student teaching by selfish Richard."

Shaking her head and wiping unbidden tears off her cheeks, Liliana emphatically retorted, "I did have Richard's attention back then, Declan. He was a man; not a fraternity boy. He lavished me with attention and treated me like a woman. Stupidly, I was flattered, Declan. I did spend a bit of time with him at school that last year; yet *you* were the only one I truly wanted., and I kept telling him that…"

"I thought that you might love me, too, because you always showed such tenderness toward me. It always gave me hope, but you kept yourself in check, Declan. I longed to kiss you and to hold you, but I had been raised to be a lady. So, I waited for you to tell me that you cared first. You *never* did. I wanted so desperately for you to love me, Declan!" she gasped out convulsively. "I finally had to accept the fact that you didn't want me. It was a very difficult thing for me."

Unashamedly, she continued, "Do you know that I counted the days until I could see you again every time that I was separated from you, Declan? Do you know that if you had just said the word, I would never have agreed to marry Richard? Instead, you just stepped aside and never even let me know that you truly cared for me."

"That afternoon, when we quarreled about Richard, you held me tightly in the cab of your truck. You kissed my cheek very tenderly and told me you were sorry, but I wanted you to kiss me until I was crazy with passion for you. Know this, Declan Ryan, if you had just said *anything* that day, I would have been yours forever." Again, she wiped her tears away.

A bit more softly, she said, "It was always you. And now, it appears that Richard's ill-timed phone call interrupted your declaration of love for me as well as our future!"

Sweet, exhausted Liliana, who was lying back on the elevated hospital bed, started to reach for him, stopped herself, then bit on her lower lip as she tried to keep herself in check. As Declan watched her try to keep her emotions reined in, the last of his weary resolve crumbled.

He quickly moved from his seat on the edge of the bed. He sat down close beside her and held her near; his hand tenderly cradling the back of her head. He kissed her on the temple and gently touched his lips to the healing scar just below her left brow, fading evidence of Richard's cruel treatment.

Declan Ryan then softly declared, "Oh, Lily! There has never been a day when I have **not** loved you." Then, holding on tightly to each other, the two of them grieved about things that could not be changed.

Finally, with their turbulent emotions spent, slumber overtook them both. The last thing Declan remembered before losing himself in sleep was Liliana grabbing a tuft of his bloodied dress shirt in her hand, and whispering emphatically, "I can't bear to ever be parted from you again, Declan Ryan!"

When Nurse Julia Edmonds' Emergency Room shift ended at seven o'clock the next morning, she went upstairs to check on Liliana Lylestrom. She had thought about that young woman's desperation throughout her shift. She could tell that those two young people were pining for each other, but she didn't know why. It didn't matter. She just wanted to make sure that they had a chance with one another.

After checking in at the nurse's station, she tiptoed down the silent hallway and peeked into Room 423 West. She smiled at what she saw: That handsome Scotsman was lying propped atop of the blanket on the upright hospital bed with his arm around his love who was bundled beneath that same blanket and swaddled in the sheet. Her brunette head lay upon his chest, and her right hand was grasping a handful of fabric from his bloodied dress shirt, as if she was fearful that he might disappear. His large hand lay gently cupped over her small wrist. Both were sleeping soundly.

Nurse Julia Edmonds drove home hoping for only the best for them, for she knew they had suffered heartache. She couldn't wait to tell her husband how true love had prevailed in the ER last night.

A NEW DAY

*L*iliana **Lylestrom** awakened feeling hope; something she had not felt in years. She was in Declan Ryan's arms; a place she had once wanted so desperately to find herself. She studied his sleeping face…so serene, so peaceful…in slumber. She breathed in his scent. His skin always smelled so good. He had shown compassion for her yesterday, when she had felt very alone in this world. "Declan Ryan," she whispered, "you are a fine man."

Declan Ryan awoke, saw that she was alert, and smiled his rare smile. His longish hair, which he wore combed off his face, was tousled. Liliana noticed that it had just a few strands of bright silver laced throughout it now, and the effect was perfect. His brilliant blue eyes shone. Declan cupped her cheek with his hand.

"How are you feeling?" he asked softly.

"Purged, Declan…better than I have felt in a very, very long time. Oh, Dec, thank you for your honesty and for staying with me."

"Liliana, you know that I would do anything for you."

Dr. Caprizo chose that moment to burst through the door of her room. "How are you feeling today, young lady? You look much better than you did yesterday. Let me just check a few things, and I have a feeling you'll be able to go home this morning."

Minutes later, the kind doctor declared her to be ready for discharge, gave her some instructions to follow for the next few days, and advised her to see her primary physician before resuming her regular schedule. He winked at Declan as he left, "You've got a lovely wife there. See to it that you give her plenty of babies! **You** are a very lucky man."

As they made the drive from Reedsburgh Medical Center to Liliana's family home, Liliana looked at Declan's profile while he drove. She knew he was deep in thought about something. She said, "Dec, I know you have someone special now. My mother told me."

"Yes, Liliana, I have been spending time with someone that I finally thought I might be able to commit to, but since I came to fetch you at the airport three months ago, I've not been able to give myself to her fully. Believe me, I tried to fortify myself by avoiding you, but somehow, my resolve eroded. Unknowingly, you have stirred my heart and my soul again. I must be honest with Kristen and tell her that there is no future in our relationship."

"Kristen Bellyer is a very good woman, but it is you who moves me, Liliana," he quietly stated. "My heart has always been yours. I know that we have cleared up things that once hindered us, and I want you to know that as much as I care for you, I will never pressure you to enter into any relationship with me, unless you desire it. It is of no matter to me how long you need for your healing; just know that when you are ready, I will be there for you."

Liliana touched his heart when she answered, "Oh, Declan, knowing that you care gives me hope that I can emerge from this nightmare to, one day, forge something new with you. But I don't ever want Richard's unfinished affairs to mar our feelings for one another. I feel a need be rid of his encumbrances before I can move on. How I hope it doesn't take forever."

Declan reached for her hand and kissed her soft palm. "As I said, Liliana, I will wait for you. Take all the time that you need."

When they arrived at her family home, Liliana sighed. "Somehow, this place seems hollow now, Declan. I had such an idyllic childhood, here in this home. It was always filled with happiness. I know that both of my parents lived good, long lives. But still, I can't help but feel that they were taken too soon. I'm so glad that I had these last few months with them. Dad was my rock while we traversed the craziness of trying to settle Richard's affairs. He and David Renton made a great team. Then, my sweet mother and I were able to spend some time just being together…something for which I had longed. I am so thankful for such precious times."

Seeing them pull in the drive, Christophe and Annie came out of the house with open arms. Liliana was exceedingly glad that they were there; it somehow made her home seem a little less empty. Declan helped her from the car, put a protective arm around her shoulders, and led her up the steps to what was left of her family.

Annie, who knew the heartache of losing three babies, held Liliana close. Christophe kissed Liliana's cheek, then Annie's, and said, "Declan, help me get my best girls packed up and home to Rosemeade Township. I suspect you'll agree with me that there will be plenty of time for Liliana and David Renton to settle things over the next few weeks. Right now, we all need to retreat to Old Vineyard Road for a while to soothe our aching hearts."

SEEING IS BELIEVING

Christophe and Annie Riordan instinctively knew something had changed overnight between Declan and Liliana. Their first suspicion came when Declan pulled into the drive at Liliana's family home. Though he wasn't smiling, Declan looked as if a burden had been lifted from his shoulders. His blue eyes had none of the wariness that had been so predominant the last few months. Then, when he emerged from the car, he quickly went to the passenger side to help Liliana out of the vehicle. Both noted the extreme gentleness he extended to her as he slipped his arm protectively around her shoulders. All the while, Liliana looked into his eyes with a devotion that was palpable.

Neither of them knew whether to be overjoyed by the change or to be wary of what was to come. Both Christophe and Annie knew how Declan had suffered after Liliana had married Richard. Though he had never said there had been anything between them; anyone, who had ever been in love, recognized Declan and Liliana's sincere affection for one another. Christophe and Annie Riordan asked themselves, yet again, "Why had she ever married Richard Rawlings?"

Once inside her family home, Declan led Liliana to a chair, and went outside to retrieve the rest of her things from the car. Liliana watched him leave with the same warmth in her eyes. Christophe dipped his head slightly as he met eyes with his wife. Both he and Annie realized that something had definitely changed between their beloved Declan and Liliana.

"Can I get you anything, sweetheart?" an understanding Annie inquired. "Did you have breakfast at the hospital?"

Liliana smiled at her and replied, "No, thank-you, Annie. I am just fine. I feel better than I have in a long time."

Since everything was in order at Stephan and Jenny's home, it took just a few minutes to pack up for the ride back to Rosemeade Township. Christophe had already alerted David Renton that Liliana would be staying with them for a few days, so it didn't take long for the four of them to be on their way back to Old Vineyard Road. As Christophe and Annie drove along the county road in companionable silence, both were wondering what was being discussed in the truck that was following them…the late-model pick-up, occupied by Declan and Liliana.

When they arrived home, Christophe and Annie again watched Declan tend to Liliana with the greatest of care. Admittedly, she looked fragile, so Declan's attention was understandable. Liliana let him escort her into Christophe and Annie's home, and deliver her to their guest room. Christophe and Annie followed behind carrying her make-up bag and a small suitcase. Christophe whispered to his wife, "Something has definitely changed here…I wonder if he'll broach the subject with us?"

Annie whispered back, "I don't know if he will, my love, but I can tell they are both quite pleased with whatever has changed."

Declan proceeded to tuck Liliana into the downy soft guest-room bed. He then ran the back of his fingers along her pale cheek and told her to rest. All the while, Christophe and Annie Riordan stood by amazed at what they were witnessing.

While Liliana slept, Declan very sadly related to them how Richard had brutally hit and injured her, how she had become pregnant with Richard's child, and lastly, **why** she had married Richard Rawlings. Christophe and Annie wept over these revelations; both for Liliana and for Declan.

Finally, Christophe Riordan wiped his eyes and said, "God heals all wounds, Declan. Now is the time for each us to revel in His care… Annie and I for the loss of our best friends…Liliana for the loss of her beloved parents and for the loss of her bond with you…and you, son, for all the suffering you so needlessly endured at the hands of a deceiver. May we all find our stripes healed."

"Annie, my love, why don't you and I prepare some afternoon tea while Declan checks on our special girl. We could all use a good cup of tea to fortify ourselves, 'eh?'"

"I couldn't agree with you more, dear," Annie smiled.

After her well-deserved nap, Liliana enjoyed afternoon tea with Annie, Christophe, and Declan in the library of their family home on Old Vineyard Road; something the four of them hadn't done in a years. She was wearing her new pajamas that Declan had chosen for her. They were red flannel pajamas, with Golden Retriever Puppies cavorting all over them. She was still a bit pale, and she wore a slightly-wonky ponytail from her nap, but she had a smile on her face. Looking at each special person around the tiny tea table, she thanked God that He had brought her back to them…beautiful silver-haired Annie, ebullient white-haired Christophe, and serious mahogany-haired Declan…these three meant everything to her. They were her family now.

Later that evening, after Declan had gone out to the nursery to button things up for the night, Christophe invited Liliana into his study. "Liliana, I want you to know that Declan has been candid with us about the physical abuse you endured at the hands of your own husband. No woman should ever be treated in such a fashion. Only the lowest of men hit their women. I am so sorry, my darling girl. If any of us had only known your trials, we would have made every effort to protect you. My heart hurts because you suffered in silence, Liliana."

"You know, too, that your parents even suffered because of Richard's selfishness. I feel that he purposefully ensured that you were estranged from them. You were forced to go for years without the love and support of your own people. It was unpardonable behavior on Richard's part to prevent you from seeing them. And lastly, both you and Declan have suffered because of Richard's deceit. Our Declan gave you up because he thought Richard could provide for you more robustly than he…it tore him up to see you leave with Richard. These things are hard for me to bear because Richard's actions have hurt everyone that I hold dear…but I must forgive him these indiscretions, Liliana, because I have been forgiven much myself."

"I know, too, that you have turned the other cheek, dear girl. Your father was very proud that you went to Richard's parents and gave them special remembrances of their son's life to cherish. You saved face for him, Liliana, even though he was most undeserving. Such kindness of character is why we all love you so much."

Christophe continued, "Now, tell me what you would like to do after we get everything squared away with both Richard's affairs and your parents' estate? Would you, perhaps, like to teach little ones again?"

Liliana sighed, "Oh, Christophe, I feel somewhat paralyzed right now. Though the house in Seattle has sold, and David Renton's people there are handling the liquidation of all the remaining assets, Richard's debts are still very prohibitive. I don't even know if there will be legal action taken by the family that Richard injured on Snoqualmie Pass with his cowardice. I had hoped that my trust would help pay off his debts, but we both know he pilfered that money, too. I will probably go back to teaching again, but I fear it will take the rest of my life to pay off his creditors."

"Christophe, you know that Mom and Dad left everything to me, but I'll have to sell my family home and liquidate all my parents' assets to pay for Richard's debt, too. David Renton tells me that after the proceeds from Mom and Dad's estate are applied, I will probably still have about $1.5 million left to pay off from Richard's outstanding debts. I guess I need to win the lottery," she sighed. "Oh, Chris, how I wish I could start my life over again…not the childhood part…that was great…just the last ten years. Sometimes, I wish that I could have a do-over…you know?"

"What would you do differently, Liliana?" Christophe asked quietly.

"Well, first off, I would never have married Richard."

"Oh, Liliana," Christophe sighed. "I am so sorry about all of it."

"I know you are, Chris."

Christophe Riordan then continued, "But seriously, when were you the happiest?"

Liliana smiled, "Right here, Christophe. Those were four very special summers that I spent working for you at the nursery. I so enjoyed helping Declan with his vocation and his research. Don't get me wrong, I enjoyed teaching, too, but working hard and honestly, working the soil, nurturing what God has created…these are joys that bring great satisfaction and happiness to me. I so desire to live simply like that again. Believe me, I treasure the time that I spent here in Rosemeade with you and Annie."

"Well then, let me give you that "do-over," Liliana. Why don't you move to Rosemeade Township? I'll give you a good job. And, you can live in Old Jim's cottage. I suspect that he is jumping for joy in his grave right now just knowing that I'm offering you his old place. It will be your own home, and it will also be my gift to you, Liliana. You need never worry about a roof over your head ever again."

"If you choose to move here, you can spend as much time as you wish with Annie and me, and if you desire to be alone, that is okay, too. You have dealt with too much sadness this year, and now, it is time for you to have a refuge from the worries of this world. You'll feel better being here with those who love you best."

"Oh, Christophe, I don't know what to say," whispered Liliana. "You are too generous."

"Well, dear, you are our girl now, and Annie and I take care of our own. You may be a grown woman, Liliana, but long ago, I pledged to care for you in the event something happened to your parents. Well, they are gone now, and I love you like you are my own daughter. Let me give you my fidelity and my support. You'll never be wont for family here."

Getting up from her chair, Liliana went to Christophe. Standing on her tip-toes, she put her arms around his neck and kissed both of his weathered cheeks. She said, "I love you Christophe Riordan, and I accept your precious gift of love and fidelity to me. I am proud to be counted as your own."

Annie, who had been shamelessly listening outside the door, burst into the room and said, "Oh, Liliana, we are the ones who are blessed to have you. I'm overjoyed to know that you'll be here with us once again. We've all missed you more than you'll ever know."

KRISTEN

*K***risten Bellyer** knew something was up with Declan Ryan as soon as she saw him. He had driven up to Reedsburgh almost two weeks ago to help friends…old friends, who had subsequently died within two days of each other, from a virulent strain of influenza. These people were the parents of Liliana Lylestrom, Christophe Riordan's god-daughter; the same woman who had just lost her husband earlier in the year.

From what Declan had briefly told her, the deceased couple, Stephan and Jenny Lylestrom, had been good friends of his since he had immigrated to the United States. Christophe Riordan and his wife were the Lylestrom's close friends, too. Chris and Annie had dropped everything when word had come that their old friends were gravely ill, and Declan hadn't been far behind them. She hadn't heard anything from him since the day he had left. She hoped that everything was alright.

At the end of the school day, she cleaned off the chalkboard in her classroom and prepared her lesson plans for the remainder of the week. She straightened the rows of little desks and looked about her colorful room; pleased with the art projects that covered the east wall, and her "Spring Kites" bulletin board. She laughed, once again, at Jimmy Hoffenagle's self-portrait. "That kid is so funny," she whispered to herself. Kristen was just getting ready to leave when she heard a soft knock on her classroom door. Though the door was open, Declan Ryan, who was always courteous, waited to be invited inside.

"Hello, Declan! Please come in…I'm glad to see you made it home safely. How is Christophe's god-daughter doing?"

Declan Ryan came through the door of her classroom and sat down in the wooden chair next to her desk. He seemed concerned about something. Kristen knew something was amiss, so she asked, "Is there something wrong?"

"Yes, Kristen," Declan replied. He looked out the window, but Kristen knew he was unseeing. They had been dating for about five months. She cared for him, and she was starting to recognize his moods. They had spent a fair amount of time together, but Declan had been somewhat detached lately…since early January really. When she thought about it, Kristen decided things hadn't been the same since Declan had been dispatched to bring Christophe's god-daughter home from the airport.

"You didn't answer my question, Declan. How is Christophe's god-daughter?" she asked, understanding starting to dawn.

"Liliana has had a very hard go of it these last few months, Kristen. She has been strong, but she still needs support, he answered."

"Oh, I see. And, you are giving her that support, Declan?" Kristen asked with an edge to her question.

"Yes, Kristen. I am helping her bear her burdens. Liliana and I have been friends for many years," Declan quietly answered.

"Well, that explains volumes," Kristen bit out angrily.

Unwilling to be reeled into an argument, Declan got to the subject at hand. "Kristen, I have enjoyed getting to know you these past few months, but I have to be honest with you about Liliana. I find that I still have feelings for her; strong feelings for her. I cannot continue seeing you any longer, Kristen. It would not be fair to you. You are a lovely woman, and I had thought that I could finally stop holding myself back and, perhaps, move forward with you; but it is not to be."

"Does Liliana return your **strong** feelings, Declan? What about her dead husband? Does she not have any allegiance to him? Why is he just barely in the grave! That poor man…she must be quite the lady," Kristen bitterly retorted.

"Kristen, you are not acquainted with Liliana. Please, don't malign her. Ours is a long history, and you know nothing of it. Please refrain from these accusations. It is beneath you."

"But Declan, she is using you. Don't you see?" she gritted out. "I am sorry that she has had to face tremendous losses of late, but she is clinging to you because she has no one left. If she cares so much for you, why did she marry someone else?" Kristin asked angrily.

Stung, Declan ran his hand through his hair. "She married someone else because I was a fool. I don't intend to let it happen again." With that, Declan rose from his seat and said, "I am truly sorry, Kristen. Please forgive me. I never intended to hurt you in this fashion." He then stood up and walked out of her Third-Grade classroom.

A saddened Kristen sat at her desk for another twenty minutes. She was angry, yet ashamed of her outburst to Declan. She had behaved badly in front of him. He was right. She did not know their circumstances. She only knew that she was thirty-two years of age, living in a tiny, little town without many available men, and Declan Ryan had been a very special guy. She hated to give him up. In a way, though, she was glad he would not be baited by her hurtful accusations of the woman he loved. It showed his integrity. She would sincerely miss him.

"Dating is such hard work," she said aloud to herself as she turned out the lights in her classroom. Her musings continued as she gathered her things to go home. "I'm going to have to apologize to Declan for my outburst, but not for a few weeks or maybe even a few months. I need to pout a while longer. I hope that Liliana Lylestrom is worthy of him." She thought on these musings as she stalked down the shiny, freshly polished hallway floor of Rosemeade Township Primary School. The bell tower on the Village Green was just then chiming five o'clock.

As she burst through the door of her school, Kristen breathed deeply of the cool evening air. She could tell that spring was just around the corner. "There isn't much left of this school year. Maybe I'll start looking for a new position in Reedsburgh," she thought to herself. "At least I won't have to be subjected to seeing Declan and his girl every time I turn around or hear the small-town gossip about their rekindled love! Yes, that is what I'll do. I'll start looking for something else!"

A FIRST BURDEN LIFTED

*L*iliana Lylestrom was finally feeling some hope. Three weeks after the death of her parents, after what everyone hoped was the last snowstorm of the season, Liliana was ready to move into the vintner's cottage. After a series of meetings with David Renton, Christophe presented Liliana with the title and keys to the cottage at David's office. It was obvious that David was very pleased for her. He shook her hand, and then pulled her into an embrace. "I hope you enjoy your beautiful little home, Liliana. It's already got your special style written all over it."

With tears in his eyes, Christophe told her how much he loved her. Liliana had wept happy tears and kissed him. With his gift, Christophe had taken a large burden off her shoulders. She now had a place to live with freedom from worry. It was a very happy afternoon in David's handsome, wood-paneled office. The lamps were lit in the waning light of the late afternoon, and his assistant brought in a tea tray filled with the steaming brew as well as sweets, and savories. For the first time in several months, Liliana visited with David and Christophe and their conversation contained nothing pertaining to debt, lawsuits, or death. It was a welcome change.

The following day, Christophe and Declan helped her to move into her new home. The last of the spring snow storm had receded, and Liliana had spied snowdrops and crocuses valiantly emerging from the slushy wet earth. It was a sign that spring and summer were well on their way. It had been a harsh and heartbreaking winter, but now Liliana had to admit that things were getting better. She really didn't have much to move to her new home: several suitcases of her clothing, a few special keepsakes she had saved from her parent's house, her old blue and white sewing machine, and a raggedy white teddy bear. Declan, who had moved Liliana's things several times before, had never seen a teddy bear in her belongings. He asked, as he held up the skinny, little fellow, "Liliana, who might this be?"

She answered as if her response was the most-natural thing in the world. "Oh, that's Eddy. I saved him from the close-out table at the student union bookstore my last year at Brineforth. It was right after Christmas, no one had purchased him, and he was wearing an ugly metallic holiday bow. So, I counted out my money and bought him. I took him back to my apartment and proceeded to cut off all his uncomfortable trappings. We've been very good friends ever since. Lately, I've taken to sleeping with Eddy because I've had a bit too much trauma in my life. He comforts me."

Declan tried to stifle a smile. He looked the stuffed bear squarely in the eyes and replied, "Well, Eddy, I suspect you are a fine little fellow, but I hope that I don't ever have to compete with you for Liliana's attention. Do you understand me, mate?"

Liliana looked at him with a knowing smile. She replied softly, "Don't worry, Declan, you need never fight Eddy nor anyone else for my attention."

Some scrabbling noises on the porch made her turn her head; Christophe entered the cottage carrying her worn French blue chairs from her first little roof-top patio. Liliana was delighted, "I **have** been given my old life back! Thank you for saving them for me, Christophe."

"Don't thank me, Lily Girl," Christophe laughed. "You can thank Declan for saving them for you. I was ready to give them to Good Will several years back, but Declan assured me that you might need them for something someday. He tucked them away for you."

Liliana looked at Declan, and with a nostalgic smile, said, "I'm glad that you felt I might need these again, Dec. Thank you for saving them for me."

With a similar smile, Declan replied, "Perhaps, we might enjoy time in them again someday," as he set slightly worn Eddy Bear upon the fireplace mantel.

That evening, as Liliana prepared to go to bed, she found a vellum envelope lying upon a cardboard box next to her bed. It was addressed to her in Declan's flowing script. Inside was a letter that read:

Sweet Liliana,

As you fall asleep this evening, please know that I, too, will be in bed thinking of you and longing to hold you. For now, I'll assign that wonderful task to young Eddie Bear, that lucky ball of fluff...

And welcome home to Old Vineyard Road again, Lily. It's wonderful to know that you are safely tucked into the old Vintner's Cottage tonight, and I look forward to seeing you in the upcoming days. I couldn't be happier to have you here again.

In the event, you find yourself questioning my affection for you, please know that I love you far more than I can adequately express, but know that I will always be counting the days until I can see you again. In the interim, let's both take comfort in looking forward together.

It has always been you,
Declan

DAVID'S DISCLOSURE

David Renton felt it was finally necessary to tell Liliana about Richard Rawlings' relationship with Sierra Monroe. So, the week after she had moved into the vintner's cottage, he texted Liliana and asked if he could drive out to Old Vineyard Road to meet with her.

Liliana's heart pounded in her chest when she answered David's text affirmatively because she suspected David had been withholding something from her; it seemed that he and her father had been exchanging phone calls frequently the last few days before Stephan became so very ill. She didn't know if she could embrace any more damning evidence that might have been uncovered about Richard, and as she readied her new home for the two o'clock meeting, she felt slightly dizzy with worry.

David, too, worried as he drove the familiar highway between Reedsburgh and Rosemeade Township. He was apprehensive about how Liliana might take the news he was bringing. Something told him to alert Declan Ryan about what was happening. Dialing Declan's cell number from the console of his car, David was relieved when Declan answered on the third ring…

"David, my friend, what's up?"

"Declan, I just wanted to alert you about something because I feel pretty strongly that Liliana will need someone with her after our meeting this afternoon. I'm on my way over to the nursery to meet with her right now. Are you going to be on-site this afternoon?"

"Yes, I'll be in all day…is everything okay?"

David began, "I don't necessarily want to violate her client privacy, Declan, as her father was the only other person who knew about the bombshell that I have to reveal to Liliana today. Stephan was heartsick about it when he found out just the day before he became so sick with the influenza. Today, I really would prefer that it be you who is her strength. Christophe tells me that you have been there for her lately; something that I am very happy to hear."

"We have worked through some impediments, David, and I have vowed to her that I will be there for her; but I'm giving her as much space as she needs for mourning her losses. I don't see her regularly at all. She lives quietly, but alone, in her cottage right now."

"Christophe told me that you were the only one who knew what to do when she fell apart after her parents' deaths," David responded.

Declan sighed, "Yes, that is true, but she was very exhausted and overwrought by the loss of both of her parents. I did what anyone would do, I held and consoled her while she cried it out; then, I just put her to bed. She slept non-stop for almost two days, David. It was hard to see her like that…"

"Listen, Declan, Christophe mentioned that even though she slept, you never once left her side. He indicated that he and Annie watched as your indifference toward her seemed to slip away. Don't try to skirt this issue, my friend; I suspect you two have some kind of understanding because I know you both pretty well. She looked closer to our regular Liliana last week when the papers were signed for the cottage than I have seen her look since she returned. Declan, I know you had something to do with it. As I've said before, you two seem to be ordained for each other. But all I am asking of you today is to check on her after I leave for Reedsburgh. I won't push you any further on the subject at all."

"Thank you, David," Declan replied. "You have my word that I will check in on her…I'm guessing your news might be a set-back?"

"You are right, Declan. What I must tell her is odious. I'm not particularly looking forward to it, but it must be done. I'll let Liliana choose if she wants to share any part of it or not. I'll talk to you later, my friend."

With that David signed off and thought about how he was going to broach such a delicate subject with Liliana.

When Liliana opened the door to welcome David to her new home, she looked apprehensive and for good reason. So much had been volleyed into her court the last few months that he really couldn't blame her for feeling anxious. After their initial greetings to each other, Liliana got right to the point for his visit. She opened the floor with a simple question.

"David, has something gone wrong?"

Looking slightly uncomfortable, David replied, "Not really wrong, Liliana, but a new facet needs to be fashioned for Richard Rawlings' class ring of a pathetic life. I'm so sorry to be the bearer of such tidings, dear one. I do hope you'll forgive me." And so, David began…

"Liliana, when I received the initial investigative reports on Richard, I noticed several entries that linked him with a woman named Sierra Monroe. Her name was attached with Richard's on three recorded titles for houses in Chicago, Denver, and Seattle. It appeared that she moved every time that you and Richard were relocated. As if that weren't enough, she was listed as the primary owner of a money market account which forensic investigators found Richard was using to hide the monies he stole from his clients and most-likely from your trust fund."

"As well, Sierra Monroe had been Richard's secret lover these last ten years. I'm sorry to tell you this, Liliana, but she is even five months pregnant with Richard's child."

"Apparently, they met on the night you were wed to Richard and had been together ever since. Yet, she did not even know that Richard had killed himself. According to recorded statements she made to the forensic investigators retained by my firm, she asserted that 'Richard was trapped in a loveless marriage to a very difficult wife who would not give him a divorce; a woman who emasculated him at every turn; and who was extremely dominating.' Once again, it appears that Richard masqueraded as a Harvard MBA graduate in addition to the same lies about the death of his parents in an explosive automobile accident."

"When Ms. Monroe found out that Richard was dead, she was devastated. Apparently, he had been with her for the entirety of the four weeks that he went missing. When he left her on New Year's Day, he told her that he was going home to ask his 'difficult wife,' for a divorce once again so he would be free to marry her."

An ashen Liliana sat quietly and listened as David continued to tell her the remainder of Sierra Monroe's history with Richard. She wasn't really surprised about any of these revelations, but what made her want to vomit was that both she and Sierra Monroe had likely conceived a child from Richard during the timeframe of his violent rampage and subsequent disappearance. Sierra Monroe was a woman who had likely been used by Richard, and she, herself, his wife of almost ten years, had been maliciously maligned to his lover. Both had been ruthlessly duped by conniving Richard. She wondered if there was anything that he wouldn't have stooped to in order to come out on top.

In her heart, Liliana hoped that somehow, someway, Richard had truly loved Sierra Monroe. Because if he had conceived a child with her in love, at least there had been some shred of decency about his wasted life. She already knew that Richard had only wanted her for a tick-mark on his corporate bucket list, and that he had purposefully set out to separate her from Declan when he realized that Declan was vulnerable from the great losses that had left him alone in this life. All these revelations truly saddened Liliana.

"What about all the money, David?" Liliana inquired. "Is there anything left for Sierra Monroe to raise Richard's child? Is there anything left to repay the clients from whom he stole assets? Is there a possible forensic trail of how the life insurance money might have been used? And, how about the trust fund monies?"

David answered, "Well, Liliana, some good has come from uncovering Sierra Monroe. The money trail from the pilfered client monies led right to Sierra's money market account, which is now frozen. So, those funds will likely be returned to Richard's former clients. It appears Richard wove a gnarly web with your trust, though, so the forensic accountants are still working on it. If it's any consolation, Sierra Monroe must sell her assets, too, just as you have done, Liliana. She knew nothing of the money fund account or the money that passed through it. Richard had forged her signature on the bank documents. I'm quite sure that the insurance monies were used to purchase the expensive homes that Richard provided for her, and when those monies were gone, that was when he bullied you to let him manage your trust fund."

"David, did my dad know anything about this?" Liliana quietly asked.

Sighing, David shook his head affirmatively. "He did, Liliana. It was only just a few days before he died that I gave him all the news about Sierra Monroe. You two were over at Jack Petty's office in Rosemeade Township, and Stephan stepped out to take my call. He was very saddened and had hoped to be the one to break the news to you." David Renton then sadly shook his head, "I'm so sorry about all of this…"

"Oh, David, this is just one more way that Richard has reached out in death to take a swing at me. Surely you know that none of this is your fault; even if you *are* the messenger. I would like to think that Sierra Monroe will not malign me any further or that she will understand that Richard's characterizations of me were false."

David reached out and squeezed Liliana's slender shoulder, "Don't worry, we're going to get this mess cleared up and launch you back into life again. You're just going to have to be patient a bit longer. But, you're sure to land on your feet, Liliana. We're all going to see to it!"

That evening, as Liliana looked out her window at the sunset and mulled over the day's newest revelations about Richard, she was surprised to hear Declan's quiet knock on the door. When she opened it, he stood there with a rounded loaf of artisan bread, a small brick of her favorite cheddar-chive cheese, and a bottle of red wine. Under his arm, he held the blue quilt she had made for him a long time ago. She had given it to him just before her twentieth birthday.

"I thought you might just be in need of special sustenance tonight, Miss Lylestrom," he smiled.

An unbidden smile stole onto her face as her eyes traveled over the proffered gifts of food loaded into a small wooden box in his arms. "Oh, Declan, did David Renton ask you to do this?"

"Not really, Liliana. He only asked if I would check in on you this evening, but the bread, wine, and cheese were my own idea. Am I interrupting you?"

"No, not at all; I am very happy to see you. Please, do come in."

As Declan entered the old vintner's cottage, he noticed that she had already started prepping the walls for painting. Most of her moving boxes had been emptied, but Eddy Bear was no longer sitting on the mantle. "Tell me, Liliana, where is your little gentleman friend?"

Liliana laughed and replied, "Young Eddy is currently slumbering in my bedroom awaiting my arrival at ten o'clock tonight."

"Well, I hope he has been good company for you of late…"

"Yes, he has been good company. He is always upright; he is never critical of me; and he is always scented of sandalwood. Kind of like you, Declan." Liliana then took hold of his hand and led him into her kitchen. "Come, let's eat your feast at Old Jim's table."

Within minutes, Liliana had produced a tablecloth, wine glasses, plates, a tiny platter of fruit, and garlic-stuffed olives to add to Declan's gift. They ate their meal in companionable silence with an occasional smile from Liliana when Declan would give her a quick wink.

When most of the food had been consumed, Declan asked, "Would you like to discuss your meeting with David this afternoon?" It was at this juncture that Liliana's composure started to slip. A tear or two rolled down her cheeks as she nodded affirmatively to Declan who rose from his seat at the table and took her hand. He led her to the sofa in the old-fashioned parlor on the opposite side of the cottage. On the way, he picked up the blue quilt.

As Liliana sat facing Declan on the sofa, she related David's revelations to her from earlier in the day. Declan witnessed a change in her countenance as she let down her guard and finally let her tears flow. All the while, Declan was astounded anew at Richard's arrogance and his ability to weave his lies around and around his innocent victims until they were so ensnared that they couldn't get away from him. It appeared that Sierra Monroe had been his latest casualty, but Declan had to admit that what shocked him the most was that Richard had slept with her on his own wedding night with Liliana. What sort of a man would do that? If that weren't enough violation of Liliana, Richard had then had the audacity to continue in a relationship with Sierra Monroe right under Liliana's nose for ten years; all the while eroding her sweet-spirited disposition by demeaning her. Yet, it was the canceled insurance policy beneficiary monies and Liliana's trust fund that had likely funded his double life with Sierra Monroe. How shamefully Richard had behaved.

After she had shared most of the details from her meeting with David Renton to Declan, Liliana said something that truly surprised him.

"Do you want to know something, Declan? I had become somewhat hardened to Richard's offensive comments over the years, but I hope that he never treated Sierra Monroe that way. Even if she is a woman of questionable morals, no one deserves such treatment. As well, I hope that he did have sincere affection for her and that their child might have been conceived with love and tenderness."

"Declan, I'm pretty sure that Sierra and I became pregnant within hours or just days of one another because she is just barely five months along. I would have been five months pregnant right now, too, if I had not miscarried. It makes sense that Richard would run to her arms that awful night, all the while attesting to my ill treatment of him, and then languish a full month with her before returning to face his consequences with me. And yet, her conception of Richard's child was likely a bit more caring, while mine was a brutal, ugly conception… born of rape. Isn't that just like Richard?"

"My prayer is that Sierra Monroe conceived with no fear of Richard in her heart. I hope that she and her child will be able to live a happy life; even if their economic circumstances will be considerably less comfortable than she has been used to living with Richard all these years. I feel he has used her just as abominably as the rest of us because she, too, is now in need of selling off all her assets in order to pay for Richard's deceitful behavior."

Declan pulled her close, but could only utter, "I am so incredibly sorry." while he held his smooth, freshly-shaved cheek against hers.

Declan held her to himself for several minutes before asking, "…and Stephan knew of all this, Liliana?"

"Yes, Declan, he did. We were visiting his old attorney friend, Jack Petty, here in Rosemeade Township, the day he received David

Renton's call. He stepped out for several minutes to speak with David, and when he returned to Jack's office, he looked tired and slightly hunched. I had never seen his countenance like that before. Dec, I don't know if he was starting to feel the onset of influenza that day or if he was just feeling plain old grieved about the news from David, but my Dad went to his grave knowing in his heart that our family had been thoroughly violated anew by Richard Rawlings. It hurts me just to think of it, Declan." With that, Liliana's tears began in earnest.

With great compassion, Declan held her closely to himself and wrapped the blue quilt around her slight frame. He began to stroke her back with a rhythmic cadence and spoke very quietly, "All will be well, Liliana. All will be well. Things can only get better."

As twilight was enveloped by the velvety dark of night and a fresh moon started to peek over the mountain, lamplight shone softly in the vintner's cottage. Declan continued to hold Liliana within the folds of the soothing blue quilt she had made for him so long ago. As Declan held her, he thought she had slipped into slumber, and found he wanted to doze off, too, when her eyes opened, and she reached up and laid her hand on his cheek. She spoke softly and said, "Declan, thank you for soothing me tonight. You are a very compassionate man; how did you get to be so kind?"

Declan smiled down at her and replied, "I'm not anyone out of the ordinary, Liliana. I was simply raised by a lovely mother who lost her beloved husband very early in life. She poured herself into my upbringing because I was all that was left of my father. She and I were very good mates, and she modeled caring and compassion. Not every child gets that gift in this life. I was very fortunate, indeed, to have had her."

"Did your mother rock you a lot when you were little, Declan?"

"Oh, yes, she did and, at the end of her life, I rocked her.

"Oh, Declan..."

"It's true, Liliana. She was so fragile the last few weeks of her life that I would carry her out to the garden to sit in the shade in my granddad's old rocker. One day, I noticed that she was too weak to even make the chair go, so I sat in that chair and rocked her."

"You've never told me that before, Dec..." Liliana quietly whispered

"I know, Lily… It was just a few days before my mum died. As I rocked her, I told her what a fine woman she was, and I thanked her for being such a wonderful mother to me. She fell into a peaceful sleep that day, so I took her out to the garden the next day, too. That day, we sang a few of the old hymns together, and she praised God for all he had done for her before she fell asleep. But the next morning when I came to her room; I could tell that she was in the early throes of death. I was stunned, but I still asked her if she would like to go down to the garden. She wheezed out an affirmative 'yes,' so I wrapped her in my dad's favorite tartan blanket and carried her out to the garden in the cool of the morning."

"Liliana, it was only about seven o'clock, but the sun was already coming up, and the birds were chirping and flitting around the yard. It was late March, but for some reason the weather was unseasonably warm. Mum always had a beautiful garden, so as I rocked her, I described what was blooming. There were primroses, blue hyacinths, pansies, and ruffled pink tulips that morning. It was almost as if God had planned their blooming just for her. Again, I was able to tell her how much I loved her, and she briefly opened her eyes, Liliana, but they weren't looking at me; they were focused on the gate adjacent to where we sat. She said, 'James!' Then, her breathing just stopped. I think she saw my father."

This time, it was Liliana who embraced and held Declan while he shed pent-up tears. He unabashedly let his tears come because he had never shared any of the details of his mother's death with anyone, and he needed to articulate the solitary sadness he had borne all alone from her passing. After sharing such sadness with Liliana, he felt as though he had just re-lived that beautiful-but-heart-wrenching morning. This time, though, he had someone beside him who cared for him; someone who held him while he finally let go of his grief that had been suppressed for way too long.

That night, Liliana and Declan fell asleep together beneath that blue quilt with a myriad of colorful stars upon it. They slept deeply on Liliana's sofa with her back against his broad chest and his backbone flattened against the backside of her sofa. Liliana called it, "spooning," but whatever one called it, the comfort of being so near to one another after a very emotional night was cathartic.

As Declan prepared to leave early the next morning, he held Liliana to himself and again touched his lips to the scar left behind from Richard's heavy hand. He inhaled the sweet fragrance of her hair but made himself step away. He said, "I am being stern with myself this morning. There is nothing that I would like to do more than spend the day with you, Liliana. As we both agreed, you need space and time to heal from these revelations in your own way. Just know that I am here whenever you need anything. Right now, all else pales in comparison. Don't ever forget that you are treasured."

Liliana was touched by his candor and stepped toward him. She put her arms around his neck and laid her smooth cheek against his now-whiskered one. She then quietly spoke from her heart. "I hope that *you* know that you are treasured as well, Declan Ryan."

QUIET DAYS

*L*iliana continued to keep a low profile in the weeks following her move to Rosemeade Township. Periodically, she borrowed Annie's old Porsche roadster and drove into Reedsburgh to meet with David Renton, but most of the time she stayed in her little cottage healing her badly-bruised heart. There were mornings when she awoke and shuffled out to her tiny kitchen for a cup of coffee only to look out the window and see Declan already working hard in the nursery. On those days, she secretly admired his healing way with both people and plants. She would never forget his kindness to her the day she had found out about Richard's double life.

Other times, she joined Annie in her sunny kitchen, and the two of them would bake together or just visit about any and everything. At last, it was finally starting to feel like spring, and Christophe's nursery was coming together. Liliana had to admit that she had been stunned by all the improvements which had been made in the ten years she had spent away from Old Vineyard Road. The nursery was just now starting to be dressed in all its seasonal finery and was adorned with handsome old-world stone walls and fencing that Christophe and Declan had erected in the years she had been away. As well, she couldn't believe how Declan had harnessed the wildness of the abandoned vineyard rows which were now impeccably groomed. Liliana had always loved the nursery and thought it very pretty, but she could now see that Declan's eye for design had transformed it into something very special.

She, too, had an artistic eye, and she restyled the vintner's cottage into her own home. It was a very quaint little house to begin with, but in her mind, it was still Old Jim's place. A fresh coat of paint on the inside, and some plantings around the yard began to make her feel that it was hers. By the time early May rolled around, the little vintner's cottage added another dimension of beauty to an already very picturesque landscape.

Though she lived at The Old Vineyard Road Nursery, Liliana still did not see much of Declan. True to his word, he was giving her the time she needed to grieve the loss of her parents and to work through what had happened during her marriage to Richard. She respected Declan for keeping his word but found that she sorely missed his company. Seeing him through her window hard at work made her want to visit with him. Early, one unseasonably-cool May morning, she found she could not wait any longer. She brewed the kind of coffee that she remembered he once enjoyed and went out to see him.

Declan Ryan was deep in thought mending a broken fence post when he thought he heard someone come up behind him. He turned around and was surprised to see who his early-morning visitor was... There stood Liliana holding two mugs of coffee. She was dressed in the familiar red flannel pajamas that he had given to her, and she was wearing her well-worn Wellington boots. As well, she was bundled into a heavy knit sweater, and her hair flowed in waves around her face and shoulders. She was smiling tentatively at him.

Completely delighted, Declan greeted her. "Good morning, Liliana!"

"Good morning to you, too, Declan," she said as wreaths of frosty breath floated around her shy smile. "I brought you a mug of coffee to ward off the chill in the air. Here…" She then handed him the mug of steaming brew.

Taking a swallow, Declan was rewarded with the flavor of a perfectly-blended cup of coffee, laced with just the right amount of cream and sugar. "Liliana, you remembered how I like my coffee." He said this with a pleased smile.

"Declan, I remember because you are the one who introduced it to me!" I enjoy it this way quite often."

"Well, thank you for such a thoughtful gesture. How have you been these last few days?"

Still somewhat shy, she answered, "Oh, I've been getting along fairly well. I'm starting to feel like the vintner's cottage is really mine, now. I guess you could say that I'm settling in. By the way, Dec, thanks to you and Christophe for preparing the soil for my vegetable garden and for mulching the flower beds. It was very good of you."

"Oh, it was nothing, we were glad to do it."

Not wanting her to leave just yet, Declan turned an empty five-gallon paint bucket over and patted it. "Here, have a seat, Liliana." He then proceeded to pull up a bucket for himself and sat down upon it beside her. It felt right just sitting next to her in the fresh, yet unseasonably cool, morning air. He noted that there was a flush to her cheeks which he hadn't seen since she'd returned, and her eyes were brighter…those green eyes which always managed to reel him in. In all, she was looking much healthier. He was pleased. Then, he said, "You're looking well…"

"I am feeling much better, Dec…Better than I have felt in a very long time, in fact." Shyly, she finally got to the reason for her visit. "Declan, as I go about my day, I often spot you out my window, and I have to admit that I've wanted to see you again. That's why I'm here this morning. You were so good to me the other night after David brought harsh news."

Feeling that familiar pleasure that Liliana always seemed to bring, brought Declan's rare smile to the forefront. Yet, what he really wanted to do was pull her into his arms and hold her, but he kept control of himself. Instead, he simply said, "I'm glad you came, Liliana. It's very good to see you this morning. Soon, the busy season will be upon us, and there won't be much time for an early-morning cup of anything! So, let's enjoy our time together while we can."

From there, they chatted easily about an assortment of subjects, and before he knew it, his mug of coffee was gone. Liliana rose to leave, Declan handed her his mug and quietly said, "Thank you, Liliana. I'm glad that you came. I've wanted to see you, too." She didn't exactly give him her beautiful electric smile, but she did present him with a very-pleased countenance.

Softly, she responded, "Then, I'll be seeing you again soon."

With that, she was on her way back to the vintner's cottage. Declan watched her walk back along the path to her home. Her long brunette hair swayed back and forth as she walked. He had to admit that she had looked refreshed and much healthier. He took these signs as progress, though he knew in his heart that she had many more miles to go until she could embrace life like she once had.

About a week and a half later, Declan chanced to meet Liliana again very early one morning as he was just returning from a sunrise ride in the foothills. She was standing on her tiny porch as he came down a small trail behind her cottage on his old motorcycle. He stopped and called to her, "Liliana, you are up early! Are you alright?" As she turned to face him, he could tell that she was smiling, yet he knew something was off. He got off his bike and tentatively opened her gate and took a step into her yard. "Liliana, you've been crying."

She smiled and gave a small laugh. "You are right, Declan. I have been crying. Sometimes, my dreams torment me; it just happened again this morning. I came out to get a breath of fresh air, but I'll be fine."

"I'm sorry. I thought you were feeling better about things," he said.

"Oh, I am feeling much better…but sometimes, I'm awakened by the subject matter in my dreams…and that's usually when Richard stars in them." She then shook her head and rolled her eyes.

"Well, if it's any consolation, I awakened way too early this morning myself. That is why I rode up the hill to watch the sun rise. Can I do anything for you?"

"No, I'm fine, Dec. Why don't you come in and join me for a cup of coffee…"

"Thank you, Lily. I could do with a fortifying brew." Feeling pleased at her invitation, Declan proceeded to walk the rest of the way into her yard and up to her porch. He noticed that her hair was still damp from bathing and that her fragrant essence brought summer to his mind.

"I'm happy to see you this morning, Declan," she said as she led the way into her little cottage.

As Declan followed her into the shiny kitchen, he noticed that she had obviously been working very hard on the place. The aged black and white tile floor had a new sheen to it that surprised him, and all the old-time appliances were sparkling. Liliana had rejuvenated the old cottage. Once again, she had infused her refreshing spirit into something quite inanimate and transformed it. He thought to himself that it was interesting how she could do that to anything…from a sorrowful young man from Scotland to an ancient refrigerator! She was really something.

Within minutes of his arrival, Liliana handed him a delicious mug of coffee and a plate of freshly toasted home-made bread, slathered with melting butter. As they sat at her kitchen table and munched on the delicious breakfast fare, Declan noticed something. Her kitchen was very comfortable, but it had no plants. This was not like Liliana at all, so he questioned her about it.

"I notice that you've neither a jug of flowers on your kitchen counter nor any African violets on your windowsill, Liliana. That is not like you. May I ask why?"

She immediately looked down at the floor for a moment or two. When she looked up, she regarded him earnestly. Sighing, she said, "Well, Declan, I guess I'm pretty much out of practice on that front. You see, Richard prohibited flowers and plants in the house, and he outlawed flowers out in the yard. I don't know why, but I've always suspected it was because they reminded him of the nursery and those dearest to me. To be candid, he never let me have any type of a garden. Our landscaping was always sterile; quite cold really."

"Liliana, I'm sorry to hear that. I know how much you used to enjoy nurturing your colorful plants. Would you like a few things from the hot house?" At his question, her green eyes lit up like a starry evening sky.

"That would please me immensely, Declan. You might remember my beautiful violets from my little garret over the bookstore."

"Indeed, I do. That is why I inquired about them…that, and the fact that I am a bona fide horticultural geek!"

Liliana's tinkling laugh then rang out. "Declan, you are so funny. It's one of the many things that I admire about you." Her face shone with affection.

Knowing when to take his leave, Declan said, "Well then, I'm off. Thank you so much for a delightful half-hour. The coffee and the toast were delicious, but it was your company that was the best. Drop by the hot house soon and choose a few things. Just text me whenever you are ready to come."

Laying his hand upon the doorknob, he turned back toward Liliana and said, "Try not to let Richard *star* in your dreams anymore, okay?"

Her electric smile then flashed his way as she said, "I'll do my best."

Declan Ryan then departed; leaving her standing in her handsome little kitchen looking pleased and slightly wistful as she watched her front door close with a click. He didn't know that after her door closed, she shut her eyes and breathed in his inimitable scent.

WAITING

L iliana Lylestrom was patient. Though she wanted take Declan up on his invitation to select some special plants for her new little home, she didn't want to appear overly anxious. She waited for a full week before texting him saying, "If you have some free time, I would love to take you up on your offer to choose a few plants from the greenhouses."

Minutes later, Declan texted back, "Can you meet me in twenty minutes at the loft? I'm just finishing up with a vendor."

Twenty minutes later, a showered and soap-scented Liliana walked up the path toward the stone barn and the stairs to Declan's loft. She hadn't been there in years, but the earthy fragrance of the ancient barn was just as she remembered. She quietly ascended the wooden stairs and knocked on his door with a thumping heart. Her trepidation was not unfounded.

When Declan opened the door, she realized that she now saw him through a woman's eyes. He was dressed in his work clothes, but she could tell he had just shaved his usual three-day stubble from his face. As well, his hair was freshly combed and was slightly damp. Lastly, his shave cream, soap, or whatever it was that left such a memorable scent that she always associated with him, took her back to their very first meeting so many years ago.

Today, she found herself slightly shaken because he had taken time to look his best for her; even in the middle of his busy work day. At present, she thought he was even more evocative of an exceedingly handsome man than he had been on their very first meeting when she was only a young coed. Her heart started fluttering within her chest, and she found herself feeling nineteen years old again.

She tried to swallow the butterflies that were buzzing around in her tummy and finally managed to find her voice, "Hello, Declan."

He looked admiringly at her. She knew he was admiring her because an errant dimple appeared on his left cheek...somehow, she had forgotten that detail about him until just now. But all he said was, "Good afternoon, Lily. Please come in."

Declan ushered her into the loft and told her to have a seat. She sat down in his favorite old chair and scanned the room. There had been changes since she was last here. Oh, his keys, a thumb drive and a host of other "Declanesque" things were still strewn about on the leather desk blotter that adorned his ancient desk…but, it was a series of small paintings that caught her eye. They lay slightly askew on the corner of his desk…they had been beautifully framed; yet it was obvious they had never been hung up, as they were still bound in a clear wrapping. She walked over to look at them. She was very surprised at what she saw.

In those little paintings, she saw herself and Declan replicated from days gone by. They were precious petite canvases depicting their times swimming and picnicking at the lake, dancing under the stars with Fourth-of-July fireworks exploding overhead, and finally, the two of them sitting up on her old rooftop patio in the salvaged French blue chairs. He had even depicted aging Iris lying beneath their feet and her cherished orange geraniums. She was so taken with his artwork that she didn't even hear him come to stand beside her.

"Those were intended to be a gift to you a long time ago, Liliana. I happened across them several weeks ago when I was looking for something in my desk."

So very surprised by his talent, she spoke earnestly to him, "Declan, these paintings are priceless. You captured the both of us perfectly. I can almost smell the wood smoke at the lake! Oh, I knew you were a fine botanical watercolorist, but you are an exemplary oil painter as well. But, Declan, why did you not ever give them to me? I would have treasured such a gift."

"It doesn't matter now, Liliana. I had almost forgotten that I had painted them, he answered quietly."

Still, she persisted in her inquiry. "Declan, why?"

Shaking his head, he said again, "It really is of no matter, Lily. Let's not go there."

"Declan?"

Sighing, Declan gave in, "Okay, Liliana, if you must know, I was planning to give them to you that very last summer you came to Old Vineyard Road for your work. I was going to declare my love for you and ask if you might consider a life with me after you graduated from Brineforth. I truly wanted to make plans for a future with you, but you arrived with Richard. I don't need to say anymore. We both know how that summer season went down."

Stunned, Liliana looked at him with the sheen of tears glistening in her green eyes. "You were right, Declan, we shouldn't have gone there. I'm sorry that I pushed you for an answer."

"Don't fret about it. It's okay." Declan then extended his hand to her, "Come now, let's go choose something for you in the greenhouses."

Declan continued to hold her hand as they wended their way through the soon-to-be-blooming nursery. Colorful pansies were everywhere. There was a smattering of early-season clients scattered about, but the nursery staff was taking care of them. Before she knew it, Liliana found herself completely alone with Declan in the slightly perfumed and heavy air within the largest of the three greenhouses on the property.

"Have you heard anything from Christophe and Annie since they left for France?" she asked. "I suspect they are having after-dinner wine and sharing a dessert at some perfect little bistro in Paris right now, if I know those two!"

Declan smiled and said, "I suspect you're right on that one. They are really enjoying life right now, and they deserve to get away together occasionally. They've worked very hard all their lives. I'm glad they are finally taking some time to relax."

Laying a hand on the small of Liliana's back, Declan led her deep within the greenhouse to a table that housed a breathtaking array of African violets. Liliana was thrilled to see such a colorful collection. That old feeling that she got whenever she was in the greenhouse came back tenfold…she poured over the violets with great pleasure and even momentarily forgot that she was there with Declan. Finally, she looked up and saw that he was watching her. They were standing very close to one another. She could hear his steady breathing.

Then, he murmured, "Do you always wear black tights and a tiny red dress when you are shopping for violets, Liliana?" She looked steadily at his very serious face and, once again, saw that same errant dimple come into view.

Equally serious, she continued to look at him and answered, "No, Declan, only when I am shopping for violets with you." She then looked away; she could feel her cheeks flushing.

Declan stepped closer to her and put his hands on her upper arms and gently pulled her to himself until they were face to face; their lips almost touching. Taking a breath, he said, "You look extraordinarily beautiful today, and I would love to thoroughly kiss you right now, Lily, but I won't. Instead, I will tell you again that I will continue to wait for you to mourn your losses and to heal."

Liliana's lips were almost poised to kiss Declan's, too. Her heart was thudding, she leaned into him just the tiniest bit further and whispered, "I long to spend time with you, Declan Ryan." She sighed and laid her cheek upon his chest.

Declan then embraced her. He held her close with his large comforting hands moving tenderly over her back and shoulders. Finally, he said, "I'll not mar your healing time, Liliana. Someday soon, everything will fall into place for us, and we will make up for lost time." He then kissed her softly on the cheek and reluctantly broke their embrace.

Liliana was visibly shaken, so Declan smiled boyishly at her and, once again, held out his hand, "Come, let's finish your shopping."

After she had made her selections from the greenhouse, Declan escorted her back to the vintner's cottage pulling her plants in a small wagon. When they arrived, he carried everything into her little house and then readied himself to leave.

"Thank you very much, Declan, for taking me to the greenhouse today. I'm so pleased to have some violets again."

A contrite Declan then said, "Liliana, I almost lost my head with you today. I'm truly sorry."

"I'm not sorry, Declan. You made me feel special today, and I haven't felt special in a very, very long time. She then smiled warmly. "I thank you for a memorable afternoon."

As Declan turned to depart, he again openly admired her once more, and said, "And Liliana…I do hope you'll wear that tiny little red dress for me again someday."

As she watched that errant dimple come into view on his cheek yet again, she replied, "You have my word on it!" She was completely unaware that her porcelain cheeks were coloring.

She watched Declan return to the nursery through her window. She thought about how things had gone down today, and she had to admit that there was a tiny part of her that was disappointed that he had been true to his word; but she also admired that he was the quintessential gentleman. "Someday soon, I do hope you'll kiss me thoroughly once again, Declan Ryan," she whispered.

DOVER

Declan Ryan was grieved to receive the phone call. His friend, John Grenville, had lost his fight with cancer. John's daughter had contacted him because her father had given her some very specific instructions before he died, "Declan Ryan, over at The Old Vineyard Road Nursery, is to be the guardian of my dog when I pass from this life. Dover likes him very much, and Declan has agreed to care for him when I am gone. Please see to it that this is taken care of as soon as I pass, Katie. I don't want Dover to be frightened." Katie Grenville had sadly agreed.

When Declan arrived at John Grenville's home, two young men from the local funeral home were carrying his body from the house. Memories from his mother's passing came flooding back. Declan's stomach clenched, "I have seen too many of my friends and loved ones leave this life," he murmured to himself as he watched the two men load John's body into the hearse. Then, he heard John's young dog's keening. Poor Dover knew something was not right.

He knocked on the frame of the open door to the house. Katie Grenville appeared.

"You must be Declan Ryan," she said sadly.

"Yes, I am. I'm terribly sorry for your loss, Katie. I thought John might just make it a bit longer. He visited me at the nursery just last week, and he seemed quite hearty."

"I thought so, too, Declan. He seemed fine when I left last night, but he didn't answer the telephone when I called to check on him this morning. Apparently, he died in his sleep," Katie responded.

Dover continued to howl in the other room. Katie started to cry, and the men from the funeral home came in asking for a signature on a release form. Declan knew he had to take charge. "Here, Katie… please, sign these forms," he instructed her. "I'll go into John"s room and try to get Dover quieted down. Can you gather up his bed and toys for me?" he asked. Saddened, Declan desired to get the young dog into a different environment as soon as possible.

When Declan entered John's bedroom, giant white Dover, a Pyrenees Mountain Dog, was sitting beside the bed howling and whimpering. Declan walked over to him and held out his hand. "Come here, Dover. Everything will be alright. Come to Declan." The dog came over to him, Declan ruffled his ears and said, "All will be well, Dover. Don't fret. I'm going to take care of you. Your new home will be at the nursery. You know how you love to come visit me there," he soothed.

Katie Grenville had followed Declan's instructions to her. She came into the room with a Tartan plaid dog's nest and a tote full of toys, leashes, and grooming equipment. Fifteen minutes later, Declan was on his way back to the nursery. Young Dover sat quietly on the seat beside him as he drove. The dog kept looking into his eyes for answers. "Poor Dover, your world has changed overnight. I know how you're feeling, big guy," Declan whispered, as he scratched behind the dog's silken ears. Dover proceeded to lie down on the bench seat facing Declan and laid his large paws and head upon Declan's thigh.

When Declan and Dover arrived back at the nursery, the dog hopped out of the truck, but wasn't interested in any of the scents on the air. He stuck close to Declan. Declan looked down at his handsome broad head and said, "Dover, I'm going to take a chance on something here. You're going to have to trust me on this one, but I'm pretty sure you'll thank me for it, big guy."

He led the giant white dog up the path to Liliana's cottage. He knocked softly on the front door and prayed he would say the right words. Liliana immediately answered her door, and a look of surprise came over her face. "Declan, who is your friend?" she asked.

"This is Dover," Declan stated simply. "He needs some healing time, too, Liliana. He lost his master to cancer just this morning."

Liliana's eyes looked into Declan's solemn blue eyes, then at the quiet white dog that was standing obediently next to him but shaking. "Oh, baby," she said as she knelt and hugged Dover's large head to herself. "You're a good boy, a very good boy. It's okay."

Declan, who looked slightly heartsick, said, "His master was an elderly friend of mine, Liliana. His name was John Grenville. Several weeks ago, John asked me to care for Dover when he passed on. He had been battling cancer for several months. I agreed but thought that John might just win the fight. Apparently, he died in his sleep last night. His daughter called me this morning because John had given her very specific instructions to get Dover out of the house and into my care as soon as possible when he died. When I arrived, Dover was trembling and keening sadly at the side of John's just-vacated bed…two young men from the funeral home were loading his body into the hearse."

"Oh, Declan," Liliana said sadly. "I'm so sorry about your friend." She again held big Dover close and spoke to him like one would to a little child.

Declan watched as the cadence of Liliana's voice reassured and comforted Dover. Though the dog was still slightly quaking, it stepped closer to her. "Liliana, I have to be candid with you, this isn't the best time for me to be responsible for a dog. With Chris and Annie traveling abroad, I just can't expend the time a dog needs. You were always so very good with Iris; do you think you might want to take on Dover?" I will help you as much as I am able, and I'll pay for his supplies. Dover needs your touch right now; he needs your nurturing. Would you consider it?"

At that moment, Dover locked eyes with Liliana. Declan watched as Liliana stared back at the young dog; she was most-likely remembering something akin to Iris…a compassionate, sweet-tempered disposition. Poor Dover was so frightened right now; all he could do was shiver and cry for his master. Her decision made, she said, "Declan I would be delighted to take over Dover's care. I suspect that he and I need each other. Besides, it does get a little lonely around here at night. Thank you for your thoughtful gift. I'll give my best to sweet Dover in honor of your friend. Please come in, I would love to enjoy a cup of tea with you, but only if you have the time."

Declan Ryan sat on one of her French blue chairs with his arm around Dover's broad shoulders and watched Liliana make tea. She made everyone feel comforted and loved. This morning, he had hoped she would take on the care of John's dog for several reasons. First, he was now assured of her safety with a dog, as large as Dover, on the premises. Second. Dover was an especially nice young dog. He deserved and needed the tender care Liliana would always extend to him. Declan looked down at Dover and whispered, "It's a good thing you are a dog. Otherwise, I might just be slightly jealous of all the attention Liliana is sure to lavish upon you. You *are* going to thank me for this, you know…you are one fortunate canine." At that moment Dover looked up and into Declan's eyes. It was as if he completely understood Declan's musing.

Liliana's soft hand had brushed with Declan's as she served him his tea and shortbread. He caught that hand, rubbed his thumb over it tenderly, and gave her his rare smile. She reciprocated with a contented smile. Neither of them said anything, but their affection was definitely communicated. As for Dover, he lay down on the black and white tiled floor and laid his handsome broad head upon his front paws, breathed out a sigh, and closed his soulful eyes to rest.

Three days later, when Liliana went through the day's mail, she found something that truly warmed her heart, a postcard from Declan. Something that she hadn't enjoyed in many years. This postcard was very similar to something she had given him while she was a senior at Brineforth University.

The printed front of the card had been painted upon newsprint, and it depicted a West Highland Terrier standing upright and dressed in a shirt and tie, a vest and blazer, and a tartan kilt in clan colors very similar to Decan's family colors. Of course, the dog looked quite gentrified as he was adorned with a sporran and held a carved wooden walking stick in his dog paw/hand. A very-delighted Liliana read:

Dearest Lily,

Thank you for agreeing to be young Dover's new dog parent. It was obvious that he felt especially comforted by your embrace and by your tender words to him the day before yesterday. Young Dover is a very smart canine, and I am positive he will reward your tenderness to him with his fidelity and obedience. Again, thank you so much. You are a very special woman.

With love,

Declan

Later that day, Liliana came to Declan's loft bearing a small tin of shortbread cookies.

She was escorted by giant white Dover, and as soon as Declan invited them into his loft, she said, "Oh, Declan, I was so happy to receive your tiny missive in today's mail! It meant everything to me, so I made these for you."

As Declan accepted her gift, he also pulled her into his arms and held her close. He whispered, "Dover is a very fortunate dog to have you for his person." He again kissed her scar just below her brow before releasing her from his embrace, and asked, "May I make you a cup of tea?" It goes without saying that it was a very special teatime that particular spring afternoon.

REFLECTIONS ON LILIANA

*D*avid Renton continued to feel badly that there was nothing more he could do for Liliana Lylestrom. In the end, the entirety of her inheritance from her parents, the sum of her assets in Seattle, her clothing, her jewelry, and her automobiles went to pay off Richard Rawlings' indebtedness. Her unscrupulous husband had left her so badly off that David feared she might never get the bulk of his creditors paid off.

To add insult to these injuries, the proof that Richard had cheated on her from the inception of their marriage forward had left a pall on an already-sad situation. Kind Liliana had worried not about herself, but about Sierra Monroe and her unborn child. Sierra Monroe, too, had to move into government-funded housing and then find a job. The luxurious lifestyle that she had once enjoyed with Richard had vanished overnight.

But the thing that made David Renton grieve was that Liliana had called him late one afternoon at his office. She had quietly asked him to set aside some of her own monies for a college fund for Richard's unborn bastard child…saying only, "His mother most likely won't be able to afford an education for him, and I don't want Richard's progeny to resort to untoward methods to pay for his or her education. That is how Richard came to find himself in such trouble in the end. It is not for Richard that I do this, David, it is in hope that his child will not end up like him."

Swinging his office chair away from his desk and looking out the window, David ruminated further on Liliana Lylestrom. In the two months since her parents had passed away, Liliana had been working hard to get their home on the market at a fair price. It truly was a charming place. It sat on an acre of land, and it was surrounded by graceful old trees. Liliana's mother, Jenny, had loved to garden, so the property's landscaping was impeccable. Recently, Liliana had tilled her mother's vegetable garden and had planted sweet peas, carrots, radishes, and lettuces. The Lylestrom property *was* looking very pretty, and the Reedsburgh real estate market had bounced back nicely from the recent recession years. David hoped that the warm weather would help "up" the market just a bit more for kind Liliana's sake.

The estate auctioneers had done a great job on liquidating the personal items from Liliana's family home, so really all that was needed was a buyer. David was just going over his mental list of potential buyers when his assistant came into his office. "Excuse me, David, but there is a gentleman outside by the name of Jeremy Pettigrew. He's asking questions about the Lylestrom property. Would you care to meet with him? You don't have any other appointments for another hour."

An amazed David answered, "Sure, Cally, show him in." He then thought to himself, this visitor must surely be providential.

A slightly familiar man entered the room and extended his hand to David. "Thanks so much for seeing me without an appointment, Mr. Renton. I'm Jeremy Pettigrew."

"Oh, call me David, and it's no problem. Are you familiar with the property, Jeremy?"

"Yes, I have a friend who is acquainted with it. He suggested that I get in touch with you. I took a chance today that you might be available to discuss it with me."

"And who might your friend be?" David inquired.

"Declan Ryan, sir. We go back a long way."

David Renton smiled. "That's why you look familiar to me…if you are a friend of Declan Ryan's, then you are surely a friend of mine, Jeremy. Declan is a great guy, and he has The Old Vineyard Road Nursery looking like a page out of a magazine. My wife just loves to take a Saturday morning drive out there during the summer season. We come home with our car loaded to the brim with blooming things!"

"Aye, Declan is the best in his field. His thumb is definitely green, but old Christophe Riordan was the one who found that diamond in the rough…all Declan did was to help him to cut the facets on that beauty."

"Right you are there," David laughed. "Tell me… you must be from Scotland, too?"

"Yes, I emigrated years ago. Declan was a mate of mine from school. He encouraged me to come for a visit, and I guess I just never went home. I'm a naturalized citizen, now. I truly enjoy this part of the country."

David Renton blew out a big sigh, "I hear you there, man. I hope no one ever finds out about this little piece of the world. It's like going back in time here…almost as if Post-World War II America never moved on. People work hard, they enjoy their families, and it is not a shameful thing to love God and country here. Rosemeade Township and Reedsburgh are two of the most-beautiful little places on the planet."

Jeremy Pettigrew replied, "That's exactly why I'm interested in, perhaps, purchasing the Lylestrom property. I have a little girl of three years, and I want her to enjoy a healthy and happy upbringing. I'm hoping that the Lylestrom home might just serve our needs."

"Has your wife seen the property, Jeremy?"

"No, David, my wife left when my daughter was just a wee babe of three months. Apparently, 'surfer dudes' from San Diego, California, were of more interest to her than her new baby girl. Three months after she deserted us, the final divorce papers were dispatched from her lawyer. She never even asked for custody or visitation rights. I've not ever heard from her again."

David Renton was shocked. He was the father of three small girls. "How any mother could abandon her little child is beyond me. I'm sorry to hear that happened, Jeremy. Has it been hard?"

"Well, it hasn't been so bad. My father had recently died when my wife left, so my mum came to care for Daphne as soon as she heard the news. My mother is a good woman, and my baby girl is being cared for by someone who adores her. I can do my job without worry. We make a family."

Jeremy Pettigrew then got down to the business at hand. "Do you know what the property has been appraised for or what the Lylestrom's daughter is asking for the home?"

"I do, in fact, know Jeremy," David answered. "Liliana Lylestrom is asking 1.75 Million for the property. The appraisal supports the listing price, too. If you would like to make an appointment to see the home, I'll be happy to have the realtor arrange a showing for you."

"Yes, I would like that," answered hale and hearty Jeremy Pettigrew.

"Let me make a quick call, and maybe we can set something up for this afternoon. Have you had a chance to get pre-approved for a loan?"

"There is no need, David. I'll be paying cash." Jeremy Pettigrew replied.

"Well then, Jeremy, let's get this **house party** started," said a delighted David Renton. He knew a cash deal on the sale of Liliana's family home would go a long way in expediting the payoff of Richard Rawlings' enormous debt. He couldn't wait to tell her. She would be delighted to know that a sweet family would be the beneficiaries of her childhood home.

In less than a week, Jeremy Pettigrew, his mother, and three-year-old Daphne had met with the realtor and Jeremy had signed the necessary papers to make an offer to Liliana for her parent's property. Liliana gladly accepted his offer. The Pettigrew family would be able to move in within a month. All parties were pleased. As well, the realtor, who knew of Liliana's financial plight, willingly gave up a portion of her commission on the sale of the property. Arrangements were made for the closing to be at David Renton's law office.

The day of the closing arrived, and Declan drove Liliana to Reedsburgh to sign the papers. Upon arrival, Liliana immediately recognized Jeremy. He was Declan's friend; the one who owned the grill pub, where Declan had taken her the night she had arrived home from Seattle. "Declan, did you have a hand in this?" Liliana had asked.

"Actually no, I didn't, Liliana. Jeremy was looking for something special for his family. His wife abandoned him and their baby girl a few years back. His mother lives with him now, and she cares for his beautiful, little girl. His daughter is such a sweet little thing. I suspect she is much like you must have been at her age. I just wanted Jeremy to have a chance to offer her an idyllic youth…much like you had. So, I suggested he look at your parent's property, since I knew you needed to sell it. You and I both know that your parent's home would never have stayed on the market very long, so I'm just happy that someone I esteem was able to buy it and to help you in the process. I know Jeremy, Mrs. Pettigrew, and young Daphne will be very happy there. I'm sure Stephan and Jenny would approve, too."

"Oh, Declan, this so delights me. Thank you for being so thoughtful to both Jeremy and to me. Please, re-introduce me to Jeremy. I am much better suited for introductions today than I was in early January."

Declan ushered Liliana further inside David's reception area to where Jeremy and David were chatting like old friends outside the conference room. Both men looked up and smiled. David spoke first, "Liliana, how are you? You look well and very pretty…and Declan, I've never seen you looking better either." He then proceeded to wink at Jeremy. "I assume you've met Jeremy, Liliana. Am I right?" David asked.

Liliana then extended her hand to Jeremy and gave him her brilliant smile. "Jeremy, I am so happy to make your acquaintance again. I'm afraid I wasn't in very good form when we met earlier this year. Please accept my apologies if I was rude in any way."

A smiling Jeremy took her hand within his and said, "I know you were in mourning that day, and, believe me, you were still very gracious. I am so happy to meet you again, Liliana. Declan always speaks highly of you." He winked back at David. Then, he extended his hand to Declan, and the two friends gave each other a combination hand-shake and "bro" hug.

Minutes later, signatures were obtained from all parties on the paperwork, certified funds were exchanged, and the transaction was finished. Liliana, again, shook Jeremy's hand and wished him great happiness in her family home. Jeremy beamed at her. "You've given us a gift, Liliana. My family and I will ensure that life *is* lived happily in your beautiful childhood home."

At this juncture, David Renton asked if he could have a minute of Liliana's time privately. He then ushered her into his office and closed the door. "Liliana, I'm glad that this transaction went so smoothly and that it will eliminate another large portion of Richard's encumbrances.

Are you sure that you don't want a bit of these monies for yourself? I know Christophe has provided a home for you, and that you're working now, but I still worry that you might need extra money; especially since it was from your personal money that you set up a college fund for Richard's child."

"David, I'm fine, really," Liliana earnestly replied. "We both know that the college trust was small but will mature into something better while Richard's child grows up. As for me, Christophe and Annie continue to stop by every couple of days with a bag or two of groceries, so I am definitely not going hungry. And, as you know, my father gave me a fair amount of cash before he died. He told me that I could not use it toward Richard's debt under any circumstance, so I have respected his wishes. It is tucked safely away in a high-yield money market fund, just in case something happens. Somehow, I don't think Dad would mind that I shared a part of it in order to give someone else a chance at a better life. So, you see, David, I am really in pretty good shape. I'm feeling so much better, too. Thank you for caring; you have been such a wonderful friend."

Seeing that she was relaxed and looking so much happier, David Renton agreed to put the entirety of the proceeds into the Escrow Account that had been set up to pay for Richard's debts, but he still wondered how this sweet friend of his would ever finish paying off the remainder of her dead husband's obligations. Somewhat sadly, he decided that he would have to ruminate on that another day.

A HEALING SUMMER SEASON

Everyone watched Liliana bloom into a version of her former self that summer. The fresh air, the beauty of Rosemeade County, and just being with her own people again went a long way in bringing her spirit back to health. Yes, there were days when acquaintances inquired about her parents, and she would find herself somewhat subdued, but overall, she found her verve again.

It goes without saying that nursery clients and vendors remembered her from years before and were happy to see her again. After hours, she still went to her cottage and spent her nights quietly, but during the days of hard work, she always seemed to infuse her sparkle into every chore, every business transaction, and every friendly reunion. In short, Liliana was once again lighting up people's lives with her charming effervescence. During these times, Christophe, Annie, and Declan watched from afar and were thankful to see her embracing life again.

When the Fourth of July rolled around, she spent it quietly with Christophe, Annie, and Declan. They did not attend a picnic, a dance, or a fireworks display, but simply spent their time together talking about Stephan and Jenny and the many happy times they had all enjoyed together over the years.

Annie prepared a lovely meal that they savored out on the patio, and Liliana baked a blueberry pie for their dessert. True to her mother's style, she spooned home-made whipping cream onto that pie when she sliced and served it. For Declan, her pie brought back memories of that first summer he lived in America. Somehow, Liliana always factored into his most-cherished memories, and that very first Fourth of July he had celebrated in America had been with her. "Some things never change," he thought to himself.

That evening when it was time to go home, Declan walked up the path with Liliana and Dover. When they stopped at the gate to the vintner's cottage, Liliana truly surprised him. She said, "You know what, Declan? Tonight, there is nothing that I want more than to fall asleep in your arms after making passionate love with you. Me, a widow of a mere six months…yes, me…Liliana, who always does the right thing! I'm sick of myself! I'm starting to be tired of always doing what is right in this life. I seem to reap heartache by doing the right things, saying the right things, and working my bum off for my dead husband who had only disdain for me. Yet, I pay for his debts, for his lying and cheating, and for his abuse of me. He may be dead, but he's still running my life…no, he's running our lives, Declan!"

"I am angry at myself, too, because I didn't have the guts to tell you that I wanted you all those years ago. I didn't speak up for myself. All my college roommates ended up with the men they desired, but I was a wimp and just let myself get steamrolled into marrying someone who misrepresented just about everything; even his love for me. Richard **never** loved me; once he knew that he had taken me away from everyone I held dear, he showed only disdain for me." But I stayed the course in an unsatisfactory, sometimes cruel, marriage because of my beliefs. I even saved myself for marriage, but that 'gift' meant nothing to Richard. We both know how that turned out, don't we…I was just one more thing that he'd conquered."

"Oh, he wanted to buy me big, obscene diamond rings, fancy cars, giant houses, and designer clothes, but I didn't want any of them. I found myself married to a man who couldn't have cared less about my feelings or what I brought to our marriage….a man who only wanted me for a trophy. You know that I was an innocent, Declan. I grew up during a pretty loose time in American culture, but I kept to my upbringing. I stayed a good girl, who always did the right thing. Now, I loathe myself for ever being impressed by Richard's supposed Harvard education and the life that he promised to me if I married him. He preyed upon my lack of experience, and all the while had a double life with his mistress."

"And you know what else? Sometimes, I'm even incensed at you, too, Declan, for always being so blasted honorable about everything. Perhaps, we both would be happier right now, if we'd just lost our heads once upon a time. I probably would have found myself carrying your child; you would have done the respectable thing and married me. And I know that we would have been very happy with each other, Declan. Yet, I somehow found myself married to a charlatan, and you lived your life alone because you had been honorable. Oh, how we were both duped. I wish you would have done something crazy back then and fought for me! I sometimes even wish that when we danced together the night of my wedding that you would have swung Richard a "facer" and stolen me away."

"Now, we both are driving ourselves insane with our properness… you are giving me time to grieve my losses and me feeling like I have to save face for my undeserving late husband by paying off his debts before I can ever embark upon a relationship with you! What if I can't ever get those debts paid off? I will have wasted all the time that I could have spent with you! I'm not sure I like doing the right thing anymore."

"And, lastly, I wish we would have been scandalous three months ago when we ironed out what went wrong in our relationship that night at the hospital right after I lost Richard's baby. I wish that we would have driven straight to Las Vegas and had a drive-thru wedding. At least we wouldn't still be waiting to get on with our lives and for me to pay off Richard's stinking debts!"

"My sweet parents wouldn't have cared if I had even married you on the day of their funeral, let alone two or three days afterward. They both told me to mend things with you on their deathbeds. Declan, my folks would have been overjoyed for us, and tonight, we could be making sweet, sweet love in that big old iron bed that I sleep alone in every night. But we aren't…just because you and I always do the right thing!"

When she had finished her passionate diatribe, she found herself engulfed in Declan's arms. "Good girl, Liliana. You're angry. I, for one, am happy to see it because it means you're healing, and the pace is only going to accelerate from here. I'm happy for you!" He then started to laugh and said, "You are quite a feisty lady when you get all riled up; making up with you after an argument is sure to be an enjoyable experience!"

"Oh, Declan!" She then scowled at him and stepped away.

Declan walked through the gate toward her porch, sat down on the steps, and then pulled her down beside him. He held her hand and kissed her palm. Then, he began, "Listen, Liliana, I know exactly what you are saying. Do believe me when I say that I unerringly understand how you feel. The only reason that beautiful vineyard that you so admire every day found itself tamed is because I was so angry at you for choosing Richard and at myself because I did what I thought was the right thing. Wanting only the best for you, I stepped away and literally gave you to Richard because I thought you wanted him."

"That awful day when you became his bride, something snapped within me. I feverishly despaired because I had not disrupted your wedding and knocked surly Richard to the ground. Believe me, I wanted to be a crazy Scotsman. I wanted to make a scene; I wanted to claim you for my own, and to carry you away. Instead, I did what I thought was the right thing. Afterward, I loathed myself for it."

"Liliana, you don't know this, but on the night of your wedding, I was so angry at what I had let happen that I came home and started a huge bonfire from cuttings taken from finally harnessing and pruning those wild vineyard rows. Christophe and Annie arrived home late that night and saw the glow from the fire several miles before they even turned off the main highway. They found me still in my wedding clothing madly pruning those wild grapes and throwing the dead wood into the roaring fire. Old Jim later told me that I was working as if the hounds of hell were after me. He was right!"

"And guess what, sweet Lily? I pruned back acres of those wild grapes like a mad man for months because I was so angry at you and so disappointed in myself that I almost couldn't stand it. Several days after I started on the project, Old Jim joined me and stayed by my side until the pruning was finished because he was fearful of what I might do, otherwise. When the project was finally completed, I still wasn't happy, but I had at least purged most of my self-loathing and anger."

An aggrieved Declan soldered on, "If you have ever wondered why I gave you such a wide berth when you returned to Reedsburgh, it was because I never wanted to see you again. But you know what, Liliana? My love for you was not really vanquished by putting those overgrown vines back in order…because, when I saw you standing alone and looking so fragile on that airport concourse last January, an entire decade later, my love for you re-ignited so powerfully that it frightened me. I was nervous of being around you again, and that fear renewed some of my anger, too. Yes, I wanted to be flint, granite, and steel toward you. It was all I could do to keep my sanity in check while staying as far away from you as possible."

"But, Lily, my wall of resolve to be angry at you just kept fracturing at every juncture. On that sad day when I drove you to the hospital, you fainted in my arms! I was so frightened that I might lose you to death that I let the last remaining shards of that wall shatter and crumble until there was nothing left of it. Later, when you shared Richard's abominable treatment with me, there was no anger left, only consuming sadness that I hadn't been able to protect you from harm. It is well and good that both of us continue to work through these issues a bit longer."

Declan then gave her his beautiful smile and kissed her cheek, "And, as to making passionate love with you in your old iron bed, I can wait a while longer if you can. There is nothing that I desire more than to show you how one's bride is to be cherished on her wedding night for her purity. Somehow, someway, we will be together again, my lovely girl. Please don't be frustrated. Part of the reason that I care for you so much is that you are, and will always be, a woman to treasure. Believe me when I say that precious ladies like you don't come along very often in this life." Declan then held her close and, again, his lips tenderly found her cheek, and he murmured loving endearments to her.

Liliana sighed, "You are right, Declan; but sometimes, I do fear that I will never be free of Richard and that I will forever be under his dominant thumb."

They had been quiet and introspective for several minutes when Declan queried, "Do you remember the day we quarreled about Richard's intentions that last summer we worked side by side, Liliana?"

"Yes, I do, Dec…I was feeling pretty low."

Declan continued, "I felt as though my guts were being wrenched from me as I helped you into my truck that afternoon as we left Annie's Diner; we both were angry at each other. You sat far away on the other side of the seat; something that hurt me. Before, you had always nestled close to me whenever we drove anywhere. Do you remember that I stopped my truck, unbuckled your seatbelt, and pulled you into my arms?"

"How could I not, Declan? You held me very close, but you did not kiss me. You tenderly apologized for being angry with me and bussed me on the cheek, but it still hurt that you didn't kiss me like you once had. You doubted my affection for you that last summer, so you never held me in your arms or kissed me until the day I left for the last time. I wanted you to kiss me so much…" A slight sob caught in her throat as she answered.

"Well, know this, my sweet Lily, I wanted to kiss you with a fury that day; I wanted you to desire me as much as I yearned for you, but your ardent defense of Richard made me believe that you no longer wanted my company. I have always been regretful that I didn't kiss you madly and tell you of my devotion to you. Perhaps, we both could have avoided some grievous sorrow if I had. Believe me when I say that I am tiring of always doing the right thing, too. It seems that Richard has us both under his dominant thumb; even though he's gone. I, too, am sick and tired of his dominance over the both of us."

A PROPOSED STRATEGY

Declan Ryan was feeling quite determined. It was the day after Halloween. The sky was a brilliant cornflower blue and there were remnants of smashed pumpkins along the streets and boulevards en route to Reedsburgh. The air was perfumed with the scent of mulched leaves and wood smoke. In all, it couldn't have been a more perfect setting for the celebration of the harvest season. Declan had been ruminating on something quite significant since early July, and he had finally made a major decision about it yesterday. Even though things were still busy at the nursery, and Annie and Christophe were off traveling in New England, he knew he needed to meet with David Renton because he would not be able to rest until he received some answers to his questions. He thought about Liliana as he drove.

This year's spring and summer seasons had brought back the girl he used to know. Oh, she was definitely a woman now, but living out her "do-over" was putting the color back into her cheeks and the vivacious personality back into her demeanor. The cloud of Richard Rawlings demeaning treatment of her was retreating. It seemed that once she had settled into the vintner's cottage, she had made great strides toward feeling better again.

As Declan thought about it, having her living so close had brought about changes for him, too. Life seemed more colorful with her around, and even though he was giving her time to pick up the pieces of her life, he knew in his heart that she cared for him. The misunderstandings that they had conquered that night at the hospital almost nine months ago, had given him the hope he needed to wait for her. Then, in July, when she had finally gotten angry about certain factors that were hindering the both of them, he had decided that some type of action was necessary. He would still give her all the time she needed to heal…he could live a lifetime just knowing that she cared…but now, he had decided to act upon an idea that he had been contemplating for several months. Today, he was finally ready to propose his plan to David.

Declan asked himself if he was, perhaps, being selfish in even considering acting upon such an idea; even though it might possibly expedite things for them both. Yet, her very passionate diatribe on the Fourth of July had told him that she was ready for her mourning, her healing, and her non-ending payments to Richard's creditors to be over.

Sweet Liliana…how could anyone fully describe her? She was very intelligent, she was fun loving, and she was so caring. Oh, how she loved that crazy white dog he had given to her! Dover had always been handsome, but he was still a dog. Under Liliana's care, his coat shone, and it was snow white. He was always impeccably groomed. Declan guessed that Dover now knew how to "take a bath" quite regularly. Dover followed her everywhere. She made sure he never frightened customers or little children visiting at the nursery, and he was amazingly well behaved. Occasionally, Liliana had substituted at the local primary school. On those occasions, Dover had stayed with him for the day. They were good mates, but Dover was never easy until Liliana was again in his line of vision. John Grenville would be happy for his big dog and that dog's good fortune in finding himself with such a wonderful caregiver.

"Things *are* getting better for all of us," he whispered aloud.

Looking up from his reverie, Declan was surprised that he was almost to Reedsburgh. As always, the quaint town looked beautiful. Large trees lined the streets, and the downtown area was ablaze with the last vestiges of fall color. There was a hint of wood smoke in the air, and as Declan drove past the local high school, the football team was practicing for an upcoming game. Yes, he thought to himself, I do like this little corner of the world. With that, he pulled into the parking area of David Renton's law office.

It was always nice to visit with David. His office smelled of fragrant wood, leather-bound books, and furniture polish. For some reason, it always reminded him of his mother and his childhood home. The handsome reception area was welcoming with its lowly-lit lamps, leather furniture, Persian rugs, oil paintings, and travel books. David even employed real living trees and plants in his foyer; and for some reason, such a gesture pleased Declan. No faux greenery!

Young Cally Westbrook, David's assistant, welcomed him. "Good afternoon, Declan," she said, "You are right on-time. David is just finishing up with a telephone call. Have a seat. He'll be right with you." Several minutes later, David bounded out of his office, and extended his hand to Declan.

"Declan, my friend, how are you today?"

"I'm doing well, David. Thanks so much for seeing me on short notice."

David stepped aside and extended his arm toward his office, "Come on in and tell me what I can do for you this afternoon. Would you like something to drink?"

While Cally brought in icy-cold Italian spring water in glass bottles, Declan had a quick "look-see" around David's office. His personal space was filled with handsome photographs of his wife and little daughters, art pieces from his travels, and framed kindergarten artwork which said, "I love you, Daddy" in brightly-colored, uneven letters. These things struck a chord with Declan. He found himself desiring similar things on his old mahogany desk in the loft. David Renton was a blessed man.

David took the lead, "Tell me why you're here, my friend. Is everything all right with Liliana?"

"Oh, yes, she's doing very well, but it is something to do with Liliana that I would like to speak with you about, David. I'm not even sure you'll be able to answer my questions, but I'm hoping you can."

"I'll do my best for you," David responded seriously.

"David, I'm going to be frank with you today. You know that Liliana and I have a history. We've lost many precious years due to misunderstandings on each of our parts. We have worked through these things, but there is something that still stands between us… Richard Rawlings' debt and the possibility of a lawsuit from the people he injured. Liliana feels that she cannot embark upon anything until his debt is significantly reduced or completely paid off.

I understand why she feels this way, but I can't help but wonder if her integrity on this issue will stall any happiness that she and I might have together for a very long time. I know Richard's debts have taken almost everything away from her and that the money she makes from part-time teaching and from working for Christophe always goes toward paying off Richard's pathetic legacy. As well, I know that she is starting to feel fatigued from the pressure of these concerns. Can you share with me approximately how much she owes?"

"Declan, you know that I'm not supposed to reveal that figure to you or anyone. It violates her client privacy. Why do you need to know?" David queried.

"Because Richard Rawlings has seemingly violated Liliana in every sense of the word, and even in death, he still continues his grip upon her. I fear she may never be free of his oppression, David. If possible, I would like to anonymously pay off Richard's obligations to free her once and for all."

David Renton was astonished. He looked earnestly across the desk at his friend. "You *really* love her, don't you?" he said softly.

"Yes, I do, David, and even if Liliana were to decide that she doesn't ever want to be with me, I would still take this burden from her shoulders. She truly deserves freedom from Richard's domination," Declan acknowledged.

David Renton thoughtfully looked at his watch, "It's half past four, Declan. Let me take you over to my club for a drink. I think we need to discuss this further." Ten minutes later, the two men walked across the Reedsburgh Town Square and entered a stalwart red brick building upon which hung a shingle, "Ramsgate Gentlemen's Association, Rosemeade Township, Established 1875."

As they entered The Ramsgate, David joked, "This old club was established so long ago, and its name sounds so old world. Yet, when one does the research, they find that this venerable establishment got its noble name simply because it was located next to the pasture gate of the local sheep rancher!" Declan chuckled, and David continued, "Its early patrons probably all had sheep dung on their boots, so don't let the high-class white tablecloths and crystal glassware fool you…it's just a place founded by local sheepherders almost one hundred fifty years ago!"

David led them to a table set slightly apart from the others in a small alcove. "I like this particular table. It will give us plenty of privacy, Declan." So, over tumblers of malt whiskey and a basket of savory crackers and nuts, David deftly guided their conversation to cover all the facets of eliminating Richard Rawlings' debt without ever violating his client's privacy. In the end, David said, "Declan, with your generosity, you will be giving Liliana her life back. It's very good of you."

Declan responded, "David I don't want to appear self-serving here. You know I would do anything for her…even give up my life; if it was required of me. She has labored long enough under the yoke of Richard's oppression. My only desire is to emancipate her."

David then asked Declan a candid question. "Has Liliana ever told you that we were once young sweethearts?"

"Yes, she has said something of it to me," Declan knowingly grinned.

"Well, then, you probably know what a little twit I was to her." Now that I am a father to three beautiful little daughters, it horrifies me to think about how I acted in those days. I've always been sorry for my bad behavior toward her. Liliana stood firmly upon her morals and her beliefs, and it wasn't until a year or so later that I even had the guts to apologize for demanding intimacy from her for a few lousy movie-and-dinner dates. She's a very fine woman, Declan, and do you want to know something else?"

"What is that, David?"

"I've seen how she looks at you, and I was never the beneficiary of such devotion from her, even when I was her beau…nor have I ever seen anyone else of my acquaintance receive the marked affection she has always shown toward you. **You** are a very fortunate man, Declan Ryan! But what am I saying? You just arranged to pay off the balance of Richard Rawlings' debt burden; a man who openly displayed disdain and hostility toward you. Yet, you turned the other cheek. You are not only an honorable man, but the only person I know of who is worthy of Liliana's devotion. I'm truly happy for you both." David Renton then extended his hand across the table and shook Declan's proffered one.

As they crossed the Square heading back to David's office, Declan thought of one more question. "David, do you think that you could hold off on telling Liliana about the debt being paid off for a while longer…perhaps, until Christmas? I think finding out on Christmas Eve would really be a nice gift for her, and she would probably ask fewer questions about who her benefactor is…"

"That's good thinking, Declan. I won't say a word until then. Any money she gives to me will just go into her escrow account and will be given back to her later. I'll be in touch with you the first thing tomorrow, and we'll arrange for a wire transfer of funds."

David Renton was so pleased with what was transpiring on Liliana's behalf, he decided to share a little something with Declan. "You know, Declan, the Phillips Family has recovered well from their injuries from the auto accident, and they were very impressed that Liliana took it upon herself to meet with them and to apologize for Richard's damnable behavior in trying to kill himself at their expense. Stephan Lylestrom and I met several times with representatives from both insurance companies. We tried to negotiate things to benefit the Phillips family as well as Liliana. At this point, both insurers have come to an agreement on an equitable settlement for the Phillips, so it looks like Liliana's fears of a lawsuit can be laid to rest. I've not had a chance to speak with her on this, but the settlement is soon to be consummated. She is finally getting a break." A smiling Declan Ryan heartily shook David's hand, yet again, and took his leave; vowing to keep his silence on what had just been shared with him.

David Renton, knowing what a lovely woman waited at home for him, couldn't wait to get home and tell his wife, Claire, about Liliana's anonymous benefactor.

A satisfied and very pleased Declan Ryan drove back to Rosemeade where the woman, he someday hoped to marry, was waiting for him to help her move a rickety nineteenth-century table from the attic into her newly painted sewing room.

It was a Thursday, the fifth day of November, and while Liliana Lylestrom substituted in the kindergarten class at the Rosemeade Township Primary School, the final payments to those who had carried Richard's debt for her were being made via wire transfers. At four o'clock that afternoon, as she waited for the city bus to take her back to Old Vineyard Road, she unknowingly became free. Cruel and insensitive Richard Rawlings' vise grip was no longer upon her.

That same day, as David Renton was finishing up the last of his case work on Liliana's file, he shook his head and wondered something, yet again. Was that old adage about the Scottish being thrifty really true? Both Declan Ryan and Jeremy Pettigrew, who seemingly looked like regular, work-a-day men, had both accrued enough monetary wealth to literally wipe away the last substantial portion of Richard Rawlings' overwhelming legacy of heavy, heavy debt. Thanks to their prudent handling of money, Liliana was to finally be free from the oppression of her late husband's poor handling of the same. Knowing she was now released from these cares, pleased David immensely.

CHRISTMAS EVE

*L*iliana Lylestrom was baking pies for Christmas Eve dinner which was to be at Christophe and Annie Riordan's home. Her little kitchen boasted black and white tiled floors, an old white enamel stove that looked brand new, and an ancient refrigerator that still managed to keep everything the perfect temperature. A year ago, she had lived in a huge, very modern home north of Seattle, but it was not very snug or comfortable. Her giant state-of-the-art kitchen had been filled with the newest appliances that any chef would have been envious of, but those things could not compare with the happiness her simple, little cottage kitchen was bringing her today. She loved rolling out her pie crusts on the old farm table that Declan had helped her salvage from a local estate sale. She always wondered who else might have prepared something special on his or her farm table whenever she worked upon it. In short, she loved the simplicity of her new life in Rosemeade Township. Yes, she would always miss her wonderful parents, but Jeremy Pettigrew and his sweet family were making memories in her old family home. And in her heart, Liliana knew this would please Stephan and Jenny Lylestrom immensely.

As for herself, Liliana was feeling happier than she ever thought she would be again. It was almost the one-year anniversary of Richard's death. Her father, David Renton, and others had worked tirelessly on her behalf to, hopefully, ward off a lawsuit and to negotiate payment arrangements with Richard's creditors. Almost all those creditors had agreed to drop additional interest and penalty fees when they found out how Richard had stolen from his clients and from his own wife's trust fund. Most everything from her former life had been sold to pay off Richard's enormous debts, and she had had to give up her inheritance from her parents to further erase Richard's egregious mistakes; but today, she was happy to be where she was in this life… living in Rosemeade Township with those who meant the most to her.

Liliana's home was spanking clean and ready to celebrate the Christ Child's birth. She had trimmed a smaller-sized Christmas tree in colored twinkle lights and had hung cherished ornaments from her childhood upon its sturdy branches. Underneath were three carefully-wrapped gifts for those who were her family now, and there was also a large package which was addressed to Dover. It looked suspiciously like a new dog bed. "Yes," Liliana thought to herself, "I've got to admit that things are getting better every day…my life is being restored." Just then, her cell phone rang and interrupted her reverie.

"Merry Christmas, Liliana!" David Renton's happy voice greeted her.

"Merry Christmas to you, too, David!" Liliana replied. "How are Claire and the girls?"

"Oh, they are all doing great. The girls are still trying to decide if they want Father Christmas to bring them princess dresses or new dolls or both! Little Adrian is worried that if she asks for too much, she might just get a rock in her stocking for being selfish. All in all, we are having a lot of fun," he replied.

"What are your plans for the holiday, Liliana?" David then asked.

"I'm spending a quiet family Christmas with Christophe, Annie, and Declan. I'm making pies for it as we speak. My parents always did the big Christmas celebration with them when I was growing up; so tonight, Annie is hosting the festivities. Tomorrow morning, they are all coming to my place to open gifts and to have breakfast. I'll be missing my parents, but it will still be a wonderful holiday. I'm feeling so much better now, David."

"Liliana, I couldn't be happier for you. It's been a hard year, I know, but the worst part is behind you. You've been strong. Many people would have never gotten back on their feet after life dealt them what you've endured. You are made of good stuff, and that is why I am calling you. I've got some news for you. Do you think Claire, the girls, and I could stop by for just a little while this afternoon?"

"Yes, David, I would love to have you and your ladies stop by. What time?"

"Would two o'clock be alright?"

"That's perfect. I'll have hot chocolate, tea, and cookies waiting for you all. May I invite Declan to join us?"

"Of course, do invite Declan! We'll see you a bit later then. Good-bye, Liliana."

"Bye, David."

BLESSED LIBERATION

ive minutes before the hour, **Declan Ryan** opened Liliana's evergreen-decorated gate, walked to her front door, and softly knocked. She opened the door and, as always, she took his breath away. It wasn't just her looks that got to him; it was her resilience and her disposition that drew him to her. Declan knew there were others who would be devastated to be spending their first Christmas without their beloved parents or others who would have given up under Liliana's same circumstances. Yet, she had forgiven Richard for his odious behavior, she had saved face for him and had reconciled him, even in death, to his family; and she was keeping a brave face as she struggled to pay off his creditors. She had strength of character, and that was why she took his breath away.

"Merry Christmas, Declan," she smiled. "I've made you your very favorite shortbread today."

"Be still, my heart," he teased. "I love your shortbread more than my mum's…God rest her soul. But I suspect she would agree that yours is the best by far."

Liliana laughed, and pulled him through the doorway into the warmth of her little home. As always, she engaged one's senses. Two handsome pies were cooling on the work table in her kitchen alongside a jug of red roses that she had cut in the greenhouse. She had set out a tray of sweets and savories, and there was a pot of tea, as well a pot of hot chocolate, sitting adjacent to the tray of comestibles. Her small living area contained a Christmas tree that was exquisitely decorated, and Dover was also dressed for the occasion in a freshly-laundered holiday bandana. His handsome coat was truly snow white. There was not an ounce of mud on those pristine paws, either. Declan thought to himself, "She really does know how to make a house a home."

Right on time, David Renton arrived with a bevy of beautiful girls with him. He was dressed in his business suit and wore a cashmere overcoat, so Declan knew he was going to mix business with Christmas cheer. Introductions, kisses and hugs abounded, and before they all knew it, Liliana had them sitting around her kitchen table enjoying steaming cups of hot chocolate and tea. Declan sat back and looked at David and his women…his wife, Claire, was lovely, and she had given him the gift of three beautiful little daughters…Julianne, Laurel, and Adrian. Again, Declan found himself envying what David possessed. He said, "David, you are a very fortunate man. All of your ladies are perfect."

Liliana chimed in, "I totally agree with Declan, David. You have a houseful of sweet women that just adore you."

David Renton practically blushed when he said, "I am, indeed, a fortunate and happy man. Life has been very good to me. But on to you, Liliana…I have some happy greetings for you today, Miss Lylestrom."

"Oh, David, do tell," chirped Liliana.

David Renton smiled at his old friend and shook his head, then announced, "Liliana, today, I come bearing certificates of your freedom, so to speak. I have signed-and-notarized letters from each of Richard's creditors stating that you have paid your late husband's debts in full. Whether those debts are from commercial loans, notes to his hard-money lenders, or IOUs to his friends, each has been paid in full. You need never worry about Richard's legacy of debt ever again."

"David, how can that be?" a flustered Liliana asked. There is still a substantial amount to be paid off. I don't understand."

"God looks out for his own, Liliana. Someone has come forward and anonymously paid off Richard's debts. You have been absolved. You can now move forward with your life without a millstone around your neck," David kindly replied.

"David, who would give me such a gift?" a slightly-tearful Liliana inquired.

David continued to smile at his old friend, "I am not at liberty to divulge that information to you, Liliana; not ever! Just know that your benefactor desires to remain anonymous, and I will take his or her identity with me to my grave. I have not shared one word of this agreement with anyone. Even my paralegal knows nothing of it. This contract and its arrangements were prepared and consummated in private. Only your benefactor and I know the terms of the agreement." He then handed her a leather portfolio that contained the notarized letters from each of Richard's creditors. "Merry Christmas, Liliana. You are finally free."

"David, you know that I owe you for all of your hard work this last year. Did my benefactor compensate you, too?"

"Your benefactor tried, Liliana, but the work on your case is my gift to you…my special gift to a wonderful old friend. But, Liliana, there is even more. Satisfactory negotiations have been arrived at by both insurance companies regarding the Phillips family, and there will be no lawsuit. The Phillips family will be well compensated for their injuries with a monetary settlement, and I am happy to report that each of them has had a full and complete recovery from their injuries," David quietly stated.

At that, Liliana jumped up from her chair. She hugged David, she hugged Claire, and she hugged each of David's small girls. She then threw her arms around Declan's neck and whispered, "Declan, I'm free. I'm liberated for the first time in years." As he held her, he could feel her trembling. She then proceeded to hug everyone again. At this point, Dover, who had been dozing by the Christmas tree, started to bark and David's three little girls squealed in delight. A wee bit of chaos ensued, with Dover cavorting around the room followed by three lively little lasses.

While all of this was going on, Liliana sat perusing each of the letters contained in the folio. She was speechless and on the verge of a good cry. Declan recognized the signs. He gave David the silent signal. David then rounded up all his women, heartily shook hands with Declan, and kissed Liliana's cheek. "Let's head home, girls. We have to get ready for Father Christmas."

While David bundled the children into their car seats, Claire came over to Liliana and hugged her once again. "Liliana, you have shown such grace under fire. I hope you can get on with your life now, because you deserve only the best. David so admires you. And, now that you're free, you and I can have some fun together."

Liliana smiled brightly, "I would love that, Claire."

"We'll make arrangements after the holidays are over, then." Claire started to walk away, but she turned back and whispered into Liliana's ear. "If I were you, Miss Liliana, I would marry that Scotsman of yours ASAP. He is a keeper."

With alligator tears threatening to spill from her green eyes, Liliana giggled, "That is exactly what I hope to do someday soon, Claire."

Claire winked at her and turned toward the car. As she started to pass by Declan, she stopped and whispered in his ear, too. "Declan, now that Liliana is free from her dead husband's oppression, I suggest you marry her ASAP."

Declan laughed and replied, "Whenever Liliana gives me the signal that she is ready, that is exactly what I hope to do. I have waited a long time, Claire, but I am a patient man. I can wait a bit longer for her."

"Someday soon, both David and I both want to raise a toast to you and Liliana at your joyous wedding," Claire softly whispered.

"I thank you, Claire. I do hope we can raise a glass someday soon," a pleased Declan Ryan answered.

After David and his family were on their way back to Reedsburgh, Declan joined Liliana in her living room. She looked bewildered, and she said, "Declan, I don't know who would do such a thing for me, but I am humbled by their generosity. Who has that kind of money to just give away?"

Declan earnestly replied, "I am sure that whoever did this for you, Liliana, knows of what you've had to endure at the hands of your deceased husband. We live in a small place, where it is hard to keep such things under wraps. You know that many of your family friends were outraged that Richard behaved so badly. He wronged both you and your parents. And, that is not the half of it. He hurt you, Lily, in so many other ways. Only Christophe, Annie, and I know of his physical abuse to you, but if others knew of these indiscretions, they would be outraged anew. Accept the gift that has been given to you, dear one. Whoever liberated you from Richard's oppression wanted to help you."

The tears finally started to flow, as Liliana realized she would probably never know who her benefactor was, but she told Declan quite affirmatively. "I don't know who gave such a gift to me, but I will be thankful for their generosity all of the days of my life. I may never be able to say thank-you personally, but I will petition God's blessing on him or her for such kindness to me."

"Your prayers will be enough, Liliana." Declan quietly retorted as he cradled her in an embrace.

Christmas morning arrived in splendor. Snow had fallen during the night, and everything was blanketed in pristine white. The lamp posts throughout the nursery were adorned with evergreens and ribbons. The fencing all the way from the highway junction to the roundabout at the entrance to Christophe and Annie's home and back again was lit up with colorful Christmas lights, and a giant Christmas wreath adorned the old stone-foundation barn. Lastly, the manger scene which was the highlight at the nursery entrance had a smattering of new snow, but Baby Jesus and his parents were safe and snug from the elements inside the small, little barn that Christophe and Declan had erected to commemorate His birth. All these beautiful reminders of the season were now dressed in a coating of crisp white snow.

Christophe, Annie, and Declan arrived at the vintner's cottage in high spirits the next morning and were greeted by a glowing Liliana. She had been cooking and baking for them, and the aroma of homemade cinnamon rolls floated out the door when she opened it. Dover knew something special was afoot, so he shot out the door and ran three times in succession around the fenced-in yard before coming back to receive his Christmas greetings from the family.

Once everyone was in the house, their coats and scarves stowed upon on Liliana's bed, the festivities began. Filled Christmas stockings were hanging from the mantle, and a wide-eyed Liliana said, "It looks very much like St. Nicholas visited here last night!" Her special guests were delighted. Liliana had sewn and hand-quilted stockings for each of her people. Though their names were not written nor embroidered upon the stockings, it was easy to tell whose stocking was whose…

each one was adorned with something that spoke quite vocally about its designated owner.

Breakfast was served on a beautifully-set kitchen table. Jenny Lylestrom's wedding china sparkled at each place setting along with her old-fashioned silverware and crystal. Candles shone brightly in polished mismatched silver holders, but it was the happy faces around that handsome table that meant the most to everyone in attendance that morning.

Christophe prayed, "Father, thank-you for the salvation your Son brought to this world, and thank you for the forgiveness you have extended to us all. Lord, you have carried each of us at this table through trials this year, and we praise you for that. Bless this food that you have so graciously given to us, Lord, and thank you for continuing to keep us in your care. Father, only you know who so graciously took away the debt that our dear Liliana was struggling with, and Father, we thank you for him or her. You are holy, Lord God. Amen."

Immediately following Christophe's prayer, each member of the family raised their glasses to honor the Christ Child, "Thank you, Lord Jesus," they all said in unison.

It was a wonderful morning inside the old vintner's cottage that day. Liliana's delicious breakfast was thoroughly enjoyed, thoughtful and precious gifts were exchanged in honor of the Christ Child's birth, and many new memories were made. At long last, Liliana Rose Lylestrom was truly free from her late husband's oppression.

CHRISTOPHE'S GIFT

Christophe Riordan knew in his heart that the time had come to share his wealth with Declan Ryan. It was mid-January, in a brand-new year, and Christophe had been considering changes for a while because losing Stephan and Jenny Lylestrom to death within the blink of an eye almost a year ago had really gotten him to thinking. Though Christophe had all his personal affairs in order in the event he died unexpectedly, those arrangements did not really take into account Declan's current role in his and Annie's lives.

It was a rare occurrence any more for Christophe and Annie to grieve that they had never been able to have children. It wasn't that they hadn't tried, but circumstances were such that Annie hadn't been able to carry a child to full term. When Declan had told them that Liliana was miscarrying her child on the day of her parents' funeral, they had sadly remembered their three separate trips to Reedsburgh Medical Center; each one with the same outcome: two broken-hearted people departing from the hospital a day later with no little baby in their arms.

Both Christophe and Annie had eventually accepted that they were never to have children, but sometimes, it was hard. Years ago, when Stephan and Jenny Lylestrom had asked them to take on the responsibility of being godparents to tiny Liliana, they had been overjoyed. They had always had a close relationship with her parents, so taking on their role as godparents had brought them much pleasure. They had shared in all the watershed events in Liliana's young life, and they knew she loved them dearly. However, it wasn't until Declan Ryan arrived in their lives that they finally knew the joy and honor of having a son of their own.

When Christophe first met him, Declan Ryan had been only eight years old. Technically, Declan was Christophe's second cousin. His lovely mother, Mary Ryan, had been Christophe's cousin and closest childhood playmate. They had grown up together and had shared many fine memories. As adults, they had remained very close, so Christophe made every effort to see his special cousin as soon as he heard that her husband, James, had died. To Christophe, it didn't seem that long ago that Mary had happily confided to him that she was in love with a young grocer whom she had recently met, whose name was James Ryan. A simple-and-wholesome village wedding had then followed for Mary and James, and within a year and a half, Baby Declan had arrived. Sweet young Mary had been ecstatic.

In the years that followed Declan's birth, Christophe had moved to America, but he and Mary had continued to keep in touch. As it happened, Christophe had been back in Scotland on his honeymoon with Annie when he had received word of James Ryan's death. He and Annie had arrived at Mary's home to find her being comforted by a sober eight-year old Declan, who was the spitting image of his father. When young Declan was introduced to Christophe, he extended his small young hand to his mum's cousin, and his brilliant blue eyes looked straight into Christophe's soul. Christophe had never forgotten that serious young boy who had taken it upon his young shoulders to comfort and care for his mother. In the ensuing years, Declan grew not only in stature, but in character as well. Christophe knew this from the letters that he and Mary continued to send across the many miles that now separated them.

Then, the telephone call that had come fourteen years ago…the call that a grown-up Declan Ryan had placed to him one evening not long after his mother's death. It seemed that Mary had suffered from cancer for close to two years, but she had never disclosed her illness to Christophe. Mary's letters simply told how Declan had graduated with honors from the University of Edinburgh and that his study emphasis had been in Plant Science. Mary had only given the slightest hint that anything might be wrong with her when she wrote that Declan had taken some time off after graduation to help her with a few things. Christophe had never known anything was wrong, so he had been quite saddened to hear of his special cousin's passing. He felt even more grief, though, when he found out that twenty-two-year-old Declan had cared for her all alone. There had been no family to help. All of them had already passed away…Christophe knew that he was Declan's only remaining familial tie. There was only one thing to do.

Knowing of Declan's character from his mum's letters, and knowing that Declan had a degree in horticulture, something told Christophe that Declan Ryan would be just the person he needed to help him with every facet of the burgeoning workload at The Old Vineyard Road Nursery. Christophe had entreated Declan to come to America for an extended stay and to work alongside him. Not long thereafter, staid Declan Ryan had arrived in Rosemeade County. Declan had been thankful for the opportunity of work in his field and had pledged to do his best for him. Christophe had never been sorry. As the years had passed, Declan had proven himself to be honorable, hard-working, and he had always shown allegiance.

Somehow, Declan had morphed from a special young relative into a son. Christophe was so very proud of him. Together, they had worked side by side, just like a proud father and his son would. They had laughed, celebrated, mourned, and prayed for strength; just as a father and son would do, too. In all, Declan Ryan had become that "beloved son" that he and Annie had once prayed for, and now the time had come for Christophe to reward Declan for his love and fidelity.

Christophe had already contacted David Renton and spoken with him about his plans, and David had prepared the documents. In short, Christophe was going to give Declan the entirety of his business now while he was still in good health. Then, he would draw a salary from Declan, and he and Annie would have more freedom to travel and see the world. Basically, Christophe knew that he would be changing places with Declan. But this change would give Declan the inheritance that he so deserved.

So, one morning in early February, Christophe asked Declan to come to the house for breakfast. They met in Christophe's office which housed a giant old-world desk, shelves of books, and a stone fireplace that was crackling with spirit that day. Declan arrived wearing a tweed jacket much like those from the old country, but this jacket had an updated and contemporary look to it. That was one of the things that Christophe admired about Declan. He still clung to the things from his home country, but he had incorporated them in a modern and stylish way. It was the same with The Old Vineyard Road Nursery…Declan had infused it with a new presentation of old-style trends, and the business had taken off to heights that Christophe had never imagined his fledgling nursery could attain. Yes, his young second cousin had been a gift from the very beginning of their friendship.

Christophe waved him in with a hearty greeting. "Good morning to you, Declan, you are looking fit and healthy this morning."

Declan responded with a handsome smile that always seemed to dispel the serious set to his young face. "Good morning to you, too, Chris!"

Just then Annie appeared at the door with a breakfast tray laden with scrambled eggs, haggis, baked beans, bacon, fried toast, broiled tomatoes, and coffee. For some reason, Annie now knew how Declan liked his morning coffee. Declan suspected that Liliana had had something to do with it.

Declan kissed Annie's flushed cheek as he took the tray from her hands and set it on the corner of Christophe's desk. He lifted up what he knew to be his cup of coffee and said, "Annie, you are one in a million. I thank you for preparing a traditional breakfast from the old country for us this morning."

Christophe responded with, "Annie, my love, why don't you stay and join us? What I have to say to Declan is really from the both of us. Let me get a comfortable chair for you to sit in, dear."

While robust Christophe Riordan sought out an appropriate chair for his wife, Declan Ryan looked at Annie and teased, "I'm not going to get sacked this morning, am I?"

Annie Riordan just threw back her head with laughter and said, "Not hardly, Declan. I don't know what any of us would do without you. Believe me, there will be no firings this morning!"

Declan then winked at her and said, "Well, that's reassuring…"

Smiling back at Declan, Annie queried, "Where's that scruffy three-day stubble that drives all the women in this county wild, Declan? You must have a luncheon engagement with someone you fancy today. Am I am right?"

Declan shook his head negatively and rearranged his smooth features into a slightly boyish version of himself and said, "Oh, no, not really…just a lady that I know has invited me for Shepherd's pie and tea this afternoon, but that's all…"

"And would that lady happen to be my god-daughter, Mr. Ryan?" Annie inquired with sparkling eyes.

At this juncture, just as Declan was going to play coy for a bit longer, Christophe reappeared carrying a carved wooden arm chair from the kitchen for Annie to relax upon while they enjoyed breakfast together. Annie raised a knowing eyebrow and said, "Just because my husband is back and we're ready to bless the food, don't think you can get away without telling me who you're to be taking tea with later today, Declan. I know you and your ways!"

Laughing, Declan responded, "Oh, Annie, you're on to me, aren't you?"

"All I know, young man, is that Liliana borrowed my car just yesterday to go to the market. She came back bearing several paper bags that looked as though they might contain the ingredients for your favorite, shepherd's pie."

"Like I said, you're on to me, Annie!"

During breakfast, they chatted cordially about the nursery and the soon-to-be-upon-them spring rush. As always, Declan interjected interesting new ideas for presenting the nursery and its bounty to their ever-widening customer base. By the time the last cup of coffee had been consumed, Christophe got to the subject at hand…

"Declan, you know that Annie and I consider you to be a son, and the time has arrived for you to be rewarded for all you have done for us. You have always shown honor in everything you do, and you have given us your love and devotion during times of trial. Son, I guess what I am trying to say is that Annie and I want to give you a portion of your inheritance now, instead of down the road when we go home to be with the Lord."

"Right now, our will stipulates that you will receive the entirety of our estate when we are gone: The land, Annie's Diner, and most of our money. As to the nursery, that is what we desire to give to you now, Declan. I've never voiced this before, but I sometimes wonder if Liliana's benefactor at Christmastide may have, in fact, been you; but I'll not press you on that point, son. What I do know is: Someone freed her from a lifetime of paying off Richard Rawlings' incredible debt, but that selfless gesture was probably to the detriment of their own life savings. I know you, Declan, and I know you are pretty savvy with a buck, but a gift like that could set a person back for a while. That is one of the reasons why I want to give you the nursery now. It already runs like a well-synchronized watch under your care, and Annie and I are indebted to you for its continuous growth…no pun intended."

"Declan, my lovely Annie and I have been blessed abundantly, and we want to share our wealth with you now, while we can watch you enjoy your gift. The gift taxes are already put away in an Escrow account, too, so you're all set. You need only do what you've already been doing since the day you arrived here."

A clearly stunned Declan then spoke, "Christophe, Annie…you are being far too generous with me. I don't think you realize what you're giving to me. This is the gift of a lifetime…especially for a horticulturist like me."

Christophe just shook his head and smiled at his serious young cousin… "You know that our travels thus far have only whetted our appetites for seeing the world, Declan. Annie and I want to take more time for travel during our retirement years, so it just makes sense that you take over completely as captain of this ship. Besides, we all know that without you, this place wouldn't be nearly as productive as it has been since you arrived. I might have found this gem, but you are the one who helped me to fashion it into such a beauty."

Declan replied, "I just don't know what to say…I've always been so thankful that you invited me to America to be a part of your lives, but this gift is far more than I deserve."

"That's crazy talk, man," chuckled Christophe. "You know that you're the one who's responsible for the incredible growth and charm of the property." Christophe continued, "Also, Declan, I suspect that you'll be wanting to marry one of these days. You'll want to have this property to provide for your loved ones. We all know it would be a lovely place to raise a family. All I ask is that you now pay me a salary for my work. Please say that you'll accept our gift to you."

Overcome with love for the two people who had become his only family, a humble Declan Ryan rose from his chair, strode around the desk and engulfed his second cousin and his wife in a heartfelt embrace. He simply said, "I am honored to be considered one of your own, Chris and Annie. Thank you." Shaking his head in disbelief, he said, "What a wonderful gift you have given me today; I can't thank you enough for your generosity to me."

Putting her hand on Declan's stubble-free cheek and looking into his brilliant blue eyes, Annie Riordan then said it best, "I watched your stalwart commitment to your mother when you were only a mere eight years of age, I have reveled in your allegiance to Chris and me, and I have witnessed your tenderness toward dear Liliana since her return... Declan, you are the kind of man that every mother hopes their child will grow into...I know I speak for Christophe as well when I say that we are so proud to call you our own." She then embraced Declan while he fought for composure.

When that embrace was broken, giant Christophe Riordan put his big, work-worn paw of a hand on Declan's shoulder and said, "Why don't you stop by Liliana's cottage on your way back over to the nursery, son? I suspect she would enjoy seeing you this morning and hearing your news." With that Christophe and Annie Riordan began to busy themselves with carrying the breakfast dishes back to the kitchen. No one would have ever known that they had just given Declan Ryan the gift of a lifetime.

Fifteen minutes later, Liliana Lylestrom opened her front door to find Declan Ryan standing on the front porch. He was smiling, but he looked slightly overwhelmed.

He simply said, "Oh, Liliana, Christophe and Annie have just given The Old Vineyard Road Nursery to me as part of an inheritance. I must admit that I'm somewhat overcome…may I please come in?"

Giving him a very pleased smile, she extended her small hand and pulled him gently over the threshold. As soon as he was inside, she closed the door tightly. Putting her hands upon his shaved cheeks, she said, "You are the best man I know, Declan Ryan, and there is no one more deserving of such a thoughtful and wonderful gift than you. I couldn't be happier for you, sweetheart."

Declan, then pulled her to himself and held her very tightly. It goes without saying, that ever-faithful Declan Ryan did shed a few tears as he shared his news with his beloved that cold February morning.

PART IV

SUMMER'S RENAISSANCE

THE OLD VINEYARD
ROAD NURSERY

It was as if the staid, **Old Vineyard Road Nursery**, knew something very special was on the horizon this year. Everything looked quite beautiful as if poised for a big event. The flowering trees had shown themselves off throughout the month of April, and with the arrival of May, late-blooming, long-stemmed, ruffled tulips and irises began their parade. The old property looked its best and across the street, lettuces and sweet peas showed evidence of forthcoming delights. The Old Vineyard Road Nursery, its extensive grapevines, and its organic gardens looked as if they were dressed in their finery for a spring dance.

Liliana Lylestrom was again cultivating and arranging the flower beds while Christophe, Declan, and young Tim Hill, Declan's assistant, were unloading newly arrived plants, roses, and trees. This year, she was to help in minding the stone kiosk on Friday and Saturday mornings where organic farm-to-market fruits and vegetables were sold seasonally. She had begun to run the little stand occasionally the previous year, and it was no surprise that customers made a weekly effort to purchase their produce from her. Who could resist her in cowboy boots and a sundress as she thoughtfully packaged their purchases in brown paper and twine?

Dover, who seemed to fancy himself, manager over the entire nursery and farmer's market operation trotted between Liliana and the three men day in and day out; always managing to swish his tail just in time to avoid getting it stepped on, or worse yet, stuck under the sturdy weight of a peat-potted young sapling. In all, the entire staff of the nursery was happy that the winter weather was behind them.

Occasionally, Declan Ryan would look up from his work to lock eyes with the love of his life. She always flashed him her electric smile, and he would nod his head to her in turn. Declan was starting to suspect that Liliana was ready to get back into living her life again. He was very happy for her. In the months since she had learned that someone had paid off the debts of her late husband, the happy young woman that he had once known began to surface once again. To see her like this brought great joy to Declan's heart.

For most of the winter months, Liliana had substituted for the Rosemeade County School District, but on the days when she was not working, Liliana found time to prepare something special and invite Declan for lunch. He truly enjoyed breaking bread with her. Oftentimes, he would arrive to the aroma of meat pie or pastry-wrapped sandwiches. She was an excellent cook and her home was very inviting. In turn, on these occasions, Declan always brought her something special from the greenhouse. It was obvious to Christophe and Annie Riordan that both Liliana and Declan were healing every day.

Now that Liliana was working full time at the nursery once again, she, too, was delighted to be working closely with Declan. Just as she had done years ago, she assisted him with his research studies. Sometimes, they would be quiet for hours just sitting side by side on roughly-hewn benches while they propagated plant cuttings for the upcoming summer season. It didn't matter what they were doing, as there was no awkwardness or wariness with one another; just the thrilling happiness of being friends and together again. Like the nursery, they seemed to sense that bigger things were on their way for the both of them. Yes, this summer season at The Old Vineyard Road Nursery promised to be a pretty special one.

A DO-OVER NIGHT OUT

*D*eclan Ryan was weary. He had been working very hard for weeks, and tonight was to be Christophe and Annie's annual **Summer at the Vineyard Dance** at the nursery. It was a highly-anticipated event by all in the Rosemeade County area. The month of June was the perfect time, too. The nursery looked beautiful, as the roses were in full bloom, the grapevines lining the terraced foothills behind the nursery were lush and newly-leafed out, and the scent of honey suckle wafted through the evening air. The third week of June always brought the perfect temperature with it, as well.

Once the sun dipped below the horizon, a bonfire would be lit, and the dancing would begin inside the barn and outside on the sprawling patio. The staff from Annie's Diner had set tables out in inviting configurations throughout the area and the scent of delicious food was floating on the air. It was going to be a wonderful evening, but Declan had been working hard for a month and a half in anticipation, and he was dog tired.

Liliana, too, had assisted in the preparations for this evening's big event. She was buzzing round the nursery tweaking things with her artistic eye. It was a joy to see color back in her face and to witness her renewed spirit. Richard Rawlings had just about broken that spirit, but she was healing now. Declan had enjoyed having her back again, and it made him feel good to know that she was tucked safely in the little vintner's cottage that Old Jim used to occupy. Somehow, he knew Jim would be happy that she now lived in his old home. Though Jim would probably not recognize the place, as Liliana had dusted, swept, scrubbed, and painted every surface in that little house, and her creative touches were showing up everywhere, from the colorful flowers planted around the yard to the tiny deck Declan had helped her to build on the east side of the cottage. Yes, he thought. Old Jim would be happy, indeed.

Declan, Liliana, and Tim had just finished the last of the day's work, and Declan was more than ready for a shower when a new red Acura pulled into the drive. Out popped Vivienne Richardson, who proceeded to wave him over.

"Hello, Viv, what can I do for you this evening? Are you and Dick planning on attending the dance tonight?" greeted Declan.

As usual, Vivienne was breathless in her greeting as she met Declan by the hood of her car. "Oh, Declan, I just wanted to stop by to let you know that Dick is out of town this week, and I was hoping that you might save a dance for me tonight." She looked knowingly up at him.

At this point in their exchange, Liliana looked up from tying some vines to a trellis with a look of amusement on her face and mouthed, "She's coming on to you." Declan winked at her.

"Well, I'll tell you, Viv, my dance card is full this evening. Kristen's Bellyer's Third Grade class has been learning to dance, and I've a bevy of beautiful little girls who have already claimed my hand for tonight. It appears that I'll be completely tied up all evening. I'm awfully sorry; maybe next time."

"Oh, Declan, how much longer are you going to make me wait for you?" sighed raven-haired Vivienne. Resigned, she wiggled herself back into her very expensive auto and backed out of the drive. "Until then, Declan!" she called as she roared off down the road.

Declan Ryan stood there shaking his head, and Liliana Lylestrom was laughing as she finished tying off a hummingbird vine. But, before she could gather her twine and scissors, a green, 1949 fastback Chevy coupe came chugging up the drive. Mavis Whittier, the retired Rosemeade County Librarian, hopped out of her classic car and ambled toward Declan. Mavis Whittier was nothing short of eighty-seven years of age.

"Oh, yoo-hoo, Declan!"

"Well, hello Mavis, how are you this fine evening? You're looking as pretty as ever!" greeted Declan.

"Oh, Declan, I stopped by to make sure that I can secure a waltz with you tonight," twinkled white-haired Mavis. "I didn't get to dance with you last year, so I wanted to stake my claim early."

"Mavis, surely you must know how sorry I am about how things turned out last June. I can assure you that I have saved two dances, especially for you, dear," a clearly-pleased Declan retorted.

"Oh, thank-you, my good man; I'll be looking forward to it. I must get home to get all gussied up for you. I'll see you then," beamed lovely Mavis.

Liliana was quite amused by what she was witnessing when, yet **another** vehicle came up the drive. This time, the automobile contained ninety-year-old Priscilla Newman, and her sixty-five-year-old spinster-daughter, Grace. Grace, of course, was driving her mother's very-sensible, metallic-blue 1970s-era Chrysler.

Priscilla Newman hobbled gingerly out of the huge automobile and said, "Declan, I'm just making sure that you dance with Gracie, tonight. She's just had a new perm, and she never realizes how beautiful she looks. She even bought a new dress for this evening, so make sure you give her a spin around the dance floor, won't you?"

"Why, of course, Miss Priscilla. I would be honored to dance with your beautiful daughter," he smiled as he inclined his head toward Grace as she cowered behind the wheel in embarrassment. "It would be my pleasure. See to it that you rest up, too, Miss Priscilla, as I would also like to take **you** for a spin around the dance floor, as well." he laughed.

Declan then proceeded to bundle Priscilla Newman back into the car. He bumped his fist quickly upon the roof twice in succession, and Grace Newman took that as her cue to begin backing the giant Chrysler out onto the drive. "Until then, ladies!" he shouted over flying gravel as the two women spun out of the drive.

Liliana smiled and quipped, "I guess my dear old Iris wasn't the only girl, blazing a trail to see you, was she? You are quite the lady killer, Declan Ryan. Do you think you might save at least one dance for an old gal like me? I can't even remember the last time anyone asked me to dance," she laughed.

Declan's twinkling blue eyes turned serious, and in the heavy brogue that always laced his words when he was being thoughtful, he quietly answered, "Liliana, I do intend to invite you to dance with me this evening. It's been a long time." He then proceeded to amble up the path with her. They stopped outside the wrought-iron gate that led into Liliana's yard. Declan looked thoughtful again, "May I walk you to the dance this evening, Miss Lylestrom?"

"Why yes, Mr. Ryan. That would be lovely. What time shall I expect you?"

"I'll call for you at eight. Will that work?" he asked.

"That will be perfect." She then entered through the gate and proceeded to her front door. There, she paused and waved. Declan nodded and continued back down the path to the ancient stone barn and that long-awaited shower.

Two hours later, promptly at eight o'clock, Declan Ryan knocked softly on her front door. When the door opened, Liliana and Dover greeted him. Her long, dark hair was still slightly damp from the shower, and it was curling sweetly around her face. She smelled of soap and looked fresh and pretty. She wore a little black dress made of lace and a pair of pink cowboy boots. "She has absolutely no idea how lovely she is," Declan mused to himself.

"Good evening, Dec, you are right on time, she beamed.

"And, you look very fetching this fine evening, Miss Lylestrom," Declan teased. "Are you ready to go?"

"I am ready, but I'm afraid Dover is nervous that I won't be coming back. He so dislikes being left alone, and he's been shaking ever since he saw me putting on my clothes for the dance. Even his favorite treat has not put the "wag" back into his demeanor. Do you think he could come to the dance, Declan? I'll tell him to stay in his 'spot,' and I know he'll mind me. He is such a good boy."

Knowing that Dover had fallen in love with his mistress and had rewarded her devotion to him with commendable obedience, Declan said, "Oh, why not? He already acts as if he is one of the staff anyway, and he *is* a gentleman of sorts. Let's bring him along."

"Liliana's face lit up in much the same fashion as when she was a college girl. "Oh, thank you, Dec. I'll be right back." She turned around and headed back to the bedroom. When she returned, she had a recently ironed light-blue bandana in her hands. "Come, Dover, let's get you ready for the dance." She lovingly knotted the bandana around the dog's neck. "There you go, my big boy. All the girls will fall madly in love with you this evening," she said as she ruffled the huge dog's ears. Declan noticed that the dog had been impeccably groomed. If he knew Liliana, which he did, he knew that she would never let a dog of hers look unkempt…just in case that dog received an invitation to the big dance.

Shaking his head and smiling, Declan took Liliana's hand and tucked it into the crook of his elbow, covered it with his other, and off the three of them walked down the gravel path that led to the special party at the barn. It was going to be a perfect evening.

When the threesome arrived, Christophe was welcoming his guests with his usual gusto. As he spotted them, he said, "Ladies and gentlemen, I want to make sure that you all know my beautiful god-daughter, Liliana, and my cousin, Declan. They both make Annie's and my life so very special. Declan is truly the son we never had, and Liliana has been our special girl since she was born. As to that giant white dog, you may call him Dover." He then put his arm around Annie and said, "Now, you've met my whole family. Enjoy the food and get ready for some serious dancing!" Christophe and Annie's guests burst into applause, and the special evening was launched.

True to his word, Declan danced every dance with Kristen Bellyer's third-grade girls, and since the third-grade boys had seen Liliana arrive with him, they naturally assumed that she was to be their partner, so the two of them were kept busy. When all the third graders were finished dancing, their attention turned to petting and fawning over Dover. The huge white dog was, indeed, a big hit with everyone.

Declan made good on his promises to Mavis, Grace, and Priscilla for their special dances with him. He also took Miss Bellyer, the third-grade teacher, for a spin around the barn and the patio. All the while, Liliana danced her feet off with every white-haired grandfather and ancient bachelor from Rosemeade County. They were no fools those older men; they knew a special dancing partner when they saw one. Declan laughed to himself as he watched Liliana glide by again and again.

When the time came for Miss Bellyer's students to go home, they were each given a ribbon of achievement for their dancing. Then, Declan and Liliana helped her to shepherd her charges to their respective parents' cars, buckle them into their seatbelts, and wave them off to their homes for a good night's sleep.

From there, they escorted Miss Bellyer to her automobile and bade her good night. Yet, neither Declan nor Liliana knew that a quiet Miss Bellyer had then watched them walk back up the path to the barn for more dancing. Kristen Bellyer saw that Declan's hand was lightly cradled on the small of Liliana's back. Then, she watched as Liliana said something to Declan that humored him. Resignedly, Kristen observed as his rare smile lit up his face in the moonlight while he lovingly gazed down at Liliana. Kristen knew in her heart that she had never been the recipient of Declan's attention like that, and so she finally admitted to herself that even though Declan Ryan had danced with her tonight and had been very cordial, that his heart's affection would always belong to Liliana Lylestrom.

Somehow, she had been hoping she might be able to change his mind about that, but she had to admit to herself that she admired his fidelity to the woman he loved. Kristen Bellyer wanted so much to dislike Liliana, but she could not; Liliana Lylestrom was quite deserving of Declan's devotion. Sighing, she drove home to her quiet, little apartment wondering if she was ever going to be able to share her life with someone that she loved.

Back at the stone barn, the remaining tempo of the summer dance changed. Since the band was an eclectic mix of musicians from the World War II era to rockers from the Sixties, Seventies, Eighties, and Nineties, and well into the new millennium, there wasn't a song request that could not be played. A fresh round of food and drink was passed, and a beautiful moon peeked over the top of the verdant foot hills. Men and women alike gathered around the bonfires and chatted. Christophe and Annie cruised from table to table visiting with their guests, and Declan and Liliana finally sat down under a wisteria-covered pergola adjacent to the patio. Dover saw them relaxing and ambled over to join them. It was the perfect evening.

"Declan…"

"Yes, sweet Lily?"

"Nothing much, really; but I just wanted you to know that tonight, I feel as though my "do-over" is getting closer to completion. You know that last year was horrible for me. Cleaning up after Richard was not easy. And, then, when both of my parents died on the heels of each other, I felt as though I might not ever be happy again. Yet, I have been healing, Declan, and tonight has been a milestone of sorts for me. I have great hope. Hope…because I feel like me again. No longer am I governed by Richard's heavy hand or his bad decisions."

She continued. "I feel as though I have been let out of prison, and I am breathing in clean, fresh air once again…sort of like what one might refer to as: a second bloom. I think you know what I mean. Surely, you know that I am so very thankful to whomever paid off the remainder of Richard's debt for me, and I have great gratitude to Christophe, Annie, and to you, Declan, for helping me through some very hard times. I love you all so much."

"I'm truly happy for you, lass," a pensive Declan replied. He then smiled as the strains of an old World War II love song floated onto the patio, and said, "Liliana, I believe this is the dance that you promised to me earlier this evening. Would you do me the honor?"

Happily, Liliana replied, "It would be my pleasure, Declan."

With moonlight flooding over the patio, Declan put his arm around her waist and drew her close. He then captured her hand within his larger one. She placed her free hand upon his shoulder and unknowingly wound her fingers in his curling hair. She looked up at him with a sparkling smile, then proceeded to follow his lead around the floor. As the music progressed, Declan linked her hand a bit tighter within his and held it down flat upon his chest. He suspected she could probably feel his overflowing heart beating wildly. They hadn't danced together since the day she was married to Richard years ago, and they had never danced to a 1940s love song. Tonight, Declan was glad his mum had insisted so many years ago that he learn to dance. From across the patio, Christophe and Annie exchanged knowing looks as Declan and Liliana floated over the flagstones, completely lost in each other's company.

When the last of the guests had departed, and the last vestiges of the party were cleared away, Christophe and Annie hugged Declan and charged him with getting Liliana safely home to the vintner's cottage. The older couple walked off toward the big house arm-in-arm. Once again, Declan tucked Liliana's hand into the crook of his arm, and they strolled up the gravel path to her cottage with Dover obediently following behind them. The air was perfumed with the scent of honeysuckle mixed with the fragrance of the old-world roses that had been planted adjacent to the path. The moon glow amplified the beauty of all the improvements Christophe and Declan had made during the years she had been away. In all, it was the most-perfect summer night that Liliana had savored in many, many years.

"It was an excellent party tonight. Did you enjoy it?" Declan inquired.

"Very much so, Declan. I really can't remember the last time I had such a special night. I truly did enjoy myself."

Declan squeezed her hand that was tucked within his arm. "I am so glad."

"Dec, it's such a beautiful evening, and I'm not quite ready for the fun to be over. Would you like to come in? I could make us something to drink, and we could sit on the porch and look at the night sky. The stars seem especially bright tonight."

"Yes, Liliana, I would like that very much…"

Fifteen minutes later, Declan Ryan and Liliana Lylestrom were sitting together, savoring sparkling lemon water on an old wooden settee that Christophe had brought home for Liliana's front porch.

Their only light was a little glass jar containing a candle. The ageless settee was really the right size for two and sitting so close just felt right. Before they knew it, they were giggling like two school kids.

"This is like old times, isn't it, Liliana? Only, we are not driving in your old blue Beetle."

"Didn't we used to have fun, Declan?" Liliana queried. "That V-Dub was the best car ever. I wish that I still owned it. We had some great times together driving on the back roads of Rosemeade County in that little car…me getting us lost, and you always managing to get us back home."

"Those days were great fun. You made me feel so welcome, Liliana."

Then, before he realized what he was doing, Declan scooped Liliana up and onto his lap, and held her. She didn't seem the least bit surprised, and she put her arms around his neck. She leaned her soft cheek against his. They sat there for several minutes that way. Liliana was the first to speak. She sat back, touched her hand to his cheek, and declared, "Declan Ryan, you are truly the finest man I know."

He laughed, "Oh, I don't know about that, but I do know I'm a pretty good navigator when lost in the backwoods with you."

She laughed, too, and said, "But, I meant what I said, Declan. You are so good to all of us, and I can see why every woman under ninety years of age in this county wants to be with you. I couldn't quite believe that parade of cars earlier this evening. Those gals definitely wanted to stake their claim upon you, and who can blame them?"

Declan's heart skipped a beat when he heard her words, and he took a chance for the first time in many months. He looked at her seriously and said, "There's only one woman I've ever wanted to stake a claim upon my heart, Liliana, and that woman is you. Here I am, a man of almost thirty-seven years, and I'm still waiting to thoroughly kiss you until we're both crazed… and yet, we've already shared so many of life's intimacies together."

"She looked seriously into his eyes and said, "Perhaps, it is time that you finally kissed me properly then, Declan Ryan."

Declan could tell that she was slightly trembling when he wrapped his arms a bit tighter around her. He kissed her with the tenderness of someone who knew the hurt and pain that she had endured at the hands of her own husband. He kissed her as a man who wanted to cherish her. When he broke their kiss, it was almost sorrowful.

She looked up into his eyes, then whispered, "Might I have another kiss, please?"

Declan obliged her. He wrapped his arms further around her waist, and he pulled her a bit more tightly to himself. He kissed her with much emotion this time, and they languished in that kiss. When they finally drew apart, Declan found that she was breathless. She embraced him tightly before she sat back from him.

She then shook her head and murmured. "Declan, I'm afraid that just one of your kisses will never be enough for me."

His heart melted at her declaration. "So, you do fancy me then, eh?"

"Oh, yes, I **do** fancy you, Declan Ryan," a serious Liliana intoned.

Spurred on after her sweet declarations, he held and kissed her quite passionately, yet he was keenly aware that the last time she had been kissed or held by anyone; she had been treated quite abominably. He kissed her with palpable devotion but kept himself in check; he could wait awhile longer. And so began a new chapter in Declan Ryan's life, too. Somehow, Liliana Lylestrom always seemed to reach into his very soul. He knew she was truly his now, and that she desired him. At last, they were to be given their second chance.

RELIVING SPECIAL MEMORIES

*L*iliana *Lylestrom* was humbled by the transparency Declan had shown to her earlier this evening. Oh, she knew him well, and she had always cared for him very much, but he had guarded himself waiting for her to declare that she was ready for something more between them. Ever since that night in the hospital last year, he had patiently waited for her to give him the cue that she was ready. That night, Declan had finally told her how much he cared. Tonight, well over a year later, he had tenderly kissed her and held her, making her feel cherished. "Oh, Declan…" she whispered aloud.

Liliana couldn't sleep after Declan had gone to his loft, so she replayed the entirety of the evening again in her mind's eye. They had been particularly connected the whole night. Then when the party was over, she had recklessly invited him to stay awhile because she couldn't bear to be parted from him. The dance they had shared together on the patio should have been enough, but she had wanted more of him. Tonight, they had reminisced about his first summer in Rosemeade when she had wanted to "share" America with him.

Liliana then thought back to that very first summer, so many years ago, that she had spent at Old Vineyard Road. She was just barely nineteen years old back then, and Declan had taught her so many new and interesting things about the plants and trees that she helped to care for at the nursery. She had been fascinated that he held degrees in both botany and business. She had watched her mother nurture her vegetable and flower gardens, but she, herself, had never caught the fever until she worked with Declan. He had brought the care and cultivation of plants to life for her. It was during his teaching that Liliana had first witnessed Declan's rare, but very beautiful, smile. He was definitely serious, but it had been a welcome change from the tedium of ever-drunken fraternity boys.

When the Fourth of July had arrived that year, she had asked Declan to join her family, along with Christophe and Annie, for their annual celebration. It had been a wonderful time for all of them. Her parents had welcomed Declan with open arms because he was part of Christophe's family. It had been a perfect day. Her mother had plied them all with delicious homemade food. Then, there had been fireworks and dancing under the stars at the city park. That evening, she and Declan had danced together for the very first time. And, as they all had walked home together that evening, Declan had tucked her hand into the crook of his arm and covered it with his own. That had been the beginning...

The remainder of that first tender summer had included plenty of rewarding work, many Sunday drives through the backcountry of historic Rosemeade County, and lots of swimming at the lake. All in all, it was the best summer of her young life, and she had been sorry when she had had to return to her university studies. She had known that she would see Declan again at Thanksgiving, but that day seemed like such a long way off to a nineteen-year-old girl who was truly falling in love for the first time. The evening before she left to return to school, Declan had come to her little apartment, and they had sat on her tiny roof-top patio.

The little patio showcased several pots of geraniums that she had purchased from Christophe. She and Declan had sat upon two old wooden chairs that she had found in the dumpster behind the thrift store. Declan had helped her to shore them up, then she had painted them French blue. The effect of the blue chairs and brilliant orange geraniums never failed to please her when she sat there. That night, though, she found it hard to enjoy her tiny oasis. She was sorry to be leaving.

Declan quietly spoke, "It's not going to be the same around here without you, Liliana. There is no one else like you in all of Scotland **or** the USA," he had quipped. "Thank you for making my first few months in Rosemeade County so very enjoyable."

"Declan, this has been the most memorable summer of my life, Liliana retorted. "I have been so delighted to have worked with you.

I do hope you're here for a long time because if Christophe will have me, I want to help out at the nursery again next summer."

"Rest assured, Liliana, that your job will be saved for you," Declan had chuckled. "Christophe likes nothing better than to have you around. That big guy would put his hand in the fire for you. He takes his job as your god-parent very seriously. And, who can blame him?"

Declan had then leaned forward in his blue chair, grabbed her hands, and said, "How about if we go have a piece of pie at the diner? It will be my treat."

"You don't have to ask me twice, Declan Ryan! You already know my feelings about pie," she had laughed.

As they had ambled down the street toward Annie's Diner, the scent of French fries had beckoned them. The evening had been warm, and many of the handsome old buildings around the square had window boxes filled with colorful summer flowers. Couples were strolling around the village green, and church bells rang the hour. Neither of them had had much to say that summer evening, but it had been so comfortable; just two friends enjoying one another's company.

That night, they had sat on the same side of the booth close to one another and had lingered over their peach pie. After they finished, they walked around the town square and admired the gardens. It had been a special time. When Declan delivered her to the door of her little apartment, he had tenderly held her face between his large palms and had kissed her. He then said, "Liliana Rose Lylestrom, I'll be seeing you soon." Right then and there, she had started counting the days until Thanksgiving break. Oh, what a wonderful summer that had been…she and Declan were innocents and neither of them had made any decisions that would alter the course of their young lives.

Liliana shook herself from her reverie and rose from her bed. She found herself at the open bedroom window where a cool canyon breeze was flowing through. She looked out toward the old stone barn; it loomed large in the moonlight. The tall trees surrounding it shimmered in the glow of the barn's architectural lighting with new fresh leaves. She noticed that Declan's lamp illuminated his window. Apparently, he wasn't sleeping, either. She wondered what he was thinking. "I'm acting like a silly school girl," she said aloud while shaking her head. "One would think that was my first kiss." She randomly walked down the hallway toward her little sewing room when she heard soft knocking at the door.

"Liliana, it's me, Declan. May I come in?"

Her heart beating in her chest, Liliana opened the door. Declan stood there in a tee-shirt, low-slung plaid pajama pants, and leather flip-flops. His mahogany-colored hair was in disarray. He was breathing deeply, and his muscular chest rose and fell with the same cadence. "Are you alright, Declan?" she asked with concern.

"Believe me, Liliana, I am more than fine."

"What's the matter, then?"

"It's you, Lily. You make me crazy! Since I held and kissed you tonight, the years we've lost just keep flying around in my head. I don't know if you are even ready to embark upon a relationship, and I've tried not to pressure you at all. Yet, ever since that night at the hospital, well over a year ago, though I've longed to hold you again, I have tried to be patient. You have needed time, and I know this…but, I have to say that I desire to move forward with you now. We both know that life is short, and I feel we've wasted too much precious time already. I care for you deeply, and I yearn to court you; to quote Old Jim." He then shook his head and grinned at her like a teenager.

Liliana went to him and put her arms around his waist while he held her in kind. She looked up at him. "The essence of your skin is wonderful, Declan Ryan. Your scent appeals to me." She looked steadily up at him and then stated, "I was crazy about you when I was just nineteen years old, and I am ready, Declan. The time for us to begin courting has finally come. I know Old Jim would be very happy for us, indeed."

After tenderly kissing good-bye for at least three quarters of an hour, a very-pleased Liliana watched as Declan Ryan walked slowly back to his loft.

He stopped suddenly and turned around, "Lily, do you know that you have saved me once again?" Smiling and shaking his head, he turned back toward the path to his loft. What Liliana didn't know was that he could still feel her sweet kisses upon his lips.

Liliana slept very soundly that night. It was the first sound sleep she had had since she had returned to Rosemeade County. Declan Ryan had saved her, too.

STOLEN TIME

L iliana was very engrossed in her work two days later when she looked up to see Declan Ryan standing in front of her. She had been watering young trees on the east side of the nursery and thinking about him while she worked. She just could not help herself...she felt as if she were twenty years old again and just about as giddy. So, seeing Declan backlit by the morning sun, while he wore a heavy canvas work kilt, a sleeveless knit shirt, and his work boots just about unraveled Liliana's already slightly unhinged emotions. His arms were tanned and quite muscular, and he looked so ruggedly handsome that Liliana found it hard to squeak out a greeting to him. Yet, she somehow managed.

"Good morning to you, Declan. How are you this fine Thursday morning?" she managed to say coherently.

Declan smiled knowingly at her and replied, "Good morning to you, too, Liliana. I find myself feeling very well today." He then looked surreptitiously around the nursery where his staff was hard at work and inquired, "Do you have a minute to look at something? I've some concerns…" He then turned around and began his ascent up the path to the greenhouse that was the furthest away.

Puzzled, Liliana followed him up the path. Nothing was said between them until they arrived at the greenhouse. Once inside the door, Declan turned around, took her hand and led her to the back of the humid structure. When he was sure they would not be seen, he thoroughly kissed her and said, "I almost can't concentrate on my work, Liliana. I had to see you alone."

Flushing beautifully, Liliana replied, "I think that makes two of us, Declan."

"You look so lovely today that I can't seem to take my eyes off of you."

Liliana smiled and shook her head, "Well, once again, I think that makes two of us! I've not seen you in a kilt before, Dec. It becomes you."

"Oh, lass," he replied. "Our working together is tricky business now." He then cupped her face between his two hands and kissed her yet again.

Liliana was breathless when he broke their kiss. All she could say was, "Oh, Declan, you are right…"

"May I see you tonight, Lily?" Declan inquired. "Please, come to the loft. Let me make dinner for you. Then, let's take a drive out to the lake."

"Declan, there is nothing that I would like better."

"Good. I'll come around for you at seven o'clock, then." Declan Ryan kissed her one more time, and then said, "Off you go, then."

Liliana emerged from the hothouse and tried to look as though she had not been engaged in stolen kisses with Declan Ryan, but it was a tall order for her. Her heart was beating quickly, and she could not stop smiling. She did return to her watering but could not shake the memory of her beloved Declan in a rugged kilt whilst she tended to her trees.

At six o'clock that evening, Declan Ryan stole up to his loft and began preparing for his time with Liliana. He showered the day's dust and mud from his being and shaved the three-day stubble from his face. Next, he ordered out for what he knew were Liliana's favorite Chinese food selections and readied his home for her visit. When all was to his liking, he walked down the pebbled path that led to her cottage.

Liliana opened the door when she heard his knock. Young Dover dog thumped his tail prodigiously on the black and white tile floor and barked a greeting. "We're both very happy to see you this evening, Declan," she greeted. "Please come in."

Stepping into the safety of her tiny cottage, Declan couldn't help himself. He reached for and embraced her, inhaling the scent of her hair. When he stepped back from her, he said, "You look very pretty this evening, Liliana. May I escort you to my place?"

"Yes, Dec, that would be lovely. Is young Dover invited, as well?" she queried.

"Of course, he is…I know that you two now come as a matched set. Do you know if he fancies Chinese take-out?"

"I don't know if Dover does or not, Declan, but I know that I fancy Chinese take-out. You remembered."

"Aye, that I did," Declan answered with a smile.

In just minutes, Declan had loaded Liliana and Dover into his shiny truck. He drove the short distance to pick up their take-out order. All the while, Liliana sat with her arm laced through his. It felt so good to be together again.

Later that evening, after a delightful meal of Sesame Chicken, Tangerine Chicken, Moo Goo Gai Pan, Fried Rice, and Egg Foo Yong, Declan and Liliana sat and sipped jasmine tea across from one another at Declan's small kitchen table. The tea was fragrant and delicious, and neither of them was quite ready to quit the cozy atmosphere of his kitchen. The windows had been opened, and the scents of honeysuckle, jasmine, and roses floated in the air.

Liliana spoke first, "Let's play Three Questions," Declan."

"I'm afraid I've not heard of that game before," a thoughtful Declan answered.

"It's easy, Dec, you go first…ask me three questions, and I'll answer them for you."

"Okay, that sounds easy enough," Declan replied.

Studying her across the table he began the game. "Do you still enjoy listening to music, Liliana?" Declan inquired as that errant dimple appeared upon his freshly-shaved cheek.

"Oh, yes, I do enjoy listening to music; especially nowadays, as it all sounds fresh and new to me," she earnestly answered.

"And why is it that everything sounds like a new composition to you?"

Liliana took a sip of her tea and her answer surprised him. "Because my late husband did not enjoy music, Declan. He would turn the stereo or the radio off as soon as he returned home each evening. He said, 'It grated on his nerves.'"

Rolling his eyes toward the ceiling and shaking his head, Declan then asked her, "May I play something for you from my collection then, sweet one? It seems that you've been a bit starved for good music of late."

A smiling Liliana then answered him, "Any chance you might have The Bill Evans Trio, *Waltz for Debby*? She thought for sure she could stump him with her choice.

In turn, Liliana was surprised when Declan replied, "Ah, yes, that one has always been one of my favorites. Let me go and queue it up for you."

When he returned, the strains of Bill Evans's pretty music floated through the loft and Liliana replied, "It's my turn, now, Declan."

"Okay, then…"

"Are you ever planning on returning to Scotland again?" a curious Liliana asked.

Answering quickly, Declan replied with an affirmative, "No!" Then, a bit more softly, he said, "Not unless you are by my side, Liliana. You are not the only one who can't bear to be separated, you know."

Knowing that Declan was referring to her passionate exclamation at the hospital over a year ago, Liliana asked quite seriously, "So do you think you might love me then, Declan?"

Declan then presented her with an especially serious countenance. Dipping his head slightly, he grinned and answered, "Aye, Liliana. My heart truly staggers with what I feel for you."

"Do you know then, Declan Ryan, that I love you equally as much?"

Declan then stood up and came around his tiny kitchen table. He pulled Liliana into his embrace and looked deeply into her green eyes. Still quite serious, he exhaled and replied, "Good…then it appears that we are both on the same page." He then kissed her with fervor. When his ardent kiss was at last broken, he said quite humbly, "I'm honored that you love me, Lily." The heavy brogue poured over his words.

A misty-eyed Liliana answered, "And I, you…"

While this tender scene played out in the kitchen, young Dover slept quietly under Declan Ryan's ancient old desk.

A SURPRISE ENCOUNTER

Christophe Riordan couldn't believe his eyes. He had just entered the greenhouse that contained young roses. The heavy air was perfumed, and he was looking for one special color of rose. When he looked up, he saw his own Declan Ryan and his little Liliana in the rear corner of the hothouse embraced in a very passionate kiss. Declan was holding her in the fashion of a man who truly cares for his woman, and she had her arms draped tightly around Declan's neck. Both were in their work attire…Declan, a blue chambray shirt, low-slung jeans, and his muddy gloves…Liliana, a pink T-shirt, a ponytail and shorts, no muddy gloves. Yet, their embrace was captivating. Christophe could hardly look away. Neither of them even knew he was there. Christophe made himself back quietly out the door. There was no denying it; those two young ones were in love. "I've got to tell Annie," he said aloud to himself as he hurried away from the greenhouse.

Annie was in her sunny kitchen, just pulling fragrant cinnamon rolls from her oven when her husband burst through the door. "What is it, darlin'…you look like you just won a prize."

"Oh, I have, Annie…I have won a special prize. Our young ones are in love!" he said, with sincere delight in his tone.

"Do you mean Declan and Liliana?" she asked.

"Yes, and it was beautiful to witness," he beamed.

"Christophe Riordan, you had better start from the beginning," Annie quipped. "I think this is very big news. Sit down and tell me over a mug of tea, okay?"

Christophe sat down at the table and wound his big fist around a mug of breakfast tea. He began, "Just a few minutes ago, I needed a particular rose for the beds outside the farm stand, so I went into the greenhouse to get it. I was looking down when I entered, but when I raised my head, I saw Declan and Liliana embraced in quite a heartfelt kiss in the rear corner; they were oblivious to my presence."

"Declan held her with his gloved hands and his fingers were splayed against her back and waist, and Liliana had her arms draped around his neck. Her fingers were tangled in Declan's hair. Oh, Annie, I may be an old codger, but I know perfect love when I see it." Christophe smiled broadly and shook his head, "Mark my words, Annie Riordan, there will be a wedding before the snow flies this year!"

"Oh, Chris," Annie smiled. "It is about time those two finally got together. It's been obvious they love each other, but the timing has never been right for them. But it must be now!" she laughed. "I couldn't be happier. Wouldn't Stephan and Jenny just be over the moon about this? They always thought Declan was her perfect match."

"Yes, they would be ecstatic, especially now that Liliana is free from the burden of Richard's debts. I still wonder who paid off the last of them for her. Though I suspect Declan, he is adamant and will not admit to it. For some reason, Liliana thinks that it might have been us. I don't think we'll ever know for sure."

"Annie looked thoughtful for a few seconds, "I wonder the same," she said, "and whoever it might be, I pray for their well-being and happiness every night."

From there, Annie got back to the topic at hand, Declan and Liliana. "I used to ache for Declan when he would bring girls home to meet us, as I could tell that his heart was not in it. Some of them were lovely young women, but Liliana always seemed to be one who was intricately woven into his heart. I'm glad he is finally getting the woman he has always desired...and she's our Liliana!"

Christophe shook his head again and smiled. "I just can't believe it. Two weeks ago, when we charged him with getting Liliana home safely from our summer dance, I never dreamed I would witness such evidence as I saw today. Oh, this *is* exciting."

A half hour later, when Christophe returned to the greenhouse for his rose, Liliana was intently watering the brilliantly-colored impatiens on their display tables. Her ponytail was slightly mussed, her cheeks were beautifully flushed, and she had a lover's secret smile on her face. As for Declan, Christophe watched him quietly hulking newly-delivered maple saplings off a truck with the same smile on his face.

Christophe Riordan then laughed to himself and whispered, "Yes, love is in the air, here on Old Vineyard Road."

Three days later, Annie Riordan shook her husband out of a sound sleep. "Christophe, wake up! You won't believe what I just witnessed."

Shaking his head to clear the sleepiness, he said, "What is it love… are you okay?" He then proceeded to look at the clock. It was only midnight.

"You're right, my dear…our kids *are* in love. I just saw them myself, Chris. I had almost forgotten how beautiful burgeoning affection like that can be."

"Please, share with me, Annie…"

"Well, it all started with that huge moon tonight. You know… the Native Americans in this area call it, The Strawberry Moon. That brilliant moon was lighting up our yard tonight like midday. It was giant, too…so big and bright in the night sky. I heard Declan's truck come into the drive, and a few minutes later, I heard voices talking softly. I looked out our window and found myself mesmerized."

"Declan and Liliana were walking the perimeter of the property arm-in-arm, with giant white Dover ambling along behind them. Declan was saying something that delighted her…I know that tinkling laugh of hers. Seconds later, Declan leaned upon the stone wall adjacent to our gazebo. He pulled her close, and he kissed her in much the same fashion that you witnessed in the greenhouse. His hands, with his fingers splayed, held her slim, young frame to himself like a man who cherished her. She was responding to him in much the same way. Her pretty, little hands caressed his face and hair. That Strawberry Moon lit up their love scene as if movie lighting had been employed. I just couldn't help watching, Christophe. It was quite moving to watch their affection for each other; especially knowing the pain they've endured."

"And, Chris, our Declan is a real man. He held her closely, but with respect; something I'm sure she needs after Richard's vile treatment of her. I couldn't be happier for those two darlings."

"Christophe smiled sleepily, "Oh, Annie, love *is* wending its way through this old vineyard, and I am so happy about it. Come back to bed with me, darlin', and let's both dream about young love tonight!"

A JULY GET-TOGETHER

iliana Lylestrom realized that the Fourth of July was soon to be upon them. Last year, she had quietly celebrated the holiday with Christophe, Annie, and Declan, but now she wanted to incorporate some of her mother's fun into the day. She invited her "people" to her cottage for a new tradition.

The Fourth of July arrived warm and sunny…the perfect day for a party. She prepared berry pies and potato salad in the cool of the morning, and hand-cranked vanilla ice cream in an ancient, old ice-cream freezer that she found in the attic of the cottage. When the shade finally started to cover her little deck on the east side of her home, she set up a slightly rickety white table, along with her old French blue chairs. She couldn't believe that Christophe and Declan had saved them for her. Recently, she had acquired two more vintage chairs at the local flea market and, again, Declan had tightened them up for her. She had painted them a coordinating color. They looked great coupled together with her old blue chairs.

Next, she covered the table with a colorful depression-era feed-sack quilt which she had found tucked away in an old chest of drawers that came with the cottage. She suspected that the pretty, little quilt had been stitched by Old Jim's mother. Last of all, she placed a large white water pitcher filled with colorful and very fragrant sweet pea blossoms in the center of the table. She had grown those pretty flowers in her small garden. The old-time look suited her side-yard perfectly.

Just before five o'clock that evening, Liliana scalded flour-dusted chicken breasts and thighs in a fry pan on her quaint, old stove. She then transferred the pieces to a glass baking dish, seasoned and popped them into a hot oven for an hour. While the chicken baked, she squeezed lemon juice from well over a dozen ripe lemons and added it to a cooled sugar and water mixture she had made earlier in the day. She taste-tested her concoction, then declared, "Home-made lemonade is by far the tastiest drink of all."

When her guests arrived promptly at six, they discovered delicious oven-baked chicken, potato salad, fresh green beans, watermelon, and berry pies waiting for them. Christophe, Annie, and Declan couldn't have been more delighted. They ate their meal at the charming table she had set for them in her side yard, while Dover lay on the ground on high alert. He was hoping something tasty might fall off that charming table.

Throughout the meal, Christophe and Annie Riordan noticed how both Declan and Liliana's eyes had shown with love when they gazed upon one another. When the meal was finished, Christophe declared that he and Declan would clear the table and do the dishes. Liliana was slightly amazed, because no one had ever volunteered to clean up a kitchen for her before. She and Annie had a special visit while they waited.

Annie looked at her god-daughter, covered her younger flawless hand with her own, slightly-aged one and said, "Liliana, I wish Stephan and Jenny could see how happy you are right now. They would be so pleased."

"Liliana smiled, "Oh, Annie, I am *so* very happy right now. I know my parents would be pleased for me, too, but I thank you and Chris for helping me to get to where I am again. You two have just loved on me and comforted me until there was nothing else to do but rejoice! I am indebted to you both for everything… Thank you for caring about me and treating me like a daughter. I love you for it. And, don't even get me started on how much I am enjoying your gift of a home to me. Each morning, I wake up and thank the Lord for you both."

"I don't think it's just your freedom from grief that's making you so happy, young lady!" laughed Annie. "I've seen the way our Declan looks at you and how he walks around smiling these days."

Just then, Christophe and Declan rounded the side of the house into the yard. Christophe announced, "The food is put safely away, the dishes are washed and dried, and there are two beautiful pies waiting to be enjoyed." He gazed toward Liliana as he sat down and said, "You are a very fine cook, Lily Girl. That was a memorable meal."

"I agree with you most heartily, Chris!" Declan added as he plucked Liliana from her chair. He sat down on her vacated seat, and then parked her upon his lap. He then grew serious, looked from Liliana to Christophe and to Annie. Then, he announced, "I love this woman deeply. She has agreed to let me court her," he said. "Christophe, may I have your permission to do so?"

Christophe Riordan, who was rarely at a loss for words, just nodded affirmatively with a pleased smile on his face, and finally said, "Declan, there is nothing that would make me happier."

Annie Riordan squealed in delight.

Liliana Lylestrom flushed beautifully and then rather shyly burrowed her head into Declan's neck and shoulder. He proceeded to lift her chin with his fingers and kiss her. Both Annie and Christophe clapped, and Dover began to bark.

FULL HEARTS

*A*ll was very quiet on the cottage porch later that evening. Now, after a multitude of fireworks had exploded from the city park, and berry pie with home-made ice cream had been enjoyed, Liliana again sat upon Declan's lap on the wooden settee. He held her lovingly in his arms, and both were very content. Dover had long since fallen asleep under a butterfly bush that was so big, it had most-likely been planted with caring hands way back in the 1930s. It was a beautiful night and the only sound was the symphony of crickets. Liliana could hear Declan's steady breathing in the quiet of the late hour. There were no lights, only the moon and the stars illuminated the night. She said, "I don't think I've ever enjoyed the Fourth of July quite this much, Declan."

"Aye, my sweet Liliana. This was one of the finest days of our acquaintance. I'll have to say, I've never seen Christophe dumbstruck before, but he was this evening when I asked his permission to court you. And, you know what? Old Jim's term is kind of growing on me. I should have thrown caution to the wind and courted you long ago; it's a pretty heady feeling," he confided as he smiled and held her closer.

"I wish that we could have courted long ago, too," Liliana sighed. "But you know what, Declan? I don't think it would have been nearly as precious to me then as it is now; because I hadn't ever known heartache. Believe me, I am happier to have your love now than I suspect I would have been when I was younger. Though I cared for you very much back then, I so admire the kind and honorable man that you are so much more now. I didn't have enough life experience back then to truly embrace what a wonderful person you are, Declan. You make me so very happy."

Humbled by her declarations, Declan kissed her.

Courting: When Declan thought about Old Jim's archaic term, he had to admit that there was something about that word that did strike a chord with him. When he thought about his first encounters with Liliana, he was glad that he had always treated her with the respect she deserved because she had been the sweetest and freshest young woman he had ever known. She had mesmerized him.

Declan ruminated on the other women he had dated during his university days, and he had to admit that all of them had paled in comparison to Lililana. Not one of those women would have been prepared to cleave to her principals and upbringing as she had. In retrospect, the word, "courting," seemed to be the most apropos moniker for what they were now embarking upon. There was still such a fresh honesty about her, that he couldn't even fathom not treating her as a treasure. Yes, courting was the only way he wanted to approach his relationship with her.

Declan also remembered something his lovely mother had told him shortly before she died, "One day, when you are ready to marry, son, find a sweet girl; a girl who hasn't been hardened by this world that we now live in." Declan knew that Liliana had been that girl years ago, and that she was still the woman his mother had encouraged him to search for today... He considered himself to be very fortunate indeed.

Courting and working so closely together brought about challenges in its own way. On more than one occasion, Declan found he had to stop his work and take Liliana into the far recesses of one of the greenhouses just to hold her for a moment and to kiss her sweet face. It was always on one of these occasions when she would take his breath away. Simply dressed in shorts with a little tee shirt and her pink work gloves, Liliana never failed to tear at his heart when he saw her. He knew that she loved him, too, and that she desired to be his alone. Her face would light up every time they happened to cross paths during their busy workday. He was always touched by her sincere affection for him.

On those occasions when he took her out to someplace special, she never even realized that everyone in the room looked at her as she passed by. She had no idea that she was beautiful inside and out. Though she didn't dress to be noticed, and she didn't flirt or invite attention, her charm just seemed to draw others to her. Waiters were at her service as soon as she asked them what their favorite entrée was; or cashiers smiled when she asked if they had had a busy day. Liliana just engendered happiness wherever she went, and she was making him feel very content right now. Courting was a beautiful thing.

IN THE MOONLIGHT

*D*eclan Ryan currently found himself mesmerized anew with the beauty of God's creation and in sharing it with his love, Liliana Lylestrom. Fairly late, one August evening, after having spent the whole of the dusk "courting" Liliana, he was preparing for bed when he chanced to look out his open window and see a brilliant light starting to appear from just behind the flattened dimensions of the tree covered mountains outside his loft. Instantly, he knew a full moon was soon to be rising, and it was sure to put on a brilliant show. He immediately called Liliana and told her to go out to her porch.

"I will be there in just a minute, sweet girl. Wait for me…"

Slightly puzzled, but trusting Declan completely, Liliana went out to her front porch in her night clothes and waited for him. Not ever wanting to be separated from his lady, giant white Dover was waiting there, too.

Soon, Liliana saw Declan quickly walking down the path to her little cottage. He was clad in his pajama pants, a tee-shirt, and his leather flip flops.

When he arrived, he took her hand and said, "Quickly, Lily, a spectacular full moon is soon to come up over the mountain. Sweetheart, I just have to share it with you." She tightened her grip on his hand, and off they went to stand at a wide-open set of sliding doors at the back of the nursery's barn on its second floor…just opposite Declan's loft. As they hurriedly made their way, Dover Dog trotted behind them.

Arriving at the huge opening of the barn doors and looking out, the flattened dimensions of the adjacent mountains appeared as though they had brilliant yellow-orange molten lava on their ridge tops, and those same mountains were backlit by very soft yellow light. It was dazzling. As just seconds ticked away, the top edge of the moon started to appear. It was slightly rounded and rose further and further into the night sky. It was breathtaking and Liliana could not contain her awe.

She exclaimed, "Oh, Declan, I've not ever seen the moon have that brilliant orange color before; have you? It is so beautiful."

"No, Lily, not like that…but of late, my life has been in technicolor because we are together again. I just had to share this moment with you."

As the seconds continued to tick by, the orange orb rose higher and higher in the sky. Soon, it was fully exposed in the full glory of its orange luster. The higher that beautiful moon rose in the night sky, the more it began to showcase its beautiful topography, and it became a brilliant bright white. In short, it was completely awe inspiring.

The two companions continued to watch the moon and could not believe its wonder. Then, they started noticing brilliant Mercury and Venus, as well as the constellations that they once enjoyed watching together years ago. Declan then held her close and said, "These are simple joys, Liliana, but with you by my side, they cease to be simple. They are restorative."

Declan earnestly continued, "Taking pleasure in things together from our shared past is quickly mending both of our badly bruised hearts, don't you think? I once thought that I would never be able to enjoy these things with you again. Thank you for sharing them with me tonight."

Just about a half hour later, Declan slid those huge barn doors closed again and walked Liliana and Dover back home again beneath the full moon's bright light.

When they arrived at her front door, they both wanted to linger a wee bit longer. Liliana said, "I feel that the words of that old World War II love song that we danced to at Christophe and Annie's Summer Dance in June are quite appropriate for us these days. You know, the opening lines, *I'll be seeing you in all the old familiar places, that this heart of mine embraces, all day through…*'". She didn't know all the words, so she began to hum.

She sat down on her little settee and Declan joined her. Dover took that as his cue to lay down at their feet. And as he had done so often of late, Declan pulled her onto his lap and embraced her. Both quietly reminisced about that June evening not so very long ago when the two of them innately knew that the time for them to begin again had finally arrived.

When Declan reluctantly rose to depart, and said, "I'll be seeing you in all of **our** familiar places tomorrow, sweet Liliana. You'll find me waiting by your front gate first thing in the morning."

As Declan walked away and opened her front gate, Liliana called out to him, "Dec, do you know that you have saved me, too?"

Declan Ryan looked very pleased in the moonlight as he nodded his head once, and answered, "Aye, and I am so happy that you're mine again, lass! Good night, sweetheart."

"Good night, my dearest man," Liliana breathed out as she stepped inside of her snug little cottage with Dover.

And, true to his word, Declan Ryan was waiting for her outside the gate when Liliana and Dover exited her cottage early the next morning at seven forty-five. He held a dog treat for young Dover, and a white waxed bakery bag of cider doughnuts.

He quipped, "I also remember how much you adore cider donuts, Lily."

Completely delighted, Liliana ran to him, and kissed him soundly while Dover ran in circles and barked out his morning greetings to his good friend, Declan Ryan. It was sure to be a great day for all three of them.

A HEARTFELT ADMISSION

*D**eclan Ryan* took Liliana to the lake late one afternoon in early September. The summer was waning; the local kids had gone back to school, so there were no people at the lake that day. They had everything to themselves. Liliana had packed a picnic for them, and at dusk, they lit a campfire. She wore his old sweatshirt over her swimsuit as she roasted bratwurst dogs over their campfire. Her hair was pulled up in a ponytail. As he watched her, she looked no different than when she was twenty years old. At that moment something pulled at him, something made him want to weep, something made him heartsick. It truly was his fault that she had married Richard Rawlings, his fault that she never knew he truly cared for her. Why had he ever held back from telling her his heartfelt feelings back then?

Declan went to her, and he quietly took the roasting sticks from her hands and laid them down. He tugged on her arm and led her to the colorful old quilt she had always brought on their outings. There, he sat down and pulled her into his arms. He told her, "When I saw you in the twilight just now, wearing my raggedy old sweatshirt over your bathing suit, I was taken back to the summer we first met. Liliana, you look no different tonight than you did then, you're so fresh and lovely." He then kissed her. "This is what I longed to do that very first summer after we met. I only wanted to kiss and to hold you, yet I didn't want to scare you off because you always teased me about being so much older than you, and I was, in a way, older. I earnestly hope that you do understand that all those years ago, I didn't want you to miss out on anything special in your young life by entering into a relationship with me too soon. I hope you recognize now why I held my declaration back. Can you forgive me, Lily?"

She looked slightly wistful, and said, "But, of course, Declan."

"Liliana, I only wanted you to be ready for a serious relationship with me. I knew there were only three years between us, yet I did feel considerably older than that. You know that I was forced to grow up early because I didn't have a father. My mother needed my help at our little grocery store after my dad died. And then, when she became so ill with cancer, I had to become a man in pretty short order. I guess I just felt that it would take you a while to catch up with me, and I don't know why I ever thought that of you. I assumed too much, Liliana! Can you *ever* forgive my stupidity? I may have ruined what could have been the happiest years of our lives. I am *so* sorry. We could be married, we could be raising our children, and we could be enjoying our life together. We could be waking up in your old iron bed each morning…"

Declan looked far away for a few seconds, then he said, "Old Jim was right when scolded me and asked me why I tarried."

He then turned his attention back to her, "Dearest Liliana, I do want to marry you. I long to hold you in my arms and to make very passionate love to you," he said as he smiled boyishly. "How much longer before I can ask for your hand in marriage? I desire only to care for you and to make you happy. When, Lily? When can I make you mine?" he passionately entreated.

A sheen of tears filled Liliana's eyes, but she smiled brightly. "Declan, the fault is not entirely yours, you know. I am just as much to blame for the time that we've lost. Because I was so young, I didn't recognize that you were waiting for our timing to be right. I just assumed that you didn't love or want me after taking Richard's innuendos to heart, so I stupidly let him manipulate me into a relationship that I wasn't ready for… and that was exactly what you had tried to protect me from, Declan." She then shook her head and said, "Back then, I should have just told you how much you meant to me. But I feared that you would think I was too brazen. We both erred. Can you forgive me, too?"

"My dearest Declan, I *want* to be your wife. I desire to wake up to you every morning and to give you those babies, and I yearn for you to make very passionate love to me for the rest of our lives. Declan Ryan, I am ready to marry you. You need only to ask me." She then pulled him to herself and tangled her fingers in his slightly long hair as she quite unabashedly kissed him.

Later that night, when they returned home, Declan Ryan went straight to Christophe Riordan and asked for his permission to marry his goddaughter. "You need never worry, Chris; I will always do right by Liliana. She is very precious to me."

Big Christophe Riordan wiped tears from his eyes and embraced Declan. He said, "Declan I met you when you were just a young lad, but I could tell that you were special; even then. Little did I know that God had designated you for our Liliana. Yes, you two have had some mean bumps in the road, but I know in my heart that you are meant for each other. Son, you have my full and complete blessing to marry our sweet Liliana. Congratulations!"

Declan Ryan returned to his loft and opened a small cedar-lined trunk of belongings from his old life in Scotland. Nestled within the confines was a velvet jewelry case that had belonged to his mother, he took out her engagement ring. His mother's ring was nothing like the rings he had seen on the fingers of American women, yet it was quite unique. It contained a large square-cut, diamond surrounded by a handsome border of emeralds. It was very old-world, but he felt that it suited Liliana perfectly. He would take it to the jeweler in Reedsburgh tomorrow for cleaning and sizing. Now, there were only a few more arrangements to be made...

LILIANA'S BIG DATE

*L*iliana Lylestrom was a bit surprised. Declan Ryan had invited her out for the evening, and he had been gone all day. It was close to five o'clock that afternoon, yet she still did not know what time to be ready for their date or if she even had one. Declan had always kept his word to her, so she tried not to fret. Yet, she began to think about Richard…he had never kept his word to her, ever. There had always been a series of excuses as to why he had not been able to keep his promises; most times, he indicated that it was her fault that he broke his word. She found herself starting to feel renewed anger toward Richard just when her dear, caring Declan came driving into the rear of the nursery in a sizable EZ-Haul Rental truck. He waved at her, and all her anger toward Richard vanished. "What is wrong with me?" she thought.

Declan hopped down from the cab of the truck. She could tell he was happy to see her. He spontaneously kissed her and said, "Would you like to have dinner at Stefano's tonight? I am in the mood for some authentic Italian. Does that sound good to you?" While they discussed their dinner plans, he guided her to the back of the furthest greenhouse, pulled her into his arms, and kissed her with feeling. He removed her gloves and laid them down on the well-used pine display table, clasped both of her hands in his, and said, "I missed you today, Liliana. I can't wait to see you tonight. Why don't you head over to your cottage and get ready; the staff and I will finish up here." He kissed her yet again and walked alongside her to the cottage gate. "I'll pick you up at seven o'clock," he said as he turned back toward the nursery.

"What's in that big truck, Declan?" she asked.

"You remember that Bob Whitney filed for bankruptcy, right? Well, I bought most of his nursery stock this afternoon. He'll make more off it this way than if he liquidated it with a closing sale. Everything is healthy and in good shape, and we'll coddle anything that might start suffering over the winter. I'm sorry things didn't work out for him, though; he's a nice guy."

"I'm sorry to hear that, too," she said with a wistful voice. "Do you think he'll be alright?"

"Yes, I think so; but it's never easy to start over," he said thoughtfully. I'll see you in a little while." He smiled at her and continued down the path.

Liliana wanted to look special for Declan, and she had some extra time, so she took advantage of it. Something about his happiness when he had arrived back at the nursery this afternoon made her want to please him, so she buffed, fluffed, lotioned, and prettied herself up for their special date. She had recently bought a new dress, so it came out of the closet for its first wearing. All the while, Dover watched her and thumped his tail.

When Declan knocked on her door at the stroke of seven o'clock, she was ready and waiting for him. She opened the door to find Declan was looking his best. He was wearing a European-cut suit, a crisply-starched, button-down collar shirt, and Italian-made shoes. His slightly-long hair was curling and combed off his face. "He looks delicious!" she thought.

Declan commented, "You always look lovely, but you look especially beautiful this evening, Liliana. I'm not competing with skinny little Eddy Bear tonight, am I?" he asked with a smile.

"No, I'm all yours, Dec," she grinned

When they arrived at Stefano's, Stefano Giancomo met them at the door. "Oh, Miss Liliana, you must wear little black dresses and red high heels more often. They are very becoming on you. Please come in," he said, as he heartily shook Declan's hand.

Stefano Giancomo led them to a table already set for two. Candles twinkled in the dimly-lit room at all the other tables, yet there were no other patrons in the place. The room's French doors had been opened onto the back patio, and a fire glowed from the vine-covered outdoor fireplace. Declan seated Liliana, and Stefano laid a starched black napkin on her lap. Once Declan sat down directly across from her, Stefano announced, "I will be taking care of you personally tonight, Miss Liliana. Please sit back and enjoy your evening."

Minutes later, Stefano Giancomo returned with several bottles of wine, and a long, rectangular box covered in golden foil and tied up with a white lace ribbon. There was a small white envelope attached. Liliana was surprised when Stefano bowed and handed it to her. She opened the small envelope and took out the card. It displayed Declan's flowing script:

My beautiful Liliana,

Though they are handsome, these roses cannot compare to your loveliness or your love for me. I will always be yours.

With all of my love and devotion, Declan

Flushing beautifully, she said, "Declan, you are very sweet to me. Thank you." She then carefully opened the box. Nestled inside were two dozen delicate pink roses interspersed with purple blooms of English lavender. The pink and purple of the blooms were framed beautifully with the grey-green leaves of the fragrant lavender. The entirety of the bouquet was wrapped in an iridescent, satin-like tissue paper that was sprinkled with tiny rhinestone flecks and tied with a satin white cord. It was all very beautiful. "You've given me some lovely gifts over the years, Declan, but you've never given me this type of bouquet before. Is this a special occasion?" she asked, looking slightly overcome.

"Yes, sweetheart, it is a very special occasion," Declan replied. His brilliant blue eyes looked very serious. "I want to ask for your hand in marriage tonight, Liliana." He then stood up and came around the tiny table. He reached for her and pulled her up and into his embrace. He kissed her with tenderness; then, he simply asked, "Will you be my bride and my love for the rest of our lives, dearest Liliana?" The heavy Scottish burr flowed upon his tender words. Liliana fought for control over her tears. She put her palms on both sides of his clean-shaven cheeks, smiled warmly and replied, "Yes, Declan. Yes, I will be your bride, and I will be your love until the Lord sees fit to take me home." She then kissed him softly.

Reluctantly, Declan broke her sweet kiss. He reached into his jacket and pulled out a small black velvet box. "Liliana, this was my mother's engagement ring. It would bring me great pleasure if you would wear it." The Jeweler in Reedsburgh sized and refurbished it, and it is back to its original beauty. Declan opened the box and held it out to her, "I do hope that you like it."

She looked into the proffered velvet box. The ring was very beautiful, and it was just to her liking…a simple square-cut diamond surrounded by emeralds. It was perfect; exactly what she might have chosen herself. "Declan, I would be honored to wear your mother's lovely ring. I'm so touched that you have given it to me. It's just perfect. Thank you." Her hand trembled as Declan slipped it on her finger. His mother's ring was truly her style.

Stefano, who had been watching this poignant scene through the round glass window in the swinging kitchen doors, was dumbstruck. He had seen more than a few proposals in his restaurant before, but it was always more about the size of the diamond ring, always more about the guy getting down on one knee to propose, always more about the woman…these two only wanted each other; nothing else mattered. Their love was beautiful. He had heard something of their story, so he was especially happy for them. He came bursting through the kitchen doors carrying champagne and proceeded to kiss both Liliana and Declan on the cheek. "Now, I will cook for you two lovers," he grinned.

And cook he did; the meal was served in the European style… slowly. Over the course of several hours, newly engaged Liliana and Declan were served Stefano's gift of food from his beloved Tuscany. The couple enjoyed Stefano's favorite dishes, and his wife, Gina, helped him serve the special celebratory meal. Their meal sounded like poetry, and it tasted heavenly:

Antipasti	Fettunta al Pomodoro	(Tomato Toast)
Primi Piatti	Penne con Piselli	(Penne with Peas)
Secondi Piatti	Bistecca alla Fiorentina	(Florentine Steak)
Verdure	Insalata di Fagiolini	(Fresh Green Bean Salad)
Dolci	Panna Cotta al Arancia	(Creamed Oranges)

When the last of their engagement meal was finished, and they had reveled in the happiness of their special night, Declan and Liliana said good-bye to Stefano and Gina with great affection. Their evening had been perfect, thanks to the servant-attitude of the Giancomos. "We must make sure that Stefano and Gina join us when we marry," a glowing Liliana mentioned to her future husband.

"Aye, Liliana, and when should we marry?" Declan asked as they walked along toward the parked car.

"Soon, Declan. I don't know if I have the patience to wait very long. I want to be yours only," she sighed as she answered him.

Declan thought about it for a bit, then, he asked, "How about in October? Maybe the middle of the month…that would give us about five weeks to prepare. What do you think?"

"Oh, Declan, that would be perfect. Perhaps, we could be married in the yard at Christophe and Annie's. The weather should still be nice. Do you think they would let us?" she asked…much like a carefree school girl.

Unaware that they were standing under the bright light of a street lamp, they held each other and kissed unabashedly until a car full of teenagers drove by and shouted, "Go get a room, you two!"

Declan laughed, and Liliana blushed.

The next morning when Liliana awoke, she looked over to where her giant baby boy, Dover Dog, usually slept, then she remembered that he had spent the night with Christophe and Annie. She saw the two dozen pink roses housed within her mother's antique glass vase on her nightstand, and she thought about the wonderful evening she had shared with Declan, and how it had been very hard to part in the wee hours of the morning. She then looked at her beautiful engagement ring and sighed with happiness. "I can't wait to tell Christophe and Annie," she said to herself. She flew out of bed and got ready quickly. She was just hurrying out the front door when Declan came through her gate. When she saw him, her heart skipped a beat.

"I'm going to marry you, Declan Ryan," she exclaimed as she flung herself into his very strong arms.

He, too, was feeling quite exuberant, and answered, "I know, my love; we are to be together at last. Tell me, did you sleep well last night?"

"Yes, and I dreamt of you," she whispered, as she draped her arms around his neck and kissed him; "I love you so much. I was just heading over to Christophe and Annie's to pick up Dover, and to tell them our special news. Please, come with me!"

Together, they started down the path, when suddenly, Liliana stopped short. There, parked prominently in the drive, was a Volkswagen convertible that looked quite a bit like the one she used to enjoy. It conjured up memories of happy-times with Declan from years ago. "Declan?"

Declan smiled down at her. "It's yours, sweetheart. You've taken the bus for almost two years now, and you've not once complained. It gives me great joy to give it back to you." Cocking his head slightly and smiling, he said, "David and I have been doing a little investigative work. It *is* your old car, love…I just had it spruced up a bit for you." His blue eyes were shining.

"Declan? How did you do this?" she asked incredulously.

"Oh, you know…David Renton and I make a pretty good team. For some reason, he had the VIN number in some old files from your Dad. We traced it and found it just a few weeks ago. It's been in storage all this time."

"Oh, Declan, you are really something," she murmured. "Was that what was in that big truck yesterday?"

"Yes, Lily, it was…along with what was left of Bob Whitney's nursery inventory. I know that you have always been sorry that you gave up your little blue V-Dub, so it gives me great pleasure to restore it to you. Perhaps, we can get hopelessly lost in rural Rosemeade County once again!" he smiled.

SPECIAL NEWS

nnie Riordan looked out her kitchen window and knew something was up! Declan and Liliana were coming up the walk arm-in-arm, and she had never seen either of them look happier.

"Christophe, I think Declan and Liliana have an announcement to make!" she chimed.

Christophe looked up from his newspaper, appeared slightly smug, and said, "I'm not surprised. Declan asked me for her hand a week ago."

"And you never told me, Christophe Riordan?" she scowled at him.

"I'm sorry, Annie, but I just wanted you to enjoy this occasion as much as those two love birds are…"

"You are a rascal, Christophe Riordan, but I love how you still make life wonderful for me, even after all these years!"

Just then, the kitchen door opened, and a delighted Declan ushered Liliana into their fragrant kitchen. Annie Riordan acted as though she had no idea of what was really going on and said, "You two are just in time for some hot biscuits and a cup of tea. Come on in…"

Smiling Declan Ryan then pulled her into his embrace and exclaimed, "Annie, our Liliana has agreed to be my wife by October!"

Annie squealed, and kissed both of Declan's cheeks. "I am so very happy for you, my dear, dear Declan!" She then pulled on Liliana's arm and exclaimed, "Get over here, missy, I need to hug my sweet girl."

Much excitement ensued over the next hour. The poignant engagement ring was admired, plans for the wedding were proposed, and hot buttered biscuits were enjoyed along with steaming Scottish breakfast tea. True joy and happiness permeated that bright family kitchen, and all of this took place while Declan and Liliana couldn't stop smiling at one another and giant Dover bounced around the room like a puppy.

Christophe and Annie couldn't have been any happier for their two cherished kids. They both knew that the upcoming wedding and the union of Declan and Liliana would, at last, purge the regrets and sadness that had been hampering them all for far too long.

When Declan and Liliana prepared to depart, he winked at Christophe and said, "I guess it goes without saying that I won't be in the office or the nursery today, Chris. My girl has a new set of wheels and has agreed to take me driving on the back roads of Rosemeade County again…just like we once did. Personally, I hope that she gets us hopelessly lost."

"Come Liliana and Dover, we have some driving to do!" Declan entreated. He then ruffled Dover's ears and said, "Dover, my boy, please be aware that I ride shotgun in this vehicle…you may take the rear seat."

As they watched Liliana's little V-Dub toddle down the drive, Christophe and Annie stood arm-in-arm. Christophe said, "You know Annie, Liliana and Declan truly are enjoying a 'do-over.' Not everyone gets that in this life… Both of our special kids have always done the honorable thing for others, and I can't help but feel that God is rewarding them. Who would have guessed that their relationship would ever be restored to them again or that Declan and David Renton could find such a special remnant of Liliana's youth for her to enjoy once more? How I wish that Stephan and Jenny could have been here to witness these special things with us this morning. They would have been so happy for their lovely daughter."

Christophe Riordan then continued, "When they entreated us to be her god-parents, I don't think Stephan and Jenny had any idea that we two would end up caring for her as an adult, but I wouldn't have it any other way, would you, Annie?"

"No sweetheart, I don't think I would." answered Annie. "Those two sweet kids have truly enriched our lives."

A ROGUE AT THE KIOSK

eclan Ryan was slightly taken aback as he walked across the road several days later and watched Liliana helping her clients at the farm-to-market stone kiosk. She had colorfully displayed the stand's late-summer vegetable offerings in woven baskets along with petite wooden berry boxes that contained strawberries, cherries, and apricots atop a red-and-white-checked cloth. Alongside those colorful offerings, cellophane-wrapped loaves of rustic breads, tied with vibrantly-colored baker's twine, were on display from Annie's Diner. It was a most handsome display of the summer's bounty.

Though the stand protected Liliana from the sun, her cheeks were slightly flushed, and her hair was beginning to curl about her face. Declan thought she looked so very sweet and straight out of a Victorian calendar illustration. Yet, each time she bent across the stand to hand a customer their brown-paper parcel, she leaned far enough over the produce display that she unknowingly let patrons see her lace-trimmed bra peeking out from her bright shirt. Though she looked truly adorable, he knew she would be embarrassed that her charms were on display.

Declan waited a minute or two before she had a break from customers and then stepped into the kiosk alongside her. He quickly looked about, kissed her, and said, "My beautiful girl, I need to find a wooden box for you to stand on today, because each time you so charmingly lean over the produce display to give your clients their parcels, you are innocently showing them your assets!"

Liliana's hands immediately flew to the slightly-lower neckline of her soft cotton shirt and she exclaimed, "I was wondering why some of those older gentlemen had knowing smiles on their faces!" She pursed her lips, looked slightly discomfited, and said, "Oh, Declan…I'm so sorry that I've been on display alongside the organic produce!"

Declan threw back his head in hearty laughter and answered, "I'm not…you are the freshest and most-beautiful thing here today, and I have to say that you certainly made my morning! I'm just not sure if you want to share such a pretty view with all of your patrons, though, my darling!"

Laughingly putting her hands on her hips, Liliana replied, "Well, Mr. Ryan, this is a new side of you. You mean you looked?"

"Aye, that I did…I do consider myself to be a gentleman, but I just couldn't help myself, Liliana. You looked so very sweet."

"Well, then, perhaps you should fetch a wooden box for me to stand upon," a slightly- breathless Liliana replied.

Turning to leave, and looking back at her, Declan tried to look penitent, but failed. Instead, he smiled boyishly at Liliana and that errant dimple, which always peeked out when he was pleased, appeared on his cheek. He stepped out of the kiosk and said, "I'll be right back with that box, then."

Upon returning a few minutes later, Declan again stepped into the stone kiosk and secured a sturdy wood crate firmly upon the floor. He then took Liliana's hand and helped her to stand atop the wooden box. "Will you forgive me, then?" he asked; his wayward dimple still on display.

Now, standing closer eye-level with him, Liliana smiled and looked up into Declan's blue eyes and answered, "You are a cheeky one, Declan Ryan. I don't know if I can overlook such an indiscretion! Perhaps, I'll have to file a complaint at two o'clock, when my kiosk shift ends."

Trying to affect seriousness and cocking an eyebrow for effect, Declan retorted, "I'll be waiting for you in my office, then. It's good to air one's grievances with the management, you know! I look forward to seeing you then, ma'am." He then winked at her and left an astonished Liliana in his wake as he walked back across the road to the nursery.

Several hours later, just after two o'clock, the door to Declan Ryan's office was firmly closed and locked, and his window blinds were drawn. Inside his office, he happily held green-eyed Liliana Lylestrom in his arms. She had completely forgotten to register her complaint!

NIGGLING FEARS

*L*iliana was very pensive when Declan picked her up for a night out on his old Harley Davidson motorcycle. Ordinarily, she was quite an enthusiast for a bike ride through charming downtown Rosemeade Township, but tonight, Declan could tell that something was bothering her. He had planned to take her to the cinema, but instead, he maneuvered the bike around the village green and stopped at Annie's Diner. Things were hopping in there, but Declan managed to get a booth so they could have a bit of privacy. Shortly after they had ordered, Declan engaged her in conversation.

"Something is bothering you tonight, sweetheart, would you mind telling me what's on your mind?" he inquired.

"Yes, Declan, something is on my mind tonight…"

"What is it, lass?" Declan was beginning to be concerned.

"Oh, Dec, something dawned on me this morning, and I'm afraid that it could have a bearing on whether you truly want to marry me or not."

Declan immediately looked heartsick, and replied, "Dearest Liliana, nothing you could ever say to me would make me change my mind. Please tell me what is burdening you."

Taking a breath and sighing, Liliana began. "You know how it never even crossed my mind that I might be pregnant when I found myself carrying Richard's child because my cycle has always been so erratic? What if I can't give you any children? What if that tiny, tiny little baby that I miscarried a year and a half ago might have been the only time I ever conceive? You may need to reconsider whether you want to marry me or not."

Declan Ryan took her hand and smiled at her. "Liliana, I would love you whether or not we ever had any children. Sweetheart, up until just a few years ago, I thought you were lost to me forever. It's you that I love and desire. If little ones come along, that will be wonderful. But if not, that's okay, too. You've already made me the happiest of men."

She had worn a ponytail that night and tendrils of hair had come loose during their ride and were curling around her face. Her bottle-green eyes looked slightly misty as she tried to conjure up her lovely smile but found that she could not. Instead, she just bobbed her head. "There's more, Dec, but I'm ashamed to tell you…"

"You can tell me anything, Liliana. Nothing you could ever say would change my feelings for you."

"Okay, then… Richard told me on multiple occasions that I was a terrible lover, and it was no wonder that he lost interest in intimacy with me. I had always suspected that he had another woman, but I could never find concrete proof until, you know… Declan, I tried to make him happy, but sex was always just for him; my feelings and needs were never factored in. Only once, did Richard ever try to make me feel special or cherished and that was just after he had behaved so abominably on our wedding night. I'm pretty sure such care came from his guilty conscience. Thereafter, it was when he got what he wanted, the love-making was over; fulfillment for me didn't matter to Richard. According to him, I was lousy. Declan, you might just be marrying a potentially barren woman who is horrible in bed."

Masking his anger toward cruel Richard, Declan instead looked at her serious face and compassionately stated, "Dearest Liliana, I know you, and you are a very passionate and loving woman. There is no question about it. Though you and I have never been together in that way, I know in my heart that we will be very compatible, and even if by some fluke we are not, then we have a lifetime to work on things. We'll get it right. Frankly, I would love to pummel Richard Rawlings for never respecting your needs, or your tender feelings! As well, his exceptionally ugly comments to you make my blood boil. Believe me when I say, he was the one who was a terrible lover."

"And, Liliana, if you are fearful that we may have problems ever conceiving a child, then let's just get a head start on things when we marry. I'm fine with trying to conceive from the start. Sweetheart, we'll see how things turn out. If we don't have success, then we'll seek out the help of a fertility specialist. Liliana, I don't want you to fret about anything. You are my special love."

Their food arrived just then, yet Declan took Liliana's other hand in his. He then gave her his beautiful smile and said, "Personally, I'm looking forward to soon being able to hold my lovely girl all night long and show her how much she means to me; my desire is to purge Richard Rawlings forever from her memory!"

Liliana's sweet smile then lit up her face. "Thank you for being so kind, Declan. You always seem to fortify me. So, I hope you understand that I don't ever want to disappoint you; especially when it comes to love-making."

"Believe me, Liliana, when I say that I have absolutely no fear that you could ever disappoint me."

Later that night as they drove home on Declan's cycle, he took a detour to the city park. They walked arm-in-arm through the beautiful rose garden in the light of the harvest moon. They then sat quietly beside a gurgling water fountain. The autumn air was cool, yet it still had the fragrance of freshly-cut grass engaging their senses. Both were deep in thought about their upcoming nuptials in a little less than a month. Liliana was the first to broach the subject.

"Declan, I hope you don't think that I'm being silly in saving myself for our wedding night. It's old-fashioned, I know, but it is what I believe is right. And, it's not like I'm really going to be a virgin bride, but I just want to give myself to you as though you are my first and only. I know virginity is a gift that can only be given once, but years ago, I had hoped to eventually give that gift to you. If there hadn't been manipulation and meddling on Richard's part, I could have come into a marriage with you unsullied. Now, years later I can't change things that happened over a decade ago, but I will come into our union as purely as I can. I love you very much, Declan."

Declan was very touched by her candor. He said, "Dearest Liliana, no matter what has gone before, I could never even begin to think of you as sullied in any way. You are so special, and I am honored that you love me."

"Sweetheart, let me also share with you some things that I have been struggling with of late," Declan quietly stated.

"You know that during my university days, I was no choir boy. I strayed from my beliefs, and it wasn't until my mum became so ill that I finally got things right with God. I have regrets too, Liliana. I am sorry that I was ever intimate with anyone, now. We both know that I can never go back, but I've been with no one in that way since we met, Liliana. At first, it was because I wanted to come to you as honorably as I could, if you would have me. Then, after you married Richard, it was because I wanted no one else. I poured myself into my work, instead."

"Lass, the last time you were with someone, it was a very brutal experience, and it was at the hands of your own husband. Liliana, these things grieve me, and I want to make them up to you somehow. I have tried to show you the utmost respect during our courtship, but I find myself fearful that in just a few weeks, when I can finally show you the breadth of my love for you, that I may somehow frighten you. You have my vow that I will be tender with you."

Liliana laid her hand on his cheek; it had three days' worth of stubble on it. His dislike of shaving…it was one of the things that she adored about him, and that stubble endeared him to her even more tonight. She said, "Oh, Dec, aren't we quite a pair…both of us are just a wee bit fragile and worrying about things that cannot be changed…"

"Aye, we are, Lily. But this I know… You are the only woman I have ever loved, and come what may, we'll face things together."

A SPECIAL HARVEST TIME

*D*eclan Ryan and *Liliana Lylestrom* were married in October. The sun was getting low in the afternoon sky. All their guests had arrived and were milling around a giant tent which had been set up in the side yard at Christophe and Annie's handsome home. Rows of white chairs, dressed in large satin bows, were lined up beside the tent. The trees and bushes surrounding the old house were brilliantly clad in full, fall regalia. Burning bushes appeared to have been colored with red lipstick. The grape vines on the foothills behind Christophe and Annie's home were still green and lush, so the contrast of the vivid fall colors and the green vines made for a perfect wedding backdrop. Garlands of colorful pink, purple, and white chrysanthemums along with grape vines decorated the giant tent and its tables, in addition to pumpkins, gourds, and decorative kales. The effect was most charming. Those same tables were also set for a sit-down meal, and the scent of roasted chicken, salmon steaks, and prime-rib floated on the air. In all, it was an inviting setting.

If one looked slightly downhill toward the nursery, he or she would see old, wooden farm carts loaded with orange pumpkins and bales of hay as well as fall flowers. Stalwart geraniums and impatiens still showed the fullness of their summer beauty. They were tucked in planters and flower beds throughout the nursery. All the trees were heavily mulched for an upcoming winter's rest, and the leaves surrounding the whole of the property shimmered in their colorful splendor with late afternoon back-lighting from the sun. Just when the guests had assembled in their seats and were thinking things could not get any more special on this halcyon autumn afternoon, the faint sound of bagpipes was heard.

Looking down Old Vineyard Road toward the highway junction, guests started to spot the procession of a striking bagpipe platoon. They were piping an old Scottish ballad entitled, *Highland Laddie*, and the pipers were dressed in finely woven kilts. Colorful flag-bearers bore the tartan colors and family crests of both the Riordan and Ryan families. The scene was breath-taking.

As the pipers drew closer, Declan Ryan appeared at the foot of the path from the stone barn. He was handsomely dressed in his father's dress kilt. His colorful ensemble fit him like a glove and accentuated his muscular physique. He looked very strong and healthy. The pleased countenance that he bore made it obvious to all in attendance that he was overcome with joy on this perfect day. He was soon to be marrying the woman he loved.

When the bagpipers marched into the drive, David Renton joined their procession directly in front of the flag bearers. He wore a tuxedo adorned with a cummerbund of plaid. Next, Jeremy Pettigrew solemnly fell in line immediately next to David wearing a dress kilt of his clan's colors. When the pipers drew close to Declan, he fell first in line and led the piper's platoon and his two friends further into the yard and up to the rose arbor which was covered in a brilliant flush of fall blooms. Each man then took his respective place adjacent to the rose-covered arbor. At last, Declan Ryan had arrived to be joined to his beloved.

At this juncture, the pipers' music stopped for just the short measure of a few seconds, as Suzette, Tracy, and Elise, Liliana's best friends from her university days, appeared at the head of the path. *Amazing Grace* then burst forth from their ancient pipes as the three girlhood friends made their way to the rose arbor to join Declan and his groomsmen. Each of Liliana's old friends were adorned in retro-style gowns that had once belonged to Liliana's mother, Jenny, and each frock had heavily-starched petticoats peeking out from underneath. They carried bouquets of ornamental kale surrounded by English lavender and pink roses.

Next, three-year old Daphne Pettigrew scattered fresh rose petals from a tiny basket. When she had finished, her father momentarily stepped out of his assigned place, and lifted her into his arms. Daphne familiarly entwined her flawless young arm around her father's neck. Her tender affection for her father brought forth many smiles from the guests. Now that the all the bridal party had taken their places, a chord was stuck, and the bridal march began from the pipes.

Finally, hearty Christophe Riordan appeared at the top of the path with Liliana on his arm. He, too, was wearing a dress kilt of his clan's tartan colors, as he led his beloved god-daughter down the meandering path from his home to the rose-covered archway to where his treasured second-cousin-turned-son, Declan Ryan, awaited his bride.

Liliana was beautifully arrayed for her wedding day that October afternoon. Every guest, young and old, stood up in deference to her arrival, and a collective, "Oh!" was heard when they witnessed her arrival to marry her beloved groom with an obedient Dover walking proudly behind her and Christophe. Dover, too, was wearing a neckerchief made of Declan's clan colors around his fluffy neck.

Liliana was clothed in her mother's slightly-refashioned silk and lace wedding gown. The antique gown's skirt billowed as she made her way on Christophe's arm, and she wore the tartan plaid of the Ryan family draped around her slender waist. She had fastened the family colors with lace, silken cords, and a large antique brooch that had belonged to Declan's mother. She did not wear a veil. She had simply pulled her brunette hair slightly off her face and had fashioned rustic lace throughout the intricate braiding and curls that spilled off her neck and over her shoulders. The effect was very pretty and suited the rustic nuptials perfectly. Her green eyes were sparkling with happiness.

Tears rolled down Christophe Riordan's tanned cheeks as he escorted her down the path to be delivered to her groom. He was so happy for his Liliana. She had suffered much loss, but she was healing. How her parents would have enjoyed seeing this special day in her life. He acted as her parent now, and he would see to it that she lived a healthy and happy life with Declan. There was no man on this earth who showed more compassion and respect to his loved ones than Declan. Christophe was so proud of his two children. "Yes," he thought to himself, "they *were* his children." He and Annie had not been childless after all. What a gift this beautiful day was…

Declan showed everyone his handsome smile when Christophe entrusted him with Liliana's hand, and their hearts melted when Declan mouthed, "I love you so," to his bride. Together, they walked the short distance to the officiating pastor who waited to join their lives. Christophe and Dover made their way to join Annie, who couldn't have been happier.

After a very heartfelt exchanging of vows, a touched Pastor McClenahan instructed Declan to, "Kiss your bride." Once again, that striking smile transformed Declan Ryan's serious countenance. He cupped Liliana's porcelain cheeks with both of his hands and kissed her quite tenderly. Nearly every woman in the crowd was ready to swoon while their spouses clapped and cheered. It goes without saying that friends throughout Rosemeade County were truly happy for these two very-special people.

For the next hour, the newly-married Mr. and Mrs. Declan Ryan greeted each of their guests as they circulated through the crowd of well-wishers. Both radiated joy that they were, at last, united. It had been a very long time in coming, but their trials had brought them back to where they had first started. Theirs was now a joyful story. Their love for each other had truly come full circle.

Though not everyone knew their background, there was one guest in attendance, who had helped to bring the two of them together again. Yes, it was Nurse Julia Edmonds. A year and a half ago, Declan had gone to the hospital several weeks after Liliana had lost her child there. He had sought out Nurse Edmonds. He had thanked her for having compassion on Liliana that day. He related how it had started out as one of the saddest days of both their lives but had ended as one of the happiest; thanks, in part, to her. Declan had concluded their conversation with, "When we are able to marry, yours will be the first name on our guest list." He had then kissed her on the cheek. Nurse Edmonds had been thrilled.

Not long after sunset, when the memorable and very delicious wedding feast had been consumed, and the family toasts had been offered, multiple bonfires began to glow around the property. A temporary dance floor had been erected for the occasion with young and old alike participating. Under the glow of torches lit for the event, guests danced to traditional Scottish music, tapped their toes to high-spirited fiddle playing, and laughed while they danced.

After Declan and Liliana had danced to their selected wedding song, Christophe led Liliana onto the floor for the dance designated for her father. As he guided her around the floor looking so regal in his kilt, he confided to her that her own father, Stephan Lylestrom, had requested on his deathbed that Christophe help her to get things patched up with Declan. Christophe smiled warmly, "Liliana, I just let nature take its course. You and Declan did the rest. Sweet girl, your dear father would be so happy for you today."

Next, David Renton had whisked Liliana around the dance floor after she had finished her special dance with Christophe. As they waltzed, David had said, "Liliana, you are truly a beautiful bride today, and I know that this time, you are going to be loved and cherished by your husband. Declan is a fine man. In fact, he is the only man I know of who is worthy of a woman like you." Minutes later, when David had returned Liliana to her new husband, he had heartily congratulated Declan and embraced him in a hug.

While his new wife had been engaged with David Renton on the dance floor, Declan had danced briefly with Kristen Bellyer. She had said, "Declan, I am still quite regretful about my behavior toward you last year. I was so out of line with the things that I said about Liliana. I have since gotten to know her when she has substituted at my school, and I find that she is a lovely person and is so very kind. I understand why you love her so much. Please, Declan, can you forgive me for maligning her?"

Declan smiled, "Kristen, there is nothing to forgive." He was about to say something else, when Jeremy Pettigrew cut in…

"Pardon me, Declan, but would you mind introducing me to this lovely woman? I'm afraid we've not met."

Declan Ryan laughed at his old friend, he then said, "Kristen, this is a mate of mine from primary school to university. Jeremy Pettigrew, this pretty lady is my friend, Kristen Bellyer. See to it that you don't step on her toes." He then handed a smiling Kristen into Jeremy's very strong waiting arms.

Many happy dances later, when a brilliant moon had risen over the foothills, Declan Ryan took the stage and bade good night to his guests. He smiled and said, "Ladies and gentlemen, my wife and I have waited a long while to be together, and now, it is our time to be alone. Please, continue to enjoy yourselves with more food and drink, and thank you all so very much for sharing in our wedding today." That being said, he lifted his lovely bride into his arms and carried her up the path to the old stone barn.

Well-wishers whistled, whooped in their joy, and called, "Goodbye!" Jeremy Pettigrew's deep voice boomed above all others. He said what many in the crowd were thinking, "Declan Ryan, you are the most fortunate man in the entire world today! But you deserve only the best in this life, mate!" Everyone cheered.

TOGETHER AT LAST

*D*eclan Ryan was carrying his bride up to his loft. He wanted to share something special with her. He breathed in her scent as he held her in his arms. She was always enveloped in the fragrance of something familiar, but he still couldn't pin down exactly what scent it was. Earlier today, she had staggered him with her beauty as she had walked down the path on Christophe's arm, but it wasn't just her physical beauty that had struck him. It was that Liliana had an unusual gift of always thinking of what might please others. He hadn't expected her to incorporate his clan's colors into her gown but was deeply affected that she had done so. It was so like her to remember what such a gesture would mean to him. Such thoughtfulness was what had first attracted him to her so long ago.

Liliana's arms were draped around his neck as he carried her up the pebbled path to his loft, and she looked deeply into his eyes and said, "You've made me the happiest woman in the world today, Declan Ryan. I love you so very much." Her declaration pleased Declan Ryan immeasurably.

"My sweet Liliana, I can hardly articulate how happy I am to be your husband. You bring me such great joy," Declan replied, again breathing in her lovely fragrance.

He easily carried his bride up the wooden stairs to his loft and paused at the entrance. Turning the knob, he opened the door. Neither he nor Liliana could believe what they saw. The loft had been transformed, and the effect was captivating. Declan had arranged for cleaning, yet this was far better than what had been negotiated…

While the wedding celebration had been in full swing, a housekeeping crew had come into the loft to prepare things for his bride. They had dusted and polished everything, including his ever-cluttered desk. Someone had arranged his books, his trade journals, and his leather folios quite attractively. Because the windows were thrown open and the cool, night air was flowing in, a fire burned in the little fireplace. Even his leather reading chair was draped with a new tartan throw. "Where did that come from?" he wondered. Someone had also turned the lights low. "This is far better than what I asked for," he whispered to Liliana.

The housekeepers had made up the bed with the handsome bridal quilt that Liliana had finished in the weeks since they had decided to marry. Annie had helped him to choose just the right linens for Liliana's creation. Everything was freshly laundered and ironed. Even his small writing desk and his night table in the bedroom had been tidied. His father's leather journal held a place of prominence on the nightstand, and two letters had been laid atop that battered, old journal. The old European armoire, which always reminded him of his home, had been highly polished, and some of Liliana's honeymoon wedding lingerie had been hung upon the door. "Whoa," he thought to himself when he saw the lacy confections. A platter of assorted breads, cheeses, and colorful fruits sat alongside a bucket filled with a bottle of champagne. There was also a stunning bouquet of mixed-color roses in a handsome old silver water pitcher. Declan had to admit to himself that it all looked quite inviting.

"Declan, did you arrange for all this?" a surprised Liliana inquired.

"Yes, I did, but this is far more than I contracted for...I suspect Christophe and Annie might have had something to do with it."

"Oh, Dec, this is just wonderful. Thank you."

"I suspect we'll need to thank Christophe and Annie, too!" Declan laughed.

Declan finally set his bride down and sat in his comfortably-worn leather chair. He pulled Liliana onto his lap. He kissed her quite thoroughly, and said, "Liliana, I have something very touching that I want to share with you."

He then walked into his bedroom and lifted two somewhat-faded envelopes from the night stand and returned to her. "Earlier this week, I dropped off my Father's wedding clothes at the dry cleaner. They had been packed away in a box for many years. Yesterday, when I returned to pick them up, the dry cleaner handed me two envelopes that he had found tucked into Dad's box. When I returned home, I opened them to find that both envelopes contained letters from my Mum and Dad. Each had penned a special note, written especially for me on the day of my marriage."

"Oh, Lily! Receiving them made me very happy. I suspect that God knew I would be missing them both today." A very touched Declan then leaned back against his desk and handed the two precious vellum envelopes to her. "Here, Sweetheart, would you read these two wonderful gifts from my parents?"

Liliana unfolded the thoughtful "gifts" which had been lovingly left for her new husband. What she read reinforced what she had already suspected of his parents. They were caring people, who had cherished their son. The following heartfelt greetings are what she read:

17 September...

Dearest Declan,

Son, if you are reading this letter, it is probably on the occasion of your wedding. I have been very emphatic with your mum about saving my dress tartans for you. If you are, in fact, looking into this box, I suspect it is because you are about to marry. If so, Declan, I send you my love and my very best wishes for a happy life with your bride.

As I write this letter to you, I know that my time on this earth is waning. But, Declan, I want you to know how proud I am to have been your father. You are such a fine young man, and it has been my honor to care for and to protect you. I know you will do well in this life, son, as you have already demonstrated great strength of character in all you do.

Declan, I'm sure you realize that you have a wonderful mother, and it has been my joy to be her mate. Today, my prayer is that you, too, may find the same happiness that I have shared with your mum. Marriage isn't always easy, Declan, but a loving mate is worth far more than any wealth.

I know you will look after your beautiful mummy, young Declan. Even though you are only an eight-year-old-lad, I have seen great evidence of the character you are already developing. Your mother will continue to guide you as you mature into a man, but she will need your small feet to fit into my slightly larger shoes for a while. You need only do exactly what you are doing now...just be her companion and friend.

Look to the Lord in all things, son. Someday, I'll see you on the other side.

I love you very much,

Dad

15 February…

My Dearest Declan,

Right now, you are probably rummaging in the box that your Father made me promise I would save for your wedding day. Well, I have, indeed, saved your father's things for you. And, you know that I have been as emphatic as your father about you wearing his tartans on your special day!

How, I wish that I were there to see your precious face again and to meet your lovely bride, Declan. Whomever you have chosen, I know you will be a fine husband to her. You had a wonderful example in your father, Declan, and you have demonstrated to me time and time again the kindness and strength of a good man. She will esteem you and your quiet strength as you stand beside her in this life.

My honorable son, I also want to tell how much I have enjoyed being your mother. You have been a *blessing to me since the day your father and I brought you home from the hospital, and it is my hope that you will be healthy and happy for all your days on this beautiful planet..*

We both know this earthly life is short; neither of us were able to enjoy enough time with James, so I rejoice that you have found a woman who brings you happiness. I know you will cherish and tenderly care for her, as that is the kind of man that you are.

I'm sure you know that your father and I had a wonderful life for the short time that we had together. And, as you and your new bride embark upon your new life together, my prayer is that you will know that same contentment.

Stay strong in the Lord, dear one, and I will see you again.

With so much love,

Mum

After reading the two poignant letters, Liliana looked up; tears shimmered in her eyes. "Oh, Declan," she breathed, "I know these must be the sweetest greetings you have ever received. How much your parents must have treasured you to make sure you were in receipt of their love on your wedding day. Oh, dearest, I am especially happy for you," she murmured with a slight sob. She then reached out her hand to him. He caught her palm and kissed it.

Looking serious, Declan said, "I am very touched that even during the last days of their lives, when I know neither of them was feeling up to the task, both of my parents took the time to ensure that I knew how much they loved me. There was never any doubt on my part, but these simple pieces of parchment, bearing their handwriting, mean so very much to me today."

"Liliana, we both have been blessed by the loving families we were born into... I know that if there had been time, both Stephan and Jenny would have made sure you received their greetings of love today, too."

"I suspect that you are right, Declan," Liliana whispered winsomely.

He then gazed at her and extended his hand. "Come, Lily," he smiled, as he gently pulled her out of his leather chair and into his embrace, "Now is the time for me to show you how much I care for you in both word and deed. To quote Old Jim, 'I want to "know you" in the biblical sense.'" Smiling, he softly said, "We have waited for each other long enough."

Shortly thereafter, Declan Ryan was awestruck. First, he had held and kissed his bride quite thoroughly before carrying her into what used to be his bedroom but was now their bridal retreat. Next, he had helped her to undo what seemed like at least a hundred tiny satin buttons down the back of her gown as she held her soft hair up and off her shoulders and neck while he worked at those tiny buttons with his large hands. She sat upon a small, armless wooden chair, and while he quietly undid her buttons, he gazed at her tender neck and shoulders and tried not to think about Richard Rawlings ever striking and hurting her...how could that man have done such a thing? She was so precious.

Declan breathed in the scent of her hair which was threaded with seed pearls and lace and thought to himself that his bride must surely be the most beguiling woman on the planet. Finally, he helped her to lift off the voluminous skirts of her wedding gown to find that she was clad underneath in a lace-infused silken petticoat that floated from her waist to her ankles. She was also wearing a very fetching strapless corset that matched that handsome petticoat. The curve of her breasts rose over the top edge of that corset with the cadence of her breathing, and her slightly tanned shoulders seemed to float above her lace underpinnings. He thought that he had never seen her look more beautiful.

Liliana sweetly pulled him close and began to help him dismantle his handsome tartan dress clothes. First, she unlatched the silver ornament that fastened the tartan scarf that was draped around and over his shoulders. She then removed that colorful scarf and wrapped it loosely around his waist. Tugging on his tartan scarf, she pulled him even closer to herself. She gave him a tender smile. He encircled her waist with his two hands and watched her with a slight smile of his own as she continued in her ministrations to him. Next, she lightly kissed his lips as she removed his dress coat and gently tugged upon his fastidiously knotted bowtie. Once his tie had been removed, she began to undo the shiny jet buttons that fastened the placket of his crisply starched and pleated dress shirt. Though Liliana had worked closely with Declan over the years, and she had swum at the lake with him many times, it was still very intimate to remove his dress shirt and to smooth her hands over his muscular chest. She looked up into his face and gave him her electric smile.

Then, she laid her head upon his bare chest and held him. She could hear the steady thumping of his heart. At last, she began unfastening Declan's colorful kilt. The leather buckle fasteners were a bit cumbersome, but she persevered. When the last of his ornamental accoutrements were finally removed, she found that she was very ready to take her honorable husband unto herself.

An unclothed Declan Ryan easily lifted her into his arms and carried her further into their bridal escape. He laid her upon the bed which had been prepared for their arrival, then lay down next to her upon his side, propping himself up on his elbow. Declan laid his hand upon her lace-clad belly and looked into her slightly misty green eyes. Quite seriously, he said, "Liliana, tonight, I hope we can purge Richard from our lives… for you, the freedom from fear of him…for me, the palpable regret that I freely gave you to him years ago. We both have been aggrieved for far too long."

"From tonight forward, my desire is that Richard will no longer punctuate the ebb and flow of our life together. You have forgiven him his transgressions, and I have tried to follow your example, though sometimes I fail. Yet, in his own self-centered way, Richard did set things in motion for the two of us to finally be together. For that, I am deeply grateful."

Declan kissed her tenderly and when he deepened that kiss, Liliana responded to him in kind. Within minutes, her sheer underpinnings had been gently removed and swept aside, and at this juncture, Declan caressed her lightly tanned bare belly and quietly stated, "Lily, your body is so very beautiful, but you are also lovely within your heart. Yet, I know that the last time you were with your late husband he treated you maliciously. So tonight, you have my vow that you and I will proceed only as far as you wish to go and at your pace. We have the rest of our lives to consummate our commitment and love for each other, so I will follow your prompting. Just let me know what you desire, sweetheart."

Upon hearing his compassionate words, a tear escaped from Liliana's eye, and she earnestly looked at her caring new husband who had no idea that he was bathed in moonlight as he leaned over her. She lightly laid her hand over his heart and could feel its solid beating as he looked so solemnly back at her. She said, "I desire only one thing tonight, Declan Ryan…and that is: **You**. Besides my wonderful father, you were the first man that I ever loved, and God has given you back to me again. Declan, I trust you and know that you will never hurt me. I love you for your willingness to take things slowly; but with your compassion and your sensitivity, I do hope to give myself to you quite fully and completely tonight." She then reached for him. Her husband, who was quite moved by her candor, wrapped her in his arms and pulled her to himself.

For the next hour or two, the love-making that ensued was very special. Declan Ryan demonstrated to Liliana how a true man shows his devotion to his wife, and she found herself breathlessly whispering his name while he intimately held and touched her.

As for Declan, he loved his woman deeply, but found that he, too, could not help whispering out her name in joy when the two of them finally became one. That crisp October night, as moonlight shone through the open window, and a spent fire barely flickered in the fireplace, Declan and Liliana were purged of their misgivings about things that had gone before. They made love to one another with complete abandon.

Later, they savored the comestibles that had been left for them, they bathed together, enjoyed champagne and lastly, prepared themselves for slumber. Finally, in the waning minutes of the day they were wed, Mr. and Mrs. Declan Ryan fell into blessed sleep in each other's arms. It had been a healing day for both.

SWEETEST LILIANA

L iliana Ryan awoke feeling elated. She looked to her side and saw her husband sleeping deeply. "I now have an honorable man for my husband," she thought to herself. "I would go through everything again, just to be here with him today. I am so thankful for a second chance."

She ruminated on what a very special occasion their wedding had been the day before. All their guests had been truly happy for them. She had felt overjoyed to be joined together with Declan. It had been a day of sincere rejoicing. "I'm so glad that both Mom and Dad confided to me that Declan was their choice for me," she mused. "I have been able to enter into this marriage, knowing they loved and admired him. Oh, how happy that makes me feel."

From there, her thoughts were taken back to their love-making last evening while moonlight had flooded through their open window. Liliana had saved herself for marriage once again, but this time, her gift had **not** been ignored. Declan had made her feel like she was his virgin bride. Though life's circumstances had forced the two of them into very personal and, quite frankly, intimate circumstances over a year ago, when she had miscarried her child, she had only wanted Declan to comfort her. He had proven his devotion to her that horrible day; he had acted as her partner. It had not been embarrassing that he had experienced such a thing with her. It had culminated with both of them being able to look toward a future with each other. Finally, being able to give the gift of "herself" to Declan last evening had been very moving for them both.

Liliana also remembered Declan's tender ministrations to her last evening. He had elicited feelings from her that she had never known in her marriage to Richard. With his touch, Declan had shown her how very deep his love was for her. He had honestly demonstrated that he cherished her in both word and deed. She had never been enveloped with such tenderness nor known such overpowering feelings. Until last nightfall, she had never yet experienced the crescendo of climax and had been overcome when both she and Declan had experienced it together as one. She had wept a few tears afterward, as he held her closely and whispered, "All is well between us, Lily. All is well." She had felt his heart beating wildly as he held her in his arms.

She was still musing on the wonder of their first night together, when Declan awoke from his sleep. His beautiful smile, which was no longer rare, lit up his face, and he reached for her and held her gently to himself. "My bride," he had whispered. An hour later, they emerged from their tangled sheets, replete in their love and just a little bit hungry.

The first three nights of their marriage were spent in the complete privacy of Declan's loft. They gave of themselves quite unabashedly, and both thought things couldn't get any sweeter until they coupled together the next time. Liliana thought her husband must surely be the most-talented lover in the entire world, and she could tell that Declan was moved by the depth of her feelings for him.

The newly-weds finally showed themselves when there was nothing left within the confines of Declan's little refrigerator for sustenance. A trip to the grocery store was in order. Liliana's face was flushed with the look of someone who had been loved quite thoroughly the last three days, and her husband's face shone with contentment. Both had eyes only for each other.

Christophe and the rest of the nursery staff, called greetings to them when they emerged from the loft. All the staff had knowing smiles on their faces, but it was evident that everyone was sincerely happy for them. Declan, not wanting anyone to intrude on their privacy, hustled her into his truck, and they drove away before anyone could laughingly inquire, "How are you two enjoying married life?" Hours later, they returned just before dark; their hair was mussed, and their clothing was in disarray, and they had no groceries…

Since they still needed sustenance, they didn't return to Declan's loft. Instead, they went to Liliana's cottage. There, they ate a delicious pasta dish that she prepared between passionate embraces with her new husband.

They spent three more nights loving one another with complete abandon in Liliana's antique iron bed. She thought Declan looked particularly handsome upon awakening each morning in the lacy sheets which adorned that old bed. To their delight, they both fit in her claw-footed tub, so they languished for hours in warm water and bubbles. They reveled in just being with one another without any constraints. This intimate time alone was quickly erasing their regrets from years past.

Their one-week anniversary dawned with a hard frost, but with brilliant, sunny skies. They emerged from the vintner's cottage clothed in jeans and sweaters carrying Stephan Lylestrom's old leather suitcases. Today, they would begin the second part of their honeymoon. Christophe and Annie drove them to theBrookings City International Airport.

"What a difference almost two years makes," Liliana whispered to Declan.

The last time she remembered being at this airport was during those last few trips to Seattle with her father to clean up Richard's affairs. Again, she thought, "I would go through the heartache again, to be here today with my wonderful husband. Oh, thank you, Lord, for giving us a second chance."

A PLEASED MAN

*D*eclan Ryan was completely content. He was flying to his homeland this morning with his new bride. He hadn't been back to Scotland since he had left well over a decade before, but he so desired to share his home country with Liliana. He wanted to show her where he hailed from, to introduce her to his oldest friends, as well as to have her meet his Mum and Dad's close friends. He wanted to show her things that had been beloved to him long before he had known her.

As they snuggled together in their seats, Declan again told her how she had made him the happiest of men. She, in turn, told him that she had never imagined that life could be so sweet with him at her side. It was obvious to one and all that they were newlyweds, but neither of them cared. The road to this point had been fraught with sadness. They only wanted to revel in finally being together.

An hour or two into the flight, Liliana slept soundly, her head on a little pillow. Declan thought about the last week of his life with her. He knew he loved Liliana deeply, yet he was humbled by the depth of her reaction to his love-making overtures. She had wept openly when they had finally come together as one, and he had never felt so overwhelmed by his feelings for her as when they had both reached the apex of their love-making that first time. Each time they had come together during the last week, she had earnestly shown him the depth of her love for him. To hear her declarations of her desire for him touched his very core. "Is it really possible to love her more than I did just a week ago?" he asked himself.

He thoughtfully decided that, "Yes, he did love her more than he had the day of their wedding!" Now, they were one, and it made him feel deeply complete. True, he had waited a long time to have Liliana for his wife, but now the hollowness of being without her that had once plagued him had been vanquished. It had been replaced with tender joy. Declan had never expected to be this happy or content. He looked at his sleeping bride and thanked his Master, "Lord, I would go through the suffering again to be here today with this woman. Thank you for giving her back to me."

After thirteen hours on an airplane, Declan and Liliana arrived in Edinburgh. The air was crisp, and the city was beautiful. They rented a car, and Declan drove them to their hotel, The Waldorf Astoria Caledonian. Declan had called ahead and secured the honeymoon suite. Though there was much to see in Edinburgh, their first day was spent in total relaxation. They slept a short while and awoke desiring one another.

Later, refreshed from their rest, they visited the Royal Botanic Gardens. The last flush of autumn's flowering hung on the manicured gardens. Somehow the waning blooms made Liliana want to weep, but she knew that her emotions had been at the forefront for the last week, so she blinked back the tears. She was completely content, and she could tell that her husband was too. It was so lovely just being together. It had never, ever been like this with Richard.

When evening came, they dressed for dinner and enjoyed a special meal in the dining room at their hotel. It couldn't have been a nicer repast, but halfway through their shared dessert, Liliana earnestly looked him in the eyes and said, "Today has been so lovely Declan… perfect actually. Would you mind if we returned to our suite?"

"Sweetheart, are you alright?" a concerned Declan inquired.

"Yes. I am fine…but, I'm mad for you, Declan Ryan. I just want to be alone with you."

A pleased Declan immediately hailed their waiter. "I find we are later than we realized for an appointment. Would you please add our meal and your gratuity to our suite's tab? Give yourself a $100 gratuity sir…Your service was impeccable."

Exiting the restaurant, hand in hand, they briskly walked back to their room. A thoughtful hotel employee had tidied and turned back their bed covers and had left chocolate on their pillows. Liliana, who was a serious chocolate aficionado, did not even notice. She only wanted to hold her husband. Mr. and Mrs. Declan Ryan were off to a very good start on their life together.

DECLAN'S OLD FRIEND

ane Ross was so excited to see Declan Ryan again. He was to arrive at her new Edinburgh home early that afternoon, and she was so happy that he was coming to visit her. Later, when she opened her door to greet him, she was surprised and delighted to find out that he had brought his American bride to meet her. Jane knew that Declan's mother, Mary, would have heartily approved of his choice. As they sat together in her front parlor, Jane watched how Declan interacted with his sweet bride. Mary's son was kind, loving, and very tender with his new wife. It was obvious that he loved her deeply. When Jane inquired how they had met, both had looked a bit uncomfortable, but Declan took the lead.

"Janey, I met Liliana the very first week that I arrived in America. She had a crazy, old dog that made sure that we were introduced, and I have to say, it didn't take me very long to fall in love with her. But, due to some mistakes on both of our parts, we were not able to be together until earlier this year, but I feel that I can speak for both of us when I say that we would go through our trials once again to be where we are today."

"Yes, Jane, Declan is right. It has been a long, circuitous road that we have taken, but we are elated to be together. We've been married almost two whole weeks. I have never been happier," Liliana interjected. A smiling Declan reached for her hand and kissed her palm. As Jane watched Declan kiss his wife's hand, she noticed that Liliana was wearing Mary Ryan's ring, too. Jane Ross was thrilled for them.

The topic then turned to Declan's work with Christophe Riordan and how Christophe was the late Mary Ryan's cousin. Declan explained that Liliana was Christophe's god-daughter, and how they had worked together at the nursery for several years. After listening to their story, Jane Ross suspected that Christophe Riordan and his wife were likely just as thrilled for Declan and his new bride as she was. She knew

Declan had been a wonderful son to his widowed mother and how he had tirelessly taken care of her the last two years of her life. Again, she thought to herself, "How delighted you would be for your son, Mary, if you could only be here right now; and James, too."

When the large grandfather clock in Jane Ross's sitting room struck two o'clock that afternoon, she offered Declan and his bride a cup of tea. Ten minutes later, she emerged from her kitchen bearing a tray, loaded with all the accoutrements for afternoon tea. When Liliana commented on the pretty china tea set that she served from, Jane's face lit up, and she replied, "This is your tea set now, Liliana. Declan's mother gave it to me before she died; but it would give me such pleasure to have you use it in your new home with Declan. I know his mum would be pleased, too."

"Oh, Jane," whispered Liliana. "Thank you, but you'll not have any remembrance of Mary, if I take it."

"Oh, yes I will, dear. Just seeing your true affection for Declan and how happy you two are, is my gift, you see. Perhaps, I'll even come to America one of these days, and you can prepare tea for me!"

"That would be my sincere pleasure, Jane. I do hope you'll come," a very pleased Liliana retorted to Declan's special friend.

"We would love to show you America, Janey," Declan interjected. "Please consider a trip. I speak from experience when I say that Liliana would heartily welcome you."

Later, at the end of their visit, Declan kissed Jane Ross on the cheek, and thanked her for being so kind to his new bride. He then pulled the two letters he had received from his parents on the eve of his wedding from his pocket and shared them with Jane. While she read the familiar scripts of her two special friends who had departed this world too early, Declan and Liliana carefully stowed his mother's boxed tea set into the boot of their European rental car.

When they returned, Jane looked up, she had tears shimmering in her eyes. "Oh, Declan, what a special gift you received from James and Mary. Oh, son, you had the finest of parents, and it goes without saying that they have passed their goodness on to you." She then heartily embraced Declan and kissed his cheek.

She said, "I will make the effort to come see you in America, Declan; you **and** your lovely bride." She handed the two precious vellum letters back to him and said, "I am so happy that you came. Thank you both for coming to visit me, dearest Declan and Liliana."

As they got back onto the bucolic road that led to their lodgings once again, Declan thought about their visit with Janey. It had been so very nice to see his mother's special friend again, and he could not believe her thoughtfulness in giving Liliana his mother's tea set. He thought back to all the help she had willingly given to him during his mum's illness, and he was so glad that he and Liliana had made the trip to see her. Janey was a true friend.

Both Declan and Liliana were quiet for a few minutes after they returned to the slightly narrow roadway leading to their lodgings. Both were savoring the time they had just spent with Jane Ross. Then, Liliana looked into his eyes and told him something that made Jane's gift seem even more poignant.

"Declan, you know how Richard destroyed all of my special things when he upended the china hutch on the night that he hurt me. Well, I know things are just that…things…they can always be replaced. But, when he destroyed everything in my china cupboard, he also smashed my very special tea set that had been passed down from my Great Grandmother Essie, to my Grandma Helene, to my sweet mama, then right on down to me. It was the only broken thing that I cried about.

Having your precious mother's pretty tea set means a lot to me; perhaps, one day, I'll even be able to hand it down to our own daughter on her wedding day. The tradition can continue, but now with your own dear mother in the family loop, too. Do you understand what I mean?"

"Yes, sweetheart, I do appreciate what you mean. I suspect that mum probably gave her tea set to Janey, knowing that she would see it through to my bride someday. It is a very special gift."

That night, Declan was awakened from his sleep by Liliana. She was having a nightmare. As she tossed fitfully in her sleep, she cried out, "No, Richard, stop it!"

"Please stop, Richard. That belongs to Declan's mother. ***Stop!***" she begged.

Declan was surprised and reached out for her. She fought him off, and cried out again, "Don't, Richard!"

As gently as he could, Declan held her until she stopped flailing. He spoke soothingly to her, "Liliana, it's me, Declan. I'll not let anything happen to you. Can you wake up, sweetheart? You are having a bad dream."

At this juncture, Liliana's eyes flew open, and in the moonlight that was streaming through their window, she saw that she was, in fact, in Declan arms. She held on to him tightly and unbidden tears dampened his chest as he held her. She quaked in fear.

"Oh, Declan, Richard was alive," she said. "He was angry with me, yet again, and he was destroying Janey's lovely gift to me. He was also coming at me with his fist, and I couldn't get away; no matter how hard I tried. Why can't he ever just leave me alone?"

Declan's heart wrenched for her. He whispered, "Everything is alright, Liliana. I am your husband now. Richard is dead; he is gone. He can never hurt you again, dearest. He has no further ties upon you. You are free of him."

Liliana lifted her tear-streaked face upward and looked solemnly into her husband's eyes in the moonlight. "Oh, Declan, I suspect that Richard was probably on my mind because I had told you about my broken tea set this afternoon. I'm so sorry that I'm such a wimp."

Wise Declan Ryan then said something quite insightful, "Liliana, in view of all that has happened to you in the last two and a half years, I suspect that you've not fully had the time to work completely through the night that Richard inflicted injury upon you. That was quite a frightening ordeal for you. Then, upon the heels of his abuse, came his death and the revelation of all his lies to you. And, as if all that trauma weren't enough, you had to face the tragic loss of both your parents. You had to say good-bye to Stephan and Jenny within a few months of just barely getting them back in your life again."

"Just one of these things would be hard to endure for anyone, sweetheart. You have been strong, you have been forgiving, and you have embraced all the hard knocks that have been volleyed your way with admirable courage. But maybe, just maybe, Liliana, you still need to face such ugliness straight on. If you want to talk these things through with me, I'll listen for as long as you need. If you would prefer a professional, we'll find the right one. But we have something very special now, and neither of us wants Richard ruining our happiness. He has already inflicted enough pain on everyone."

Liliana sighed heavily. "You are right, Declan. That night *was* so frightening."

"Liliana," Declan replied, "You are my love, and together, we will purge these things from your dreams. We will vanquish Richard's grip." With that, he held her until they both fell asleep again.

So far, the entirety of the honeymoon trip had been most-enjoyable. Declan was the perfect guide… They toured The Holyrood Palace and later enjoyed "Cream Tea" across the street from the Parliament Building two days after they had arrived in Edinburgh. Several days later, Liliana was completely delighted when they visited the ancient Edinburgh Castle, and she was very enthusiastic to also visit the many eateries and pubs her husband had enjoyed during his university years in the beautiful, old city. Edinburgh with its historic stone edifices was so very different from where she had grown up in the relatively-young western United States.

From Edinburgh, they traveled north and slightly inland to the famous Balmoral area where Great Britain's late Queen Elizabeth II and the Royal Family spent their summer vacations. Both enjoyed its wondrous castle setting and its wildlife. From there, they continued to Inverness to see where Declan had been born and raised.

Once in the Inverness area, they stayed in a beautiful old stone mansion in Lochend which was attached to an ancient church. The large paned windows of the mansion afforded them a beautiful view of the narrow end of Loch Ness. As they looked across the loch, they enjoyed a view of a castle which was being restored. Using these lodgings as their home base, Declan and Liliana enjoyed a daily junket to see notable castles, and local historic sites. Of interest in this area was the Battlefield at Culloden. Liliana had read of Bonnie Prince Charlie and of the Jacobite clansmen, who had fought to restore the royal throne of Scotland in 1746. But, to see the battlefield in person, and to view the clan flags and stones of remembrance was sobering for tender-hearted Liliana.

Declan had chosen each of their honeymoon stops very thoughtfully, and Liliana was so happy to explore where he had grown up and to meet those who had been influential in the young life of her husband. It was obvious that each person she met had true affection for Declan and for his late parents. While on their wedding trip, Liliana finally also got the answers to some questions she had been harboring for some time, too…

She knew that both Christophe's and Declan's last names were not of Scottish origin. They both were, in fact, Irish surnames. She had always wondered why. One afternoon, as they motored through the autumn-flushed Scottish countryside, she ventured to ask him.

"Dec, I have been questioning something for a while now. Why is it that your last name and Christophe's last name are of Irish origin, and both of your clan colors are Irish as well? Why do you each hail from Scotland and claim its heritage when I suspect that somewhere within your family line, your people were from Ireland?" She flashed him an inquisitive smile as she made this inquiry, and her husband began to laugh.

"Oh, adorable Liliana, do you fear you may have married a reprobate or a horse thief?" Declan Ryan queried his bride.

"I love you no matter what your sullied lineage might just be, Declan Ryan, but I *am* curious for an answer," she laughingly replied.

"Well, my love, I hope you will still fancy me once you get your answer!" Declan retorted. Then he began to tell her the story…

"Liliana, in your mind's eye, imagine life early in the Nineteenth Century. Then, imagine a large man…much like Christophe; only his name is Matthias Riordan. Imagine, too, his cousin, whom everyone called, Johnnie, and you will have met Chris's and my forebears. These two young men grew up in County Cork, Ireland. They might have well been brothers, because they spent the entirety of their youth in each other's company. When they were both twenty, the adventure bug bit them, and they decided to cross over to England to work in the burgeoning industrial revolution there."

"These two characters did pretty well for themselves and managed to send money home to their starving families. As fate would have it, one evening, they were enjoying a pint in the local public house when a fight broke out. It seems that someone tried to accuse Matthias of picking their pocket. The authorities tried to arrest poor Matthias on those false charges. And, Liliana, because both Matthias and Johnnie were Irish, there were always those who tried to mete out harsher punishment and cruel treatment. Matthias and Johnnie knew that if Matthias found himself in the local jail, that he would likely never see the light of day again. Johnnie jumped into the fray and fought alongside Matthias, and they were able to escape from the local constabulary."

"Because they both knew the police were after them, they high-tailed it out of town and through the night. For days, they traveled, but only at night; and soon, they found themselves in Scotland. Once in Scotland, they continued further northward until they felt they were far enough away from their pursuers to let down their guard a bit. They still traveled off the main roads, and one day, they found an older fellow lying beaten and bloody near a copse of trees adjacent to a lonely stretch of road. Though they didn't have much between them, Matthias and Johnnie ministered to the man who had been assaulted and robbed by highwaymen."

"As fate would have it, this old fellow was a member of the Macfarlane Clan which had migrated to Scotland from Ireland many, many years before. When the old man was restored to his family, and his people realized these were brothers from Ireland, they offered Matthias and Johnnie refuge. Once the old man recovered from his injuries, he asked the two of them to stay on, and he offered them sanctuary with his family. Because of the Macfarlane generosity, both Matthias and Johnnie were still able to provide a wee bit extra for their loved ones back in Ireland. From there, the story continues with Matthias and Johnnie each marrying one of the old man's beautiful, red-haired twin daughters. Family legend has it that these two beauties not only had deep-red tresses, but also violet-colored eyes. Who knows, Liliana…maybe someday, those Macfarlane genes might just find their way into our family tree!"

Liliana laughed, "Oh, Dec!" Then, she inquired, "Is there still a chieftain, so to speak, for the Clan MacFarlane?"

"No, love. It is my understanding that the male lineage of the family died out around the mid-1880s…but from what I have read, there is a clan society today; both here in Scotland and in the United States."

"That was a wonderful story, Dec. But you are descended from neither reprobates, scalawags, nor horse thieves…I find I'm just a little disappointed because I rather fancied the idea of you being just a little bit of a rogue."

Declan Ryan then threw back his head in laughter. "Liliana, if you fancy just a little bit of a rogue, we're not far from our B&B. Perhaps, we could have an early dinner, and then I could show you just a bit of the rogue that resides within me!" He then winked at her. It goes without saying that Liliana was eager to witness this new facet of her husband's disposition as they pulled into the picturesque drive leading up the hill to "The White Manse."

That evening, after a memorable meal, a walk around the scenic grounds of their lodgings, and plenty of flirting, Liliana dreamt of Matthias Riordan and Johnnie Ryan and how they had found their way to Scotland. Yet, in her dream, Matthias looked much like her beloved Christophe Riordan, and Johnnie Ryan could have been her husband's twin. When she awoke, she had to chuckle to herself as she thought about how her psyche had most-likely "replayed" those two Irish fellows just about right! She also secretly wondered if those violet-colored eyes might ever find their way into her and Declan's gene pool.

DECLAN'S HOMECOMING

*L*iliana Ryan was enchanted several days later with what she saw as her husband drove the car up the steep hill to a tree-lined, somewhat terraced, street. The stone row houses which also lined the terraced neighborhood were quaint and very stalwart. It was easy for Liliana to visualize the families and friends who had surrounded Declan's parents when he was a boy, as lamplight cheerfully shone from front windows where late-afternoon tea was likely being enjoyed with lively conversation and tartlets. It all looked so very cozy.

Declan continued to drive the automobile toward the end of the street before he stopped. There at the end of the row was his boyhood home. Being located at the street's end, which was bordered by a stone wall with grazing sheep adjacent, his family home also boasted a beautiful side yard with a gate which led to the backyard garden. Taking in such quiet beauty explained much to Liliana as to why her husband was so even tempered and ready to give back to the land. He had simply grown up in a setting that was quietly serene and far from the world's chaotic busyness.

At this juncture, Declan cut the auto's motor and commented, "Lily, this is where I lived the entirety of my life until I left for my university studies in Edinburgh. It is also where I cared for my mum during the last years of her life. I love this place."

Sighing, Liliana put her hand softly upon his shoulder and said, "My darling man, this is very close to what I had envisioned for your family home. Oh, Declan, it is so very charming, and the yard is just lovely. Has it changed very much since you left?"

"Quite the opposite, sweetheart. It looks even prettier than when I left it and moved to America."

"Did you know the people who bought it very well, Dec?" Liliana inquired.

"Well, I didn't exactly sell it…I gave it to some dear friends of my parents on a thirty-year lease since I already owned it outright after my mother's death. They maintain it, pay an equitable leasing payment to me, and look after the payment of the taxes on it, too. Yet, if you ever wanted to live here seasonally, I could likely make arrangements for us to take it back at some point…"

"Declan Ryan, you are an amazing man. You probably guessed that I would fall thoroughly in love with Scotland and want to come back again and again. How could you know that? When you leased it to family friends, we hadn't even met yet!"

"I just couldn't quite give it up, you know… I knew that I might want to bring my future wife and my children back here someday, and look at me now, Liliana, I'm doing just that!" he smiled looking every inch like the quiet young Declan whom Liliana had fallen for when she was just barely nineteen years of age. "I don't have those children just yet, but I have no worries on that front. We seem to be very compatible when it comes to making love, don't you think Liliana?"

Liliana could tell that the apples of her cheeks were taking on the heat of a blush, so she just sighed and answered, "You're definitely right on that one, my love."

Declan chuckled and said, "Come, Lily, let's take a little walk…"

Through the bucolic pasture land and stone turn-styles, Declan shared treasured vistas and childhood haunts with Liliana. She truly enjoyed seeing the animation and joy in her husband's face as he took her on a tour of where he had grown up and into the man that she loved so dearly. As the late afternoon sun was beginning to wane, they arrived back at the car to find the front window of Declan's old family home lit up with light flowing from beneath a burgundy-wine-colored lamp shade. The light showcased a carved mantle adorned with family photos and Staffordshire china dogs. The scene charmed Liliana to her core.

Just as Declan was bundling her into the rental car, an attractive silver-haired woman came out of the front door. She skipped down the front step and called, "Declan Ryan, is that you?" She spoke with the same heavy brogue that Liliana adored in her husband.

"Aye, Katy, it is, in fact, I… Though I'm surprised that after all these years, you would even recognize me! I was just showing my wife where I grew up."

At Declan's declaration, the woman sped up her cadence and drew up alongside Declan as he held open the door of the car and engulfed him in a hug. "Who could ever forget you, Declan? You have always been pretty easy on the eyes!" She winked at an astounded Declan, then bent and offered her hand to Liliana who was already in the car and announced, "It's my pleasure to meet you, lass, I'm Katy McLeod."

Very pleased, Liliana clasped Katy McLeod's hand and answered, "Hello, Katy, I'm Liliana. It is lovely to meet you."

And so, began a late afternoon tea with Katy and her husband, Thomas. Both McLeods were engaging people, and they chatted with Declan as though almost fifteen years had never elapsed since they had last seen one another. As for Liliana, both Katy and Thomas adored her for the handsome smile that they now witnessed on their old friend's face. And, as far as Declan was concerned, he could not have been any happier to include his new bride into his late parents' circle of friends. Somehow, it made him feel as though his mum and dad had finally met Liliana, too. Everyone was in high spirits when it was time for them to depart.

"How long are you and Liliana to be in Inverness, Declan?" Katy McLeod inquired as Declan helped his wife into the car.

"Well, Katy, I plan to take Liliana to Nairn to go antiquing tomorrow. She and I share an interest in old things and their history. If we find something, we cannot pass up, we plan to ship it back to Rosemeade Township. Then, on Thursday, we will be travelling to the Isle of Skye. I've booked a suite at the Kinloch Lodge for us."

"Oh, Declan, what a wonderful excursion you and Liliana are about to embark upon! When you return from Skye, I would love to have a little social in your honor. We'll enjoy some of Thomas's autumn cider, and his hand-made sausages. I'll invite some of your mum and dad's old friends, so that they can see you again, too, and meet your bride. I know you've visited Janey Ross already, but everyone would love to see her again, if she would like to make the drive. Maybe she would consider joining us for the weekend. We've missed her a lot since she moved to Edinburgh. What do you think, you two?" Katy asked.

"Dearest Katy McLeod, I think that my bride and I would be more than honored. What do you think, Liliana?"

"I know that we both would be very pleased, Katy! Is there something that we can bring?" Liliana queried.

At Liliana's inquiry, Katy McLeod threw back her head in laughter and said, "Are you daft, young woman? This little get-together is to be in your honor. You just find yourself here at five o'clock on Saturday afternoon with Declan in tow. My lovely Thomas and I will do the rest."

On Saturday evening, Liliana found herself being embraced into Declan's old circle of family friends, just as he had been welcomed into the heart of her family and friends years before. She felt honored that because they loved and esteemed her wonderful husband, they loved and esteemed her, too. Once again, she found herself thankful for all of life's special blessings in this new season of her life.

A TENDER TIFF

Though they were most compatible, **Declan and Liliana Ryan** did have a falling-out during their honeymoon. Whatever they had argued about was of no matter to either of them by day's end. Both had suffered enough by the time their evening meal was served to them at a quaint place where they had been staying for several days, but both were still stubborn with each other. So, they ate their meal in silence, shared a delectable dessert that went down as if it had been prepared with sea sand, and walked back to their private room without touching one another. Once inside their bed chamber, Declan picked up the small local newspaper that he hadn't yet fully read, and Liliana stood looking out the window at the setting sun.

What remained of the setting sun was half of a brilliant orange orb just barely slipping behind the flattened dimensions of the deeply shaded rolling land. The clouds in the sky were an intense purple hue fading into vivid pink streaks. Liliana was silhouetted against this colorful canvas, not knowing that Declan watched her in lieu of reading his newspaper. At last, both could take no more; they both spoke to each other at the exact same time. "I'm sorry," they echoed.

Declan quickly rose from his chair and covered the space between them in just a few steps. Liliana nestled into his embrace and reached for his face. They kissed tenderly and held one another tightly. Liliana spoke first, "Oh, Declan, I don't want to be at odds with you! You are my wonderful husband and my tender lover. Sweetheart, I don't ever want to fight with you. I'm so sorry if I was out of line."

Declan then cupped her face within his hands and spoke, "No, no, Lily; it was all my fault. I was curt with you and for what I can't even remember. Please pardon my behavior. I don't ever want to treat you in such a fashion again. Liliana, you are my beautiful bride; a bride that God restored to me, I don't ever want to be undeserving of such a precious, precious gift!"

Again, they embraced each other tightly during the last violet-hued minutes of the day. Declan was the first to break their embrace. He stepped slightly away from his wife, soberly looked into her eyes and asked, "Liliana, will you have me now? I have been longing for you since we quarreled this morning."

Liliana's eyes shone slightly with just a sprinkle of unshed tears that sparkled in the waning light, and she answered, "Yes, Declan, I want you too. I won't feel completely soothed until you hold me."

Later, as they lay in each other's arms completely sated from their loving and succumbing to the cocoon of sleep, Liliana quietly inquired, "Dec, do you want to know something?"

"What is it, love?"

"On the day that Richard did away with himself, I was leaving his hospital room to go upstairs to the cafeteria for dinner. He called out to me as I opened the door to leave. When I turned and looked back, he stared at me for several seconds, his lips slightly twitching with a sneer. Then, he callously said, 'Liliana, do you know that you sometimes call out Declan Ryan's name in your sleep?' I was surprised but said nothing in response. His veneer of a man in dire pain quickly fell away. He exhaled disgustedly, then smirked and shook his head just slightly, rolling his eyes as I turned to go again. Somehow, I knew he was going to do something dreadful, Declan. And, that was the last thing Richard ever said to me," she whispered.

"Taunting me was how it began the night that Richard battered me, too," she added. "I've had enough angry seasons of life to last me forever. It bruised my soul today to harbor any ill feelings toward you. I never want to be incensed with you again."

Quietly, Declan answered, "Today, I was more torn up about things than I care to admit, Liliana. I can't abide feeling any resentment toward you, either. It brought back an ache that felt far too familiar. I don't want to go there any more. With that, Declan Ryan held his wife just a little bit closer and whispered, "Now, we can start with a clean slate tomorrow."

Mr. and Mrs. Declan Ryan were closing out their honeymoon junket very well; very well, indeed!

NIGHT SHIFT MEMORIES

eclan Ryan was busy with a project. Though he had only just recently returned from his month-long honeymoon in Scotland and was still making up for lost time with his bride, he felt compelled to finish a project that he had started some time ago. Completion of this task had kept him from coming home and enjoying time with Liliana for several evenings in a row, and he was finding himself feeling restless without her company, yet he soldiered on with his work.

Stealing away to his loft for several evenings, he kept company with two small blank canvases, his oil paints, and his brushes. You see, he was adding to the tiny grouping that he had painted for his love years ago but had never given to her. The framed, though never hung, depictions of the early years of their relationship had captured the purity and affection they had felt for each other. Liliana had been delighted when she had accidentally found them months ago, but the time had not been right to give them to her. And now, Declan was capturing the newest chapter of their lives; the night they became engaged and their memorable wedding day. He wanted to add these special events to the collection he had painted for her years ago. And now, he planned to give the little grouping to her to mark their upcoming two-month wedding anniversary.

As Declan had mixed the oil-paint colors on his artist's palette and then watched them flow from his brush, he could see Liliana in his mind's eye. He was taken back to the evening he had proposed to her at Stefano's. That night, she had looked so very beautiful, and she really had had no idea how affected he had been when she had so lovingly agreed to spend the rest of her life at his side. As the paint colors continued to fill the petite canvas, a miniature likeness of Liliana appeared wearing a black dress and red high heels; she was glowing with happiness. Declan also found himself appearing at her side as they stood outside Stefano's picturesque eatery. As he continued to layer the colors on the diminutive canvas, the joy that they had felt that night began to feel palpable.

A day later, Declan painted Liliana and himself standing beneath the rose-covered arbor on the day of their wedding. Her wedding dress, with his family's clan colors so handsomely bound about her waist, and her dark hair entwined with seed pearls and lace also found their way out of his artist's brush. Before he knew it, his likeness was standing beside her on the canvas dressed in the full regalia of his father's treasured dress tartans. The autumn colors of that day were depicted, too, and Declan found that he could almost breathe in the scents that had floated on the air that afternoon and evening. He relived the joy of his wedding day once again as his brush continued its trek across the small, yet expanding, canvas.

On the third night of work on his gifts to Liliana, Declan felt that he was missing something, but he couldn't quite determine what it was. The tiny paintings were perfect, but something was still missing; even though he had thoughtfully captured their lives in his renderings. As he was preparing to return to the vintner's cottage and to his waiting wife, a memory struck him quite profoundly. It was then that he knew what he needed to paint. There was one more facet in his memory bank that he needed to capture, but it was not to be captured in miniature. He hurriedly sketched out what he wanted to paint on a larger gesso-prepared canvas, and then went home to his captivating wife.

Liliana's face lit up as he entered their bedroom. She was sitting in the ancient iron bed reading a book, and she wore a very fetching lace snippet of sleeping attire. Her hair spilled sweetly around her face and shoulders, and with open arms she reached for him; her book completely forgotten. Declan crossed the room and returned her embrace; moved that she was so devoted to him. When he had loosened their embrace, she quietly inquired.

"I've missed you these last few evenings, Declan Ryan. What are you working on so late into the night? I've seen the light in your loft… I know you are up to something!"

"Aye, my Liliana," he retorted. "You know me well, don't you?"

"Yes, I do…but, I hope you are not tired of my company or feeling the need to distance yourself by returning to your work each evening."

Declan's heart wrenched when he heard her words. He pulled her to himself and kissed her tender lips. Richard's thoughtless treatment of her had struck again. It saddened him that such a standard had been set in her mind. With a heavy brogue, he replied, "Oh, love, I had to return home to you early this evening because I could not find it in my heart to stay away any longer. Please don't let Richard's former treatment of you dictate your feelings now. Liliana, I am only working on something special just for you. That is all."

Liliana put her soft hand upon his cheek with its three-day stubble, "I'm sorry, Declan."

He took her hand, turned it over, and kissed it, "No, sweetheart, it is I who should be sorry. I never even considered the precedent that had been set. It was thoughtless of me to steal away and to be secretive about it. It smacks of Richard. Can you forgive me?"

"Of course, Declan, I adore you."

Kissing her, he said, "I'll be right back; don't move!"

Minutes later, Declan came back to their bed. He was shaved, showered and ready to show his complete commitment to her. That night, he purposefully made love to his wife with no expectations for himself in that old iron bed. He caressed her and tenderly ministered to her needs because he realized that she was feeling slightly fragile. She responded to his overtures with a passion that humbled him while she breathlessly whispered out his name. Afterward, he held her in his arms until sleep overtook them both. There was no question that Declan Ryan was totally devoted to his wife.

Several days later, Declan walked with Liliana to Annie and Christophe's home. She and Annie were driving to Reedsburgh for a girls' day out. They planned to shop, have lunch, and to attend an art exhibition. Declan kissed and hugged the two of them before watching them drive toward the highway junction. Again, he thought of her solemn question several nights earlier as to whether he was tiring of her, and he was saddened. He could not believe that Richard Rawlings had been so malicious and mean-spirited toward her that she questioned herself.

Knowing that he had several hours to expend, Declan told his crew that he would be working in the loft most of the day. He wanted to complete his project without any more evenings away from Liliana. Since Declan had already sketched what he wanted to portray on that waiting canvas, he got right to the subject at hand.

As the day progressed, Liliana's face began to look back at him from the large canvas. She was dressed in the same lace-infused corset and petticoat that she had worn under her wedding gown. She was sitting on an antique reproduction chair that he had painstakingly refinished years ago. Both pieces of her underpinnings shone somewhat diaphanous, and her petticoat slightly revealed her limbs while her hands lay folded in her lap. Her tanned shoulders were shown beautifully on his canvas. Her corset, with its golden cording, was still fastened and was shielding her lovely assets from view. She looked angelic.

As Declan painted what he could clearly see in his mind's eye, he relived the precious unveiling of his wife's body on their wedding night. After unfastening a myriad of satin buttons down the back of her gown, he had helped her to step out of that billowing garment. He was then dumbstruck by how lovely she had looked in her glistening lace underpinnings. Her smooth skin had looked almost pearlescent. Though Declan had seen her in a bikini and every type of summer apparel many times before, he knew that she had chosen her bridal lingerie very carefully and just for him. She had looked virginal, yet ready to become his. Such thoughtfulness was one of the many things that he so admired about her. Earlier that wedding night, he had refrained from unfastening her undergarments; he had simply waited for her to remove his wedding clothing first.

Slightly shy, but with loving hands, she had removed his formal tartan clothing, piece by piece. While she labored at her task, she would occasionally look up into his eyes, then tenderly kiss him. When there was nothing else to be removed from his being, she had put her hand

upon his beating heart and had said, "I am ready to be yours, Declan."
He had then carried her to their marital bed.

It was there that he had, at last, unfastened the laces of her corset.
It had taken a minute or two to loosen them, but his labor had not
been in vain…she had then allowed him to caress and to kiss her lovely
curves while she, in turn, touched and familiarized herself with his
body; all of this from a woman whose last encounter with her late
husband had been a brutal rape and beating. Liliana's loving touch
only served to increase his commitment to her. Their love-making that
brisk October night had rocked him. It was nothing short of perfect.

And now, as he looked up from his musings, he saw Liliana perfectly
captured on the canvas by his own hand. Oh…how thankful he was
that God had brought her back to him. Pleased with his work, Declan
transferred the wet canvas into the loft's now empty walk-in closet to
dry for several weeks. From there, he would take it to Reedsburgh to
be framed along with the new miniatures.

RECURRING THEMES

Liliana awoke with a start and realized she was in her own bed with Declan. Once again, she had dreamt of Richard. As before, he was coming at her; and this time, he was determined to beat her within an inch of her life. In her dream, she had tried to run out the door, but he had wrenched her back by pulling on her long hair and was pummeling her with his fists. Try as she might, she could not free herself from his vise grip or his brutal punches. Now that she was fully awake and in her respite from the world with Declan, she decided something monumental. She would seek out professional help to eradicate Richard from her dreams.

As she turned over and nestled back into the downy cotton sheeting of her bed, sleeping Declan reached for her and pulled her to himself. As she lay with her back against his chest with his arm draped about her waist, she marveled, that even in his slumber, he sensed that she needed reassurance. Feeling secure once again, she fell into a deep sleep. She awoke feeling refreshed but determined.

After sharing a breakfast of tea, toast, and scrambled eggs together, Liliana followed Declan into the bedroom and watched him dress for a day of his late-autumn tasks at the nursery. His smooth skin was still slightly damp from the shower as he put on his undergarments and his low-slung jeans. She loved seeing him with no shirt and no shoes… only wearing his jeans. There was something about watching him this way that spoke to her heart. This very appealing man was hers. He was honorable, caring, and kind, but he was also strong and protective. She considered herself blessed to have such a wonderful mate.

Declan looked up and said, "What are you thinking, Liliana. You're pensive, but you're wearing a smile."

"Oh, Dec, I was just enjoying watching you get ready for the day. I sometimes can't believe that you're mine, and I was just reveling in it; that's all," she dreamily replied.

"Do you know that I felt exactly the same way, as I watched you prepare breakfast for us this morning?" Declan replied with a knowing smile.

"Good!" she chimed. Then, she decided to tell him her decision about counseling.

"I know I'm changing the subject here, Dec, but I wanted you to know that I've made a determination regarding professional counseling. Last night, I had another horrible dream about Richard, and was so relieved when I awoke that I decided to finally seek some help. I'm getting fatigued from waking up terrified."

"I am glad to hear it, Liliana. It hurts to see you awaken so upset. Would you like for me to attend the counseling with you?"

"Yes, I would, Declan. You fortify me, and there are so many fragments about my years with Richard that I think you need to understand, as well. Perhaps, we could both benefit from several joint sessions, as he undermined you, too."

"Then it's settled. We'll embark upon it together, sweetheart. What we have now is too special to let Richard interrupt our joy; even if it is only in your dreams."

"You are so very right, my Declan."

In just a matter of days, Liliana had chosen a therapist whom she felt would be caring of both their needs. Their first session was scheduled in the early evening on a Thursday night. Declan and Liliana arrived at Dr. Reese Winston's office to find that she was, in fact, a friendly and very caring person. Her office was painted in a calming palette of colors. The lighting was low and very soft, and she had soothing music playing in the background.

Dr. Winston invited them to sit down on a white-on-white striped fabric sofa that was splashed with embroidered and needle-pointed pillows that looked to be antique. As she opened their session, she inquired how long they had known each other and how long they had been married. When Liliana called her, 'Dr. Winston,' she smiled and said, "Declan and Liliana, please call me Reese. If we are to probe through things that are very intimate and sometimes difficult to articulate, we need to be on a first-name basis. Agreed?"

"Yes!" chorused both Declan and Liliana.

"Liliana, why don't you tell me how you met Declan, as your story seems to begin with him."

"Okay, Reese, I'll begin…I met Declan just a few weeks before I turned nineteen years of age. I'll be candid with you…he was so different from anyone that I had ever dated or known from my school days that my interest in him was piqued within just days of meeting him. I had a wonderful father, and Declan exhibited characteristics that I so admired in my dad. Yet, I wasn't looking for someone just like my father, I only desired a friend of the opposite sex who was moral. I found that in Declan. He had family ties with my god-parents, and we worked closely together at my god-father's tree-and-flower nursery. Declan was newly arrived from Scotland then, so we quickly became friends." At this point, Liliana shook her head and continued, "No, it was more than friends, it was something deeper."

Reese continued to guide the conversation, "Declan, is this how you would describe your meeting?"

"Yes, Reese, it is… I had only just arrived in the United States a few days before I met Liliana. Her god-parent, Christophe Riordan, is my second cousin. When I met my wife, I found her to be very kind and caring. At the time, the compassion of her character appealed to me, as I had just suffered the loss of my only remaining parent."

"My father died when I was just barely eight years old, and I had lost my mother three months before I immigrated to the United States. I was almost twenty-three, and I was feeling very alone at the time. My world had been fraught with heartache, as I was the one who had cared for my mother for most of the two years that she suffered from cancer. It was Liliana who had the courage to inquire about my losses not long after we were introduced. Though she wasn't quite yet nineteen years old, she had the social grace of someone considerably older. It seemed as though I had known her all my life after just a few conversations. Liliana is right when she says it was more than friends. We were companions, and I'll admit that I was quite taken with her… right from the start."

"Liliana, when did you meet your late husband?" Reese inquired.

Breathing a deep sigh to fortify herself, Liliana began to relive events that she would have rather forgotten, but she stayed the course and explained to the therapist the incidents that forever changed both her and Declan's lives. It was hard on her, as Reese asked many questions pertaining to her life with Richard and wrote down copious notes. At this juncture, Reese began to ask Declan questions regarding his feelings as he had listened to Liliana relate the happenings.

Declan could only answer, "Reese, I have to admit that listening to Liliana relate both the first four years of our relationship and how Richard duped the two of us makes me feel renewed anger at him and renewed disappointment in myself. I harbor no anger at Liliana, because it was my cues that she misread, so she entered further into a relationship with Richard after I stepped away from her. Richard Rawlings **did** appear to be exceedingly successful, and because I felt that I had nothing to offer her at the time, I literally handed her to Richard. I thought he could give her things in this life that I could not…yet, by stepping away, there was never any natural progression in our relationship toward an end or toward something more. Knowing how he undermined our bond years ago; I now feel Richard played the both of us like a fine violin. I know he sensed vulnerability in me and the peace-maker in Liliana."

"Liliana, would you agree with Declan on the things that he just shared?"

"Yes, Reese, I would." Liliana softly replied. "I agree with Declan that our relationship was never truly finished. Even though Declan stepped away, I still wanted him. Richard was pretty savvy in his efforts to plant doubts into my mind about Declan's affection for me, too. After a rocky last summer spent working alongside Declan at the nursery, Richard had pretty much managed to convince me that

Declan had no feelings for me at all. It was very hard on me to come to terms with such a realization…"

"Yet, I have myself to blame, too, because before arriving for my summer job at the nursery that last year, I had let Richard escort me to several expensive events, dinners, and concerts. Though I loved Declan dearly, our relationship had always been simpler; quieter really. Declan had taken me to exciting places in Brookings City, too, but we had always come back to my parents' home or to the nursery afterward. I had always been cared for with him. What Declan and I had always enjoyed was liken to an intricately woven tapestry, and it was very special to me. Yet, Richard ensured that my time with him was always fast-paced and exciting. Often, staying out very late and waking up too tired to drag myself to class the next morning. Somehow, I did manage to get myself to class on those occasions, though."

"At that time, Richard treated me like a woman which was flattering to an inexperienced twenty-one-year-old girl, whereas, Declan had always been thoughtful of my upbringing and the protection and respect I had been cocooned within while growing up as an only child. My parents didn't even conceive me until they were well into their forties. I wasn't smothered by my parents' affection for their long-awaited child, but I was able to grow up at my own pace; not by any frenetic standard. My parents always cherished me right where I was, and Declan did the same. That is why I felt so much affection for him at such an early age. He never tried to push me." Smiling and looking over at her husband, she said, "I still love and admire you for that, Declan. Thank you for your esteem when I was a young university student."

Dr. Reese Winston watched with some fascination as Declan took Liliana's hand into his and replied, "How could I not have been respectful to you, Lily? It was obvious even then that you were going to be a one-of-a-kind woman." Both seemed to have forgotten that she was there.

Getting back to the subject at hand, Dr. Winston asked. "Liliana, did Richard pressure you to give up your relationship with Declan?"

"Yes, Reese, but not blatantly; he just continued to put doubts in my mind about Declan's true affection for me. He constantly referred to Declan as a "***mere émigré***," who could offer me next to nothing in this life. He tried to paint Declan as someone who was weak."

Liliana continued, "Now, I understand how Richard could sniff out vulnerability of any kind, and I know that he sensed that Declan's loss of both parents had left him hurting; so, Richard's mission became one of eroding our relationship at every turn. Today, I understand that Declan stepped away because he felt that Richard possessed the extended education and the money to provide a comfortable life for me. What Declan didn't know then was that I would have given up everything to spend the rest of my life with him. His strength of character, his kindness, and his ethics spoke to me more vocally than any wealth ever could have…so you see, Reese, both Declan and I were cruelly played by Richard Rawlings."

So began Declan and Liliana's sessions with Dr. Winston. Some appointments were spent together sifting through how things had gone so awry over a decade before. Other times, they met with Reese singly. On those occasions, Dr. Winston addressed specific incidents that had been pivotal to them both.

When the time arrived for Liliana to work through the details of Richard's brutal treatment, she was feeling apprehensive, but knew that her nightmares would likely not stop until she purged the ugliness of abuse from her psyche. That evening, she made great strides…she shared the details of that frightening night with Reese Winston and candidly answered Reese's many questions.

While Declan sat just outside the closed door of Dr. Winston's office, he felt trepidation for the things that Liliana was likely reliving just a few feet away. As always, he wanted to take away her pain, but that night, he knew that he could not. Instead, he lifted his lovely wife up in prayer.

Back inside the office, Reese asked Liliana if she could, perhaps, assign a number between one and ten to the severity of the incidents that she had just articulated to her. A sober Liliana assigned the number, ten plus. Reese noted that her face was tear-stained and that she trembled after reliving her beatings and her subsequent personal violation, but she knew they must press on…

"Liliana, if you were to assign a color or colors to that night, what would they be?"

"There would be several colors, Reese," Liliana replied. "There would be a very dominating dark blackish purple blending into a fiery orange red, then melding into molten yellow around the edges. There would be a hot wind encouraging the colors to burst into flame, and there would be flying shards of very sharp glass being spit from within the cloud of colors. If you want me to assign a sound to it, it would be a deafening roar with a cacophony of screaming sirens."

As she said these things, Reese watched Liliana return to the scene of the crimes that were committed upon her that night. Personally, she was very saddened for Liliana Ryan, but her physician's gut told her to keep pressing on as Liliana was making strides toward resolution of lingering fear.

"Liliana, tell me what emotions you were feeling as these violent events were taking place?" Reese continued.

"Even though it had been a decade since I had seen him, I wanted Declan to come for me and take me home to my family. As I was locked inside my bedroom that night, I recalled how Declan was the one person, besides my father, who had always looked after my welfare when I was young; just on the cusp of womanhood. But those feelings shamed me, too, as Richard had completely convinced me many years before that Declan had never even cared for me at all. I felt embarrassed for desiring Declan's concern, but I wanted him only because I knew he would never have let such a thing ever happen to me."

"Lastly, I was humiliated, and so very demeaned. I knew that I could never tell my parents what Richard had done to me. They, too, would have felt completely violated, as I was their one and only child. In short, Reese, I felt so abject that I chose to hurt alone; scared beyond measure."

Quietly, Reese asked, "Liliana, can you continue to spend some more time concentrating on the night Richard violated you in so many ways? Can you let every fiber within your body be enveloped with the feelings that affected you that night? Close your eyes and just continue to feel the concentration of every emotion that you suffered through that December evening. Walk through it again, Liliana, and just *feel* everything that happened to you."

"Take note of how each member of your body feels while you concentrate on these feelings. What hurts, what aches, and lastly how your psyche feels. Take all the time you need to feel these emotions again. Once you've concentrated, really concentrated, on these emotions, the fear will begin to erode."

Liliana did as she was asked. The room was very quiet. All that could be heard was the resonant timbre of the Vivaldi music that played softly in the background.

Soon, Reese heard Liliana begin to breathe erratically, then she heard Liliana gasp and say, "Reese, I think I'm going to be sick." Reese Winston jumped to Liliana's aid and led her into an adjacent powder room beside her private office. There, Liliana fell to her knees and vomited up the contents of her stomach into the spanking clean white commode. Reese then handed her a cool washcloth and helped her back into her chair. Liliana continued to keep her eyes closed and concentrate on how she was feeling.

Several minutes later, when Liliana finally spoke, she said, "Reese, I'm sorry about sullying your sparkling bathroom, but I wish I could have been that violently sick several years ago. Every part of my being felt so incredibly ill reliving those feelings again tonight. My head ached as though there was thunder inside, my heart was pounding, and my entire body felt as if it was reeling convulsively through space; completely out of control. It certainly was hard to cope with again."

Kind Reese Winston then replied, "You are not the first of my patients to react in such a way, Liliana, and you certainly did not sully my powder room. Let me get you some bottled water and a disposable toothbrush, dear."

Minutes later, a freshened Liliana smiled shakily, then said, "Amazingly, I do feel better, Reese. For one thing, when I walk out that door in just a few minutes, I will not be suffering alone in abject silence. This time, after reliving Richard's violations, I have my self-esteem intact, and I have my steadfast husband and my devoted godparents there for me. The first time that I lived through Richard's abuse, there was no one to ease my torment. Thank you, Reese, for supporting me tonight."

When the door finally opened from within Dr. Reese Winston's office that evening, Liliana emerged pale and slightly shaky. Declan Ryan immediately reached for her and pulled her into his embrace; his large hand cupping the back of his wife's head, as he whispered encouragement to her. Reese Winston watched as Liliana's honorable husband touched his lips to the only visible scar of her abuse just below her left eyebrow.

Looking into Declan Ryan's troubled blue eyes as he again held his wife within his embrace, Reese smiled at him and shook her head affirmatively. "She did very well this evening, Declan. I'm very proud of her."

Two weeks later, Declan took his turn reliving events for Dr. Reese Winston. And, as he had done for her, Liliana waited just outside the door of Reese's office and prayed for her resolute husband.

That night, Declan tackled several issues relating to Richard Rawlings and how he had changed the course of both his and Liliana's lives. The session was intense for Declan as well. At long last, Declan admitted that for years, he had felt as if his heart might implode from his regret. Declan, too, had to relive several pivotal issues associated with losing Liliana to Richard Rawlings as well as to articulate his remaining anguish and absolute sorrow about things that had gone before.

Together with Reese, Declan was finally able to embrace the palpable remorse and the paralysis he had felt when Liliana became Richard's wife. He shamefully admitted to her that he had gone to Liliana's wedding secretly wanting to knock Richard Rawlings unconscious to the floor and take Liliana for his own. Interestingly, Declan assigned a similar number and colors to the events associated with Liliana's wedding. Finally, Declan relived his extensive pruning of the abandoned vineyard rows for months after Liliana's marriage; admitting how much he had loathed himself for doing what he felt was appropriate by letting her go...

In the end, Declan Ryan thanked Reese for her compassion and for her earnest counsel to him during the intensive therapy session. He left exhausted, but encouraged, that he was at last learning to forgive himself...no more wallowing in regret. He told Reese that "He knew that God had given him much to be thankful for..."

Dr. Reese Winston watched as waiting Liliana Ryan hurried to her husband's embrace, and then stood on her tip-toes to kiss him soundly on the cheek, as he exited her office. The three of them then briefly discussed Declan's session and his great strides toward forgiving himself. The couple then exited the building arm-in-arm. Dr. Reese Winston watched them depart and wished that all her patients were esteemed by their spouses like the Ryans.

Both Declan and Liliana knew there would be more sessions with Dr. Reese Winston. They both felt that their preliminary sessions with her had done much to soothe the fear, the fragile feelings, and their related issues that had brought them to her. Yet, they also knew that delving further into these issues with Reese Winston would help to truly eradicate some troubling memories that might tend to linger a bit longer.

A HOLIDAY GETAWAY

Declan Ryan was making arrangements for a two-night stay at the historic Hotel Bellingwood in Reedsburgh. After weeks of Thursday evenings spent in therapy with Dr. Reese Winston, both Declan and Liliana were ready for some time away. Since the Christmas season was in full swing, and the Hotel Bellingwood provided a wonderful holiday experience for its guests, Declan decided to book a suite. Though Liliana had lived in Reedsburgh for the first twenty-two years of her life, she had never stayed at the lavish Hotel Bellingwood. He knew she would be very pleased to enjoy a few days and nights of pampering as well as afternoon tea in their renowned tearoom.

Declan then invited her to have a special dinner with him at a small restaurant they both loved to escape to in Reedsburgh, called Isaac's. As well, Declan told her to pack her suitcase for a special two nights away with him. It was to be a surprise where they were to spend their time. Liliana was very pleased with his invitation; especially when she found out that he had already planned arrangements for Dover's care and had given Tim Hill a bonus for minding the nursery in his stead.

That special night over dinner at Isaac's, Declan presented her with the miniature paintings of their history. As she was opening the colorfully-wrapped box, he simply said, "You already know that I was once going to present these to you and then ask if you would be mine, Liliana. But now, so many years later, I only want to humbly give them to you to say thank you for being my bride. There are really no words that I can use to convey what I feel. My renderings are a poor representation, but they were created from memories that I'll carry always."

As she pored over his miniature paintings, he could tell that she was somewhat overcome. "Don't you like them, Liliana?" he asked in a heavy brogue.

She looked at him with winsome eyes, and replied, "Oh, Declan, I absolutely adore them! You have captured our relationship perfectly…

my only regret is that there is a ten-year gap in our history. When I think about what could have been, it hurts, but we have been working through these things with Reese Winston."

Declan completely understood her feelings. He answered with candor, "We've both made mistakes, on that we can agree. But I think when we look at our memories of things that went before; we can consider them a bridge to something that turned out far stronger because of those mistakes. I loved you then, Liliana, but what I feel for you now has no comparison." He paused, took one of her hands in his, and suggested, "Perhaps, we should break the paintings into two groups. We'll hang the early years in my office at the loft and our present love in the vintner's cottage. That way, as watershed events come along in our new life together, we can add to them. You know what I mean, our travels, our children…What do you think?"

"I think that is a wonderful idea, Declan, but I do have one request, though…it is for those paintings that will be hung in our cottage. Could you paint another miniature of you, me, and Dover on the night we attended Christophe and Annie's summer dance last June? That evening was truly what I consider to be a watershed event in our lives, and I treasure the memories from that night." She continued on, "When I think of your affection for me that evening, I get misty-eyed. You made me so very happy…"

Declan continued to hold her hand in his and looked pensive for several seconds. When he again looked into her eyes, he said, "I'll do just that, Liliana. That was a night to remember. Yours is a fine suggestion!"

Ten days later, very early on Christmas morning, Liliana awoke and saw Declan quietly leaving their bedroom. Next, she heard rustling paper in their living room. Minutes later, he quietly returned to their bed, saw that she was awake, and murmured very softly, "Liliana, I think I just heard Father Christmas clattering in the parlor. We both must get back to sleep before he finds us awake!" Pulling the quilts up and around their shoulders, he kissed her cheek and pulled her close. They both slept deeply until Christmas bells ringing throughout tiny Rosemeade Township and the snowy countryside, heralded the Savior's Day.

That Christmas morning, while they opened gifts with Christophe and Annie, Liliana found two brown-paper wrapped bumps deep inside her Christmas stocking. When she pulled them out and opened them, she was very pleased. Declan had not only painted her requested rendering of them at the Summer Dance at the Vineyard, but he had also painted her cottage as it had looked on the Fourth of July. Old Jim's colorful quilt covered the table, along with a jug of fragrant-looking sweet peas and a pitcher of home-made lemonade. Declan had also captured the image of Christophe, Annie, himself, and, of course, her sitting together around that inviting table. Even Dover sat at their feet! That day, too, had been a watershed event…it was the day Declan had announced to his family that he loved her and had then asked Christophe's permission to court her. Declan's thoughtful re-creation of these two memorable events on canvas made his wife very happy.

Late in the evening on Christmas Day, after spending memorable time with Christophe and Annie, Declan asked Liliana to take a walk with him. They both bundled up for a snowy walk. Since daylight was waning, Declan carried a lantern. The air was crisp and the colored lights that Christophe and Declan always hung along the stone fences surrounding the property twinkled merrily in the winter evening. Liliana inquired where they might be headed, and Declan indicated the loft. He said, "Liliana, I have one more gift for you; but it's a bit private."

Holding Liliana's hand and leading the way through the darkened barn, Declan led her up the stairs to the loft. Since he no longer lived there, he used his old quarters as his office and as his studio. He ushered Liliana into the bedroom which still housed the bed where they had consummated their marriage. Yet, tonight that room also held Declan's gift for her. Finished in a slightly-ornate, old-world framing which shone both silver and gold in the soft lamp light was an oil painting of her mounted on the bedroom's east wall. Liliana immediately recognized that he had captured her image from his memories of their wedding day. He had painted her sitting quietly on a refurbished antique wooden chair which they had bought together years ago. She was dressed in the lace-trimmed corset and petticoat which were the underpinnings she had worn beneath her mother's refashioned wedding gown. Declan had also painted the minute pearls, bits of lace, and ribbon that she had also woven through her hair that day.

Liliana quietly took in the detail, the brush strokes, and the layering of paint from his palette knife. Her husband had captured everything. Her image displayed all the contentment and love she had felt for Declan that day, too. In all, it was a wonderful painting, but Liliana was so taken aback by his talent that she could barely breathe.

As always, when he felt emotional or somewhat vulnerable, the heavy Scottish burr laced the cadence of his speech. "Do ye not care for it, Lily?"

Liliana quickly turned from the painting and covered the few steps to him. She wound both of her arms around his neck, stood on her tip toes and held him tightly. When she broke their embrace, she shook her head and looked intently up at him. "Declan Ryan, you are the most-wonderful man in the world. I adore your gift to me...somehow, you've captured what I felt that night in every way."

Holding her around her waist and pulling her firmly against him, he replied, "You are a very comely woman, Liliana, and when I helped you to remove your wedding gown that evening, I knew I had never seen you look more beautiful. But what made me want to capture you on canvas was how you had adorned yourself just for me. Bringing the gift of your intimate self to our marriage and how you so demurely let me know you desired me by your embellishments rocked me to my core, Liliana." Again, his quiet declaration was woven through with the heavy inflection.

Declan then lifted her up into his arms and strode to his old bed. It was covered in the wedding quilt that Liliana had stitched with her own hands. He threw back the covering and laid his wife on pristine sheets. For the remainder of that Christmas evening, Declan Ryan and his bride made tender love to one another beside his exacting artwork hanging on the east wall.

CELEBRATING THE GREEN

*L*iliana Ryan was thoughtfully cooking up a special meal because it was St. Patrick's Day, and she wanted to have a little party to celebrate. Her husband had been outside in the cold working hard with Christophe all day long, so she had prepared a very special meal for him. Liliana knew that soon the nursery's busy season would be upon them, so she wanted to take advantage of any time that they could spend together.

Later, when Declan arrived home to the vintner's cottage, he was very pleased. The table had been set for two, the kitchen smelled of something delicious, and there was a rustically-shaped, round loaf of Irish soda bread cooling on the rack. The kitchen table had been draped with a green and white checked table cloth, and there was a slightly chipped water pitcher filled with red roses sitting in the middle of the table. It was all so cozy looking that Declan knew good things were afoot. It was always that way with Liliana, she could turn a simple meal into a memorable event, and over the last five months since they had married, she had made life so very sweet. He called out for her, but there was no response.

Checking the bedroom, there was no sign of her. Next, checking her sewing room, there still was no sign of her… Lastly, he checked the bathroom, and there she was…waiting for him. She had drawn a hot bath for him in the old claw-footed tub, there were fresh towels stacked on an adjacent low wooden stool, along with soap and his shaving gear. But it was his wife that pleased him the most; she was sitting on a chair next to that steaming tub clad in some of the prettiest underwear Declan had ever seen her wear. She was reading a book. When she saw him, she jumped up from her seat, crossed the room, and threw her arms around him. He was dusty from his work with Christophe, but that didn't seem to deter her.

"Liliana, you look pretty as a picture!"

"Oh, Declan, Happy St. Patrick's Day!" she chirped. "I have a special evening planned for us, but first, I'm popping you into a nice hot bath." She then proceeded to strip Declan's work clothes off and guided him into the tub. From there, she massaged his back and neck with a bubbly soap concoction. Next came the shampoo…Liliana massaged his slightly long mahogany-colored hair with shampoo and squealed when he tried to grab her into the tub with him. "I can't join you in the bath this evening, Dec! As I said, I have quite a special night arranged for us."

"If those pretty knickers are any indicator, I suspect we're going to have a fine time, Liliana! Tell me more of your plans…"

"Well, I have prepared a meal of Irish food for our St. Pat's dinner, and later on, we are going to a new pub that I know of." She was grinning from ear to ear.

Declan cocked a soapy eyebrow at her and queried, "What new pub?"

"You'll see!"

Liliana then turned and started to walk out the door. "You're on your own for the rest of your bath, Dec…I have to get myself ready for our special night, too!"

Declan watched her walk out the bathroom door. He couldn't believe how special she was…the last few months of marriage to her had been wonderful. There were so many dimensions that Liliana had added to his life, and there was one tiny little element that he especially liked about her: her underwear. She did not own any plain, white utilitarian underwear. No, her lingerie drawer was filled with an array of things that were very feminine and unusually pretty. Sometimes, it brought a smile to his face to know that even though she might be wearing her work clothing and muddy garden boots, underneath those trappings, was a pair of lacy panties adorning her very cute bum. "Yes," Declan said to himself, "I am a lucky man."

A half-hour later, a clean-shaven Declan Ryan sat at the dining room table feasting on Irish stew and soda bread. He was fresh from the bathtub with slightly wet hair curling and combed off his face. Across from him sat Liliana. True to her promise from quite a while back, she was wearing that memorable tiny red dress along with her black tights. Tonight, she looked even more enticing in that little dress than she had months ago when Declan had taken her to choose violets in the greenhouse. And, as he studied her across the table from him, that same errant dimple on his cheek indicated his approval. She just blushed and said, "Oh, Dec…"

Promptly at half-past eight, Declan drove into the parking lot behind the new little pub to which Liliana had directed him…it was tucked away on the far corner of the Rosemeade Village Green in what had once been an old bank. The property had been empty for years, and Declan was surprised that he hadn't even noticed it was being refurbished. But, admittedly, he had been very busy loving his new wife the last few months to notice anything, but her! He had to laugh at himself.

The old-fashioned, arched windows across the face of that old building were lit up and gleaming in the night air. Through those windows, Declan saw several people that he knew, yet there was no identifying sign showing the name of the new pub. Liliana just smiled at him and pulled him toward the door. Once inside, both Declan and Liliana were greeted heartily by many of their friends, but Declan was still surprised when Jeremy Pettigrew burst through the kitchen doors and engulfed him in a friendly hug.

"What do you think, Declan…do you like my new place?" his hearty voice boomed out. "Your bride keeps a secret very well. I really did want to surprise you, and from your expression, I find that I have done so. Well done, Liliana!" Jeremy Pettigrew then proceeded to lift Liliana into his strong arms and dance a jig around the room. Then, all of Jeremy's guests erupted into laughter. The evening was off to a wonderful start.

A thoroughly surprised Declan watched with amusement as Liliana was whisked around the room with her feet barely touching the floor and was then passed back into his keeping. Declan queried his friend, "Jeremy, how can this be? You've always had your pub across the county line in Brookings."

Jeremy happily retorted, "I know man, but these days, I find myself wanting to be home with my baby girl. She's growing so fast. So…I have a great manager taking care of Pettigrew's Place, my grill pub in the city, and a partner taking care of Pettigrew's Public House, right here in little Rosemeade Township. Since I live halfway between Brookings City in one direction and halfway between Rosemeade Township the other, I can visit both of my business entities quite easily!"

Just then, a curly-haired young man in his late twenties walked up to shake Declan's hand, and Jeremy's deep voice resounded, "Declan, do you remember my little brother, Nevin? He co-owns the place with me!"

Once again, Declan was taken aback by Jeremy's younger brother whom he hadn't seen since the kid was a teenager. He happily proceeded to shake Nevin's hand quite heartily and said, "Nev, let me introduce you to my wife."

A smiling Nevin Pettigrew then winked at Liliana and said, "Believe me, Declan, I've had the pleasure of meeting your lovely bride; you lucky dog!" Then, turning to Liliana, Nevin laughed and said, "This husband of yours used to be quite the character, but it appears that both he and my brother have turned out pretty well. Perhaps, there's hope for me, yet!"

Liliana's laugh chimed out as she said, "Nevin, I would venture to guess that there is a good man rattling around inside of you, no matter what kind of a rapscallion you profess to be!"

At this point in the conversation, Declan noted, "I conclude that you've known Nevin for a while then, Liliana?"

"Yes, my darling, I met him several weeks back, but Jeremy swore me to secrecy. Your friends have really pulled off a surprise for you, haven't they?"

Laughingly, Declan responded, "Yes, you **could** say that…"

Jeremy then chuckled, "Well, man, I've got one more surprise to volley your way."

"What is it, mate?" Declan inquired.

Jeremy's expressive face then sobered, and he quietly said, "It's Kristen. Declan, I am indebted to you for introducing us. She is my lady these days. My little Daphne adores her, too. She is the reason that Nevin and I are opening the new restaurant. I have been spending a lot of time in tiny Rosemeade Township myself. You just didn't know it because you've been romancing your new bride behind closed doors all these months! Declan, I am a very happy man, and I can tell that you are, too, my friend."

Sincerely pleased, Declan shook his friend's hand and engulfed him in a friendly bear hug just as Kristen Bellyer walked up to join them. Happy Jeremy put his arm around her waist and pulled her closer to himself. It was obvious that the two of them were, indeed, smitten with one another.

Liliana chirped, "Oh, Kristen and Jeremy, how lovely!" She then proceeded to hug Kristen and Jeremy alongside her husband.

Sheepishly, Kristen said, "Oh, Liliana, I really tried not to like you when we first met at school, but it quickly became apparent to me that you and Declan truly belonged together. Now, I find that I am indebted to Declan for introducing me to Jeremy. I am happier now than I have ever been."

A smiling Liliana then squeezed Kristen's hand and said, "I understand. And it's okay. I think that the two of us are pretty lucky women. Things have turned out perfectly."

"I couldn't agree more, Liliana," a glowing Kristen answered as she looked over at Jeremy.

Jeremy's deep voice then resounded again, "Let's get this party started; all of my guests are here, now!"

Huge trays of food and drink were then brought out from Jeremy and Nevin's shiny new pub kitchen. Traditional fish and chips wrapped in cones of newsprint were the big hit of the night, but the steak-and-ale pies proved to be a close second. It goes without saying that green beer was the favored beverage that evening, but something told Liliana not to partake of it. Instead, she sipped green-colored soda water with lime.

Around ten o'clock that evening, the dancing began in earnest as soon as the little band that Jeremy had hired started playing traditional Irish celebratory songs. It was a lovely launch party at Pettigrew's Public House that night, and all of Jeremy and Nevin's guests vowed to return the next weekend when the new, little pub would be officially open for business.

As they drove home at midnight, the stars were brilliant in the night sky. Both Liliana and Declan were in high spirits when they arrived home. Declan plucked his bride from his truck and carried her in his arms into the vintner's cottage. Once inside, kisses and giggling ensued as Liliana sat on her husband's lap at the kitchen table. Later, while Declan waited for her to finish preparing for bed, he again thought about how special Liliana had made his life. He had to admit that he felt quite content.

When Liliana, at last, stepped into their bedroom, she said, "By the way, Dec, I can't seem to get my little red dress unfastened. I might just have to wear it to bed tonight…if I can't get the zipper moving. You don't mind, do you?"

Declan looked up from his reverie to find that she was, in fact, still wearing that tiny carmine snip of cloth, but she had taken off her shoes and black tights. As she bent to turn down the lamp, those handsome underpinnings that she had welcomed him home in earlier that evening peeked out. When she snuggled into his embrace in their cozy bed, Declan Ryan said, "I knew good things were afoot when I arrived home at twilight! Here, lass, let me help you with that zip."

A week later, Declan awoke early one morning to find Liliana gone from their bed. He went to search for her and discovered her sitting on the black-and-white tiled floor in the bathroom. She was resting her head on the rim of the commode. She had recently vomited. There was the sheen of perspiration across her cheeks, and she looked quite pale.

"Sweetheart, are you alright?" a very concerned Declan inquired.

Liliana raised her head up, smiled wanly, and replied, "Dec, I'm not sure, but I think I might be pregnant."

A very surprised Declan Ryan then sank to his knees on the floor and held his sweet wife as she again laid her head on the rim on the ancient toilet. She whispered, "Oh, Dec, I think I'm going to vomit again."

Later that morning, Declan made a trip to the local apothecary to purchase a home pregnancy test kit. The results confirmed Liliana's suspicions; she was, in fact, pregnant with their child. Declan was elated. Liliana was equally elated but felt a bit too nauseated to show her enthusiasm. Instead, she cried crocodile tears and said, "I really am happy, Declan…really."

Several days later, Declan took his bride to see Dr. Eric Crocker, the newest obstetric physician in historic Rosemeade County. Dr. Crocker's office was forty miles away in downtown Reedsburgh. Young, red-haired Dr. Crocker confirmed everything; Mr. and Mrs. Declan Ryan would be parents by Christmastide. As the happy couple emerged from Dr. Crocker's office, the good doctor, Anthony Caprizo, was just entering the building. He immediately recognized them and shook Declan's hand. He then said, "I remember you two, and judging from whose office you're exiting, and those big smiles on your faces, I would venture to guess that you took my advice to give your lovely wife plenty of babies. Well done, young man!"

Declan happily pumped the doctor's hand; then, he turned serious. He put his arm around Liliana and spoke to Dr. Caprizo in earnest. "Dr. Caprizo, thank you for being so very kind to my wife during what was a very difficult time for her. And, yes, we will welcome our first child in December."

Dr. Caprizo was then serious, too. He looked at Liliana and smiled. "Congratulations. I am very happy for the two of you. That little baby will be blessed to have two committed and loving parents. Not every child gets that these days, you know." As Dr. Caprizo started to walk away, he turned around and winked at Declan and said, "You just keep heeding my original advice, young man!"

"Aye, that I will, doctor!" Declan Ryan happily laughed while his sweet Liliana blushed quite beautifully.

A DISCONCERTING VISIT

eclan Ryan was waiting for a new client to arrive. It was mid-August, and Declan had prepared a bid for landscaping services for Patrick Benton, who was the new CEO of a technology firm in Brookings City. Patrick was making the trip to Rosemeade Township to meet with Declan and to see The Old Vineyard Road Nursery because he was building an expensive new home on the outskirts of Reedsburgh, and he had heard that 'Declan Ryan was the best in the business.' It seemed that the commute over the county line to his office in the giant city was of no matter to Patrick, as he was enamored with the bucolic atmosphere of the whole Rosemeade County area.

While Declan waited, he looked out his window and watched Liliana emerge from the vintner's cottage and walk toward his office. She was well into the second trimester of her pregnancy, and she was, at last, feeling like herself again. The first few months of her condition had been very difficult for her, and severe morning sickness had prevented her from working in the nursery at all. Declan was relieved. He knew he was probably being over-protective, but he did not want her to suffer from heat exhaustion or to hurt herself or their baby by moving heavy things around the nursery. He wanted both Liliana and their unborn child safe from overexertion, so it had been agreed that Liliana would retire for a while.

When Liliana arrived minutes later, Declan was moved by his affection for her. She was looking healthy once again, and her body was blooming with subtle outward signs of impending motherhood. To the casual observer, however, she did not look pregnant, but Declan knew that her physique was ripening with curves that hadn't been nearly as predominant before as they were now. In short, she looked a perfectly-sculpted woman. Today, Liliana was unknowingly wearing a curve-hugging knit dress that made her look very handsome.

As it happened, Liliana had come to his office to tell him that she had planned a special evening for the two of them and that she hoped he might be able to arrive home a bit earlier that evening. She was just leaving the stone barn when Patrick Benton arrived. Declan watched from the landing outside his loft as Patrick openly admired her while she exited.

Seconds later, when his client came up the stairs to the landing, Declan greeted him with, "You must be Mr. Benton," as he extended his hand in greeting.

"Oh, please, call me Patrick," his visitor replied.

"Aye, and you may call me, Declan," he retorted. "Please come in, Patrick," he said as he extended his arm toward the door. May I get you something to drink?"

Declan then led the way into his loft. Since the loft now served as his office, conference area, and creative getaway, its atmosphere now bespoke much more of his Scottish heritage, his love of plants and art, and his recent travels with Liliana. It was a welcoming place to meet with clients. Today, as Patrick entered the loft, he commented on what a handsome environment it truly was.

After Declan and Patrick Benton had gone over some preliminary sketches of the proposed landscaping as well as its pricing, a contract was agreed upon and signed. The two men continued to visit about business and the economy. All the while, Declan couldn't quite put his finger on what it was about Patrick Benton that bothered him. Just as Patrick was readying to depart, it hit him. Patrick Benton was akin to Richard Rawlings in his looks, but not in his demeanor. Declan had found him to be straightforward in his opinions and considerably more affable in his attitude, but nonetheless, Patrick Benton bothered him. As Patrick walked out the door of the loft, he turned around on the landing and innocently asked Declan the wrong question.

"Say, Declan, do you know who that woman was that I passed on my way in earlier? That lady is very attractive, and I would love to get to know her. It's been lonely since my wife and I separated. I would enjoy escorting someone like her around the city."

Declan tried to rein in his angst as he answered, "Sorry, Patrick, I'm afraid I don't know who you mean."

Patrick's response was, "Oh, that's really too bad." He then proceeded down the stairs oblivious that he had just offended Declan Ryan.

Two weeks later, Patrick Benton again made the scenic drive from Brookings City to Rosemead Township to give Declan the down-payment for the upcoming landscaping project at his new home. As he arrived at the entrance to the nursery, he chanced to see Liliana again. This time, she was walking with snow-white Dover at her side, and she looked quite becoming. These days, everything that Liliana wore accentuated her physique because her fertile body was rapidly changing.

Patrick Benton pounced on his opportunity to meet her. He looked at her with open admiration, and said, "Excuse me, but I'm new to this area. Could you recommend a place to eat in Rosemeade Township after I'm finished here at the nursery later this morning?"

When Liliana looked up to answer his question, she was slightly taken aback. It was as if Richard had returned from the dead. The man looked enough like Richard Rawlings that it was discomfiting, and though his attitude wasn't sullen, the way he engaged her in conversation was eerily familiar. Poor Liliana was shaken; so much so that she was barely able to give directions to Annie's Diner. As she turned to leave, Richard's lookalike inquired if she would, perhaps, consider joining him for lunch.

Liliana's trembling hand latched tightly onto Dover's leather collar as she replied as graciously as she could. "No, thank you, I'm afraid that I cannot." She quickly changed her direction and walked away.

A slightly puzzled Patrick Benton then watched her walk up the path to a picturesque stone house at the base of the beautifully-manicured vineyard. Now that he had seen her up close, his interest was piqued, and he wanted to find out who this woman was…

Declan Ryan was reviewing the final plans for Patrick Benton's landscaping contract, when the man arrived. Declan stood up to greet him, and said, "Patrick, you are right on time. I've just been going over your plans. Please, come in and sit down." Though he tried to be cordial to Patrick, Declan found it was not as easy a task as it had been two weeks ago.

Patrick Benton took a proffered seat and handed Declan a cashier's check for the project's down-payment. The two men then coordinated their calendars for the proposed work schedule, and Patrick was preparing to leave when he said, "Declan, I saw that same attractive woman that I inquired about the last time I was here. She was walking a large white dog through the front entrance to your nursery just as I arrived. I tried to engage her in conversation, but she seemed skittish. She dismissed me in pretty short order, but I saw her enter that small stone house adjacent to the vineyard. Surely you know her if she lives on the premises."

Declan tried to reply, but Patrick interrupted him. "I truly am in need of a handsome woman like that to spend some time with…"

At this point, Declan could take no more. He interrupted Patrick, and with a face devoid of any expression and answered, "Patrick, it would behoove you to not inquire any further about the young woman who lives in the vineyard."

Patrick was still unfazed, and asked, "Why? Is she your sister or something?"

Declan was finding it difficult to keep his temper in check, and so he resorted to humor, "Patrick, that lovely young woman you are so interested in…she is my wife, and she is carrying our child. Any more inquiries on your part, and I might have to show you the crazy Scotsman side of my disposition! I'm afraid your musings are making it a bit difficult for me to do business with you."

A flabbergasted Patrick then held his hands up and in a submissive gesture as he sat across the small conference table and said, "Oh, Declan, I'm sorry. I didn't mean to insult you. She was not wearing a wedding ring, so I just assumed… I'm truly sorry."

Declan then looked a repentant Patrick squarely in the eye and responded, "At present, she wears no wedding ring because of her condition. She's not had an easy go of it."

A very surprised Patrick then continued in his contrition to Declan. "I *do* apologize, Declan. I guess I've just become accustomed to getting things that I want whenever I see them, because of my corporate position. I've made an ass of myself, and I hope that you can forgive me."

Then, as he was accustomed to doing, Declan Ryan turned the other cheek. He held out his hand to Patrick in a gesture of forgiveness. Patrick Benton gratefully pumped his proffered hand and said, "Thanks for overlooking my stupidity, man."

Following the remainder of their consultation, Declan walked with Patrick to the landing outside of his office and bade him good-bye. But, as Patrick began to descend the first step, Declan quietly mentioned, "You know, Patrick, if you've any love left for the wife of your youth, why don't you mend things with her?"

Patrick Benton then looked seriously at wise Declan Ryan. He said, "I do love my estranged wife very much, but I'm afraid things between us have festered for too long, and the fault is all mine. I know she would never consider joining me here in Rosemeade County."

Declan looked thoughtful for a moment, then retorted, "Then do it the Highland way, Patrick. Put on your best kilt, go to her and apologize for being an "arse," then lift her into your arms and carry her home. You won't regret it, my friend."

A thoughtful Patrick answered, "Thanks, Declan. I'll see you soon."

Though the situation with Patrick had had a satisfactory ending, Declan felt off balance the rest of the day. As he ruminated on what had happened, it brought back memories of the summer Richard Rawlings had delivered Liliana to Old Vineyard Road for her work. Somehow, just thinking about what had happened that year made him heartsick. He thought, too, about the things that he could have done differently that summer, and for some reason, such rumination made him feel renewed anger toward himself. He thought that such feelings had been put to rest with his sessions with Reese Winston.

Later that evening, when he arrived home to the vintner's cottage, he found that he was not the only one experiencing bad memories. The moment he cracked open the door to their respite from the cares of the world, Liliana flew into his arms and clung to him fiercely.

"What's this, sweetheart?" he soothed as he held her close.

She whispered, "Oh, Declan, I just want you to know that I am so thankful that you are my precious husband."

Declan Ryan then tenderly cupped her vulnerable countenance with his large hands and softly kissed her. He sighed and commented, "I understand that you encountered Patrick Benton, my newest landscaping client, today. He is Richard Rawlings' twin in both looks and stature, but he has a much better demeanor. I find that I'm feeling somewhat out of sorts this evening because he has inquired about you each time that he has met with me to finalize his landscaping schematics. Today, I finally set him straight that you are my wife. He was quite repentant and apologized profusely, but I find myself ruminating on things that went down with Richard Rawlings from years ago."

"Well, that's two of us who spent the afternoon pondering things that we both would rather forget," a subdued Liliana responded. "Declan, both his looks and his confident demeanor reminded me of Richard when I first met him. Then, when he inquired if I would be interested in joining him for lunch, I found myself wanting to flee from him. I'm sure he thought I was a crazy woman…I know that I was visibly shaking. I even had to hang onto Dover's collar to fortify myself."

Declan looked down at her upturned face, as she looked soberly into his eyes. "I know, Lily. Patrick's looks are eerily similar to Richard's, but we can't fall prey to our misgivings about what happened before. Let's change the subject. Instead, let's talk about plans for this evening. Would you like to do something special?"

"Well, Declan Ryan, it has been almost a year since we became engaged, so I was thinking that maybe we could stop by Stefano's restaurant for dinner and share our happy news with him and Gina.

As you can see, I won't be able to hide this little baby of ours much longer!"

"That is a wonderful idea…reminiscing about our life together tonight sounds superior to letting old memories of Richard ruin our evening. Let's do it; let's get dressed and head into Reedsburgh for a night out and some authentic Italian food. I think we both need a slight change of scenery tonight."

An hour and a half later, just as the late summer sun was setting in a brilliant array of color, Declan and Liliana were ushered to their table at Stefano's handsomely appointed restaurant. Seeing them arrive, Stefano Giancomo crossed the room and passed through the French doors that led to the Italian patio and stood beside their table. He kindly declared, "Oh, Miss Liliana, you are always lovely, but tonight, your beautiful face speaks of impending motherhood. Am I right, dear one?"

A happy Liliana put one hand on her slightly rounded belly and held her husband's broad hand with her other and proclaimed, "Yes, Stefano, we wanted to share our happy news with you and Gina tonight." A proud Declan then put his arm around his wife and kissed her cheek; from there, he pumped Stefano's hand in a hearty shake.

From across the patio, Patrick Benton, who dined alone in the evening shadows, watched the three of them with envy. He saw what his new friend, Declan Ryan, possessed in happiness and contentment. Declan had been decent and kind to him today when he had made a fool of himself by inquiring about Declan's lovely wife. Then, Patrick thought honestly to himself…he might have it all professionally, but he had lost a great deal personally to get where he was tonight.

A saddened Patrick considered what his estranged wife might be doing without him this evening; he knew she was purposefully avoiding him. He wondered if his marriage could be salvaged…he had been so busy attaining his goals that he had lost sight of what meant the most to him, and he now worried that he had had his revelation too late.

A WEEKEND JUNKET

*B**elinda Benton* sat and looked out over the Chicago skyline. Somehow, the bright lights did not hold her attention quite like they once had. The panorama from her rooftop patio had once thrilled her, but now that Patrick was gone, those lights no longer held her attention. A lot of hard work had gone into securing such a view of her hometown, but she had no one to share it with… Tonight, she felt hollow, and the anger she had been harboring toward her husband for months no longer seemed worth the effort…not when she ached for him and his wonderful company. How had she and Patrick arrived at this point? She sighed, and pondered the same question, yet again. Until the extreme fatigue finally kicked in later tonight, she knew she could not fall into bed for some sorely-needed sleep.

While she sighed and girded herself for yet another sleepless night, she didn't even hear the ringing of her cell phone; it lay forgotten on her nightstand, in her lonely bedroom. Many miles away, Patrick Benton, ended the call without leaving a message; disappointment flooding his soul.

Unbeknownst to Belinda, her estranged husband's disappointment in not being able to speak with her that night had spurred him into action. He would take Declan's Ryan's advice and try to salvage his marriage. Never one to tarry once he had made a decision, Patrick dispatched a private jet for take-off very early on Saturday morning. He knew his wife, and he knew exactly what she would be doing that day, all he had to do was catch up with her…and maybe, just maybe, if he caught her unaware, he could finally speak with her.

As Patrick sat and watched the patchwork of farm fields hundreds of feet below his airplane window, he reflected on how things had gone down the last time he had seen Belinda. She had been hurting and had lashed out at him saying things to him that he knew he deserved, but he had been too caught up in the euphoria of his new position to see that he was losing the woman who had stood steadfastly by his side as he rode the wave of his success; that is, until he had put her needs second, one time too many.

All Belinda had ever asked of him was the simplicity of a private life with him; she had postponed her aspirations time and time again for him. Yet, when he had finally achieved his life's dream, her ambitions had been shelved for so long that she felt she could no longer resurrect them. In short, something within her had withered and died. Her beautiful countenance had seemed strained the day when word had come that he was to be the new CEO of Sonata Data Systems. She had simply caressed his cheek and said, "I'm truly happy for you Patrick." Three days later, she had asked him to leave. There had been no spirit left in her that day; she had wanly stated that she no longer had the stamina to take on the obstacles within their marriage.

A month later, when he was readying to move fifteen hundred miles away for his new position, he had approached her and asked her to come with him. She had quietly refused. That day, she had told him she would always love him, but she could take no more of merely being an appendage to him because she was his wife. She could no longer suffer the disdain shown to her by his talented young work colleagues… They thought she was old, though she was only just barely thirty-nine years old. Patrick was forty-two, he had a distinguished look about him, but to his twenty-something colleagues, he was truly fascinating. She, on the other hand, was someone whom they felt Patrick should discard for one of them.

Belinda quietly told him that she could no longer ignore the blatant flirting of younger women who had never sacrificed anything for their husband. They came on to him so often and so aggressively that she felt she was in danger of being replaced by a newer, younger version; a beautiful new trophy wife who would enjoy the fruits of success in her place. That woman would be the one to give him the family that she had waited patiently for…that woman would travel with him to places that the two of them had once dreamed of visiting. In short, she feared she was soon to be usurped. She had summed up her feelings by saying,

"You need to admit that I am not off base in these accusations, Patrick. I see how flattered you are by their attention, and I can no longer subject myself to it. It hurts too much."

Fierce anger had welled up within him, and he would not accept this fatal turn of events. He had said things to Belinda that day that now shamed him, and she had retaliated with accusations that were true and those same accusations shamed him even further. They had raised their voices in anger at one another; she had rallied to match him insult for insult; all the while, her beautiful countenance had become strained and pallid. She had finally looked into his soul with wounded eyes, "I'm setting you free, Patrick. Enjoy your hard-fought success. I will not impede you or your young collaborators who make plays for you any longer." Three days later, the separation papers had been delivered to him by a courier. That had been a little over six months ago…

In the months following the separation, Patrick had found himself in the company of many beautiful and talented female associates. Several of them had even indicated their interest in him; yet, none of them were appealing to him…it was Belinda who had always captivated him. She had been so interesting that she had mesmerized him. No one else ever had. When he had seen Declan Ryan's wife, she had been the first woman in the last six months who had truly piqued his interest. With just a passing glance, she had intrigued him. He now knew why… she had reminded him of Belinda…his wonderful Belinda.

In the cool morning air, Belinda Benton, scanned the baskets of freshly-picked peaches and pears. She smiled to herself and thought… "Wouldn't Patrick have loved a peach pie from these beauties! I'll, at least, take some home to eat fresh." Next, she walked over to her favorite bakery tent. A tiny baguette of French bread beckoned to her, so she handed over several dollar bills to the bakery attendant.

From there, Belinda headed down the grassy path that led to Mr. Mastiacoli's pasta tent. "Mmmm," she thought as she scanned the colorful noodles, "my home-made vodka sauce would taste fabulous over Mr. M's home-made fusilli regati." She also purchased a single serving of dessert cannoli, her favorite…with sweetened mascarpone cheese infused with chocolate shavings, grated orange rind, and pistachio nuts. Now, she thought to herself, just one more thing to purchase for my Saturday night dinner.

Patrick knew he would be able to find her at the Farmer's Market. It was what she enjoyed during the warm summer months. He knew his wife, and he knew she loved to do her marketing early before the crowds came out. It was just barely half past nine in the morning, and it didn't take him very long to find her.

She was poring over huge bunches of fragrant, flowering sweet peas under a sizable blue market umbrella that protected the flower merchant and his offerings. She carried a colorful market tote already brimming with carefully-chosen greens and a loaf of rustic bread. Patrick would have known her anywhere…the curve of her hips, the pale blue of her shirt, and those shiny red toenails peeking out from her silver sandals.

She was just reaching for a bouquet that was dominated by pink sweet pea blossoms when Patrick walked up and quietly said, "Hello, Bee… may I buy those for you?"

His estranged wife whirled around in surprise and disbelief. She breathlessly asked, "Patrick, what are you doing here?"

Looking penitent and slightly nervous, Patrick Benton quietly said, "Baby, I've come to take you home."

LATE HARVEST SEASON

Declan Ryan was working hard that day, but his mind was focused on only one thing. It was mid-afternoon in late October. Some of the trees boasting their fall colors were already spent, but the sun was bright, and there was an earthy fragrance in the air from decaying leaves. Declan Ryan briefly stopped his project and thought of his wife. She always seemed to occupy a place in his thoughts, but right now, she seemed to be at the forefront. He felt that he should go to the vintner's cottage to check on her.

He told Tim Hill and the crew that he would be gone for about a half hour. From there, he made his way home from the far end of the vineyard rows followed by snow-white Dover. When he arrived at the cottage, all was quiet.

The kitchen had the delicious aroma of something freshly baked, and the table was already set for dinner. Declan thought that Liliana had, perhaps, gone over to Christophe's to spend time with Annie, but before he went looking for her, he thought to check the bedroom. When he walked in, his heart became knotted with emotion.

There upon the bed lay Liliana, deep in slumber. The afternoon sun streamed through the open window and lit up the room with its brilliant light and its warmth. Her cheeks were flushed pink, and her limbs were no longer under the bed covers. She was sleeping on her side. Her chest rose and fell with the cadence of her breathing. Her hand was folded protectively over her very rounded abdomen. She was wearing only her black cotton panties and a tiny black tank top that was stretched tightly across the swollen belly that protected their unborn child. Declan was moved to see that even in slumber, she shielded their child.

At that moment her eyelashes fluttered, and she opened her eyes. She sleepily smiled up at him. Declan sat down on the old iron bed and ran his hand through the dark wavy hair that had fallen over her cheek.

He looked deeply into her drowsy green eyes, and said, "Are you okay, sweetheart?"

Liliana nodded affirmatively, and said, "Yes, I'm fine, but I'm just a wee bit tired today. After I put our supper in the oven to slow cook, I thought I might just have a little rest, but I fear I've been asleep much longer than I intended."

"That's okay, Liliana, enjoy some rest while you can. Soon, sleep will be a special treat for the both of us." Declan then ran his hand gently over the burgeoning bump in her belly. "How is our little baby doing today?"

Shaking her head, Liliana replied, "I think our baby fancies him or herself an acrobat or a rodeo cowboy. This little one has been very active today!" She then grew serious, "But, I wouldn't want things any other way, Declan. I'm so happy to be carrying our child." She then proceeded to blush quite prettily.

Declan Ryan, who once thought that Liliana was lost to him forever, kissed her and said, "I would love to make even more babies with you, Mrs. Ryan. You have made me a very happy man."

"Oh, Declan," she murmured, coloring yet again. "You are too sweet to me! Can you stay for a cup of tea? I can have it ready in minutes."

"Believe me, I would love to stay here with you, sweetheart, and spend some time enjoying your company, but I have to get back to my project. I'll be home in just a couple of hours. We'll have our cup of tea then, okay?

She smiled affectionately at her husband, "That sounds lovely, Dec."

Declan Ryan again smoothed his hand over her belly and kissed her. "Take care of yourself until then."

As he walked back to the furthest edge of the vineyard, Declan thought how blessed his life had been over the last year. He was a very-satisfied man.

When Declan arrived home later that evening, Liliana was refreshed from her rest and, as always, was very happy to see him. As they relaxed after dinner over a cup of tea and dessert, Declan suggested that they drive out to their favorite lake to watch the sun set. He needed to broach a tender subject with her.

As the sun slowly dipped behind the pine-crusted mountains leaving the last vestiges of orange, pink and purple marking its exit, Declan lit a campfire and pulled a blanket tightly around his wife and himself. He picked up Liliana's hand, kissed her palm and dove into the subject at hand.

"Guess who called me today, Lily?"

"Perhaps, Vivienne, Priscilla, or our lovely Mavis, retired librarian?" she joked.

Chuckling, Declan replied, "No, it was Patrick Benton. He invited us for lunch this weekend. He wants us to meet his wife, Belinda, and to see their new home. What do you think, sweetheart?"

"Well, Declan, he does smack of Richard in looks, but you've assured me that he is a much nicer person, so I guess that I could probably gird myself for an afternoon with him."

"You know, he has referred several other clients to us since we did the landscaping on his new place. I did get to know him while our staff worked on his project. He's really quite a nice fellow. I no longer see Richard when I'm in his company; only a truly good man."

"Declan, I would do anything for you, so if you would like to go, I'll do my best to enjoy myself…"

"Thank you, sweetheart. Patrick is very happy to be back together with his wife, too, so you needn't fear any invitations for a date with him," Declan quipped.

"Well that sounds encouraging!" Liliana laughed.

When they returned home from the lake, Liliana invited Declan to shower with her. Her body was taut from the growing child inside her, and Declan was moved as he held her clasped within his arms under the flow of the warm water. Safely within her small frame, which was pressed tightly up against him, he could feel their child moving. The happiness he felt at that moment was almost tangible, and he was humbled once again by what God had restored to him.

When Saturday arrived, Liliana was still reluctant to see Patrick Benton, but she faced her challenge head on…she wore a new outfit that Declan had recently bought for her, and she readied a colorful fall bouquet that she had arranged in a red-glass mason jar. Lastly, she carefully put a freshly-baked apple pie into a carrying container, and she was ready.

Declan, who had watched her do these things was struck anew by his steadfast wife. He knew she was dreading an afternoon of what she thought would be in Richard's company, yet she had agreed to go for him. His wonderful Liliana, who was kind and thoughtful had, yet again, proven herself to be valiant in facing hard challenges. Crossing the room to where she was working at her rustic farm table, he said, "Let me stow these things in the car for you, sweetheart."

When Declan returned, he held both of her upper arms with his hands and bent to kiss her. He then commented, "You look especially beautiful today, Liliana. I know you are not looking forward to this afternoon, but I suspect you'll agree with me about Patrick by day's end. I thank you."

HEALING TIMES

Patrick and Belinda Benton awaited Declan and Liliana Ryan's arrival on the wrap-around porch at their new home. Their home sat upon the rise of a small hill and, as such, afforded them a wonderful view of the countryside surrounding Reedsburgh. The house was very pale in color; soft yellow to be exact, and was trimmed in brilliant white. It was built in the Colonial style…architecture that Belinda had always adored. Patrick had chosen the design while he was estranged from his wife, and to his surprise found that everything he had wanted in the house was exactly what Belinda had once dreamed of having in her home someday. When he had brought her home to Reedsburgh several months ago, she had wept when he had carried her over the threshold of their new home and had proceeded on up the stairs to their bedroom...the only room in the house that had any furniture. There in that upstairs suite, they had re-consummated their marriage in a bed that Belinda had been desirous of having for many years. She had always kept a photograph of it tucked away in a box.

Today, they sat in white rockers amidst large colorful containers of potted impatiens which had grown huge in just the short time since they had been planted. Belinda was glowing with happiness and Patrick felt a warm satisfaction in knowing he had made her feel cherished. For Patrick, today's get-together would serve to thank Declan for all that he had done for him; not just in the wonderful job that Declan's team from The Old Vineyard Nursery had done on his yard, but for encouraging him to work things out with Belinda. Taking Declan's advice had been a turning point in his life, and he sincerely wanted to thank his new friend. As well, he hoped that he could make amends with Declan's fetching wife.

For Belinda, as she sat holding hands with her husband, she reflected on how her life had changed so tremendously in just a few short weeks. Looking back, she realized that she had always worked…

from the time she was a teenager until now, she had worked…first, waiting tables to put herself through college. Then, after she had married Patrick, she had worked to support them both while he studied for an MBA. Later, when Patrick was working his way up the corporate ladder, she had juggled work and school while studying for her master's degree. Finally, after things had gone horribly awry with Patrick, she had decided that she would, at last, dust off her dreams of a doctoral degree in Art History. She had once been very close to completion of her dissertation but had shelved her aspirations when Patrick's job had demanded as much from her as it did from him. In all this, Belinda had never had any time for herself. Now, she was enjoying freedom from her cares; today, the balm of her happiness was overflowing in many ways; not just in well-deserved relaxation.

Seeing Declan and Liliana motoring up the long, tree-lined drive, Patrick hopped up from his chair and offered his hand to Belinda. She smiled affectionately at him, "Patrick, you seem especially happy to entertain your friends today, why?"

"Oh, Bee, I am…because if Declan Ryan hadn't been candid with me a few months ago, I fear we wouldn't have been making love like two honeymooners these last several months. That guy gave me the gift of his wisdom, and for that, I'll forever be grateful."

"Well, then, let's meet this dear man," Belinda beautifully smiled.

Arm-in-arm, they walked down the steps, as Declan Ryan's shiny vehicle rolled to a stop on the newly-paved drive.

A SPECIAL OUTING

The autumn afternoon spent with Patrick and his wife sped by for both Declan and Liliana. Immediately upon arriving, the Bentons made sure that their guests felt comfortable. Liliana's thoughtful gifts had touched both Patrick and Belinda, too.

While Liliana and "Bee" got to know each other in the kitchen, Patrick and Declan walked the perimeter of Patrick's property. As the two friends rambled through the newly-planted landscaping, they visited about a variety of things. Finally, Declan felt he had to be frank with Patrick.

He started out, "Patrick, before we go back to the house, there is something I think you should know about Liliana."

"Is she alright? She's not feeling ill, is she?"

"No, she's just fine, but it has something to do with the last time you saw her…"

"Is she in need of my apology to her, Declan?"

"No, not at all," Declan answered. "Patrick, she had good reason to be 'skittish' that day. For ten years, she suffered through a marriage to a calculating and abusive man who left scars upon her; both emotionally and physically. Patrick, I broach this subject with you only to let you know that you could have been his twin. The likeness is quite uncanny, but that is where it stops. You've a completely different disposition, yet, the day you spoke with her at the entrance to the nursery, she was so surprised by your resemblance to him that she was taken aback."

"Oh, Declan, I'm sorry if I upset her in any way. Does this guy still harass her?"

"No, he purposefully killed himself two and a half years ago, but the wake of his selfish actions has been pretty far reaching. It took courage for her to accompany me here today, but I have assured her that if she gets to know you, she will no longer see him anymore…only Patrick Benton, whom I know to be a very good man."

A surprised Patrick stepped back and shook his head, soberly, "Declan, I'm regretful for what she's endured, but it explains something to me. That day in August, when I approached her, she latched onto her huge dog's collar with a trembling hand. She was gracious but could not quit our conversation fast enough."

"And you, man, had good reason to want to smack me; first, for blatantly inquiring about your wife; not once, but twice! Then, I upset her by trying to engage her in conversation. Declan, you probably wanted to pummel me. But I'm glad that you've shared these things with me. I'll do my best to make sure that Liliana feels comfortable today. I can only guess what she's been through." With that, Patrick Benton offered his handshake to his new friend.

Declan heartily pumped Patrick's hand in return, then put his hand on Patrick's shoulder and said, "Now that I've met your Belinda, I can see why Liliana would pique your interest. Those two beautiful ladies are cut from the same cloth."

Minutes later, when Patrick and Declan entered the house, Belinda and Liliana were already fast friends. It was obvious the two of them had hit it off on their very first meeting.

As they were just finishing their meal, Patrick raised his glass of iced tea and said, "Today, I would like to propose a toast to Declan. He is the only man of my acquaintance who encouraged me to mend my relationship with my lovely Bee. For that, I will always be grateful, so here's to you, Declan."

Patrick and Belinda watched as Liliana's dazzling smile lit up her face. She held up her water glass. "To Declan," she said softly.

"Yes, to Declan!" cheered Belinda. "Thank you."

Now that each of them was sated with Belinda's memorable meal, the after-dinner conversation began in earnest. Belinda began, "So tell me how you two met…"

Liliana took Declan's hand in her own, smiled up at her husband, and replied, "I'll let you take that one, Dec."

Declan Ryan gave her a quick wink and began, "Well, it all started with Liliana's old dog, Iris…thanks to her, I met my lady when she was not quite nineteen years old. It was in the middle of the night, right outside of my loft at the nursery. I had only just arrived from Scotland a few days before, and my body clock was still off, so I was up working a bit. First, Iris bounded through the open barn doors, then Liliana followed on her heels. It was almost as if her dog wanted to make sure that we were introduced; even if it was the middle of the night and Liliana was clad in her pajamas! I thought Liliana was special right from the start, but when she took me out for a cup of tea a day or two later, it didn't take long for me to find myself falling for her. I'm still indebted to that Golden Retriever."

Smiling, Liliana responded, "Yes, Declan has a way with women; be they Golden Retrievers or eighty-seven-year-old retired librarians! As for me, a day and a half later when he helped me to move my things into my first little attic apartment, I couldn't help myself. I invited him out for tea afterward to thank him for all his help, but it was when the check came that I found myself slightly besotted. Since I had invited *him*, I tried to pay our bill. He laid his hand over mine when I reached for the check and said, 'Where I come from, we pay for the fairer gender.' I can admit this now but sparks definitely flew when he touched my hand and spoke such genteel words with his Scottish burr."

She then unknowingly withdrew her hand from her husband's and laid it upon his shoulder. Both Patrick and Belinda watched as Declan looked into his wife's eyes and communicated his affection with a smile and brief nod of his head.

"Oh, so you two have been together quite a while then, haven't you?" Belinda queried.

Declan Ryan took the lead on this question and responded, "Actually, we've only been married not quite a year; but it has been a fine year, Belinda." Nodding toward Liliana's burgeoning belly, he quipped, "As you can see, we have been very busy."

Liliana tossed her head slightly at his joke and chimed her melodic laugh.

"But, seriously," Declan continued, "we spent four lovely summers together before we went our separate ways. Ten years later, I was fortunate to find her again. Now, how about you two, Patrick and Belinda?"

At this juncture, Patrick Benton smiled broadly and started to reminisce, "Oh, I fell for Bee long before we ever met...I used to walk by the little café where she worked every morning on my way to the office. She was always buzzing around taking care of everyone in a tiny little black and white waitress outfit; it was a very-short little dress with a pint-sized apron just like you would see in the movies. She wore her hair pulled up in a ponytail, and I would admire her through the window every morning. One day, our eyes finally met through the glass, and she smiled at me. That was it; I just knew she was going to be the one."

"I had also watched Patrick walk by each day," Belinda added. "But I wondered if I would ever get to meet him. Then, very early one Tuesday morning, he just appeared during my shift and told the hostess to make sure that he was seated in my area. I was very flustered, but quite thrilled that he had come in. When I went to his table to take his order, he said, 'This *is* table number six, right? I was supposed to meet the most-beautiful girl in the world here today... May I buy you some breakfast?' Even grisly old Tommy, my boss, was very pleased for me that day. He insisted that I sit down and enjoy a meal with Patrick, though it was the morning rush. Three months later, Patrick asked me to marry him."

Belinda shook her head as if she, herself, couldn't believe the story that they were telling their new friends. "Patrick and I didn't even have the fortitude for an engagement...we just hopped on a plane to Las Vegas and were married at a place called, The Little White Church on the Boulevard."

Patrick chuckled, "Both of our families were pretty surprised, but they forgave us for our recklessness in pretty short order. My mother said that she knew Belinda truly loved me when she never once complained about going out in my old beater car with my incorrigible dog, Bernie, sitting between us."

"After Patrick and I returned from our honeymoon in Las Vegas, I moved into his place, and poor Bernie did raise his scraggly eyebrows at me like I was an interloper," Belinda laughed.

"Yeah, he really did," Patrick chuckled, "but about a week later, Bernie changed his allegiance completely to Belinda, though. She bathed him, trimmed his scraggly eyebrows, and he smelled like shampoo!" Pointing to Belinda, then circling his finger round and round, he added, "This girl even used the money from her tip jar to buy Bernie a new dog bed…and you need to understand that the money in her tip jar was being saved for a trip to Europe to see all the treasures housed in their art galleries and museums…I couldn't even borrow money from that tip jar! Yes, I knew Bee truly loved both me *and* Bernie, then."

"Belinda," Liliana interjected, "I am so impressed that you have a doctorate in art history. What an accomplishment. How long did it take you?"

"Oh, I just barely defended my dissertation a few months ago."

"I'm afraid that Bee is being modest. She gave up her aspirations for me to get an MBA and to climb the corporate ladder," Patrick interjected. "I'll have to admit that she put me first for far too long. It was during the time that we were separated, that Bee was finally able to defend her doctorate, Liliana. It's something that I'm not very proud of…Belinda always taking a back-seat in order for me to excel."

"You've more than made it up to me, Patrick," Belinda said softly to her husband.

Patrick then asked quietly, "Bee, do you mind if I share our news with our new friends?"

Belinda Benton flushed slightly and answered, "No, Pat, not at all."

"Well, in all of Bee's sacrifices for my career, we never really got started on a family; but we find ourselves in the family way, now! We're pretty sure that Belinda conceived the weekend that we were reconciled. I, for one, couldn't be happier."

Belinda Benton then started to laugh, "I may have my teaching credential and a doctorate in art history, but all I want to do right now is languish in my impending motherhood and nest with Patrick!"

Liliana then responded as her own hand touched her sizable belly, "Oh, Belinda, I understand you loud and clear. I never thought I would experience these joys, but here I am despite every obstacle that beset Declan and me."

Declan Ryan then held up his glass, "Patrick, I think another toast is in order. "To Belinda and Liliana, for the gifts of life they are carrying for us."

"Yes, Declan, to Belinda and Liliana!" Patrick toasted. Then inclining his head toward Declan, he added, "We are very fortunate men, indeed."

Late that afternoon as Declan and Liliana drove home, the panorama of the fall colors was heightened by the back-lighting of the late afternoon sun. The colorful red, orange, yellow and lime green leaves shimmered in the light breeze, and there was the scent of newly plowed earth in the air, reminding them both that the harvest season had passed, and soon the weather patterns would be changing. Both were quiet with their own thoughts, when Liliana broke their respective reveries.

"You were right, Declan. Patrick Benton may be Richard's twin in height and looks, but he is his own very-likable self. He couldn't be any more different from Richard if he tried. I'm glad you encouraged me to get to know him. It was a lovely afternoon sitting out on their veranda getting to know each other. I quite like Belinda, and I got a kick out of Patrick calling her his 'Busy Bee.' I can't help but feel that in getting to know Patrick, I'll be able to stop recalling Richard when I see him. Patrick's happy disposition seems to cancel out Richard's surliness. You were wise to encourage me, my darling."

Declan drove on for several seconds before answering. "You know, Lily, I understand why you piqued Patrick's interest at first sight. You and Belinda both have a freshness and a kindness about you that one doesn't always see these days. I'm sorry to say it, but I think this busy world sometimes erodes that special loveliness that women innately display when they are young and on the cusp of their adult lives. By the time they have spent several years in a competitive educational or work environment, that loveliness can sometimes get trampled. The fact that they are someone's precious daughter, a husband's loving mate, or a young child's caring mother often gets forgotten by the world at large. Not always, but it seems that when ladies play hardball with the men for, often, lesser pay for a commensurate job, the world forgets that they are someone to be cherished for their femininity. I guess what I am trying to say very inarticulately, is that both you and Belinda have retained that loveliness, and I'm sure that is why Patrick inquired about you when he was separated from Belinda."

"That is a very kind compliment to both Belinda and me, Declan." Liliana replied. "But it was for the same reason that I fell in love with you when I was just nineteen years old. You were so very different from all the guys I knew from Brineforth University. Nothing had ever been handed to you, and you weren't expecting anything from me except my friendship. Instead, you were kind, compassionate, and you treated me with respect. To be frank, your manliness was quite intoxicating, and look at me now…I am the happiest woman in historic Rosemeade County…and for that matter, in the whole world! And, our friend, Patrick Benton, will forever be grateful to you for your candor with him. Both he and Belinda are so pleased to be reconciled with one another and to be expecting a child. As I have said before, you are the finest man I know, Declan Ryan."

A humble Declan responded, "Lily, you must surely be blinded with your love for me, but I thank you for your generous compliment."

Six weeks after spending the afternoon with Patrick and Belinda Benton, Declan Ryan arrived home one evening to find his wife packing one of her father's old leather suitcases. Fear gripped him. "Oh, Liliana, are you alright?" he asked. It's still too soon for the baby to come. Are you in pain?"

Moved by his concern, Liliana smiled at her husband and answered, "I'm fine, Declan, I just realized this afternoon that we don't have much longer, so I wanted to get my bag packed. This way, we'll be ready to go on a moment's notice."

Sitting down at the kitchen table, Declan ran his hand through his mahogany-colored hair and sighed. "My life just flashed before me, Liliana. I thought for sure our little one was coming, and I haven't felt such panic since the last time I had to take you to the hospital." He blew out his breath and ran his hand through his hair, yet again.

Liliana came to him and sat down on his lap. She put her arms around his neck and laid her soft cheek upon his, "Oh, Dec, I'm just fine. I'm feeling so well, in fact, that I prepared your favorite, shepherd's pie, today. Don't worry about anything." She then put his hand over her sizable belly, and their little baby kicked with perfect timing. It was as if he or she wanted to give encouragement to its concerned father. "See there," she said. "Our little one is reassuring you!"

Declan Ryan then laughed, but quickly lapsed into his serious mode once again. "I know that childbirth is nigh on routine these days, but it still strikes me with fear. I can't help but feel slightly wary about it, Liliana."

Touched by his candor, Liliana looked into his sober blue eyes, "Oh, Declan," she said. "We've both had more than our share of losing loved ones, I know. But birth is a happy event, and I am more than willing to go through its discomfort to give you a son or a daughter. It's the culmination of what we feel for one another. Please don't worry, my love. All will be well."

She chuckled, then chirped, "See, I'm quoting you, now!" Declan Ryan had to smile. He then held his wife just a little bit tighter and replied, "Yes, you are right, but I have to admit that I don't want you to suffer in any way."

Later that night, Declan Ryan easily carried his pregnant wife in his arms into their bedroom. As he carefully laid his wife atop of their readied bed, she quietly asked if they might make love. Slightly surprised by her request, Declan answered, "My darling, our baby has been growing so rapidly these last few weeks, I fear that I might hurt you or the baby if we do…"

Liliana still spoke softly to him, her voice just above a whisper, when she retorted, "We won't have many more opportunities to just be lovers once our little baby arrives. I just want to give of myself to you while I'm still your bride."

Touched by her candor, Declan answered, "Lily, you will always be my bride no matter whose mum you might be or how many wee bairns we might have, you will forever be my beautiful bride that was restored to me. That will never change!" Then, cradling his wife closely to himself, thoughtful Declan Ryan began their lovemaking gently, but in earnest.

DISCOMFORT

*L**iliana Ryan** knew the pain she was experiencing was just a sign of this season of her life, but she was feeling too off kilter today; her back was aching terribly, and she felt she could, perhaps, vomit up the contents of her stomach. Her husband was out this morning, so she called her godparent, Annie Riordan.

When Annie answered her phone, Liliana started to succumb to panic…just barely above a whisper, she spoke into the phone, "Annie, can you come to me? Something is not right, and I'm feeling a little nervous."

Annie responded, "I'll be right there, baby girl. Don't you fret."

Minutes later, Annie burst through the front door of the vintner's cottage and strode down the hall to find Liliana lying atop the already-made bed. She was quite pale and held her hand to the small of her back. "Lily, tell me what's wrong," she said, feeling a rush of concern herself.

"Oh, Annie, I don't feel well at all this morning, but I don't think it's the baby coming. I don't want to be neurotic, but do you think I should call Dr. Crocker? My back almost feels like it blew out, and I feel quite sick to my stomach."

"Honey, you are quite pale this morning, and we are just days away from your due date, let's just check in with your doctor to be safe. That's what he is paid for…"

Liliana handed Annie her cell phone and said, "I think I might get emotional if I speak with Dr. Crocker or his nurse. Could you please make the call for me, Annie?"

Not particularly prone to panicking, Annie grabbed Liliana's phone and found Dr. Crocker's number in the contact directory and dialed…

"Dr. Crocker's office, this is Amy. How may I help you?" a young woman answered.

"Yes, this is Annie Riordan calling regarding Dr. Crocker's obstetric patient, Liliana Ryan. She's not feeling well this morning, and she is having excruciating spasms and pain in her lower back. Could she possibly be in labor?"

"Let me patch you through to Dr. Crocker, he is between patients…"

Several minutes later, the young physician was on the line, "Hello, Mrs. Riordan. It sounds as though your Liliana might be experiencing labor. Back pain is not uncommon when the child is ready to be born. Has her water broken?"

"No doctor, it hasn't broken, but she is feeling quite nauseated, as well."

"It sounds as though she's having a hard go of it. I know that you are about a forty-five-minute drive from here, so why don't you bring her to the Medical Center, and I'll meet you there."

Annie was just signing off with Dr. Crocker when Declan entered the cottage. He was surprised to see Annie there, then said, "I rescheduled my last appointment this morning. Liliana didn't look right to me when I left earlier, is she okay?" He strode into the bedroom and found Liliana in the throes of another back spasm. She became teary-eyed when she saw him. Declan crossed the room and sat down on the bed; Annie followed him in.

Annie began, "I've spoken to Dr. Crocker; he feels she is in labor. He is to meet us at the hospital. We should probably get going, Declan. Since Chris is in Reedsburgh this morning, he will meet us there, too."

A surprised Declan immediately stood up and looked uneasy. "Annie, her suitcase is packed and just inside the front closet. Let me get her out to the car." With that he turned back to his wife, brushed his knuckles lightly across her cheek and lovingly said, "Let me help you up, sweetheart, it appears that you and I are to welcome our little one today."

When Liliana stood up, she looked quite pale and ill at ease, so Declan embraced her and kissed her slightly feverish cheek. He pushed several errant curls away from her face and said, "Don't worry, Lily; all will be well. I'll be with you every step of the way."

Annie, who had witnessed the caring exchange, had to turn away because she knew Declan, and she knew he was calmly masking his concern for his wife.

The drive to Reedsburgh Medical Center was to be through lightly falling snow. Annie sat in the backseat while Declan helped Liliana into the SUV. He gently touched her completely expanded belly. Then, he again trailed his knuckles across her cheek, "Liliana, you are giving me a gift, you know. Don't be nervous, sweetheart." Once again, Annie had to turn away. She felt as though she was witnessing something way too intimate for her eyes.

The snow continued to dance and swirl across the road as Declan drove carefully into Reedsburgh. When they arrived at the hospital, true to his word, Dr. Crocker was waiting for them on the obstetrics floor while an anxious Christophe was pacing right outside the unit. After examining her, Dr. Crocker turned to Declan and smiled, "It looks like you two are going to be parents today. But she still needs some assistance in breaking her water, so let's get this young lady into a labor room."

Declan looked down at his wife on the examining table; their eyes held... "Looks like our little rodeo cowboy or cowgirl is on the way," he murmured. A nurse entered with a wheelchair for Liliana, just as another painful spasm kicked in, but Declan gently helped to ease her off the table and into the waiting chair. From there, along with Christophe and Annie, Declan and Liliana Ryan entered a new season of their lives. It was uncharted territory, but they were eager to meet their progeny.

BABY

*L*iliana Ryan was exhausted. Today, she had worked harder than she had ever worked before in her life. Admittedly, she *was* tired, but she was delighted. Just minutes ago, while fresh snow had swirled around the evergreen-and-holly accented entrance to the Reedsburgh Medical Center outside, Liliana had given her husband an early Christmas gift of a tiny son inside that said medical center. Her husband's face was shining as he sat next to her hospital bed and cradled a little blanketed baby whose thick, damp hair had been combed off his tiny face; he looked exactly like his father.

Their sweet baby was perfect in every way. Tiny seven-pound Stephan James Ryan, who was named after both of his late grandfathers, simply looked up and listened to his father's voice; his large dark eyes taking in his new world. Christophe and Annie were there too. At last, they were to have a long-awaited child in their family. Liliana and Declan had made such a gift possible for them.

Looking at her special family and then ruminating on the great joy they brought to her, made Liliana start thinking. Almost three years ago, she had spent the entirety of the Christmas season alone and shaken; recovering from both physical and emotional wounds that had been heaped upon her shoulders by her spineless late husband. That holiday season, there had been no Christmas tree, nor gift giving. She had no idea where her abusive husband even was, or if he was ever coming home again. On that Christmas, she never would have guessed that her circumstances were soon to change so very dramatically. In a very short span of time, she would lose her hardened husband to a death of his own making. Then, three months later, her beloved parents would pass away too soon. At the time that these events were playing out, she would never have guessed that just a few years later, she would feel so very blessed.

She thought back to that day in early January almost three years ago when Declan had been dispatched to pick her up at the airport. It wasn't poised to be a particularly happy homecoming, as she had been bringing deceased Richard back to Reedsburgh for burial. There had been snow that day, too. Feeling slightly shell-shocked when she had arrived at the airport, she had been surprised when she had seen Declan Ryan making his way toward her in a sea of humanity. He, too, had spotted her in the crowd. It had been ten years since she had last seen him, yet, she would have known him anywhere. Somehow, when he had embraced her in greeting that day, she had felt comforted.

After Declan had helped her to make sure that Richard's body had been claimed by the funeral home and was on its way to Reedsburgh, they had begun the arduous trip from bustling Brookings City across the county line to her family home in Reedsburgh; all this during a heavy snow storm. That night, an always-considerate Declan had inquired if she was hungry. When she had answered affirmatively, he had then taken her to eat. As they sat across from each other in a slightly secluded alcove at Jeremy Pettigrew's grill, Declan had kindly covered her fidgeting hands with one of his own and had asked if she wanted to talk about things.

In that one simple gesture, the wellspring of her affection for him had come gurgling back to life. At first, that affection was only tiny ripples barely ruffling the surface, then three months later, a small bubbling fount that had gently eroded barriers between the two of them and, finally, two years later, the pristine and tumbling waters of love when she had become Declan's bride. Feeling blessed and very loved, a contented Liliana reached for her husband and son. Declan moved onto her hospital bed and sat close to her. He carefully handed her their tiny son, who was now mewling for his mother. Christophe and Annie stood at the foot of her hospital bed, grinning from ear to ear, as they watched the new little family.

Taking young Stephan James into her arms, Liliana was struck by the thought of another young mother many years ago on a similar winter's night in Bethlehem. That new mother had neither traveled to the birth place in a comfortable, climate-controlled vehicle, nor had she been surrounded by a staff of physicians and nurses ensuring her safety. Yet, that sweet young woman, who traveled more than a hundred miles on the back of a donkey to a lowly and, likely, aromatic stable to give birth to her child, gave the world the most-impactful gift it has ever known, the Messiah. Young Mary and her loving Joseph, who sought only to protect her and the Christ Child from a crazed and merciless King Herod, most likely, sat back upon the mounded hay savoring the joy of their young son's birth just as she and her husband were doing right now.

For some reason, the impact of the Christ child's birth struck her anew. Liliana Rose Ryan then closed her eyes and thanked her Lord again for her new son and for the forgiveness He had extended to her and to her family. Even during the times of her greatest trials, when she wondered if she had the strength to go on, she realized, yet again, that she had been carried by a tireless and loving Savior whose own mother had freely given him to the world. Liliana, too, pondered these things in her heart.

Two days later, a very-proud Declan Ryan and his bride arrived home with young Stephan James Ryan in tow. The tiny sweet boy was appropriately wrapped in a tartan bunting woven in his family's clan colors. His "grandparents," Christophe and Annie Riordan, and a very-special "Auntie Janey," who had come all the way from Scotland to meet him, couldn't wait to admire him. It was a perfect Christmas morning. Everything was covered in a fresh blanket of snow. The new little family arrived home just in time for a holiday breakfast of fragrant cinnamon buns, currant scones, fried cottage potatoes, sausages, poached eggs, and fresh hot-house tomatoes arrayed upon the kitchen table. Annie and Janey had become fast friends as they had prepared the food to honor the Christ Child's birth.

Both Declan and Liliana were delighted to have their loved ones with them on this very special Christmas morning. Joyfully, they passed their new son to each one of the beloved people around their Christmas table. Declan couldn't have been happier as he looked at his entire family. He held Liliana just a wee bit tighter, kissed her softly on the cheek and said, "Christophe, we have so very much to be thankful for this beautiful Christmas morning. Would you do us the honor of blessing the food today?"

A smiling Christophe Riordan then said it best, "Lord, you've given us a gift…You've given each of us the gift of salvation, and you've given each of us healing from the oft-times burdensome cares of this world. Lord, you have even given each member of my beloved family new beginnings, too. And, Father, as we celebrate both the birth of your precious Son and the safe arrival of tiny Stephan James Ryan, we thank you for your loving kindness. We thank you, too, for the paths that all of us have taken to be here together today. It hasn't always been easy, Lord, but in your infinite wisdom, you have orchestrated things perfectly. Thank you."

As the steaming breakfast offerings were then passed around the table, Declan again put his arm around his wife and whispered into her ear, "All is well this morning, sweetheart. All is well."

Liliana, who was holding their tiny sleeping boy, earnestly looked into her husband's eyes and whispered back, "That snowy January evening, almost three years ago, when you came to the airport to bring me back home to my parents, you told me, Declan… That evening, you covered my trembling hands at Jeremy's restaurant and quietly said, 'All will be well, Liliana. All will be well.' You were right, so very right, my honorable husband." Liliana then touched his cheek and kissed him with loving affection.

Christophe, Annie, and Janey, who had just witnessed their poignant exchange, nodded knowingly at one another with happy hearts, for each knew the many seasons of sorrow and waiting this new little family had endured to celebrate with such joy this happy Christmas morning.

Christophe Riordan then whispered into his wife's ear, "Annie, you know that as far as "do-overs" go, this one has turned out quite perfectly for our Declan and Liliana."

"I completely agree, my love. Just look at the two of them. They are so engrossed with each other and their new little baby that they haven't even taken a single bite of their Christmas repast!"

That unforgettable Holy Christmas morning, each Riordan and Ryan family member reveled in their respective thoughts as they enjoyed a family breakfast with one another. For Christophe and Annie, each of them knew that God had, indeed, blessed them with children and a grandchild in His own infinite way. Little had they known that when the late Mary Ryan had encouraged her adult son, Declan, to stay in touch with her beloved cousin, Christophe Riordan, that Mary's wonderful son would become the loving child that they had longed for so many long years.

As well, Christophe and Annie had always loved and adored Liliana, but had never expected that they would end up her only family when Stephan and Jenny Lylestrom had asked them to be Baby Liliana's godparents when she was born. Both Stephan and Jenny had been taken from this earthly life too early, but with God's perfect timing, again giving Annie and Christophe a precious adult daughter.

For Jane Ross, she found her heart overflowing with happiness in seeing kind and loving Declan Ryan embracing life heartily again after having lost both his mother and his father way too early in his young life. Yet, in her gentle and compassionate heart, she knew that both James and Mary Ryan had indelibly stamped their goodness into their son before they departed from this earthly life. Declan had always called her, "Janey," for the whole of his life, and now, he had declared her to be "Auntie Janey," to his tiny new son.

All these joys had been given to Jane Ross later in her life, yet she knew innately that God had always carried her throughout her solitary days and nights. He was now encircling her with Declan Ryan's rewoven tapestry of life, too, and that she would now always be included in a new mortal family in addition to the Family of God. Jane quietly offered up her thanks to her Savior as she savored breakfast with these loving people who also counted her amongst their own.

EPILOGUE

*Y*oung **Stephan James Ryan** was surprised when he toddled into the bathroom to find his mother sitting on his father's lap in a chair next to the bathtub crying softly.

When you are just barely two and a half years of age, it can be very daunting to find your mother weeping and your father girded only in a large navy-blue bath sheet comforting her. Stephan's footed pajamas made a soft swishing sound as he quickened his pace toward his mummy and daddy.

Little Stephan had never seen his mummy upset before, and all he could manage with his soft lower lip trembling was, "Mummy, why you cry? You okay?"

Mummy then smiled and her regular face returned. Stephan James was relieved. Daddy scooped him up onto the chair, too. Then Daddy kissed his cheek and inquired, "How is my little man this morning?"

"I fine, Daddy. "Why my Mummy sad?"

"Oh, your Mummy's not sad, my little laddie. She is crying happy tears!"

"Why, Daddy?"

"I'll let your sweet Mummy tell you…" Daddy answered.

At this point, Daddy transferred young Stephan into his mother's outstretched arms. Mummy kissed him a lot, then answered. "Baby, do you remember yesterday afternoon, when you stayed with Nana Annie and Papa Christophe while Daddy and I went to see a photograph of our baby at Dr. Crocker's office?"

Earnest young Stephan answered, "Uh huh."

"Well, guess what, Stephan? Mummy doesn't just have one baby in her tummy, she has ***three***… three babies just for you. Isn't that wonderful?"

"You're not only going to be a big brother, but you will be Daddy and Mummy's big helper, too!"

Mummy kissed him some more then said, "Three babies are a lot of work, so we will need you and Dover Dog to assist us with all sorts of things. Do you think you could do that for Daddy and me, my little doll?"

Shaking his beautiful mahogany-colored curls affirmatively, Stephan James Ryan, who was a diminutive carbon copy of his father, laughingly retorted, "Oh, Mummy, I **not** doll. I Stephan James!"

Then with the pure honesty of an innocent toddler, young Stephan James Ryan answered his mother's question, "Yes, Mummy, Dover Dog and I be your big helpers." And thinking for a second or two, he earnestly added, "You no more cry, Mummy…" My Daddy say, "'All be well. All be well.'"

To be Continued…

ABOUT THE AUTHOR

*J*anis Johnson Reese is a passionate storyteller. Her love of writing began with a childhood spent immersed in books, especially historical fiction, biographies, and the writings of influential figures like President Thomas Jefferson and British horticulturist Gertrude Jekyll. Inspired by literary voices such as Laura Ingalls Wilder, Rosamunde Pilcher, Irving Stone, Thomas Hardy, and Jane Austen, Janis developed a deep appreciation for narratives that capture the complexities of life and history with heart and elegance.

Her debut novel, *Seasons of Change*, Book 1 of *The Rosemeade Chronicles*, was born from nearly a decade of reflection and a heartfelt desire to share a story rooted in truth. Although the names have been changed, the experiences portrayed are real, and the book offers a gentle message of hope to anyone navigating similar life challenges or simply seeking an uplifting read.

Outside of her professional and writing life, Janis finds joy in her garden, which she considers a quiet retreat for inspiration. She's also a novice quilter and takes pride in her scratch-made pies. Above all, Janis treasures her family: her husband, two adult sons, two daughters-in-law, and a brilliant teenage grandson who she believes is destined to make a meaningful impact on the world.

Learn more at **JanisJohnsonReese.com**

www.ingramcontent.com/pod-product-compliance
Lightning Source LLC
Chambersburg PA
CBHW062106290726

48975CB00001B/124